The Millionaire Rogue

"The quest to find the elusive French Blue diamond in Regency England is fraught with danger in the clever second installment of Peterson's Hope Diamond Trilogy . . . The romance is enticing, with a strong mystery propelling the story forward, and the characters are witty and real." —*Publishers Weekly*

"Romance and intrigue make an irresistible combination in Peterson's latest, in which an intrepid woman and an enigmatic man find true love, despite the dictates of society."
—*Booklist*

"The Hope Diamond Trilogy continues with a wildly exciting and steamy adventure that captivates and intrigues, luring readers into the mystery surrounding the infamous jewel. Peterson keeps the romance and the danger moving forward at a rapid pace, and with all the surprising twists, readers will be left breathless and highly satisfied." —*RT Book Reviews*

The Gentleman Jewel Thief

"Overflows with adventure, suspense, and fast-paced action . . . A fresh new voice in historical romance."
—Shana Galen, author of *The Spy Wore Blue*

"Deliciously fun! What a lovely, witty book—I can't wait to see what Jessica Peterson does next!"
—Kate Noble, author of *If I Fall*

"The fabled Hope Diamond is the centerpiece of Peterson's charming trilogy, where she mixes one very bad-boy gentleman with a headstrong heroine, a stolen gem, a duel, a band of acrobats, and an exiled French king. If that isn't enough, she peppers the Hope Diamond series starter with steamy love scenes, wild escapades, and a laugh or two. Peterson keeps the pace flying and readers hanging on to their utter joy." —*RT Book Reviews*

The Undercover Scoundrel

JESSICA PETERSON

BERKLEY SENSATION, NEW YORK

BERKLEY
SENSATION

Published by the Berkley Publishing Group
An imprint of Penguin Random House
375 Hudson Street, New York, New York 10014

THE UNDERCOVER SCOUNDREL

A Berkley Sensation Book / published by arrangement with Peterson Paperbacks, LLC

ISBN: 978-0-425-27209-1

PUBLISHING HISTORY
Berkley Sensation mass-market edition / June 2015

PRINTED IN THE UNITED STATES OF AMERICA

10 9 8 7 6 5 4 3 2 1

Cover art by Aleta Rafton.
Cover design by George Long.
Interior text design by Kelly Lipovich.

Penguin
Random
House

*To my friends, who've been there for me
when boys—and hope, and sanity, and opportunity—
disappeared over the years. Thanks for helping me
keep the faith, ladies—I love you!*

Prologue

Their vows echoed off the chapel's mottled ceiling, rising and swooping like birds to surround the couple in soft whispers of faith and hope and love.

"Rings?" the vicar said, arching a brow.

For a moment the groom's eyes went wide, and then, plucking the pale green ribbon from his queue, he released a curtain of red hair about his shoulders. He used his teeth to cut the ribbon in two. Tying one length into a small circlet, he slid it onto the bride's fourth finger.

A sea of flickering candles held the darkness at bay as Lady Caroline Townshend was kissed for the first time by her husband. Joy welled up inside her and she smiled against the warm press of Henry Beaton Lake's lips.

He kissed her far less chastely than was proper at a wedding, even a secret one. He kissed her as if every stroke, every pull, every move of their lips roused, rather than satiated, a growing need inside him.

Henry held her face in his hands, guiding her toward him as he pressed a kiss to one corner of her mouth, then the other. Breathless, Caroline stood on the tips of her toes to meet his caresses, streaks of light and bursts of color illuminating the backs of her closed eyelids.

The vicar, a rather less romantic fellow than Romeo and Juliet's priest, shut his ancient Bible with a censorial *thwunk*.

Blushing, Caroline fell back from Henry, their hands entwining between them.

Lips pursed, eyes wide, the vicar glared at them. "God. Sees. *Everything*."

In a whirl of black he turned and stalked down the aisle, shaking his head at young people these days and their carnal proclivities. Caroline's lady's maid, Nicks—the one and only witness—hurried after him.

Beside Caroline, Henry shook with repressed laughter.

"How much did you pay him?" she whispered.

"Clearly not enough."

"Will he tell our parents?"

Henry ran his thumb across the back of her hand. "I should hope not. Though he doesn't seem to like us very much."

"Then we haven't much time."

"Do you mean to ravish me, Mrs. Lake?"

"I do indeed."

"Let's get on with it, then," he said, and swung her into his arms.

Caroline grasped the windowsill and, as Henry gave her a boost from below, somersaulted into his bedchamber. Inside the room it was quiet and dark, save for a single lit taper on the bedside table.

"Really," she panted, wiping her hands on her skirts. "Why not use the kitchen door? Your parents are still at my house for the ball."

Henry landed noiselessly on his feet, closing the window behind him. "Where's the challenge in that? Besides, I like all this sneaking about. Suits the secret marriage bit, don't you think?"

He took her outstretched hands and pulled her a smidge too

enthusiastically to her feet. Her nose bumped against the hardened center of his chest.

"Oh," he said, thumbing her chin. "Oh, Caroline, I'm terribly sorry. Are you all right? I only meant to, um . . . I forget sometimes that you're so little, you see; I'm used to my brothers, as you know they're rather large . . ."

Caroline looked up at Henry. Large was an understatement; like his older brothers, Henry was a broad-shouldered, ginger-haired giant with the wickedest cheekbones she had ever seen. His green eyes were even wicke*der* (if that was a word)—so brightly suggestive, so darkly penetrating, Caroline feared she might burst into flames every time he looked at her.

"I'll have a devil of a time explaining that to my mother." Henry angled his neck and brushed his lips to her injured nose. "Bloody business, marriage."

"Mm-hm," she said, burrowing farther into the circle of his arms. Her ring of ribbon slipped from her finger—it was a tad too large—and she coaxed it back into place.

His hand slid from her cheek to cup the back of her neck. With his thumb he tilted her head and caught her mouth with his. He kissed her deeply, passionately, as if he were out to steal not only her heart but her soul, her body, her being.

Henry took her bottom lip between his teeth. She saw stars.

His hands were on her face now; Caroline clung to his wrists, fearful the rush in her knees might cause them to give out. She felt the scattershot beat of his pulse beneath her fingers, the jutting architecture of his bones. Strength rippled beneath the surface of his skin, strength she felt him struggling to restrain.

And yet he touched her with great care, gently, as awed by her shape as she was of his. His fingers tangled in the hair at her temples as his mouth moved to her neck, working the tender skin there with his lips.

Caroline let out a breath, desperate, suddenly, to be free of her stays and ridiculously ruffled muslin gown. She couldn't breathe, couldn't think; she was lost in the longing she'd felt for Henry from the moment they met eyes across the garden, three weeks before.

She was hardly seventeen, set to make her debut at St. James's the following spring. Even so, Caroline knew the intensity of her feelings for Henry was a rare thing, rare and fragile. The world seemed fanatically intent on nipping such reckless affection in the bud before it ever had a chance to bloom.

But Caroline was intent on blooming. Beneath Henry's careful, confident touch, his insistent caresses, she felt herself unravel and open, giving as Henry took, and took, and kept taking.

She slipped her hands beneath the lapels of his jacket. Henry rolled back his shoulders and shrugged free of the garment, tossing it aside. He began to move forward, pressing his body into hers as he guided her farther into the room. His fingers found purchase in a row of buttons between the blades of her shoulders, working them free one at a time.

"Hold up your arms, darling," he murmured against her mouth, and gently coaxed the gown over her head.

It fell with a rustling sigh to the floor. The night air felt coolly potent against the bare skin of her arms. She shivered.

Henry gathered her in his arms, surrounding her body with the heat of his own. She could smell his skin, the clean, citrusy spice of his soap. Her desire soared.

In a hushed frenzy of movement, they unclothed one another: his waistcoat, her stays, his neckcloth. His head caught in his shirt, and after several futile attempts to remove it, Henry ripped it open. Buttons ricocheted about the room, landing with small *ping*s as they rolled across the floor.

Caroline stared at his bare chest. She swallowed.

Henry took her hands and placed them on the center of his breastbone. She inhaled at the shock of warmth that met with her palms, the spring of wiry hair. She could feel his heart beating proudly within the cage of his ribs. Proudly, wildly, an echo of her own.

In the darkness she bent her neck, and pressed her lips to his chest. He inhaled sharply, his chest rising and falling beneath the working of her lips across his collarbone, up the corded slope of his neck.

Heavens, but she hoped his parents would not return for some hours yet; Caroline couldn't have kept quiet if she'd wanted.

His fingers tugged at the neckline of her chemise as he took her bare shoulder in his mouth. The heat between her legs burned hotter. Henry coaxed the garment down the length of her body, releasing one breast, then the other. Quickly his mouth moved to take her nipple between his teeth, rolling it in the velvet touch of his tongue. The sensation was so poignant it hurt.

"Henry," she breathed, tangling her fingers in his hair. "Please. Show me."

He raised his head, eyes luminescent, translucent; they were warm and soft and they were on her, gleaming with desire.

"I was hoping you'd show me," he replied.

"You've never? Never . . . you're almost twenty, I thought . . ."

"This is to be the first time for both of us, I'm afraid."

"Then I really *am* to ravage you."

He grinned. "If you don't mind terribly."

His mouth came down on hers, and he was digging at the pins in her hair with impatient fingers. She heard them fall, one by one, until at last her hair tumbled in soft waves about her shoulder blades. Henry drew his hands through its tangled mass to rest on the naked small of her back. He pulled her to him, skin to skin; the hardened knots of her nipples brushed against his chest and she nearly cried out in agony, in desire.

The backs of Caroline's thighs met with the bed. Henry grasped her hips, and her breath caught in her throat as he tossed her lightly onto the mattress. The coverlet felt cool and deliciously soft against her bare skin.

Henry looked down upon her with narrowed eyes, his face suddenly tight.

"Caroline," he said roughly, slowly. "You are so . . . so very lovely. Beautiful."

He ran a hand up the side of her rib cage, cupping her breast; he thumbed her nipple and she arched into his touch.

And then both his hands moved to her legs, sliding off her stockings; his fingers were in the waistband of her pantalets, tugging them over the smooth expanse of her belly, her knees.

Caroline was naked. She winced at the sudden rush of cool air against the beating throb of her sex. *Please*, she prayed. *Please let it be soon.*

Henry unbuttoned his breeches and swept them down to his ankles. He rose; Caroline stared at his cock, heavy with need, as unrepentantly enormous and thickly veined as the rest of his body. It jutted out from the sharp angle of his hips, unembarrassed, and she was at once hesitant and terribly curious.

"Caroline," he said.

She swallowed. "I'm all right."

"Caroline," he said again. "We don't have to do this. I couldn't bear it if I hurt you, if you weren't ready."

For a beat he did not move, as if waiting for her to change her mind, waiting for her to roll over and demand he escort her home, take back all they'd said and done this night.

"I want to," she said. "We're married now, remember? We get to do this at last."

Caroline sat up and reached for him. He drew a breath as her hand followed the narrowing trail of hair down his hardened belly; his whole body tensed when she wrapped her hand around his cock. He felt hard and soft all at once, the skin impatiently hot and silken. She put her mouth on his belly. One of his hands went to her hair while the other moved down to cover her own around his manhood.

"How?" she whispered.

"Like this," he said, and together their hands moved up and down the length of his cock, once, twice, until he groaned and pulled away, suddenly, as if she'd hurt him.

"Caroline," he said, his face in her hair. "I love you."

"I love you," she whispered.

"I can't wait much longer. I want—I need you. Badly. Here." He reached behind him, producing his rumpled shirt. "Lie down on this, love. I'm afraid you might bleed."

Bleed?

She swallowed for what felt the hundredth time that night. He wasn't kidding about marriage being a bloody business.

Wedging the shirt beneath Caroline's bottom, Henry coaxed her back onto the bed. He took her knees in his hands and moved them apart, stepping forward so that he was wedged between her legs. She was wide open to him. She was afraid; she was overwhelmingly aroused.

Henry reached down and they both drew a breath when his first two fingers slipped between her slick curls, revealing a warmth, a wetness, that neither of them expected. Her desire soared; she ached for him to be inside her.

"You're"—he swallowed—"ready?"

"Yes," she panted. "Please, Henry."

"Once we . . . I can't stop then."

"I don't want you to stop."

He stepped forward. The bed was set high, so high that, even while standing, Henry's hips were level with hers. He put his hands on the inside of her thighs, pushing her legs even wider.

"Bend your knees about me," he said.

Caroline did as she was told. He wrapped her bent legs about his hips, hooking her feet at his buttocks. She felt his fingers on her sex, holding her open as, with his other hand, he guided his cock into her folds. He nudged against her, wincing.

"Is it . . . Are we going to work?" she asked.

"Yes," he breathed. "It's very small in there."

"Is it, um, as it should be?"

He closed his eyes, lips curling into a pained half grin. "You're perfect."

She tried not to recoil as pressure mounted between her legs. She felt herself stretching. Her pleasure was edged with pain.

"Caroline," he said. He was looking at her now, eyes wide with concern. "Tell me how you're feeling, all right?"

"I'm all right."

He guided himself farther against her, using his fingers to keep her open to him. He moved his hips, pressing into her. He pressed harder, sucking in a breath as the first bit of him entered her.

The pleasant throb between her legs heightened to burning discomfort. Her eyes smarted. Henry was saying her name but she told him to keep going, and he did. Slowly he slid into her wet warmth; they both paused when he met the barrier inside her. He looked at her. She nodded, overwhelmed by the sting, by the sense of fullness he brought her.

I'm all right, Henry. Keep going.

He inhaled through his nose, and then he bucked his hips. In a single heartbeat, he sank to the hilt. A sound escaped Caroline's lips, something between a cry and a whimper.

He was bent over her then, taking her cry into his mouth as he set his forearms on either side of her head, surrounding her. His body was wound tightly; she could tell he wanted to move between her legs, but he waited.

He gritted his teeth.

The sting began to subside, her pleasure—her heart—rising in its place. Oh, this felt lovely. A little full. But lovely.

Her hips began to circle against him, asking for more. Henry let out the breath he'd been holding and gently rocked his hips, withdrawing, entering again. Their skin, damp with sweat, slid and stuck.

She surrendered.

She surrendered to the pounding beat of her passion. To the heavy weight of her love for him.

She surrendered to Henry.

They moved against each other ardently, lost in a whirl of pain and limbs and pleasure. Her hands moved over his shoulders, marveling at the roping and bunching of his back muscles as he worked between her legs. His lips trailed over her jaw and throat.

He slowed, suddenly, and then his eyes fluttered shut; he stilled and she could feel his cock pulse inside her.

"Christ," he said when the pulsing subsided. His lips fluttered over her eyelashes. "I'm sorry, Caroline, I didn't mean . . . I meant to be more careful, but you felt so good, I couldn't stop. I wanted to stop."

"I didn't want you to stop," she whispered. "I don't want you to ever stop."

Slowly he withdrew from inside her; she felt his seed seeping warmly from between her legs.

He cursed again when he looked down at the shirt beneath her.

"What is it?" she said.

"Blood," he replied, mouth drawn into a line as he used the shirt to clean her. "A lot of it. Are you sure you're all right?"

Caroline flexed her stiff legs. She felt very sore between them. "All right. Sore. A little sore."

He crumpled the shirt between his hands and tossed it to the ground. He tugged the coverlet aside, holding it open for her. "Here, lie down. I'll get a towel."

She crawled between the bedclothes, smiling as she drew them up to her nose. They smelled like him. Like her husband.

He returned from the washstand with a damp towel, climbing into bed beside her. Thankfully he was still naked as the day he was born; he pressed his body against hers as he coaxed her legs apart, pressing the towel between them. It felt blessedly cool.

"I love you, Caroline," he murmured in her ear, nicking the lobe with his teeth. She felt him smiling against her skin. *"Wife."*

She smiled, too, a wide, irrepressible thing she felt in every corner of her being. Despite everything—despite how it appeared, her ten-thousand-pound dowry and his lack of position—despite their youth, their parents' disapproval . . . despite all that, she knew this was where she was meant to be.

Caroline loved him. She felt loved by him. And wasn't that the end of everything?

Henry spun her around and tugged her against the hardened mass of his body, her back to his front. He pulled the sheets over their heads and she, giggling, yielded to his hands as he took her body again and again and again, until the sun burned away the darkness.

It happened the next afternoon. As she was wont to do when in need of solitude and space, Caroline disappeared into the garden. Henry—her *husband!*—had a habit of sneaking from his father's house to meet her there besides; she had half a mind to toss him beneath a bush and ravage him soundly, as she promised she would last night.

She was on her knees, digging at a half-dead holly, when she heard the telltale rustle in a nearby boxwood. Her chest lit up with excitement; she was smiling, hard, when she brushed back her hair and turned toward the noise.

Only it wasn't Henry. George Osbourne, Viscount Umberton, heir to the wildly wealthy Earl of Berry, and Henry's very best friend, emerged from the hedgerow. Caroline's joy hardened in her throat at the sight of Osbourne's well-formed, if slight, figure. His face was hard, his dark eyes soft.

A tendril of panic unfurled inside her belly. She didn't like that look; something was amiss.

"My lord," she said hopefully, as if she might will good news with the tone of her voice. "What an unexpected surprise. Have you . . . er . . . come for tea?"

Osbourne bowed. "My lady, I am sorry to meet you like this, but I came straightaway."

"What?" So much for the soothing tone of voice. "What is it?"

He wiped the sweat from his thick eyebrow with a trembling thumb. When he spoke his voice was low, hoarse.

"He's gone. Henry—Lake—he's gone. I—" Here Osbourne looked away. "I thought you should know. I understand the two of you have . . . become quite close this summer, and I—"

The brass-handled garden trowel fell from her gloved hand to the earth with a muted thud of protest. "Gone? Where? But how . . . I don't understand!"

Osbourne's face was tensed with pain as he looked down at her. He swallowed. "Emptied his drawers into a valise—there's nothing left, and he took the five pounds his older brother was hiding in his pillow. He left a note for his parents, something about duty, and not coming to look for him. He said he wouldn't come back. Lady Caroline, Henry is gone."

Caroline's vision blurred; tears burned her eyes, and she fell back on her haunches. "Perhaps it's a mistake," she said. "A misunderstanding with his father, or maybe it's a joke, or—or—"

"I know Henry," Osbourne said. "He's gone, Caroline. I don't know where, and I don't know why. But he's gone."

She was sobbing then, and George Osbourne fell to his knees beside her and held her to his chest. They sat like that, damp with the heat of one another's tears, until the garden was tawny with twilight.

That was the last Caroline heard of Henry Beaton Lake, her husband, before he disappeared from Oxfordshire, from England, from her life.

Before he disappeared forever.

One

Brunswick Castle, Occupied Kingdom of Westphalia
Winter 1812

Passing under the grand iron arch of Brunswick Palace's gates, Henry Lake ducked into the shadows and, with a wince, peeled off his beard and moustache.

Bloody things itched like the *devil*; during his audience at the palace he (rather stoically, it must be said) fended off a fit of sneezing when the waxed ends of his moustache lodged themselves in his nostrils. A self-indulgent addition to his disguise, that moustache, but well worth the trouble.

Henry had got what he came to this godforsaken country in a most godforsaken winter for.

He'd found the French Blue at last.

Burrowing into an alcove between two buildings, Henry leaned against a wall and closed his eyes. His ragged breath shot from his lips in an opaque cloud as he struggled to catch his breath.

It was just as he suspected.

Just as he feared.

The diamond he'd hunted for ten years was in London.

Had it already been ten years? Dear God, he was getting old.

London. He hadn't set foot in England for more than a decade, and for good reason. *She* was there. Which meant he couldn't be.

He winced at the twist of pain in his chest, that familiar sensation, that old friend who'd accompanied him across the Continent these past years.

He had no choice; the French Blue was in London, and so to London Henry Lake would go. The diamond was far too precious a bargaining chip to let slip through his fingers. He had to obtain it lest it vanish again, the way it vanished from Paris some twenty years ago at the start of the Revolution.

He didn't have much time. No matter the danger his presence in England posed to her, to his family. He'd go, do his duty, and with any luck be back in the thick of things here on the Continent without anyone the wiser.

Besides, London was an enormous city. She was but one of thousands, hundreds of thousands of bodies occupying that soggy spot beside the Thames. No, he wouldn't see her. Definitely not. He was an *agent* of His Majesty's most esteemed *Alien* Office for God's sake; disguise, disappearance, and dashing were his trade. If he wanted to avoid detection, he could.

Only when it came to her, he didn't trust himself.

Tucking the remains of his disguise into his pocket, he limped through the blustery twilight. He drew a sharp breath; lately the bone-deep ache in his leg had heightened to a white-hot, searing sting. Even as he welcomed the pain, on cold nights like this he had a mind to swallow a pint of bourbon and cut the damned thing off. Weren't peg-legged pirates all the rage in novels these days?

Over the years, Lake found work to be the only antidote to his rising pain, and so as he limped, he let loose his thoughts. He'd suspected the Princess of Wales was in possession of the diamond from the moment his hunt for the missing crown jewels of France began. His suspicion proved correct, as his suspicions were often wont to do.

Her Majesty's father, that wily bastard Karl Wilhelm,

Duke of Brunswick, was dead, but his jeweler was not. In fact he was making quite a heap off his lusty French occupiers here in Germany, who admired jewels almost as much as they admired themselves.

A heap he would indubitably forfeit, should his French clients learn he played them for fools as an agent of his former master's son, the exiled Black Duke.

It didn't take much: a bottle of wine, a threat of blackmail, and an hour later Henry squeezed the information from Karl Wilhelm's jeweler like juice from a lemon.

And he was one goddamned juicy lemon.

The jeweler didn't know how, exactly, Karl Wilhelm came to own a fifty-carat blue diamond. A diamond that once graced the royal breasts of French kings. But he *did* know Karl passed it to his daughter, the Princess of Wales, after he'd had the jeweler reshape the French Blue to fool Napoleon's agents.

All that was left to do was ply the French Blue from the princess's grasp. Doubtless she was holding the gem hostage from her buffoon of a husband. But perhaps with the right words, a bit of flattery, the jewel might be coaxed from her treasure chest.

Henry shrugged his chin into the collar of his coat, ears ringing with cold, and turned down an alley. Usually a smelly cesspit, tonight it appeared clean, quaint even, thanks to a downy blanket of snow that glittered in the light streaming from the tavern window.

Henry paused, checking the leather strap of his eye patch. Not for the first time he was glad he had only one eye. It eased the pain, the velvety blackness that enveloped what had been his right eye; the blind spot that hid from him half the world, and half his body. The half that hurt.

He didn't deserve to be whole. Not after what he'd done to her.

Patrons near the front of the tavern glanced up at the bitter gust that accompanied Lake into the tavern. They all looked familiar, and quite drunk. Good, very good; he and Moon might have a conversation without fear of it leaving this room.

Making his way to a table near the fire, Lake winked at the tall, reedy woman wiping a mug behind the counter.

"Ah, Brunhilde! You are looking well today."

Brunhilde harrumphed, a loud, throaty sound. "Wink at me again and I'll break your balls."

"Such an elegant flower you are! How I do love the women in this country. Might I request a mug of your best beer, and a crust of bread?"

"Out of bread, and the beer is piss."

"Well, then. I shall take some of the piss if you please, Brunhilde."

Brunhilde harrumphed again. Henry took a seat across from a conspicuously square-jawed woman and took off his hat with a sigh.

"Too much?" the woman asked in French.

"Tell me, Mr. Moon, are you trying to look like a man dressed as a woman on purpose?"

Moon blinked. "No."

"Then yes, I'm afraid it is too much."

"Blast! The wig alone took me two weeks to make."

"I shall not inquire as to where you obtained so much hair."

"Better if you don't."

"Excellent." Lake leaned back as Brunhilde dropped a mug on the table before him, beer slopping onto his lap. "Now that that's settled, we might get down to business."

Lake sipped thoughtfully at his beer. Not bad, that; Germans were such snobs about their brews. "The Blue's just where I thought it'd be. We leave in the morning; the sooner the gem is in our possession, the sooner we can begin to negotiate with our toad-faced friend the emperor."

He smiled at the familiar tingle of excitement burning to life at the base of his skull. "Think of it, Moon. You and I could very well save the lives of hundreds, thousands of good British soldiers, soldiers like you and me. Who knows what Old Boney might trade for the diamond? I daresay even his tiny little manhood is on the table."

Mr. Moon scratched at his wig. "You haven't been back home in some time, have you, sir?"

Lake scoffed. "I hardly remember what England looks like."

But he did remember, in startling, painful detail, what *she* looked like. Dark hair, dark eyes, pale skin like alabaster, the warmth of her body curled into his . . .

Henry finished his mug in three long, hard pulls, head pulsing at the sudden rush of cold.

"I say, sir, are you all right?"

Henry tried not to wince. "Quite."

"So, the plan," Moon said. "We can't possibly afford to buy the diamond off the princess. Are you going to steal it?"

"Bah, theft is for amateurs. Besides, she'll assume her husband did it. I daresay she'd try to stab him."

"Surely you're joking."

"Sadly, I am not." Lake smacked his lips. "No, we won't thieve the jewel. And we won't buy it, either."

Moon furrowed his brow. "But I don't understand."

"*We* won't buy the diamond from Princess Caroline. But someone else will. I've got just the man for the job."

"One of your agents?"

"No. The man who gave me this." Lake pointed to his right eye. "Oh, heavens, Moon, put your eyeballs back in your head. It was an unfortunate accident—storm-tossed seas, falling mainmast, that sort of thing. If it wasn't for me, he'd be lying in a hundred broken pieces at the bottom of the Channel. Needless to say the man owes me a favor."

Moon swallowed. "Several favors, I should hope."

"Convincing the Princess of Wales to sell a prized jewel under false pretenses *is* a rather large favor, but I am never one to say never." Lake clapped his hands and rubbed the palms together. "Well, then. As much as I'd love to stay and chat up old Brunhilde, we must be off."

Two

---✦---

Mayfair, London
Late Spring 1812

Fragrant in the best—and worst—of ways, Hyde Park was just as Lady Caroline Townshend, Dowager Countess of Berry, remembered it: achingly lovely, poignantly familiar.

The springtime sun threw the park's multicolored charms into stunning relief. Blooms perfumed the warm breeze and almost (though not quite) masked the more earthy smells of manure and mud. The meadows and hedgerows were so violently green her eyes watered; the day's dying light streamed through the gaps in the trees and pooled in honey-hued stillness beneath their branches.

For a moment Caroline closed her eyes and inhaled the sensations of this place. She hadn't been back in over a decade; last time she frequented the park she was seventeen, in town for her first—and last—season. She'd been so lost then, so lonely.

And now she was lost again.

Her throat tightened at the rush of memories from that year. In the space of a single summer she'd fallen in love once and married twice; how young she was then, how unprepared for the crushing pleasures and disappointments of womanhood! Even now, so many years later, thinking about *him*—she could not bear to put a name to her longing—made her heart swell with something so forceful it took her breath away.

Caroline swallowed, hard. She could not cry. She *would* not cry, not here, not in Hyde Park, and during the fashionable hour at that; though she was a widow, and thus entitled to live as eccentrically as she wished, spreading gossip was always preferable to being its subject.

And so Caroline did not cry; she tripped instead.

"Heavens, Caroline, do mind your step. That's the third time today!" With a sigh her brother, William, Earl of Harclay, drew her upright by the elbow. Nodding apologetically at a nearby matron, he said, "I've half a mind to put you in a pram so that our fellow pedestrians might be spared injury. I thought you'd grown out of your awkwardness."

Caroline untangled her foot from her skirts. "No such luck, I'm afraid, but it does make our strolls much more exciting, don't you think?"

"No, I don't. Let's sit."

Caroline kept her arm tucked into the crook of his elbow as they sat on a bench set into a hedge of boxwood. She hadn't realized how much she'd missed William, his clever smiles, the way the skin at the edges of his dark eyes creased when he laughed. She'd forgotten how safe he made her feel. How welcome.

Besides, the attention he received from his admirers—they were like bees, swarming, buzzing, out for the kill—was worth the exhausting, muddy ride down to London. Caroline had never before seen a woman deliberately drop her beaded reticule into a gentleman's lap, only to retrieve it practically with her teeth.

"Ah, Lady Bonham," William had said. "We must give her credit for trying, however misguided her efforts."

Grinning at the memory, Caroline looked out over the lawn before them. A dozen children skittered across the emerald expanse.

"But heavens, aren't they darling," she said, winking at a dark-haired baby burrowed into his nursemaid's neck. Even as Caroline smiled, longing gripped her heart and squeezed.

"They're *everywhere*," William said, and pulled up the edge of his coat at the approaching twins who'd somehow managed to escape their mother's lap.

Caroline caught each of the children by the arm and handed them back to their mother. "They don't bite, you know. Unlike a certain person of our mutual acquaintance."

"That was merely a phase, *dear* sister, and lasted only a month or two besides."

She grinned. "I was fourteen the last time you bit me. Here, you can see the mark on my arm—"

William waved her away, laughing. "If I had known you'd come all the way to London merely to torment me with tales of my sordid past, I would've never invited you in the first place."

"Ah, your sordid past! I'm so glad you brought it up," she said, looping her arm through her brother's once more. "While it's quite dashing to live the life of a rakehell when one is two-and-twenty, I daresay dissipation is outré as one approaches thirty."

"Even for an earl?"

"*Especially* for an earl."

William gave the ribbon that dangled from her bonnet a soft tug. "Then you will be glad to know I've found London, and its dissipated amusements, rather dull these past months."

"Dull?" Caroline arched a brow. "Even with all those debutantes to despoil?"

William sighed. "Even so."

"Whatever shall you do?"

A small, secret smile flickered at the corners of his lips. "I've an idea or two."

"Not marriage, surely?"

"Dear God, no."

Caroline narrowed her eyes. William was up to something; she recognized that look in his dark gaze, the playful, if dangerous, intent lurking there. The look of the devil.

"It's got something to do with Mr. Hope's ball tonight, doesn't it?" she said. "Is that why you won't allow me to attend? I confess I am disappointed; I do think that theme of the Sun King's family jewels or what have you is quite clever."

William turned to her, his face studiously blank. "I am

merely protecting your good virtue, Caroline. Hope's soirees are notorious; everyone knows he spikes the punch with that damnably good stuff from his cellar. I won't have you seduced by some idiot in a powdered wig and pumps thinking he's a Sun King. It's too soon."

Caroline grinned. "I like wigs."

"I know you do. That's why you can't go." He took her hand and squeezed it, gently. "I understand you are just out of mourning, Caroline, and eager for diversion. We shall have a grand season, you and I; I shall show you all that London has to offer. But I beg you trust me about tonight. Get some rest and tomorrow we shall begin our tour."

Caroline sighed, leaning her head against his shoulder. "All right. On one condition: we start our tour this afternoon with an ice at Gunter's."

"Excellent idea," he said. "I do hope they still have the cheese-flavored ice. It's my favorite."

"A cheese-flavored ice?" She wrinkled her nose. "You always did have a taste for the bold."

William took a long breath, let it out through his nose. "And what of you and marriage? You seem determined to enjoy your solitude."

It was Caroline's turn to smile. "For once, you and I see eye to eye on the matter. As much as I miss my late husband, bless him, I wasn't expecting to find widowhood quite so . . . freeing. I go where I wish, whenever I wish it. I don't need a chaperone; heavens, I *am* the chaperone."

"I think you'd make a terrible chaperone."

"Thank you, Brother, I know coming from you that's a compliment." She grinned. "Besides. I don't think I could bear another man's follies. His moods."

I couldn't bear more heartbreak. Caroline had experienced enough of that to last a lifetime. Even now, she saw in the faces of the men who passed another scheme, another lie, another heartbreak to be suffered.

"Well," William said, "since you wish to go to Gunter's, I suppose we should scratch that itch before you launch into another speech."

She rapped him on the shoulder. "That was a good speech."

"Very good. Let's be off."

William rose and with excessive caution helped Caroline to her feet. Heads bent, they began to walk—"Slowly," William counseled, "*care*fully"—when Caroline looked up. She blinked, and blinked again when her gaze landed on a vaguely familiar outline some distance across the park.

He was enormous, a broad-shouldered, ginger-haired predator with legs like tree trunks. His color was high, the cheekbones slicing across his face flushed pink, as a small grin of—was that satisfaction?—curled at his lips. Cords of vein and sinew stood out against the bare skin of his neck. Something about it—his neck—made Caroline feel warm, suddenly, like the sun had regained its noontime strength.

Her heart stumbled inside her chest.

The figure was moving quickly—not walking, not a run, it was more of a limp—down one of Hyde Park's well-groomed pathways. His eyes were narrowed in concentration; one of his hands was tucked into the soft folds of his plain, if well-cut, kerseymere coat.

He moved confidently, discreetly through the crush (as discreetly as could a ginger-haired giant, anyway). He ducked behind a thick-trunked tree, only to reappear halfway across a verdant lawn. He ducked again; Caroline frantically searched the crowd for his face.

The last time she'd seen that broad-shouldered figure was twelve years ago in the garden at her family's house. It couldn't be *him*, he'd disappeared and for all she knew he was dead, or living out his days as a pirate in Damascus.

Besides, who hurried about Hyde Park with his hand shoved in his pocket, and during the fashionable hour at that? It was so farfetched it bordered on the ridiculous.

Which meant, of course, that it *had* to be him.

Him, her husband.

"Caroline," William was saying. "Caroline, wait, where are you going? Is it a bee? Wait, you know I'm afraid of them, the last time I was stung my toe swelled to the size of an apricot . . ."

She was charging across the park, legs moving in time to the wild echo of her pulse. The ribbons of her bonnet fluttered in her face, tickling her nose; she pushed them away. Her slippers squished in the damp grass. She kept moving.

Like a shadow dissolved into night, he disappeared into Hyde Park's hedgerows, into the tinkling bustle of the crush. He would vanish, only to reappear moments later; she could see the muscles in his jaw were drawn tight.

She dipped and trudged and changed course as best she could in time to his movements; people began to stare but she stumbled over them, breathing a hurried thanks to a gentleman who caught her by the arm before she launched heels over head into the Serpentine.

Her legs ached and her lips burned, strangely, a prickle of sensation she felt in the center of her chest.

At last she saw him. He was drawn up behind a copse of trees, sheltered from the prying eyes of passersby.

He turned his head, and through the dappled green of newborn leaves Caroline and Henry Lake met eyes.

A swell of pain, a tingling rush that was hot and cold and hard and soft all at once, moved through her. The ground tugged at her feet as if it might swallow her; she felt dizzy.

His eye—his *one eye*, the other was gone, masked by a black leather patch—was as green as she remembered, translucent, probing. A searing flash of memory blinded her as she saw him as she had for the first time: vexingly handsome, alluringly mysterious. Although this time the skin at the edge of his eye did not crinkle quite so pleasantly; deep lines were etched there, creases that crept downward as if born of glowers and grimaces.

Her stomach clenched. He was the same. He was different. Who was this man, this stranger—?

"Heavens, Caroline," William panted, bending over to rest his hands on his knees, "since when were you so light on your feet? Did you spot a particularly delicious child?"

Caroline blinked, turning to look at her brother. "No. No, I thought . . . well, I thought I saw . . ."

She turned back to the copse. It was empty; the half-naked trees groaned as a breeze rustled their branches.

She shook her head. "It was nothing."

"Are you quite sure?" William asked, drawing upright. "It didn't *look* like nothing. You were running like the devil."

Looping her arm through his, Caroline tugged him onto the path. "Shall we make for home? I do believe the hour for libation draws near."

"But what about Gunter's? I was looking forward to that ice."

Forget Gunter's, she wanted to say. Perhaps, if she got William drunk enough, he might not recognize her at Hope's ball tonight. Surely she and her maid, Nicks, could cobble together a passably decent Madame de Montespan costume? A little powder and more rouge, and no one the wiser.

At least she hoped powder and rouge would do the trick.

For she had a funny feeling Henry would be in attendance at Hope's ball. Despite her better judgment, despite the creeping sense that her brother was up to no good, despite her anger and her regret, Caroline would be, too.

She couldn't stay away. Not tonight. Not after all this time.

Henry was back.

Three

Henry brought the bottle to his lips and took one enormous, savage pull. The cognac burned brightly as it slid down his throat, but it did nothing to loosen the knot in the center of his chest.

He'd seen her.

The her. Caroline.

Out of the tens and hundreds and thousands of people in London, he'd locked eyes with the one person he didn't want to see across the emerald expanse of Hyde Park.

The one person he'd sworn, twelve years before, to keep far from the violence of the life he'd chosen.

Violence that found him even in the midst of Hyde Park's shimmering tranquility. He'd had the distinct feeling he was being followed, hence his mad dash, the way he kept his fingers clamped down on the pistol tucked into his waistcoat.

Nothing came of his suspicion, praise God. Still, she'd seen him. And he'd seen her.

Even now his blood rushed hot at the memory of her face. She was just as beautiful as she'd been at seventeen, impossibly lovely. Those wide brown eyes, the dark, curling lashes he'd found so provocative a decade ago; the soft curve of her chin, the windswept way her temples sloped to sharp cheeks and smooth lips.

God, those lips.

She was beautiful, yes. But in that beautiful face he'd seen no trace of a smile, none of the lines that came from laughing too hard and too often. His entire body tightened when he thought about the look in her eyes: soft in all the wrong ways, like a wounded animal's, and watery. She'd been pale, almost drawn, and thin; he saw no evidence of the curves he'd enjoyed so liberally in his bed twelve years before.

Henry told himself she was still heartbroken over the loss of her husband; in Paris he'd received the news of the Earl of Berry's passing. That explained her pallor, the wet unhappiness in her gaze. He couldn't stand the thought that she'd loved, and been loved in return, by someone else (and his former best friend, at that). And yet the idea that Henry was responsible for her sorrow, that she had not found contentment in his absence, was even worse.

His best friend. Caroline had married him not two months after Henry left England. Even now he still burned with jealousy that Osbourne had given Caroline what Henry could not. A home, a title, a family.

Things a lovely girl like her deserved. Things that would make her happy.

He slid his fingers into the hair at the nape of his neck and pulled, hard. God but it was complicated. He couldn't tell if he felt relieved, riled, remorseful. He drowned in all those things and more. Henry turned at the sound of ungainly footsteps—more clomps, really—and took another swig of cognac to keep from laughing.

His old friend Mr. Thomas Hope tripped onto the balcony of his Mayfair mansion, leaning on his gilded walking stick as if for life itself. Immaculately, if gaudily, attired as the Sun King Louis XIV, Hope wore a towering wig of black curls that lent him the air of a disheveled pirate. The deep cuffs of his ivory silk coat, embroidered with gold thread, glimmered in the light of the setting sun above. The sash slung about his breast was studded with an impressive collection of rare jewels.

Henry looked down to see the culprit of all that clomping: red-heeled pumps, fastened by diamond clips.

Hope was nothing if not thorough. Henry allowed himself a small smile at the memory of their time together on the Continent. As partners in service to His Majesty the King of England (in crime, too), they'd taken Paris by storm; armed with Hope's intimate knowledge of French banks, they'd managed to foil several of Napleon's more nefarious plots. Hope was a good man and a better agent; even so, he'd left the service to establish Hope & Co. here in London.

Now, as England's preeminent—and wealthiest—banker, Hope had the blunt Lake did not. Which meant, of course, he had the means to purchase the French Blue from the Princess of Wales; which is exactly what Hope did some two weeks ago after Lake called in that favor.

With the diamond in hand, Lake need only attract the attention of the French so that negotiations might begin. Hope hatched a plan to display the jewel at one of his infamously opulent balls, this one titled "An Evening at Versailles: The Jewel of the Sun King." All of London had been abuzz for *weeks* after last year's ball (its theme had something or other to do with those poison-loving Borgias), so what better way to set fire to Old Boney's arse than with this debauched little soiree?

"Give me that," Hope said, swiping the cognac from Henry's grasp. "I look ridiculous."

Lake shrugged. "But I thought you liked costumes? In France you were all too eager to don a disguise. Remember the time you played a one-armed butcher—"

"*This*"—Hope impaled his wig with the gilded walking stick—"is a rather different scenario, don't you think? The wig, the shoes . . . it's a bit much, even for me. And dear *God* my head hurts."

"Small price to pay for king and country, my friend. Though it does make you wonder how old Louis managed it. Fellow must've been bald as a bat to wear a wig like that."

Hope set down the cognac on the stuccoed balustrade between them. "He was a masochist, no two ways about it. Actually, I'm beginning to think we have quite a lot in common."

They both turned toward the house at the piercing sound of an opera prima donna warming up her instrument. The glass doors lining this side of Hope's well-appointed residence were flung open to the warm breeze, revealing the ballroom within. Footmen and scullery maids and all manner of staff criss-crossed its marbled expanse in a frenzy of preparation; Hope's first guests would arrive at any moment.

Lake inhaled, the intoxicating, sweet-fresh scent of the lilies strewn about Hope's ballroom filling his head. The knot in his chest tightened; that scent, those flowers, they reminded him of Caroline's perfume. He would never forget the way she smelled: like spring, like warm nights, like sweetness and promise and possibility.

He grasped the cognac between his thumb and forefinger and gulped, wiping his lips with the back of his hand.

Back to business. Business on which the lives of thousands of British soldiers depended; he did not have time to think about the past and its regrets. "When Bonaparte's men make contact, send for me straightaway. And don't lose sight of that diamond."

"And you"—Hope grabbed the bottle—"don't drink all my cognac. It's bloody impossible to get these days. Who do you think is going to steal the French Blue, anyway? Everyone who's coming tonight can buy their own damned jewels. If I were to peg anyone, it'd be you. Besides, I hired twenty extra men to patrol the ballroom, just in case. Trust me, Lake. *Nothing* is going to happen."

Ah, if Henry had a copper for every time he'd heard that.

"I don't have to remind you there are no more famous last words than those," he said.

Hope turned to the ballroom at the sound of female voices, his first guests; Henry turned and in one swift, silent motion, launched himself over the balustrade.

It was an admittedly self-indulgent move—he did so enjoy witnessing Hope huff and puff over his theatrics—but Henry had business to see to, and the night was getting on.

Henry landed noiselessly on his feet in the mews behind

the house and limped round to Duchess Street. His leg ached fiercely tonight; with every step his being rang with misery.

Getting old, Henry decided, was a most depressing endeavor.

Above him, night began to bruise the sky, and faded stars gained pulsing strength. The air was warm and calm and pleasant against his skin. Tucking a stray lock behind his ear, Henry wove determinedly through the growing traffic gathered about the imposing façade of Hope's town house. To Cheapside, he wondered, or was it best to head for the bridge . . . ?

That was when he saw her.

It was only a glance, a quick sweep of his eye to the shadowy alley tucked between two houses. But he would know that face anywhere; he could pick out the proud set of her shoulders in a crowd.

He drew up suddenly, pressing his back to a nearby wall. His heart beat unevenly, insistently inside his ears. He turned his head, daring another glance over his right shoulder.

With the help of a liveried footman, Lady Caroline Townshend—no, wait, she was Caroline Osbourne now, wasn't she?—descended from a gleaming carriage lacquered a brave shade of blue. Even as she stepped carefully, she caught her slippered foot in the silken expanse of her skirts and pitched forward, arms flying above her head.

Henry's belly turned over and his hands shot up as if he might catch her from where he stood. Praise heaven the footman broke her fall, and together they tumbled in an elegant knot to the ground.

For half a heartbeat Henry's chest flared with jealousy. Even though the man had rescued Caroline from a nasty spill, Henry hated the sight of his hands on her person. It was all he could do not to leap from his hiding place and help her to her feet himself.

But he couldn't. He would not embroil her in his plot. He'd learned, twelve years before, the suffering his bloody doings could bring to those he loved. Caroline would be spared.

He squeezed his eyes shut, breathing hard. He felt dizzy. His palms were sticky with sweat. His heart felt as big around as the moon.

"Oh, oh, thank you, Collins, I'm afraid this won't be the first time I'll be mauling you," he heard her saying. Her voice sent a shiver of recognition down his spine; he winced against the longing that surged through him.

". . . and please," she whispered, "please keep this . . . outing of mine between us. I shall meet you at this very spot."

Henry's eyes flew open. Caroline wasn't supposed to be here? He snuck another glance. She was indeed alone, without an escort; her rakehell brother the Earl of Harclay was nowhere in sight.

Caroline looked up and Henry ducked just in time. He held his breath as she passed an arm's length from him onto Duchess Street. He watched her back disappear into the crush; her hair was swept high onto her head, leaving the nape of her long, swanlike neck bare. He could see the tiny hairs there glimmer in the light of the streetlamps.

He swallowed. His fingers began to twitch.

Holding a fan up to her face, Caroline slipped between two carriages and mounted the front steps of Hope's mansion.

Of course. Her intricately embroidered ivory silk gown and enormous panniers should have given it away.

Caroline was going to Hope's ball.

Sneaking into Hope's ball, more like it.

Henry brought one of those twitching fingers to his lips. He shouldn't do it. Really, he couldn't. There was the diamond, and the whole of the British Empire to serve and protect . . .

He thought about Caroline's bare neck, and her perfume.

Henry stalked across the street, ignoring the catcalls and curses of the drivers he passed. Safe in the shadows on the dark side of the street, he ducked into an alcove beside a bay window.

He did not wait long. A gentleman dressed in a ridiculous robin's-egg blue coat and white satin knee breeches passed by, obviously bound for Hope's Versailles-themed ball.

Lake stepped out into the street. The man's wife or mistress was nowhere in sight; even better, he swayed a bit on his feet.

He was drunk.

It was all Henry could do not to rub his hands together with glee.

Reaching out, Henry grasped the man by the back of the neck. Before the drunkard could cry out, Lake brought his fist down on the top of his head. For a moment the unfortunately attired chap wavered, and then he fell into Lake's arms.

Looking up to make sure no one was about, Lake quietly dragged the man into the alcove and got to work. He left a handful of coins in the man's clammy palm; clothes this ridiculous must have cost a small fortune.

Tugging at the embroidered lapels of the robin's-egg blue coat—it was more than a little snug, and the breeches, dear God!—Lake emerged from the alcove a few moments later.

The crush to enter Hope's ball was already immense; costumed guests jostled and pushed against Henry's elbows, his shoulders. As he ran a hand over the powdered expanse of his wig in an attempt to smooth it, his palm brushed against his leather eye patch. He hesitated.

And then he pushed on. He was a head and a half taller, his shoulders twice as wide, as any gentleman in attendance— since when had Englishmen gotten so damned small?

Besides, considering the selection of costumed guests— and bared bosoms—he'd already seen, no one was going to pay him much mind.

With a speed of which he did not think himself capable, Henry darted up the steps, weaving and ducking between bejeweled guests like a boxer in the ring. He slipped through the doors, narrowly avoiding a run-in with Caroline's scalawag brother, the Earl of Harclay, who wore a purple waistcoat of so vibrant a hue it made Henry's eye smart.

He stalked through the hall and into the colonnaded gallery that ran the length of the ballroom. He stopped to survey the crowd: lots of wigs, lots of indecently exposed skin, but no Caroline.

Swiping a coupe of champagne from a passing footman, Henry watched as Hope's bewigged head crisscrossed the ballroom, nodding here, sagging there; his grim-faced guards waited in the shadows. Still no sight of her.

Henry began to panic. What if she'd already left, snuck away while he was busy assaulting a stranger behind a bay window? Worse, what if she was ensconced in some private room upstairs with an unscrupulous gentleman, intent on indulging the freedoms allowed her as a widow?

It wasn't any of his business, he reminded himself. She wasn't his. Not anymore.

His blood rushed hot at the unwelcome thought, nonetheless;

he downed his champagne in a single gulp and set the glass down none too gently on a nearby table. He took another from a nearby footman, and downed that one, too. Taking a third, Henry pushed his way into the ballroom.

Still no Caroline.

Just when he was about to give up and give in, across the ballroom he caught sight of a familiar pair of shoulders.

She was alone (thank God); even so, his heart fell.

Lady Caroline Osbourne was looking for someone. He could tell by the way she was trying to look like she was doing anything *but*.

She turned, stray wisps of hair brushing against the skin of her nape as she looked over her shoulder.

She looked right at Henry.

His heart tripped inside his chest. The pressure in the ballroom changed, suddenly, and Henry could feel his pulse moving inside his head.

Her eyes were heavy and full. Oh, but she was lovely.

Caroline looked away, color rising to her cheeks. He watched the rise and fall of her chest. He wondered who she was looking for, what she meant to do with him.

She moved through the crush, and he moved with her, always maintaining a safe distance even as he drew closer, bit by bit. He had no idea what he was doing. What would he say, if he drew close enough? Would she even speak to him?

But he couldn't help but follow her. He trampled toes, mauled debutantes, overturned a footman's tray; Henry hardly noticed the wreckage he left in his wake as he trailed Caroline across the ballroom.

Every now and again she would turn and look at him, knowing he'd be there, staring at her like a man possessed. She would meet his gaze, and then, her blush deepening, she'd look away.

He watched her sidle up to the refreshment tables and accept a coupe of punch. He grinned when, after taking her first sip, her eyes watered and she let out a little sputter of surprise. Hope's punch was a criminally potent brew.

Her eyes flicked up to meet Henry's over the rim of her crystal coupe. Her eyelashes were long, and darker than he remembered. Girlish, and pretty.

Her costume was neither fashionable nor daring, but it was

her: slightly careless and entirely unique; she looked elegant, a creature from another place and time. Her dark hair was pulled back, revealing the profile of her face. Strong jaw, soft chin, raspberry red lips.

So distracted was he by those lips that Henry was caught up in the swell of the crush. The press of bodies urged him to the edge of the ballroom, toward the tables where Caroline now stood. He panicked, and then he gave in.

Her eyes went wide as he approached. She tipped back the coupe, finishing her punch in a single gulp. She watched, regretfully, as a footman took away her empty cup.

Henry was so close he could smell her perfume; his entire being ached at the strange familiarity of her scent. It was shocking, to be so close to her. He'd never expected to see her; he'd never allowed himself to imagine it happening. It was too dangerous.

What he felt for Caroline was too dangerous.

And then she met his gaze, her head tilting back as he got closer, and closer, pushing aside bodies with increasing urgency.

Four

Caroline had been ducking in and out of the crush with exhausting futility all evening.

Holding her fan just beneath the reach of her bottom eyelashes, she'd searched the ballroom, from the balcony to the floor and back again. She hoped she was as discreet as she *thought* she was being in her pursuit; surely in the midst of all this merriment and mayhem, no one would notice her looking, quite ardently, for a pale-haired giant?

Yes, surely.

Caroline's eye caught on a flash of gray-blue brilliance across the ballroom, widening at the realization that it was a diamond—*the* diamond, King Louis' French Blue. It was enormous, even from a distance; there was something distinctively seductive about the way the jewel sparked and glittered in the low light of the chandeliers above, winking red one moment, flashing white the next.

Perhaps it was the lady wearing the French Blue who was so alluring. She was tall and shapely, and wore a gown of diaphanous pale gauze that left very little to the imagination. The jewel hung from a collar of wisplike diamond threads, resting just above the inviting crease between her breasts. Like the diamond, her eyes flashed a bold shade of blue; but even as the pert slope of her nose, the knowing smile of her lips exuded confidence and coolness, the woman's color was high.

One need only look slightly to the left to know why.

Caroline's brother, William, despoiler of debutantes, voluptuary extraordinaire, was grinning down at the lady as if he might enjoy that ample bosom for dessert.

Caroline rolled her eyes. So much for finding London and its dissipated amusements dull; a few coupes of punch and William was back to his old tricks. Hopefully the poor girl knew better than to indulge him.

Who was she, Caroline wondered, and why had this Mr. Hope chosen her to wear his prized jewel? Perhaps he wanted to display his wealth before all the world, or at least all of London, and there was no better way to do that than to wedge it between a pretty girl's breasts.

But even as curiosity prickled in the back of her mind, Caroline's thoughts returned again and again to Henry.

Was he here at the ball? She was beginning to feel foolish for even thinking such a thing; she was beginning to feel foolish for thinking she'd seen him at all earlier this afternoon in Hyde Park.

Yet it was him. It had to be him. She'd felt it in her skin, in her heart. Henry Lake was back in London.

But even if he *was* back, even if he was here, what did she hope to accomplish by chasing him down? He disappeared twelve years ago with hardly a handshake; no one had heard from him since. It was obvious he did not want to be found.

Caroline turned, and so did her heart inside her chest.

He was here. He was real, and alive.

And he was looking at her.

She looked away, heart pounding, heat rushing to her face. She felt unsteady on her feet, as if the ground had suddenly shifted, jolting her to life. Her ribs fought against the prison of her stays as she struggled to catch her breath.

Meeting his eyes—his one eye, which at the loss of its partner seemed to have taken on twice the intensity, twice the heat—made Caroline feel as though she was going to cry; like she was falling into the deep well of emotion that had lain hidden inside her all these years.

Caroline began to move, if only to keep from fainting. She inched sideways through the crowd, feeling the heat of Henry's gaze on the back of her neck. Was he following her?

She glanced over her shoulder. Oh, he was *definitely* following her.

Stumbling blindly through the crowd, Caroline at last found respite at the refreshment tables. She didn't need to look to know that Henry was getting closer.

Caroline hooked a trembling finger through the handle of a crystal coupe and threw back the punch.

Dear. *God.* It was more brandy than punch, burning a ribbon of fire down the length of her throat. She coughed heartily, running the back of her hand across her lips. She looked up. Henry was close. Very close.

She looked down at her empty glass, waiting for what her brother called liquid courage to light a fire in her belly.

She waited.

And waited.

And was none the more courageous when, sadly, a footman removed the coupe from her hand.

Taking a deep breath through her nose, Caroline looked up.

Henry was an arm's length away; as he moved to stand before her, he captured her eyes with his, her chin drawing higher to meet his gaze.

He drew up in front of her, a respectable distance separating their bodies until a crowd of drunken dandies jostled enthusiastically behind him, pushing him closer.

Too close.

His face lit with panic.

"Oh, oh, how clumsy, and the crowd . . . I, um. Are you all right?"

She blinked, startled by the sound of his voice. A chill shot down her spine; that voice of his, deep, rumbling, was at once foreign and familiar.

"Yes," she breathed. No. Not at all. "All right, thank you."

Henry's green eye, wide, glowed in the half-light of a thousand candles. For a minute the room fell away and she was beneath the arched ceiling of her family's ancient chapel, the echo of her vows ringing in her ears as she met Henry's gaze.

She blinked and the spell was broken. She could see stray

white strands of his wig clinging to the damp skin of his forehead; heavens, he was bigger than she remembered, and more handsome, and intimidating, and so . . . so very *much*.

"Hello," he said softly.

She met his eye. "Hello."

Caroline could smell the scent that rose from his skin. He smelled fresh, like lemon soap and laundry. There was something else there, too, something visceral and spicy, something that sent a rush of recognition through the base of her skull.

The eye patch was more sinister up close; its surface shone dully, and Caroline wondered what, exactly, was hidden beneath it. She resisted the impulse to reach up and feather her fingers across its surface.

The drunken dandies returned, forcing Henry to lurch forward; Caroline caught him in her arms. His face was bright red.

"I, uh, I swear I'm not doing this on purpose—here, once I can move I'll, um, move?"

Caroline squeezed her eyes shut, her body pinned against his. She willed herself to be still.

His chest bowed and scraped against her own. They were both breathing hard.

Behind them the music started, a rising melody that permeated the sounds and sighs around them. Henry glanced over his shoulder.

"There's more room near the dancing," he said.

Caroline ignored the excited thump inside her chest. "Are you—?"

"Asking if you'd like to breathe? Yes. Although to do that we'll need to dance."

"But it's a waltz."

Henry furrowed his brow. "What's wrong with a waltz?"

"I don't know how."

Really, she hadn't a clue; considering she often had difficulty walking, it was safe to assume she was going to be miserable at it. Never mind that Henry was looking down at her like *that*; she was likely to break her leg, his leg, perhaps even *both* their legs . . .

No matter the threat to their lower extremities, Henry's left hand dipped to the small of her back. He grinned.

"Then I shall teach you."

The protest died on her lips when his right moved to clasp her own in the steady warmth of his palm. He pulled her against him; his breath tickled the hair at her temples. She felt terrifyingly present, her body coming alive as he pulled her yet closer. She looked down at the bare skin of his throat, the ridge of his jaw covered in the barest velvet of pale stubble, and swallowed.

They began to move. Caroline blushed at the intimacy of their movements, the way Henry guided her body to glide in time to his. Her gown sighed as it brushed against the gilded buttons of his courtier's coat; his thighs pressed insistently against her own.

The ballroom surrounded them in a whirl of dark shape and sound, and yet the sensations bursting to life inside Caroline were all bright, all color. She could feel his eye on her as they moved. She did not dare look up.

Oh, heavens, what was she doing? All these years later—the heartbreak, the regret—she should know better than to waltz with Henry Beaton Lake.

And yet here she was, rising to the touch of the man whose memory had tortured her for a decade.

Despite his size and limp, Henry moved as if on air. His steps were confident, smooth. She wondered where he'd learned to waltz; in which corner of the world had Henry thrilled other women with his surefootedness, his steely command?

In the circle of his arms she felt safe and stranded. She felt lost and more than a little strange, as if it all were a dream: not entirely unpleasant, but certainly impossible—thrillingly, terribly so. She'd already woken once to find him gone. She was not fool enough to do so again.

Besides, she was widowed, and possessed of a hard-won freedom she would not give up for the likes of Henry.

But oh, that look in his eye . . .

Her stays felt too tight, suddenly, and Caroline struggled to breathe. She stumbled, but Henry was quick to right her.

Just when Caroline thought she might swoon, or die, or both, an enormous clatter reverberated through the ballroom. It was a throaty, tinkling sound. Henry froze; Caroline bumped her nose against the inviting little slope of chest where his collarbones met. They both turned at once in the direction of the noise; a wave of stunned silence washed over the crush.

There, on the far wall of the ballroom, a handful of figures costumed in black crashed through the high arched windows, showering the crowd below with broken glass. The figures somersaulted through the air before coming to land—impossibly!—on the monumental chandeliers spanning the length of the room. Pistols held high in their hands, they wrapped their arms and legs about the gilded cables from which the fixtures hung.

Caroline and Henry together ducked at the *one-two-three* discharge of the guns; the acrid smell of gunpowder filled the room. She cried out, and Henry held her head to his breast, covering her ear with his hand. With her heart in her throat, she watched the intruders pull knives from their belts, and begin sawing at the cables.

"Oh my God," Caroline murmured, and on cue the ballroom erupted in a cacophony of screams, shouts, prayers to our Lord and Savior.

An ominous groan crackled above her head. She looked up and saw an intruder leap from the chandelier to land solidly on the ground beside them; he took off into the crowd. A moment later the chandelier bore down upon their heads.

"Oh my God," she said again, backing away.

Henry pulled her against him from behind, her back to his front, and with his arm about her waist pressed her to the ground, shielding her body with his own just as the chandelier hit the floor with a shuddering, monumental crash.

The ballroom was plunged into darkness.

Her shoulder was in his mouth and his knee was wedged between her thighs and she could hardly breathe. Not for the weight of him—though that was no small consideration—but for the shock of so much sudden, searing closeness.

For half a heartbeat, Henry lay sprawled atop her, chest rising and falling against her back as he struggled to catch his breath. She could feel the scattershot *thump thump thump* of his heart through the hardened expanse of his breastbone.

Caroline wondered if he could feel her heart.

She dearly hoped he couldn't. It would give her away.

Another half heartbeat later, he was propping himself up on elbows and knees, his knees planted on either side of her hips. She turned over. His wig had thankfully disappeared, and his long, pale hair hung down about his face and tickled her nose.

"Are you," he panted, tucking the strands behind his ear, "all right?"

Caroline swallowed. Around them people were scrambling, screaming. "I believe so. What's—who—?"

"I don't know," he said grimly, glancing over his shoulder. "But we've got to get you out of here. Now."

He hovered above her, blocking out the night, the world, surrounding her in a heady mix of sight and sound and scent. His green eye stood out boldly against the darkness, wide as he looked at her, and looked, and kept looking.

The look—that *look*!—in his eye made her belly fall to the backs of her knees. No one had looked at her like that in years; intently, softly, as if he liked what he saw, and wanted more of it. As if he wanted her. She struggled not to look away; the onslaught was unbearably brash.

Caroline could see the small droplets of sweat that dotted his eyebrows and temples; the smooth, vexingly inviting flesh of his lips.

No.

The word rose up through her with propulsive force. She had to remember he'd left her, remember all he'd taken and what he'd left behind.

With surprising agility—hadn't Henry been limping when she saw him in the park this afternoon?—he leapt to his feet and pulled Caroline up beside him. People pressed and pushed against them in an attempt to flee; Caroline looked over the crowd to see three black figures making a beeline for the far side of the room.

Her gaze followed them through the darkness. Where the devil were they going? Who—*what*—were they after?

A red-blue spark, a white flash of brilliance caught Caroline's eye.

The French Blue.

Of course.

Those scalawags were after Hope's diamond!

"Oh my God," Caroline said for what felt like the hundredth time. "They're after Hope's diamond!"

She watched in mute horror as the thieves pounced upon the blue-eyed woman wearing the gem. Beside her, William struggled to push them off, his arms swinging, fists battering against the assault.

Henry palmed the back of Caroline's neck, placing his fingers and thumbs gently—if firmly—on the outside slopes of her throat.

He dipped his head. "We've got to go," he murmured in her ear.

She pointed across the room. "But William! They're attacking him. And the diamond—"

"The diamond is gone. Let's go."

Caroline looked up at the sudden edge in Henry's voice. She started; his face had transformed, seemingly within the space of a single heartbeat, into a mask of rage; his mouth was drawn into a tight line.

She followed his gaze back to the woman and her brother. The thieves had all but disappeared, and the lady's hands were clutching her bare throat. She was shouting something, crying, and then she promptly bent at the waist and appeared to empty the contents of her stomach onto William's shoes.

Well, then.

Caroline turned back to Henry. He was watching the pair of them—William and that woman—intently, his eye flashing with something she'd never seen in him before. Something that looked like suspicion.

She drew back. "Wait, wait. Are you—do you know about—?"

"Let's go."

Henry pushed her forward into the crowd, one hand at her neck as he stalked through the chaos beside her. Using his free arm, he cut a path for them across the ballroom; together they ducked through a pair of doors out onto the terrace.

Like frightened children, Hope's guests flitted about the terrace in circles, knocking one another down, bumping into the balustrade. One poor fellow had even managed to get his head stuck between two stone balusters; he wept softly while beside him his wife, hands on her hips, chastised him through gritted teeth.

"Come," Lake said, pulling Caroline toward the edge of the terrace. "Here."

"Here?" Caroline peered over the balustrade. "You mean for us to—?"

"Yes." He placed his hands on the stone railing and lifted himself onto its edge. "Don't worry, it's not as far down as it looks."

"You've done this before?"

"Just this afternoon."

Before she could protest, he flung himself from the railing into the pit of darkness below. Some seconds later she heard a small *crunch*—the gravel beneath his boots.

"Henry!" she cried. "Henry, are you all right? Good heavens, are you even alive?"

"Alive and well!" came the reply. "Your turn."

"My turn?"

"Your turn. Jump."

Caroline squinted into the darkness. Far—*very* far—below, she could make out Henry's massive shape. His arms were akimbo, fists on his hips; he was looking up at her, intently.

"I can't jump that far," she said.

"I'll catch you."

"I can't."

"You must. Now that those bastards—pardon me, my lady. Ahem. Now that those *blackguards* have what they came for, they might wreak other kinds of havoc. Kinds I cannot mention in your presence."

Caroline glanced over her shoulder. The scene behind her was like something out of a particularly melodramatic opera; inside the ballroom, a woman's wig had caught fire and she dashed about madly, arms outstretched.

Caroline looked back down at Henry and swallowed.

"All right," she said. "I'm coming!"

With shaking limbs Caroline climbed over the balustrade. Henry held out his hands.

"Are you sure you can catch me?" Her voice shook.

She could hear the smile in his reply. "Let's hope so."

Caroline screwed her eyes shut. She let go of the balustrade behind her.

For a moment she hovered on the ledge of the terrace, and then she was falling, falling, her stomach in her throat as her arms flailed inelegantly above her head.

She landed heavily in Henry's arms. Her skirts had flown up to her ears, and the padded skeleton of her panniers had somehow detached from her waist and now hung from the tip of her satin slipper. She felt the heat of Henry's palm on the back of her naked knee.

She was naked.

Well, practically.

And she was *in* his *arms*.

"Oh," she said, struggling against her gown. "Oh, dear, this won't do, blasted thing, I should've never—"

She freed her face from her skirts and met Henry's gaze. He was looking at her like that again. Like he had no right to. Like he shouldn't.

There was a violent rush of heat to her face as she elbowed her way to her feet, kicking the panniers off her toe.

Henry nodded to her skirts. "Might I?"

"You might—may—might most certainly not," she said, straightening them the best she could. Which was not very well at all.

Henry reached down anyway and gave her gown a firm tug. It traitorously rearranged into a close version of its former self.

He straightened before her; he stood very close, looming over her in the darkness.

Oh God, she thought. Oh God, what now?

Caroline looked anywhere but at him. They were at the back of Hope's mansion; she could smell the mews, hear the horses stomping and crying out at the chaos upstairs.

She was wondering what the devil to do next when a handful of slight figures appeared at the balustrade on the terrace.

The thieves.

Without thinking, Caroline took Henry's hand and squeezed, pointing up.

In half a heartbeat Henry was tugging her toward the mews; she reached out to grab her panniers from the ground just in time. He moved quickly, his long legs affording him an enormous stride. Caroline tripped behind him in an effort to keep pace.

Now the warmth of his palm was seeping through the fine kidskin of her glove.

Henry drew up short when they entered the mews. They were as much a disaster as the ballroom. Grooms scurried about, shouting directions to waiting coachmen; the coachmen shouted back with curses that made Caroline's ears ring.

"This way," Henry murmured, shoving aside a groom as he led Caroline to a nearby stall. In one of its dark corners, a glistening black mare cowered, her eyes wide and wet.

Henry opened the stall door, quietly removing a saddle from its hook as he began cooing to the horse.

"You're going to steal Mr. Hope's horse?" she whispered.

"Yes."

"Oh. Oh, all right. You're sure he won't—ah—mind?"

Hope aside, the horse certainly did mind; when Henry approached she reared up onto her hind legs and, kicking against the stable walls, screamed.

So, too, did a nearby groom, who rushed toward them with shouts that put the coachmen's expletives to shame.

"Oh dear," Caroline said, backing away.

Henry threw down the saddle and ducked beneath the groom's swinging fist. With savage ferocity, he caught the man's arm and twisted it, hard, behind his back, until the poor groom whimpered for his mummy. Henry tossed him aside and was about to pick up the saddle when another groom appeared, and another.

Henry groaned aloud. Caroline looked from Henry to the grooms and back again.

She looked down at the twisted mess of her panniers in her hand.

She looked back up at the grooms.

Across the stable she met Henry's gaze.

And then with all her might, she launched the panniers at the grooms.

Tangled in a mess of wire hoops and misshapen pads, the grooms were, for a moment, too stunned to do much of anything.

Henry didn't waste a second. He leapt over their wrangling mass and, taking Caroline's hand in his, made for the exit.

They both turned at the thunderous sound of an approaching horse. For a moment Henry's face hardened, and before she knew what he was about, he was pressing her into the shadows beside a nearby stall, urging her to silence with a finger at his lips.

She ventured a peek past the stall's rough-hewn wall.

Mr. Thomas Hope, their magnanimous and thoroughly

costumed host, drew up his enormous horse before Henry. A very pretty—and very young—woman sat astride the saddle in front of him, her diaphanous gown drawn up about her knees. Hope held her firmly against him, his front to her back; the fists in which he held the reins rested on the slope of her hips. There was something about the way he held her—the ease of his touch, the color in his cheeks—that made Caroline wonder who, exactly, she was, and what she meant to London's most eccentric, and richest, banker.

Hands on his own hips, Henry glared at Hope. Even though Hope sat atop his horse, Henry's sheer size, the burning look in his eye, made it appear as if he were staring Hope down, rather than the other way around.

"Hope," he said, "what the devil is thi—?"

The banker held up a hand. "You head east, toward the Thames. The thieves are nimble and likely faster than we'll ever be on horseback or even on foot. Tell no one what has occurred this night. Godspeed."

But Henry did not make to move, and neither did Hope; for an overlong moment they stared one another down, the air crackling with—well, Caroline didn't exactly know what it was, except that it was hard and heavy and probably not good.

She drew a shaking breath as she turned back into the shadows. She'd known Henry was some sort of agent or other, an officer in His Majesty's Alien Office. She knew his trade was secretive and often dangerous; she knew he was probably a spy or a pirate or, in her adolescent late-night fantasies, both.

Still, the reality of it shocked her. First his appearance in Hyde Park, his hand tucked into his waistcoat; there was that look he'd given her brother across the ballroom, and now this charged exchange with Thomas Hope.

Never mind Henry's reappearance in England after all this time. Why was he here? In what sort of sinister web of deceit and daring was he ensnared?

She waited, breathless, until the thunder of hoof beats filled the stable once more. She felt faint with relief.

Henry was at her side then, holding out his hand. She took it.

"Why hide me from Hope?" she asked, following him as he led her out of the mews. "And who was that girl? Why is she with him if he's going after the diamond?"

Henry's mouth was a tight line again. "You don't want to know."

"About the girl? Or the diamond?"

"Both. Neither. Come."

He led her out into the night, their arms clasped between them as they scurried across Duchess Street and away from the crowd surrounding Hope's limestone manse.

The air felt blessedly cool against Caroline's skin. It was a fine evening, the sky soft and close, like velvet. She closed her eyes and lost herself in the sensations of this moment: fresh air, warm night, the scent of spice and lemons—Henry's scent—filling her head.

Her eyes flew open at the sound of an approaching carriage.

She looked over her shoulder to see an enormous lacquered vehicle bearing down upon them. A nearby gas lamp illuminated a familiar coat of arms splayed proudly across the carriage door.

The Harclay coat of arms.

Good God, it was her brother, William! If he saw her, he'd have her head; if he saw her in the company of Henry Beaton Lake, he'd have his head, too.

"Quickly!" she hissed, breaking into a run. "It's my brother!"

Henry did not hesitate. His limp all but disappeared, he fell in line beside Caroline, and together they dashed down the street, careening into a nearby alley.

They ran down one lane after another, Henry guiding them through Mayfair's carefully kept squares and its less so lanes and mews. Heart thumping giddily inside her chest, Caroline followed him into a small, if charming, square somewhere west of Regent Street.

Or at least she *thought* it was west of Regent Street; how much the city had changed since she'd been here last, all those years ago!

Henry stopped before the redbrick façade of a stately town house, a single gas lamp flickering beside its shiny black door; the windows were all dark, save for one on the top floor.

Together, Henry and Caroline bent over and placed their hands on their knees, gasping at the cool night air.

"Why," Henry panted, "are you. Running from your. Brother?"

Caroline looked up. "You don't. Want to know."

One side of his mouth curled into a grin, revealing the curve of a dimple in his cheek. For a second Caroline felt dizzy; that grin, and good heavens that dimple, was charming beyond measure.

She turned toward the house. "Where are we?"

Henry took a deep breath and drew upright. "My older brother's house. His wife was delivered of a daughter last month, and they were unable to travel to London for the season. So now I'm staying here, at least for the time being. Come, let's have a drink or five, shall we?"

Caroline rose, tilting her head to one side. "You did this on purpose, didn't you?"

"Did what?"

"Led me to your house."

Henry's hand went to his chest. "You insult me, my lady. I merely followed your orders and made a dash for the nearest alley. That we happened upon my house is purely coincidence. Now come inside before one of those frighteningly limber thieves swings down from the roof and steals you away."

Five

Of course he'd done it on purpose.

What could Henry say? He wasn't prepared for the visceral strength of his reaction to seeing her for the first time in twelve years; he wasn't prepared for the rush of possessiveness, of guilt, that swept through him at the sight of her alone and lost in the crush of Hope's ballroom.

He should be hunting down the French Blue. The audacity of the thieves shocked him; it took a set of stones to pilfer a fifty-carat gem in front of five hundred people. He should be staying very, very far away from Lady Caroline, Dowager Countess of Berry, for her sake, and his, too.

And yet here he was, handing her a heady pour of musty red wine in a teacup. (He hadn't been able to find the proper crystal glasses.)

"Thank you," she said, turning the cup in her hands.

"Sorry about the cup." He sipped at his own and winced. "And the wine. Bah, that's bad stuff."

Caroline brought the cup to her lips, trying—and failing—not to choke. "How charmingly . . . vintage," she said, coughing.

"I tried to find something else, but my brother must've taken the decent bottles back to Oxfordshire. I suppose one *does* require a bit of wine when a new baby's in the house."

Caroline cocked a brow. "He doesn't know you're staying here, does he?"

Henry sat in the faded armchair across from Caroline's and cleared his throat. "Not exactly."

She smiled down at her cup. "Is that why we're taking te— wine in a bedchamber?"

"I'm afraid so." Henry slurped at his wine. "I haven't any staff with me aside from my colleague Mr. Moon. He makes for a rather dismal butler, and an even worse maid. This is the only room we've managed to turn out. I don't need much."

He crossed and uncrossed his legs, rearranging his limbs into an even more uncomfortable position before the pitifully tiny fire. He could not sit still, not with Caroline in the room.

Especially not with his brother's enormous four-poster bed hovering in the half darkness behind them, an oppressive shadow that, despite his best efforts to ignore it, called out to him like Odysseus's sirens.

Henry slurped more wine. Desperate times did call for desperate measures, and this wine was desperate indeed.

Caroline set the cup in her lap and looked up, meeting his gaze. His entire being started, heart hammering inside his chest. The lovely familiarity of her dark eyes made his stomach clench.

"I do wish you'd take me home." She rolled her lips between her teeth. Her voice was low. "It's getting late, and if my brother finds I'm not in my rooms . . ."

His ears perked up at that. Why would Harclay not have escorted his sister, recently out of mourning, to one of the season's most infamous—and well-attended—events? He obviously did not want her there. But why?

He decided not to pursue the matter, at least not for now. She'd thwarted his questions earlier, and he did not wish to push her away. This could very well be the last time he would ever have her like this, to himself. He didn't want to waste these precious few minutes interrogating her; he was weary of it.

"It's too dangerous," he replied steadily. "The thieves are on the loose, a priceless diamond in hand. God forfend we should meet them in the street, for they would shoot our legs off sure as Sunday. You are safer here, with me."

Caroline's eyes flashed. "Somehow I doubt that."

She swallowed; he watched the working of her throat, hypnotized by the smooth skin there, the inviting slopes and sinews.

He shifted in his chair yet again at the ominous tightening inside his breeches. As if the bloody things weren't tight enough.

He crossed an ankle over his knee so that he might not frighten off Caroline with his worsening—er, condition.

"Who were you looking for?" he asked, as a rather awkward means of changing the subject. "At Hope's ball. I saw you looking for someone."

The only light in the room was that put off by a half-dozen tapers strewn about the chamber; even so, Henry could see Caroline's cheeks burn pink.

"No one," she said, shaking her head as she looked down at her lap. "I wasn't looking for anyone."

A beat of silence passed between them. Henry began to sweat.

"And you. Why were you there? I didn't know . . ." She was swallowing again. Dear God, was she trying to kill him? "I suppose I don't know many things."

"Well." Henry cleared his throat. He'd lied his way through the past twelve years; deceit was his trade, damn it, so why was it so hard to make use of that skill now?

"Well," he said again. "Hope and I are old friends. So."

Even as he said it he struggled not to wince.

"So," she said.

"So."

He dug a hand into the hair at the back of his neck, riling his neatly tied queue. His face was burning.

"Your hair's gotten long," she said. "How fashionably unfashionable of you."

One side of his mouth went up in a smile. "I'll have you know I take great pride in my hair. My brother may have the title, but I have my flowing locks. Poor old chap's got nary a strand left."

"I remember Robert." She bit her lip. He wanted to ask her to stop; it was beyond—*beyond*—distracting. "He finally married?"

"Just last year," Henry said. "To a girl half his age. She's darling, really, and far too good for him. From what information I can gather, they are obnoxiously happy."

"But you two were so close," she said, frowning. "You don't keep in touch?"

Henry's smile tightened. "I'm afraid the"—he searched for the right words—"demands of my position prevent me from corresponding with my family as much as I'd like."

"Of course. I can only imagine the adventures you've encountered. The things you've seen." For a moment her gaze lingered on his eye patch. The look in her eyes made his heart hurt. God, how he wanted to tell her. Tell her everything.

Of course he couldn't; the strength of the impulse surprised him nevertheless.

"But you are back." Her eyes flicked to his lap. "And, from the looks of it, very much alive."

Panic descended upon him as he followed her gaze; he nearly cursed aloud as he covered the very obvious evidence of his arousal with both his hands, the teacup dangling from the hook of his first finger.

Heavens, he'd forgotten about that wicked tongue of hers. He'd loved that about her, once; her ready wit, the often perverse bent of her thoughts. She may have been an earl's daughter, and an heiress at that, but she had the mouth of a sailor.

Needless to say, her comment had the opposite of its intended effect. He was so hard he thought he might burst.

"I'm . . ." He cleared his throat, shifting in his chair. "It's the breeches, they're not mine, I stole—I mean borrowed them, who steals *breeches,* really? They're dashedly tight, you see . . ."

She bit her lip again.

He thought he might die.

"Right, then," she said.

"Yes, quite." He lowered his voice, gaze trained on the offending organ as if he might stare it into submission. No such luck.

"And you," he said. "Are you in London to seek a new husband? I see you're out of mourning."

"Heavens, no."

"I don't mean—I heard of Osbourne's passing, you see— terribly sorry, he was so young—"

Caroline scoffed. "It's not that."

Henry waited for her to explain; when she didn't, he cleared his throat, and said, "I am sorry. He was a good man."

She looked away. "He missed you."

"I missed him."

A beat of uncomfortable silence passed between them. "I'm sorry, my lady. I can't—," he began.

"I know," she said.

He looked up from his lap. They met eyes. Hers glowed in the low light like opals, dark, unknowable, full. So full and so powerful, her gaze was akin to an assault. Heavens, but he was almost glad he had only one eye; knowing her with both eyes, meeting the assault fully naked and bare, would have slain him more surely than any foe he'd yet encountered.

He looked and she looked and as the heartbeats passed, something moved between them, something that was at once arousing and painful. The amusement in her eyes faded, as did her small smile; her lips fell apart and so did her composure, and he could tell by the rapid rise and fall of her chest that she was struggling to breathe.

She was open before him. She was lovely.

His heart—his *everything*—felt swollen to twice its size as he looked at her. He wanted to smile at the disheveled, swirling tilt of her hair. He wanted to weep at the hurt in her eyes and in the crease between her brows.

The air rushed out of his lungs to make room for the rising tide of desire, of regret, that moved through him. He was leaning forward in his chair, all but numb to the sharp pain of protest in his bad leg; his cup fell with a clatter to the floor.

Her face. Oh, her face; it seemed impossibly small, impossibly vulnerable. He remembered cradling it in his hands as he'd kissed her that night in the chapel. The desire to run his thumb along the edge of her chin, touch the warm smoothness of her skin, overwhelmed him.

Caroline did not move toward him, but she didn't back away, either. She sat very still, her gaze watchful and weary, her color deepening as he drew closer. He could smell her perfume, the lilies and that fresh cleanness that was *her*.

Henry reached for her face. He was about to touch her when she winced against a rush of tears. She stood, abruptly, swiping his fallen teacup from the floor as she did so. He blinked, stunned.

"More wine," she said. It was less question, more command.

He said nothing. His throat felt tight.

Caroline sidled around the chair to the bureau that was serving double duty as a sideboard. She coaxed the cork from the bottle; wisps of hair, fallen from their pins, trailed down the back of her neck. He watched them move idly in the breeze from the open window.

She set the bottle down on the bureau, suddenly, and placed her hands on either end of its marble top; she sagged against it, her head dipping.

"Caroline." He was on his feet on an instant and standing behind her. "Caroline, are you unwell?"

She looked over her shoulder. His belly turned over at the expression on her face. Damn it, she was crying.

"Caroline," he said again.

"Don't call me that."

"I'm—I'm sorry, I just—"

She was clutching at her stays then, gasping for air as she turned toward him. "I can't breathe. Please," she gasped. "Please, if you could—"

Henry spun her back round, his movements succinct, violent almost, as he tore at the back of her gown with his hands. He felt the sobs tripping in her chest as he tugged free the laces of her corset, coaxing, pulling with his fingers; he winced as her bottom pushed far too invitingly against his erection.

As if the damned thing could give him any more grief. Jesus.

His fingers brushed against the bare skin of her back. He could see the last knobs of her spine rise above the top of her undergarments before sloping into shoulders and neck; the lace edge of her chemise peeked teasingly through the gap in her stays.

Her skin was hot to the touch.

Henry swallowed, hard, as Caroline leaned against the bureau. Now that her gown was open at the back, its sleeves worked themselves farther and farther off her shoulders with every breath she took. After a beat one of them slipped. Her shoulder was bare.

The same shoulder that had been in his mouth when he'd practically mauled her in the ballroom.

Dear God.

He swallowed again.

She breathed against him, and he breathed against her. He wondered how a naked shoulder could be infinitely more erotic than other, more private naked parts.

Her left hand went to her forehead; with her right, she poured wine into her cup and threw it back in a single gulp.

"Henry," she whispered. The sound of her voice made him feel the burn behind her closed eyes as his own. "Mr. Lake."

"Don't call me that."

She scoffed. "Maybe we shouldn't call each other anything."

"Of course. Yes," he said. A pause. He was holding himself an inch away from her. It was killing him, the impulse to close the distance between them, to press his body against hers. Resisting it was like resisting the end of night, the approach of morning: inevitably idiotic, vexingly futile.

Frustrating. Waiting out the passing of this moment, and then the next, frustrated him to no end.

He wanted to touch her. God, he wanted it more than he'd ever wanted anything.

But he was hurting her. She was hurting, and it was because of him. He closed his eyes against his guilt. He'd married her, claimed her as his own, and left her the next day.

Henry had no right to touch Caroline. He'd lost that right twelve years ago. He'd lost her. He was a cad, a blackguard, a scalawag of the worst sort.

Still, the desire to claim her again glowed brightly inside him.

He stared down at the skin of her neck; that *skin*. His fingers burned with the need to touch her there.

Those stray wisps of her hair were stuck to her glistening nape. Without thinking—without meaning to—he reached up and brushed them aside with his thumb.

Caroline sucked in a breath as the skin along her neck and shoulders broke out in a wave of goose bumps. She didn't say anything.

And then Henry was leaning forward, angling his neck as he lost himself in her nearness. He pressed his mouth, gently, to the bottom corner of her neck, the place where it sloped into shoulder. Her skin singed his lips; he tasted salt, and her.

A flood of memory crashed through him. He knew her, he knew her taste and the curves and hollows of her body, the breathless sounds she made. Across the ballroom she'd been a stranger; but now, up close, she was as familiar as she'd been that summer night so many years ago.

She was his.

At least for now.

His lips were moving up the elegant length of her neck now, slowly, as he savored every inch of skin, and felt the furious working of her pulse in the curve beneath her ear.

Caroline's eyes were still closed as she tilted her head, baring her throat to him. He held her neck in his hands, holding her closer against him, steadying her against his increasing hunger.

His mouth moved over her jaw to graze the corner of her lips, and then he was turning her toward him, trapping her legs between his own as he at last took her face in his hands and pressed his lips to hers.

A levy broke inside him at that moment, releasing a torrent of emotion, of feeling he hadn't known he'd been holding inside his chest until now.

Behind his closed lid he saw stars, and then he saw nothing, blind to everything but the riot of sensation that pulsed through him from this place where skin met skin.

In half a heartbeat he was wild with desire. It took his every ounce of self-control to kiss her carefully, thoughtfully, as she ought to be kissed; as he wanted to kiss her.

He wanted to do a thousand other things, too, things he'd learned in the misguided hope that he would one day be able to do them to *her*. Things that one could only learn in Paris; things that would make an Englishman blush, or die, or both.

God, but her lips were soft. Yielding. Her mouth tasted sweet, like wine, and clean. She allowed him to open her lips with the gentle press of his own; he groaned aloud, eyes rolling to the back of his head.

He dug his fingers into her hair, his thumbs hooked beneath her chin. He moved her head against his kiss, tilting her to the right, then to the left, taking her bottom lip between his teeth.

Henry took and she gave, willingly, meeting him stroke for stroke. She was falling into his caress; he could feel her sway beneath him.

The wildness that ran hot just beneath his skin—he struggled to control it.

And then, in the next instant, he couldn't.

He stepped forward, wanting to feel more of her against him; instead he managed to push her, hard, into the bureau.

Caroline cried out against his mouth, a pitiful sound that made his heart twist inside his chest. At once he fell away, holding up his hands.

"Oh—oh, Car—my lady, I didn't mean— Are you all right?"

She was weeping again, tears streaming from the corners of her closed eyes. Her bottom lip wobbled as she struggled to catch her breath.

Christ, what had he done? He was a pig, a randy, rutting pig, and a vile bastard, too. He was thirty *bloody* years old; he should have learned to control his baser impulses by now.

Henry had done enough damage. He could not bear the thought that he'd hurt her yet again.

"Please," he begged, desperate.

She opened her eyes; they were sharp with pain. He couldn't help himself; he reached for her. She froze.

"Don't," she said, her voice thick with tears.

"But I—"

Anger flashed in her eyes. *"Don't."* And then: "Take me home. Please, Henry, take me home."

He looked at her. "I'm sorry."

She looked back. A beat passed between them. She reached out, and brought her hand down, hard, on the side of his face.

His ears rung at the force of her blow; his skin stung as he blinked, stunned, holding the offended cheek in his hand.

For the first time in his life, Henry didn't know quite what to say.

Caroline looked away, her chest rising and falling; and then, quickly, she made to move past him. He reached out and grabbed her by the arm, pulling her against him.

"Don't touch me," she said, fighting his grip.

He gritted his teeth. "I'll not allow you to walk home unescorted. It's dark, and those blasted thieves are on the loose."

"I don't want you to escort me. My brother lives three streets over, I'll be fine—"

"No."

"No?" She drew back. "Don't think I won't slap you again."

He met her eyes. "But you won't."

She hesitated. Tears streamed down the sides of her face as she closed her eyes, shaking her head.

"Why are you here?" Her voice broke. "Why have you come?"

His grip loosened on her arm. "Business. I'm here on business. I would've never—"

She scoffed. "*Business*. Of course."

"I'd tell you more if I could."

She tore her arm from his grasp, backing away. "I don't want to know more."

"What do you want?" he said, softly.

Caroline met his eyes. "I want you to take me home. And then I want you to stay away from me, for good."

"All right." He licked his lips.

"I thought you were dead," she said, swiping her cheek with the heel of her hand. "Sometimes I even wished you *were* dead. That made it hurt a little less. I couldn't stand the thought of you being alive anywhere else but with me. I never heard from you, nor did anyone else. The way you disappeared after taking all that I had to give—the grief, Henry, you cannot know the grief I have suffered. And now, to know that you've been alive all this time . . ."

I know, Caroline, he wished to say. I know the weight of your grief, for I have carried it as my own these past twelve years.

"I thought you were dead," she repeated. "Then you appear out of the ether, running from God knows what through the hedgerow in Hyde Park. Did you follow me to Hope's ball?"

"No." He swallowed. "Yes. Maybe. Not exactly."

She scoffed again. After a beat she drew a deep breath and squared her shoulders. When she spoke she sounded weary, defeated. "Take me home, Henry. And for God's sake, don't ever come near me again."

He chewed on his bottom lip. "If that is your wish."

"It is, very much."

"Your gown." He nodded at her bare shoulder. "Let me help you."

Caroline turned her back to him, pulling her loose hair over that damnably beautiful shoulder. She was shaking.

He took the laces of her stays in his hands and gave them a soft tug; her body rocked in time to his movements. He wove the silken laces through each of the heavily embroidered grommets, his fingers brushing her skin as he tied off the laces at the small of her back.

His throat was so tight he could hardly breathe.

Henry brought her sleeve back over her shoulder, and then he went to work at the buttons of her gown. His fingers trembled and slipped, and he cursed under his breath. Her scent filled his head.

"I can do it," she said, reaching back.

"No." He tugged her toward him. "There's only a few more."

He coaxed the last button through its tiny hole. Resisting the impulse to put his hands on her, he stepped away, releasing a long, low breath.

"There," he said. "A little crooked, perhaps. But otherwise all set."

Caroline tucked her hair back over her shoulder and placed her hands on her ribs. "Thank you."

She shivered at a sudden gust of chill night air. Henry crossed the room and closed the window, untangling one of his coats from a nearby settee. He really should look into hiring a valet, and soon; Mr. Moon was better at being a woman than he was at tidying up.

"Here," he said, holding the jacket up to Caroline's back. "Might I?"

She glanced over her shoulder. "Yes."

He wrapped her in the jacket, carefully; she pulled it by the lapels closer about her breast.

Her breast. He couldn't even think the word without feeling like his cock would leap out of his breeches.

You cad, he screamed at himself. *You bastard.*

"Let's go, then," he said gruffly.

She followed him out into the night. The air felt blessedly fresh, a welcome foil to the desire still burning inside him. He could not bear to be close to her—honestly, his cock *would* leap out of his breeches if he so much as looked at her—and so he walked a pace or two ahead, stalking through Mayfair as quickly as his feet would take him.

Henry knew her family's town house well; it was one of the oldest—and largest—mansions in Hanover Square.

She moved quietly behind him, her footsteps falling lightly on the cobblestone street. At last they drew up at the back of her brother's house. Curiously, several windows glowed with light. It must be half past one, at least; what the devil was Harclay up to at this hour?

"Do you need help getting in unnoticed?" Henry asked, hopefully. "It appears your brother might still be awake. We might—I mean *you* might—climb through the window?"

Caroline glanced up at the house, a small smile playing at her lips. "Oh, he's awake, but I daresay he is much occupied at the moment—either with wine or a woman or both. Probably both, now that I think about the way he was looking at that girl tonight. Though I must confess I am relieved he—she—they both made it out of Hope's ballroom alive. He won't notice me sneaking in."

"Of course." Henry rocked back on his heels. "Well, then."

She turned to look at him. "Here, your coat—"

"Keep it."

"I couldn't. One of the maids might find it, or William. It's far too large . . ."

"Keep it," he said. He gave the sleeves of his robin's-egg blue coat a good tug. "I find I am rather partial to this lovely frock, and may have several made in its pattern. Something about the cuffs, and the sheen of the silk—rather glorious, isn't it?"

She smiled, a sad thing. Her eyes gleamed in the blue light of the moon above. "Good-bye, Mr. Lake."

"My lady." He bowed, struggling to keep his voice even. "I—I confess I do not know what to say."

For a moment she hesitated. "Neither do I. Good night."

And then she was gone, the squat kitchen door closing noiselessly behind her.

Henry stared at the door for several minutes, not moving, hardly daring to breathe. He didn't know what he was waiting for. She wasn't coming back; she wouldn't fly through the door and in a fever of romantic impulse toss him into the nearby bushes and have her way with him. That light in her eyes—the one that belonged to the seventeen-year-old girl he knew a decade ago, the one that flashed with mischief, and the intent to indulge such impulses—had been extinguished.

Finally he turned and strode back out to the street.

He didn't make it very far.

Somewhere between Hanover Square and Regent Street, Henry drew up, suddenly, in the shadows of what was probably some royal duke's half-completed palatial manse. Leaning his forearm against the naked scaffolding, he smothered the sounds of his grief in the crook of his elbow.

Beneath him, the wooden beam shook in time to his shoulders.

He managed to compose himself sometime later, wiping his nose on his sleeve. His ribs felt bruised, as if he'd been beaten from the inside out.

Well, then.

There would be no sleep for him tonight. He looked up at the moon; it would be dark for hours yet. As he'd discovered years ago, there was no better cure for heartache than chasing scalawags through slums in the dead of night. He would hunt down the thieves and recapture the French Blue, and once Napoleon took the bait, Henry would be on the first ship bound for France. He'd forget tonight, forget the look in Caroline's eyes when he'd called her by her name.

His work had always distracted him from what he'd done; he could not think about *her* if he was in motion, constantly. And tonight he needed to be distracted.

To Cheapside, then.

Six

Caroline moved silently through the shadowed halls of her brother's house, not daring to breathe lest she release the sobs tightening at the back of her throat.

She stopped short at the suspicious sounds emanating from behind the closed doors of the drawing room. It was shameless of her, but at nine-and-twenty she was too old for such trifles as shame, and so she drew closer, angling her head so that she might better listen.

There was the tinkling of laughter—*female* laughter—and then, a beat later, a voice.

"Wait a moment," the woman said. "How am I to double my stakes? I've only one virtue to offer, after all."

Caroline blinked. Surely this woman was not wagering her virtue over a game of cards with William? It was preposterous to even think—

"I shall just have to take you twice," her brother purred. Caroline could hear him shuffling a deck of cards. "Shan't I?"

She surely *was* offering William her virginity. Caroline wondered what William wagered in return. Really, where did he find such willing victims? And which games of chance invited bets of a sexual nature?

The mind, in all its perversions, boggled.

Caroline straightened and continued her progress through the house, trying very hard not to think about what, exactly, her brother was up to behind those closed doors. She had the distinct feeling the woman with only one virtue to offer was the lady who'd been wearing Hope's diamond at the ball, the one whose eyes were the same gray-blue shade as the jewel.

The jewel that was now gone, thieved in the chaos of an epic crush. She wondered what Thomas Hope would do to find it.

She wondered if Henry Lake was involved in its sudden appearance in a London ballroom; she wondered if he was involved in its theft, if that theft was the "business" that brought him back to England.

She slipped into her darkened rooms, pressing her back against the door as she closed it, quietly, behind her. Her eyes fluttered shut as she remembered the feel of Henry's lips on her skin; her fingers brushed the place on her throat where his caress had begun, marveling that there was no mark there.

She marveled that he had not branded her with his searing heat.

She had wanted to push him off, and tell him to go to hell. It was what he deserved. Did he think that in the twelve years since she'd seen him last, she would forget that he'd claimed her soul and her body and disappeared the next day? That she would forgive him, and forget his trespasses, and welcome his embrace?

She'd come *this close* to doing just that. Not the forgiving and forgetting part—for she would never forget, and *never* forgive—but good God, the sweetness of being in his arms again had caught her unawares.

A shiver went down her spine as she remembered the feel of his hands on her face, the way he kissed her as if the world were ending, and this their last night together. It *was* their last night together.

Caroline shivered again. She drew the lapels of his coat more tightly about her; his scent, the spice, clung to the fabric, and she inhaled, filling her being with *him*. She'd met many men in her lifetime. None smelled so damnably good as Henry Lake.

She felt exhausted, wrung out, her eyes heavy from crying.

She felt aroused, incredibly so, the pounding beat between her legs impossible to ignore.

During that summer twelve years ago, after he'd left her, she'd wept for a week, and then another, always in secret, always hiding the sounds of her grief in her pillow. On the third week she swore she wouldn't miss him, that he did not deserve her pain. And so she gave herself over to her hurt one last night, and when the morning came, she washed her face and went to breakfast and never wept over Henry again.

Perhaps she might do the same tonight. Perhaps Caroline might give herself over to her hurt, and her desire, one last time, and in the morning begin her liberated life as a widow; it had, after all, been more than a year since Osbourne's passing. An eccentrically aloof, steadfastly unattached widow.

But tonight—tonight she would be with Henry. *One last time.*

Wrapping herself in Henry's coat, she fell back upon the bed, the ropes beneath the mattress sighing in protest. Closing her eyes, she remembered the slide of his mouth over her shoulder and throat, the demanding press of his lips against her own, and the way he'd pulled her bottom lip between his teeth—

Dear. *God.*

Surrounded by Henry's scent, Caroline tugged at her skirts, gathering them in her fists at her waist; toeing off her slippers, she heard them fall with soft thuds to the carpet below.

Her entire body broke out in a sweat at the image of him—him, Henry—looming above her, his shoulders blocking the night as he angled his head to kiss her. He took, and kept taking, and in that moment she'd offered up all she had to give.

Her heart took off at a gallop.

She tugged aside her chemise, palm brushing against a bare knee, and with impatient fingers reached inside her pantalets.

Her thighs fell apart at the first stroke of her middle finger against her sex. She was slick with desire, slick and very warm, swollen; she saw stars at the sensation that spiked through her. Her nipples pricked to life against the confines of her corset, pleading to be set free.

His face flashed across the backs of her closed eyelids, the concentration in his narrowed gaze as he'd stalked her across the ballroom.

Henry.

The breath caught in Caroline's throat. Her fingers worked slowly between her legs, tracing slippery circles over the center of all this maddening, delicious sensation.

And oh, the feel of his skin against hers, the inviting warmth of his body beneath the layers of that ridiculous, and strangely charming, costume . . .

She gritted her teeth as her desire pulsed hotter, her fingers moving quickly now, pressing and tugging and pushing as her body burned. It had been so long since she'd felt such searing need; she couldn't remember the last time she felt so awakened, so frustrated, so insatiably hungry.

The feel of his arms around her, the heat in his eyes as he'd looked down on her, and said her name—it hurt, that memory, because it would be the last time she'd ever feel that way again. It hurt, and it aroused.

The tightness between her legs became unbearable. Her body arched off the bed, her hips bucking against her hand. Her eyes flew open as the beat beneath her fingers turned sharp, spiraling higher and higher.

Henry.

What she would give for him to be here, now, so that they might finish what they started in his brother's bedchamber! How she longed to run her hands over the muscles and slopes of his bare shoulders, to feel the gentle press of his weight against her as he moved between her legs.

She bit her lip and fell back to the bed and with one last stroke of her fingers sent herself over the edge. Tears trailed down her temples into her hair as she gasped against the force of her climax, legs curling as if they'd wrap themselves about Henry's imaginary hips.

His hips, heavens, those hardened slices of temptation—

Her desire pulsed hard, hot, one last time. Her pulse rushed in her ears.

"Henry," she whispered.

Her fingers stilled and the beat of her completion slowed. Gradually she came back to inhabit the heaviness of her own body, the rush in her ears fading until she could hear the soft *whoosh* of her breath. In and *out*, in and *out*.

Caroline swallowed, the back of her right hand falling to

her forehead as she stared at the ceiling. His scent was everywhere, mingled with that of her arousal.

Well.

Perhaps she might make an exception to her rule that she would never think of Henry again; perhaps she might only think of him when—er—the *need* arose.

For that was bloody lovely.

And lonely.

She blinked back the tears that threatened to begin anew. It didn't make sense that she would desire him after all that he'd done to her; heavens, she was possessed of some modicum of self-respect, wasn't she?

Still.

Even now the heat between her thighs throbbed at the memory of his legs wrapped around hers, trapping her against the bureau. His legs, and his eyes, the way he smelled and smiled.

She turned onto her side, tucking up her knees to her chest. She vowed that, when the sun rose, she wouldn't think of those things anymore.

Wincing, Caroline turned over in her bed at the quiet knocking on her door. She opened an eye and was met with a glorious spring morning, the light arching through the open window bright pink with promise.

Promise that, at the moment, Caroline found intensely annoying.

Her mouth felt dry and sour; she groaned, recalling Henry's unfortunate choice of libation last night in his brother's chamber.

Henry.

She was awake suddenly, the memory of last night's events rolling through her in a tide of poignant emotion. Meeting eyes with Henry through the trees in Hyde Park, Henry covering her body with his own in the chaos of Hope's ballroom (chivalrously, and thrillingly), Henry's lips and teeth nicking her jaw.

Not one minute awake and already her heart was pounding.

So was the person at her door.

Caroline rolled to her feet, noting with a small measure of distaste that she was still in her costume from last night.

But her thick-hipped panniers, those were thankfully missing. Where did I lose them? she wondered.

Oh, yes, she'd thrown them at one of Thomas Hope's
grooms while Henry tried—and failed—to steal a horse.

Of course.

She risked a glance in the mirror above her gilded vanity,
and was shocked the glass did not shatter on account of her
reflection. With trembling fingers, she quickly smoothed the
swirling bird's nest of her hair. She squared her shoulders.

It didn't matter what happened last night.

Today was a new day, the day on which she would begin
her life anew as Dowager Countess of Berry, a widow free
from the complications of coupling. There would be no Henry.
There would be no Hope, or his missing diamond.

Those things did not concern her.

"M'lady!" a familiar voice hissed from the other side of the
door. "M'lady, if you please, it's urgent!"

Caroline opened the door. There, standing in the dim hallway, was her maid, Nicks; the girl from Hope's ball—the one
with the blue-gray eyes, who'd worn (and lost) his diamond—
peeked over her shoulder.

Caroline struggled to contain her surprise.

"But you're still here?" she said, quite rudely, to the girl.

"Oh, God," the girl replied, blushing a little, "you didn't—"

"Hear you last night? Of course I did. Do come in." She
ushered them inside her chamber and quietly nudged the door
shut, turning back to her visitor. The girl's gown was practically in shreds. "From the looks of it you lost that bet."

"Actually," the girl said, looking up to meet Caroline's
gaze, "I won. It's just that his lordship your brother is an
awfully sore loser."

Caroline found herself grinning. "You should've seen him
when he was little. If he lost a game, or came in second in a
race, he'd cry so hard he would faint."

"He *is* stubborn," the girl said, glancing at her hands.
"Among other things."

Across the room, Caroline met eyes with Nicks; she saw a
good deal of disapproval in her maid's gaze, a touch of curiosity. Taking in her mistress's deflated costume and disheveled

hair, the disapproval in Nicks's eyes darkened. Caroline did her best to ignore her.

"Apologies to bother ya so early in the mornin'," Nicks huffed, turning to straighten the pillows on Caroline's bed, "but Lady Violet here needs to borrow a bit of clothin'. Can't go down to breakfast lookin' a right mess like this; she'll scare the wits out of the servants and—er—*rile* his lordship, if yer know what I mean."

"Lady Violet," Caroline said, nodding her head. "I don't think I've had the pleasure. You aren't—?"

"Married? Heavens, no. I am Violet Rutledge." Here she bobbed a curtsy. "And I'm afraid I am in need of a morning gown."

Caroline liked Lady Violet already, her wit, her forwardness, her disdain for all things matrimonial in nature; she had an inkling William liked her for these very same reasons.

She was a pretty girl, youngish, but old enough to be nearly on the shelf; surely with eyes—they were wide and very blue, a startling foil to her raven-hued hair—and a bosom like that, she'd received any number of offers from gentlemen. Why, then, had she chosen spinsterhood?

"It's a long story," Violet continued, reading Caroline's thoughts. "But your brother practically kept me prisoner here after the unfortunate events at Thomas Hope's ball last evening. We had champagne, and . . . and then, well"—she looked down at her dress—"things got rather out of hand."

"I see," Caroline said.

Violet's gaze traveled up the length of Caroline's costume. "And I see you were in attendance at the ball as well, though William made no mention of your presence."

"He doesn't know I was there," Caroline said, sidling up close to Violet. "Nor does he need to."

Violet looped her arm through Caroline's. "I do so admire a woman with secrets; there are precious few of us these days. Come, let us dress; I've a diamond to hunt down, and you, a very *secret* male admirer."

"What? Who? What?" Caroline felt her face flush with heat. "I don't—er—know what you're talking about—how do you—?"

Violet pressed a cool finger to the back of Caroline's neck.

"He left his mark," she said softly. "And his jacket, there on the bed . . ."

Caroline's hand flew to cover the offending spot. Damn Henry and those lips. If she ever saw him again, she would be sure to slap him one last time for good measure.

"Nicks," she called. "If you please, do lay out the blue morning gown—the one with the high neck. Yes, that's the one, thank you."

Arm in arm, Lady Violet and Caroline entered the well-lit warmth of the breakfast room at a quarter to eight. It was hellishly early to be awake, especially after last night's late hours and all that dreadful wine she'd had; Caroline couldn't tell if her belly ached because she was hungry, or because she was about to empty its contents all over her brother's pristine upholstery.

Even in her state of half-dead misery, Caroline did not miss the way William's face lit up when Lady Violet came into the room. His color was high, and as he rose to his feet he fumbled, quite adorably, trying to fold the newspaper in his hands.

Violet, too, was blushing, and as Caroline looked from one to the other she wondered what, exactly, Violet meant when she'd called William a sore loser.

"Ladies," he said, bowing awkwardly. "Lovely of you to join me, and at so early an hour. I trust you have made each other's acquaintance?"

Caroline raised a brow, biting back a smile. "Indeed. The maids informed me of Lady Violet's presence this morning, and I went straightaway to see her. Poor dear told me about the tragic events at Mr. Hope's ball. To think, a thief made off with the French Blue in the midst of a crowded ballroom! I wonder how he did it."

"Well"—William's cheeks burned a brighter shade of red—"hardly worth thinking about, seeing as it's over and done. We must focus our energies on helping Mr. Hope capture the perpetrators, so that the diamond might yet be found."

Caroline's gaze narrowed as something—something that felt vaguely like suspicion—caught inside her head. It was obvious William did not wish to discuss the theft; was he being dodgy, or merely polite before his blue-eyed paramour?

She shook the idea from her thoughts. Henry, that black-hearted bully, had rubbed off on her. Not everyone, she reminded herself, was embroiled in a sinister plot; she need not be suspicious, especially of her dear—if often daft—brother.

Nevertheless, Caroline was so entertained by his obvious excitement at Lady Violet's presence that she accidentally elbowed the footman, Kane, who at that moment happened to be carrying a tray of fragrant little sausages. Kane went flying and so did his sausages; one of them landed, tellingly, in Caroline's lap. She tried not to blush.

They passed the rest of breakfast pleasantly, Caroline wondering all the while if Lady Violet's poor mama would buy their tale that Caroline, being a widow (and, at thirty, an ancient one at that), had been a most rigorous chaperone for Violet and William last night. The circumstances that had brought the two of them together were, admittedly, irregular; still, if anyone discovered Lady Violet had spent the night at the residence of a known rakeshame, she would be ruined.

They were just getting to the juicy bits of last night's events when William's slick-haired butler, Mr. Avery, appeared at the door. Unlike his master, Avery was strangely pale.

"Forgive me, my lord, I've rather urgent news from Mr. Hope. One of his men waits now in the front hall. It seems they have caught the thieves and are keeping them at Mr. Hope's house for questioning. Mr. Hope also asks after Lady Violet Rutledge."

Utensils dropped with an impolite clatter to plates; napkins were tossed across the table; Caroline, Lady Violet, and William jostled one another out of the breakfast room into the gallery.

"Where do you think you're going?" William murmured in Caroline's ear.

Her heart beat loudly inside her chest, an insistent, heady pace that drowned out her thoughts and, apparently, her reason. "I'm coming with you to Hope's."

"But you've nothing to do with the French Blue, or its theft."

She didn't, but Caroline had the funniest feeling that Henry did.

Besides, she owed him a solid slap for the mark he'd left on her neck.

"You're staying," William warned.

"I'm going," she said.

And even though it went against everything she'd said, everything she'd promised herself in the small hours of last night, even though it was foolish, and probably dangerous, and definitely irresponsible, Caroline was *going* to Hope's, whether her brother wished it or not.

Seven

Henry had found the thieves in—where else?—a close, smelly tavern in Cheapside.

It had been a quick, if unexciting, chase. After collecting Mr. Moon from another close, smelly tavern (this one in Whitechapel), together they tore their way through the darkened streets until at last they cornered their quarry in a dark little hole called the Cat and Mouse.

But even as Henry reveled in the thrill of yet another job well done, he could not shake the memory of Caroline. Caroline across the park; Caroline across the ballroom; the back of Caroline's neck, the taste of the skin there.

He finished his fourth cup of scalding-hot coffee, blinking back the exhaustion he felt at not having slept a wink. He was in the bowels of Hope's Mayfair mansion, standing just outside the kitchens in a high-ceilinged hall flooded with early morning sunlight. Behind the door to his right, the thieves were bound in the servants' dining room.

The door opened and Mr. Moon emerged, jaw speckled with the shadow of dark stubble; he held a pipe, long ago extinguished, between his teeth.

He appeared ready to collapse.

"No luck," he said quietly, and shook his head. "Searched 'em, threatened to pull out their fingernails and cut off their b—"

"Too early," Lake growled.

Moon cleared his throat, plucking the pipe from his teeth. "Right, then. Performed the usual tasks, but so far, no sign of the diamond."

"Hm." Lake crossed one ankle over the other and leaned against the wall. "You think they sold it?"

Moon shrugged. "They claim they don't know a thing about the French Blue. Say they've never even heard of it."

Lake yawned so thoroughly it made his eyes water. He dropped his cup to its saucer with a clank. "Out of all our assignments, why does this one have to be so difficult? I sincerely hope we don't have to cut off their ba—"

"Lake! Any luck?" Hope hurried down the hall, running a hand through his disheveled curls. Lady Violet Rutledge and Lord William Townshend, Earl of Harclay, followed closely behind.

At once Lake's pulse quickened; he straightened, uncrossing his ankles. William Townshend, Caroline's brother.

What was he doing here?

And, more importantly, had his sister accompanied him on this early morning jaunt across town?

Henry glanced at the ceiling; was she waiting upstairs in the drawing room at this very moment?

He looked back down and met eyes with Hope. "Nothing yet. But we could use more coffee."

Lady Violet peeked over Lake's shoulder at the door. "Let me talk to them. I've got an idea."

It was all Henry could do not to roll his eyes. If this little twit hadn't lost the jewel in the first place, they wouldn't be in this mess.

Then again, he didn't have any better ideas.

With a sigh, Henry pressed open the door and led them into the room. The thieves glowered, faces red as they tugged at the bindings that bound their hands to the spindles of their chairs. The room was ripe with the smells of coffee, sweat, and sour ale.

Half expecting Lady Violet to run screaming for the door, Henry was surprised to find a saucy grin on her lips, her eyes flashing seductively as she sashayed toward her rapt audience.

She flirted and whispered, talked and touched; Harclay watched from the corner, face tight, fists balled at his sides.

It took her all of five minutes to make them sing.

"What big hands you have!" she said, running a finger along one of the thieves' arms. "And these muscles—my, my! So strong and manly. How popular you lot must be with the ladies."

The man smiled, revealing more gums than teeth. "We's acrobats, m'lady, been with th' show at Vauxhall free years now, crowd does luv our tricks, ladies, too," he said. His accent was so thick he could chew on it—if, that is, he had more teeth.

Violet sat on the edge of the table, fingering the man's lapel. "Tell me, then, how you ended up in Thomas Hope's ballroom last night."

The man glanced down at Violet's hand. Henry could practically feel the Earl of Harclay's simmering wrath roll to a boil.

"Was 'bout a week ago," he said. "We was down the pub—yeah?—when a man wiv a fake-like beard, teeth rottin' out ov his head—yeah?—sat down," the lead man said. "Said he'd give fi'ty pounds to the each ov us for making a right nice mess of your fancy-pants party. Twen'y-five before, twen'y-five after. We's still waitin' on that last payment—yeah?—if any of yous know where I can find tha bugger."

Henry brought a knuckle to his lips. An obviously fake beard? That was one he'd yet to encounter until this very moment.

"But what of the diamond?" Violet pressed. "What instructions did the man give you about stealing Mr. Hope's diamond?"

The acrobats replied with blank stares.

A pulse of dread shot through Lake.

They didn't do it. These men may have been scalawags, and stinking ones at that, but they were not thieves.

But if they didn't steal the diamond, who did? This was bad; very bad news indeed. Henry had to find the diamond, and soon. So many lives depended on it.

And he had to get out of London. Away from Caroline, before he broke the promise he made twelve years ago to protect her. Keep her safe from the violence posed by who he was, what he did.

"We ain't bover wif no diamond," another man said. "Make no mention ov it, just paid us to make a nice right racket."

Violet drew back, tucking her folded hands into her skirts. Henry could tell she was just as perplexed as he.

"And what of the other twenty-five pounds the man owes you? Have you received it yet?"

The man shook his head. "Nah. Seein' as we been caught, we ain't expectin' to see the rest. Though that ain't exactly fair now, is it?"

Violet met Henry's gaze. Something didn't add up here. The diamond couldn't have disappeared into thin air; someone had to have taken it.

But who?

Dread knotted in his belly as he glanced across the room at Lord Harclay. From the looks of it, the earl's head was about to explode. Was he jealous of the lust flashing in the acrobats' eyes as they followed Lady Violet about the room?

Or was that panic Henry saw in his lordship's pained expression?

This interview was creating more questions than it answered.

Lake closed his eyes, pulling at his eyelids with his thumb and forefinger. His head ached fiercely. He wondered if, in his exhausted delirium, he'd begun imagining things.

He wondered if Lady Caroline Osbourne was still upstairs in the drawing room. (If she'd ever been there in the first place.)

He felt impatient, suddenly; it was stifling in here.

He followed Lady Violet and Lord Harclay out into the hall, closing the door soundly behind them; the air felt fresh as a field of flowers compared to the close smells of the dining room.

Mr. Moon looked up hopefully from his coffee. Henry shook his head.

"Keep them here for now," he said, making his way down the hall, "until I figure out what to do next."

Moon leapt to his feet. "Right then, sir," he called after his superior. "And when might that be?"

Henry threw up his hands. "Tomorrow. Today. Never, probably."

Lady Violet appeared at his elbow, trotting breathlessly beside him. "I," she panted, "can help you, Mr. Lake."

He arched a brow. "You've been helpful enough, my lady, thank you."

"No." She tugged him to a stop by his arm. "The diamond was snatched from about my neck. It is my responsibility to get it back. Besides, I've a good deal of money invested in Hope and Company stock. If word gets out that Hope cannot safeguard his own assets, much less anyone else's—well, I don't need to tell you that the bank will be ruined, and so will I. Please, Mr. Lake. We've got to find the French Blue. I've got to find it, before I lose everything."

If only she knew the safety of England, and all her brave soldiers, were at stake, too, he thought. If the diamond was lost, Violet would not be the only one to suffer.

Henry tugged a hand through the hair at the back of his neck. His heart beat an uneven tattoo inside his chest. Even with all this danger and talk of destitution—even with the very real threat of defeat looming over him—all he could think about was getting up to that damned drawing room.

"I suppose I need all the help I can get," he said, sighing. "We've got more information than we started with this morning, but it's still not enough. You might contact me through Hope if you find out more."

Without waiting for a reply, he bounded up the narrow kitchen stairs. Even as he told himself he was heading for the front door—it would be the first, and likely only, time he would use it—his gait slowed as he approached the drawing room.

The doors were slightly ajar; a beam of bright sunshine separated them, illuminating tiny motes of dust as they floated drunkenly through the still air. He could hear the murmured purr of conversation.

He stepped closer, peering through the crack between the doors.

His heart fell with a squish to the floor.

Caroline sat on the edge of a sofa, her hair provocatively mussed; she wore a virginal morning gown that did not suit her, not one bit. Even though there were dark smudges beneath her eyes, they appeared very much alive, and hopeful, as if she were keen to see someone as much as he longed to see her.

She bent her neck to politely laugh at something; the high collar of her gown pulled back, revealing a telling raspberry that marred the smooth skin of her neck.

Good God, in his wanton abandon he'd marked her.

Henry wasn't sure if he was horrified, or proud, or (secretly) a little of both.

He hadn't time to decide, for at that moment Caroline looked back in his direction; she met his gaze through the crack in the door. Her eyes flashed with surprise. The smile faded from her lips; they parted, slightly, as the breath caught in her throat.

"Caroline!" Henry jumped at the sound of the earl's voice behind him. "Caroline—oh, hullo, Mr. Lake, pardon me, I've just got to collect my dearest sister—Caroline! Let's go."

Harclay poked his head into the drawing room. "Come along, love, you look like you could use a rest—no offense."

"None taken," she murmured, her eyes never leaving Henry's. She rose, and appeared about to say something—to him, to Harclay, he couldn't quite tell—when Lady Violet appeared at his elbow. She and Harclay exchanged a heated look before she turned back to Henry.

"Ah, Mr. Lake, there you are," she said, tugging him aside. "You're coming with me. You know, two minds are better than one, that sort of thing."

He would've groaned aloud had the realization not dawned on him at that very moment. It was obvious Lady Violet titillated Lord Harclay to the point of distraction; he was taken with her, and would probably follow her to the gates of hell (which is where that blackguard belonged anyway). And Caroline, being Harclay's dearest sister, was close with him.

It was safe to assume, then, that wherever Lady Violet was, Lord Harclay would soon appear. And where Harclay turned up—well, Caroline wouldn't be far behind.

Yes, yes, Henry had pledged to leave Caroline alone so that she might spend the days of her widowhood in peace. He had no claim, and certainly no right, to her company.

Not that he was glad the French Blue was stolen from under his nose, but it appeared the theft would throw the lot of them together, himself and Lady Caroline included.

And Henry was certainly glad for that.

He followed Lady Violet out to the street.

Eight

Caroline stuck out her lip and blew a stray wisp of hair from her eyes. She glanced out the window, open to a cool spring breeze, and sighed. The sun still shone brightly, same as it had when she'd last checked. The hours were passing at a snail's pace.

Would this day *never* end?

She'd begun reading quite some time ago. Even so, the book on her lap remained open to the first page—obviously a very boring first page. With another sigh she closed it and held it in her hands. Around her the house was oppressively quiet.

So far, "liberated widowhood" was proving mind-numbingly dull. Perhaps she needed a different book, or maybe a different sofa. Was it too early for a drink? Wine didn't count as a proper drink, really, when one considered the strength of other libations, brandy, cognac, rag water . . .

Caroline closed her eyes. She was being silly. There was no cure for the way Henry had looked at her through the crack in the door, not even gin.

There was no cure for Henry.

She wanted to feel rage at his appearance at Hope's. She'd

told him, in no uncertain terms, to leave her be. And he was very good at leaving.

What she felt for him was strong, and wild. But it wasn't rage.

Caroline tossed the book aside and leapt upright. Her slippers pinched her feet as she paced across the stars and constellations embroidered into the carpet, hands tucked into the small of her back. She couldn't sit still; the future that once promised peace, and solitude, and plenty of time in her garden, now seemed unbearably enormous and barren, somehow. She couldn't bear another hour like this, much less a day, a week, a decade.

After what felt like an eternity spent pacing (but was probably less than three minutes), Caroline's ears perked up at the sound of footsteps in the hall.

She crashed through the doors and slid out into the hall's marbled expanse. William was there, gathering his hat and gloves from Mr. Avery. She did not need to ask where he was headed; her brother appeared as exhausted, and just as restless, as she.

Caroline put her hands on her hips and lifted her chin and asked anyway.

"I am going to call on Lady Violet," he said, slapping his gloves against the palm of his hand. "I feel rather terribly for her, what with the missing diamond and all that. It's only proper I see to the condition of her nerves."

"The *condition* of her *nerves*? I don't believe you for a moment." Caroline sniffed. "But if you allow me to accompany you, I promise not to pursue the matter any further."

William huffed and rolled his eyes, but after making a mad dash upstairs for her spencer jacket and bonnet, Caroline found him waiting for her a few moments later.

"Don't worry." Biting back a smile, she took his hand in her own; it was clammy. William was nervous. "I take my duties as a negligent chaperone quite seriously."

Caroline's heart pounded as she and William were ushered through the rambling, if faded, expanse of Lady Violet Rutledge's house.

Henry wasn't here, she told herself. Why would he be? He had no business with Violet. Unless, of course, he was somehow involved in the saga of Hope's missing diamond, in which case he would *certainly* be here.

Caroline cowered behind the fortress of William's shoulders, as if he might lessen the blow of Henry's presence—or his absence. She heard Violet's voice—"*Our thief might be . . . someone with the cheek to steal a fifty-carat stone in front of five hundred people . . . but who?*"—and then the butler flung open the doors and Caroline was peeking underneath William's arm.

Her gaze landed on a familiar strawberry blond queue, tied neatly with a narrow green ribbon; her eyes traveled over his thick neck and broad shoulders. The scent of lemony spice filled her nostrils.

He was seated in a chair, facing away from her. At the commotion, Henry turned around. They met eyes, and then Caroline ducked, foolishly, behind William, as if she might hide there.

Oh, God.

"Lady Violet," William was saying, "would you do me the honor of accompanying me on a stroll about the park? I feel a bit of fresh air might better clear our minds of last night's unfortunate events. My sister, Caroline, has generously offered to chaperone us."

William turned just as Caroline was making to stand; he caught her head between his arm and torso.

Oh, *God*.

From her perch she peered into the room, hair pulled over her eyes, and managed a smile even as she wished, for a moment, that she might suffer an apoplexy and die.

In a heartbeat Henry was on his feet, looking down at Caroline as she struggled to her own.

In the next heartbeat William was leading Violet into the hall and toward the front door.

"Well, then." Henry held out his arm. "To the park?"

F or the first several minutes of said stroll, Caroline and Henry spoke in fits and starts.

"Oh," she said, trampling his foot. "Sorry . . . er, about that."

"Yes." Henry cleared his throat. "Indeed."

"Indeed, a lovely afternoon. Look there, a swan."

"Yes." An awkward pause. "The swan."

"It is white."

"White, yes. Like. Ah. Snow. Pretty?"

Caroline did her best to ignore the burn that shot up her arm from the place where his elbow swallowed her palm.

Beside her, Henry shuffled along; his limp had returned with a vengeance.

"Are you—um—all right to walk? We might sit—"

"No," he said. He sounded angry, suddenly. "Let's keep moving."

"Oh. Yes, yes of course."

Caroline glanced about the park—it was the fashionable hour, and crowded—worried that someone was watching them; that their shared secret could be read in the tightness of Henry's mouth, in the heat that mottled her face.

A few paces ahead, William's head was bent toward Lady Violet's; she turned and smiled at something he murmured in her ear. Desire was writ clearly on their faces; neither seemed to very much care who saw them.

Watching them filled Caroline with longing.

"I am sorry," Henry said. His voice was low and rough.

She started. "Sorry?"

"I promised to let you be. You never wanted to see me again after last night, remember?"

Caroline looked up at him. He glanced sideways at her. His temples were damp with sweat.

"I remember," she said slowly. "But this is hardly your fault. I volunteered to chaperone, and William—well, he can hardly keep his pants on when it comes to Lady Violet."

Henry's shoulders lifted with a scoff. "Your brother can't keep his pants on, period."

"I know. He claims he's getting better. But there's something different about this one." Together they stepped around an enormous Irish wolfhound tugging a poor footman about by a thick leather leash. "The way he looks at her, and how attentive he is—I haven't been with him much these past years, but I can tell he likes her."

Henry turned to her. "He treats you well, your brother?"

"Yes. As best he can, anyway. He can be annoying, a bit

patronizing. I wish he'd realize that I am close to thirty and far too tired to get into any sort of trouble."

A beat of silence passed between them as they walked; this one wasn't companionable, not by a long ways, but it felt less painful than the last few.

When Henry spoke, his voice was low. "Does he know about us?"

"No." Caroline trained her gaze on the ground. "You remember, he was away at Eton when we . . . when it happened. I haven't told him. Besides, by the time anything—I was married to Osbourne that August. No one knew anything."

"I'm still shocked our old friend the vicar didn't betray us."

It was Caroline's turn to scoff. "The vicar. I think he was too frightened of you to give us up to our parents. You forget how intimidating you can be."

"What?" Henry blinked innocently. "Is it my hair?"

Caroline found herself biting back a grin. "Yes. It's that glorious hair of yours. Gives you the look of a Viking, or a pirate. A Viking-pirate."

"I like the sound of that."

"I knew you would."

"I confess I would make a better Viking than a pirate. I like having my teeth, and besides, don't you think I'd look fetching in one of those horned helmets?"

"Along with a sinister beard, and your hair done in a pair of braids. I daresay villages wouldn't be the only thing you'd be invited to pillage."

Henry tapped his fingers against his eye patch. "The ladies do so favor cripples."

Caroline smiled. "No one would pay much mind to your eye if you were wearing that horned hat." And then, lower, after a pause: "How did it happen?"

They rounded a bend; the pathway stretched out before them in a great swoop through cleared parkland, the leaves and the grass and the air gilded by a late afternoon sun. Caroline held a hand to her forehead against it.

"It's hurting your eyes," he said.

"It's hurting yours, too. And you've only got one left."

He smiled. "Here, let's rest a bit, then."

Caroline called out to William; he and Lady Violet idled on the edge of the path.

Henry maneuvered Caroline into the shade of a nearby tree. It was quiet there, and warm, the sounds of the passing crowd a muted murmur. Caroline's arm slipped from Henry's; he leaned his back against the tree, crossing his arms over his enormous chest as he looked at her. She looked away.

"It was Thomas Hope," he said at last. "We were on a ship from Calais, sailing straight into a storm. I saw the mainmast falling; he didn't."

Her throat tightened at the image. "You must love him as a brother, to risk your life for him like that."

Henry bent a knee—his good knee—and pressed the sole of his foot against the tree trunk. It was his turn to look away. "I've missed them, my brothers. Hope was"—he grinned—"an eccentric substitute."

"Does it always hurt? Your leg?"

"It's gotten worse over the years, especially during winter. Can't seem to shake the cold. Although"—here he looked at her, intently—"well, it comes and goes, I suppose."

She resisted the impulse to reach for the patch and push it aside. She wanted to see the damage—what it looked like. The damage the life he'd chosen had done him.

The damage he'd suffered being away from her.

"What?" he asked, scoffing. "Are you disappointed? That I don't look like I used to?"

"No. I'm not disappointed." She swallowed. "Besides, what kind of Viking-pirate would you be without an eye patch and a limp?"

"An unconvincing one, I should think." Henry stood and offered her his arm. "Come, your brother's looking at Lady Violet as if he might eat her. You're not very good at this chaperoning bit, are you?"

"Abysmal."

"And quite proud of that fact, I see."

They trailed William and Lady Violet through the park until they reached the glittering expanse of the Serpentine. The sun was so warm there it was almost hot; strolling arm in arm with Henry Lake didn't help matters, either. She felt like weeping and running and mauling him all at once.

She felt confused. And a little angry with herself for enjoying his company so much. Caroline never forgot how well she and Henry got on, how easily words and ideas and feelings flowed between them. And while twelve years' distance stretched between them, there were moments when it felt like they'd never been apart at all.

"You said you were back in England on business." She looked at Henry. "Is that business Hope's diamond?"

He nodded, a single dip of his head. "We'll hunt down whoever stole the French Blue and give that scalawag what he deserves. I'm afraid I'm rather"—here he searched for the right word—"*unforgiving* when it comes to my enemies. And then I'll leave. Leave you be. Leave England."

"So eager to be gone, to leave, then." She grinned, sadly, at her feet. "Just like before."

Henry turned to look at her.

Twelve years ago, she thought, he left her, and in so doing confessed his indifference for her. He never loved her, had used her to get what he wanted and then tossed her aside. Everything he ever said to her was a lie. *He never loved her.*

Why then, that *look* in his eye, the softness that made her belly turn inside out? The heat in his gaze made Caroline feel, for a moment, anyway, that she was the only woman on earth. That she was seventeen again, and beautiful, because the way he looked at her made her feel that way.

"Allow me to confess a secret, my lady," he said, pulling her closer. His breath felt warm on her ear. "I didn't want to leave. Not you, not Oxfordshire, not my family. I left because . . . well, because I was forced to."

His confession knocked the wind from Caroline's lungs. The world whirled around her in a dizzying rush of light; a strangely metallic taste thickened inside her mouth. She was shocked. Her anger flared to new heights.

Henry was lying. It was the only explanation. He'd lied to her before, and he was lying now, perhaps with the sinister intent of tricking her once more.

What a fool she'd been all this time, to let him close again.

Caroline pulled him, hard, off the path to a halt beside her. The Serpentine lapped at their feet. "But what . . . why . . . ?" She threw up her hands. "Bah, what the devil does it matter now?"

"Please, my lady, I cannot tell you more—"

"Of course you can't. You haven't changed, Mr. Lake, not one bit."

"Somehow I don't think you mean that as a compliment."

"I don't."

He held his hands out before him. "I want to tell you, I've always wanted to tell you. Caroline—"

She turned on him, the warning not to call her that on her lips. But she tripped on her dress and careened backward, arms circling over her head as the sickening feeling of inevitable disaster descended upon her.

"Caroline!" Henry leapt forward, attempting to restore her balance.

But Caroline, quite suddenly, didn't want her balance restored.

She wanted to fall, and she wanted to pull Henry down with her. It was only what that blackguard deserved, making her feel worthy when he'd destroyed whatever worthiness she felt a decade ago, making her believe he felt anything but indifference for her.

And so Caroline's arm darted out, clasping Henry by the elbow. They were falling, falling, the momentum of her body pulling them down.

Together they cartwheeled with a monumental *splash* into the Serpentine. The water was a shade colder than freezing; the shock of it paralyzed Caroline as the weight of her skirts dragged her down.

A tendril of panic unfurled in her chest. Perhaps falling into the Serpentine hadn't been the best idea. Her skirts felt as if they were weighed down with rocks; she kicked furiously, pulling herself toward the surface with her arms, but to no avail.

She was drowning.

To think she would die just when Henry confessed *I didn't want to leave you.* She would never know what in hell he'd meant by that; she would never know what happened after their wedding night some twelve years ago.

Not that she had the courage to ask any of these questions, not that knowing the answers would ease her grief.

Still.

Caroline kicked harder. She pulled. Still she went down.

Her lungs burned. She struggled against the impulse to inhale.

And then something was wrapped around her chest and squeezing, tugging her upward.

Her head broke the surface of the water and she gasped for air. Water dripped into her eyes. Her back was pressed against a familiar front.

Henry's front.

His arm was slung about her torso between her breasts, and he was pulling her toward the shore. With one last tug he laid her out upon the muddy bank, his hand sliding to grasp her waist. She tried to slap it away but she kept missing.

People were staring, drawing close but not *too* close. (God forfend they should actually help.) William appeared at her side; apparently he'd also gone for a dip, because his wet curls hung over his brow.

"All right," Henry panted. "I deserved that."

"Deserved what?" William snapped.

"It's nothing," Caroline said. "Help me up."

Together William and Henry lifted Caroline to her feet. The water that streamed down her person was very cold, but her skin felt hot; the combination made her shiver.

"Caroline," Henry said.

William stepped between them. "You aren't to call her that. She is a countess."

"Not anymore," she said. "I'm fine, William, really."

After a beat, William turned back to Lady Violet. Henry turned to Caroline.

She tried very hard not to look at the way his clothes clung to his body. Really, she did, but like every other red-blooded woman gathered in their small circle of spectators, Caroline couldn't resist reveling in the view.

She could see every muscle, every slope, the pucker of his nipples.

Her eyes slid down the length of his body and then made their way back up. His hair hung in loose abandon about his face, its golden strands trailing over his shoulders. Water dripped from his brows down his cheeks; his one eye was burning.

And it was on her.

Henry's mouth was drawn into a grim line. A muscle in his jaw roped against the smooth skin there. "Are you all right?" he ground out.

"Oh, don't worry about your secret, Mr. Lake," she hissed, rolling her eyes. "I swear to you, I shan't tell a soul, nary a soul!"

By now Caroline was shaking so hard her teeth chattered. He reached for her. "You're freezing."

"What do you care?" She stepped aside, making a beeline for William, who, annoyingly, was sharing a jolly laugh with Lady Violet over the indecent condition of his breeches.

"Caroline—my lady—wait," Henry called after Caroline.

She glanced at him over her shoulder. "Whatever your 'business' with Hope and his diamond and Lady Violet, leave me out of it. It's better for both of us that way."

B ut the world, it seemed, was conspiring against Caroline getting her way this afternoon.

For it appeared Henry Lake wasn't the only man in her life with secrets.

She and William were ensconced in the quiet, velvet-lined safety of his carriage, swinging in time to the vehicle's jolts and lurches as they made their way home from Hyde Park. Caroline sat across from William, the coachman's coat spread out on the squabs beneath her so that her soaking skirts might not ruin the upholstery.

"Lady Violet accused me of stealing Hope's diamond," William said.

Caroline blinked, her gaze shifting from the window to her brother. "Pardon?"

"Lady Violet thinks I was the thief. She told me so on our stroll."

Caroline scoffed. "Girl's got a sense of humor. You *would* make a dashing criminal."

She said it playfully, sarcastically, but William did not share in her humor.

"I know," he said. "That's why I did it."

A pause. A very *stunned* pause.

And then: "What?" She bolted upright. "Wait. You—"

"Well, that's part of the reason why I did it. I was bored, if you want to know the truth, and what with all of Hope's bragging about the jewel, and that ridiculous ball of his . . . well, I couldn't very well resist."

For a moment Caroline stared at William. She recalled, in startling detail, Henry's words.

I'm unforgiving when it comes to my enemies. We'll give that scalawag what he deserves.

Of course her brother should prove to be that scalawag— the one who stole Mr. Thomas Hope's priceless diamond in the midst of the season's most well-attended ball.

Caroline reached across the carriage and slapped William's head. "You idiot."

He shrugged. "Don't worry, I plan to give it back."

"Like that makes it any better!"

"It should."

"It doesn't."

William furrowed his brow. "Not that I planned on telling you any of this, Caroline. But I wasn't expecting such prudish wrath from you."

Caroline was so furious, it took all her powers of self restraint not to box his ears once more.

"Do you have any idea what sort of trouble you're in, William? You've just kicked the biggest damned hornet's nest in all of England!"

"Of course I know!" He grinned, a smug thing that set Caroline's teeth on edge. "Why d'you think I did it?"

Caroline fell back on the squabs with an exasperated sigh. So much for living out the days of her widowhood in contented, unmolested peace. It was only a matter of time— hours, minutes—before Henry Lake would climb through the window of William's house and demand answers about Hope's missing jewel.

Answers that, when her brother refused to share them, Henry would look to Caroline to provide.

She reached out and slapped William once more for good measure. Crossing her arms about her chest, Caroline turned to the window. A puzzling tightness in her chest made it difficult to breathe, suddenly, at the thought of seeing Henry again; a tightness that was either anxiety or excitement, she couldn't quite tell.

Nine

A gentleman jewel thief.

Lake would've laughed at the absurdity of such a notion if it didn't make perfect sense.

He took a healthy swig of watery Scotch instead, cursing his brother for not leaving better stuff behind.

Lady Violet was the one to put the pieces together into a glaringly obvious, in retrospect, whole. She'd fingered the earl as the thief, had even accused him of the crime to his face. Henry had to give her more credit; she was made of solid, smart stuff.

He stood in his bedchamber before the open window. The setting sun cast a blush-colored shadow over a wide, unblemished sky; the air was warm and still. In the street below, well-appointed vehicles jostled London's finest to the evening's first entertainments. He could hear the tinkling of laughter, the creak and slam of doors. He drained his teacup, willing the impossible knot of his thoughts to loosen, but the Scotch, or whatever it was, wasn't nearly strong enough.

He'd had an inkling William, the Earl of Harclay, was involved in the theft from the moment Henry watched it happen across the ballroom. The earl had singled out Lady Violet earlier that night, and never left her side; he was with her when she was attacked by the acrobats.

Acrobats William doubtless hired to create a distraction while he swiped the diamond, discreetly, from Violet's neck himself.

It was genius, really—to play at fighting off Violet's attackers when the earl had hired them to do just that: attack her, distract her, so that she wouldn't see her fawning paramour steal the jewel slung about her breast.

It was a brave move, a cocky move, one that Lake would've applauded if it didn't place him in a damnably impossible bind.

Twice he'd sworn to leave Caroline be, and twice he would break his oath, just as he'd done a decade ago.

He had to stay away from her. He *should* stay away from her. His was a bloody business; he'd learned, the hard way, the danger his profession posed to those close to him.

But now that her brother the earl was their primary suspect in the theft of the French Blue, she would play a part in Henry's hunt, whether he willed it or not. It was imperative Henry reclaim the diamond so that England might use it to bargain with France; with a dash of diplomatic savvy, he might negotiate for the lives of thousands of British soldiers, the surrender of a Spanish city, perhaps even peace. There was no telling what that potbellied pig Napoleon might forfeit in his quest to reassemble to French crown jewels.

Nothing—and no one—would stand in the way of Henry's hunt for the French Blue. Especially not Lady Caroline Osbourne, Dowager Countess of Berry.

He knew better than to believe she would prove helpful in condemning her brother as the thief, even less so in seeking out the diamond. If pulling him down into a freezing lake, quite viciously, was any indication, she *really* didn't want anything to do with Henry.

"You're thinking about her, aren't you?"

He set his cup down on the bureau and turned to face Mr. Moon.

Lake cleared his throat. "I don't know what you're talking about," he said, crossing his arms and ankles and leaning against the casement.

"That woman who was here the other night. Harclay's sister. The one you're in love with."

"Pffssh," Henry scoffed. "I'm not—how did you—what?"

Mr. Moon rolled his eyes, and turned back to the mirror as he attempted to shrug into a wig of long auburn curls. "Whatever you say, sir. If I may be so bold as to offer some advice—"

"You may not."

"Tread more softly this time. I mean this as a compliment, really, I do, but you're something of a bully. Women don't like that."

"You would know."

"Yes." Mr. Moon straightened, tossing his curls over his shoulder. "I would. Go slowly with her. Be kind. Handle her with a light touch. What's the old saying? Oh yes: 'Honey attracts more bees than a blow to the gut.' No, no, that's not it." Moon furrowed his brow, lips puckered. At last he waved away the thought. "Anyway. From what I overheard last night, she might appreciate that."

"The honey? Or the blow to the gut?"

Moon bent his neck at an accusing angle. "Say what you want. You're going to lose her *and* the diamond if you don't tread lightly."

"I'm not after her." Feeling his face grow hot, Henry turned back to the window. After a beat, he said, "How do you know? About—"

"Your voice," Moon said. "I heard it in your voice. The way you spoke to her."

Henry placed his palms on the windowsill and took a deep breath through his nose.

"What are you going to do?" Moon asked softly. "She's his sister. And you and I both know he's our thief."

"Maybe he'll confess, and hand over the diamond without event." Henry glanced over his shoulder at Moon. "No, you're right, he won't. It's obvious he stole the jewel for a thrill. And there's no thrill in surrender."

Henry looked at the gilt clock on the mantel. "Once it's dark I won't have much time—what, it's almost June, I'll have a few hours of darkness, if that?—but I'll poke about the earl's residence, see what I can find. With any luck he's as stupid as he is cocky, and he'll be using the diamond as a paperweight."

* * *

Alas, the earl proved cocky *and* clever. With rising frustration Henry moved from one room to the next in Harclay's Hanover Square house. The moon was new, the darkness complete. It was almost a gift, Henry's one missing eye; for years he'd honed other senses, including touch, to compensate for what he lacked in vision.

He tore through desks and laid waste to wardrobes. He felt behind paintings and rolled up carpets, running his palms over the walls and floorboards in search of a telltale gap or knob, a loose plank. He trailed his fingertips over furniture, china, linens, paper. Always silent, always careful to put things back to rights.

All this work, and there was no sign of the French Blue.

A dozen rooms, half a dozen hours, and nothing, nothing, nothing.

For the most part Henry moved silently, intently, without disturbing so much as a mote of dust. But bending his knee to keep from limping was a painful endeavor, especially as the hours passed. He bit the inside of his cheek against the pain, but once, when he was creeping through the earl's bedchamber, the sharp spikes of sensation became too much to bear.

Hand on the knob of Harclay's dressing room, Henry drew a noisy breath through his teeth.

And then, horrified, he froze, heart thumping in his ears as he waited for the inevitable.

It came a beat later—the rustle from the great tester bed across the room.

Henry's mind raced as he glanced down at the knob in his hand. He could slip inside the dressing room, but surely the earl, if he was awake, would hear Henry close the door. And what if this door was the only way in or out? He would be trapped. He couldn't risk it.

He looked to the windows. Too far; already dawn shone through the curtains. There was no time to wait. His only option was to sneak back to the chamber door, slip out before the earl was fully roused.

Which meant he didn't have time to search the dressing room. He cursed silently, annoyed that he was forced to leave this particular stone unturned.

Then again, a dressing room was hardly a good hiding place for anything, much less a diamond. Harclay's valet was in and out of that room several times a day; the drawers were his domain, not the earl's.

Still, the fact that Henry did not know for certain what was behind this door rankled. The diamond was not in the drawing room, the study, the kitchens. It was not anywhere Henry had already searched. Which meant the jewel could be there, inside the Earl's dressing room.

Harclay tossed and turned again in his bed, let out a noise that could've been a snore, a slurred word.

Henry didn't waste any time. He bolted from the room, careful to close the door quietly behind him. The house was stirring; he could hear footsteps on the back stair. He had taken too long, was careless with the few hours he'd been given.

He didn't see the crisply attired maid until it was almost too late. Henry was racing down a shadowy hall, focusing all his energy on not making a sound, when the woman appeared, quite suddenly, a few feet to his left, brush and pail in hand.

Without thinking, Henry turned and, sending up a small prayer that the woman did not see him, ducked into the nearest room.

Closing the door behind him, he turned to face his surroundings, blinking furiously as a bead of sweat made its way into his eye.

Oh. Oh *no*.

Out of all the rooms in his bloody mansion, of course he had the bad—good?—luck to find himself in hers.

Caroline's.

Caroline, who stared at him from her perch on the bed. She dropped her teacup to its saucer with a clatter, and tugged her robe closer about her bosom. She straightened against the mountain of pillows at her back.

"Mr. Lake!" she said, voice low. "What in the world—?"

"I'm not. I wasn't sneaking—I wasn't *searching*—"

"Then what are you doing in my room at six o'clock in the morning, dressed head to toe in black?"

Henry looked down at his costume. She had a point.

He managed a tight smile. "Just doing a bit of reconnaissance. Harmless, I assure you."

And then, remembering himself, Henry bowed. Was that a blush staining her cheeks? Or merely the late springtime heat?

"You shouldn't be here," she said.

"I know. I am sorry, my lady, I am, but the maid—and the time . . . " He sighed, tugging a hand through his hair. Perhaps a change in subject was in order; it might buy him a bit of time.

"You're up early," he said. "I trust you slept well?"

She looked at him for a moment; he saw the weariness in her eyes. "It seems sleep has eluded us both."

He clasped his hands behind his back. "Are you at least recovered from our spill into the Serpentine?"

She looked down at the breakfast tray in her lap. Running her first finger through the petals of a daisy drooping in a tiny cut glass vase, she said, "You *did* deserve that, you know."

His heart began to pound. "I know."

Silence stretched between them. The morning sun was hot on Henry's back.

"Well, then." She set her hands on either end of the tray. "If you've come to ask about William, I've nothing to say."

"Ah. So you know of Violet's accusation."

Caroline nodded. "I do. But let me assure you, Mr. Lake, I know nothing about the theft or the diamond or where it is now. I spent the last year in mourning at my late husband's estate in Oxfordshire; I came to London less than a week ago. If William was planning something, I—well, I knew nothing about it."

Henry took a breath through his nose, reining in the impulse to pepper her with more questions. He recalled what Moon had counseled the night before.

Bees like honey more than a blow to the gut. Or was it *honey attracts more bees than a fist?*

Whatever it was, Henry was determined to heed Moon's advice, however unsolicited and inane that advice might be. Caroline would never forgive Lake for what he'd done—he didn't begrudge her that—but he could certainly work to make her hate him a little less.

Besides, he had a missing diamond to find and a country to save; the more help he could enlist, the sooner he'd find the gem, the sooner he could leave London, and Caroline in peace.

At least that's what he told himself.

"Very well," he said, rocking back on his heels.

She blinked. "Very well? That's all you've got to say? I half expected you to arrest me, or at the very least torture and interrogate me until I confessed."

"Messy business, torture, and I've only one good coat to my name. Well, two, if you count the one I—er—*borrowed* for Hope's ball. Can't spare either of them, I'm afraid, and blood does have a tendency to stain."

Caroline's eyes widened, just a bit. "You're joking."

He smiled. "Of course I'm joking," he replied. "About the coat. After you so graciously sent it back, I donated it to my associate Mr. Moon. Man does so love a good costume."

Caroline ran her tongue along the inside of her bottom lip in an attempt not to smile.

Henry took a step into the room. He felt unaccountably nervous, all of a sudden. "I would never ask you to betray your brother, Caroline. But I must find the diamond, and soon, if only to remove myself from the widowhood you do seem to so enjoy. If you see anything, or overhear a tidbit that could help . . . perhaps I might see you, ask some questions, look about?"

"See me?" Caroline arched a brow. "You've been away from England too long. You don't just *see* a dowager, and one recently out of mourning. William will know you're up to something."

The words came before he could stop them. "Perhaps I could gather my reports under the guise of a social call or two, so William does not suspect me? That way I might poke about without him knowing."

"There will be no *poking* about."

"Of course." He swallowed. *Poke*—an unfortunate choice of word, he saw that now.

"I told you I know nothing."

"Please," he said, his voice small. "Help a fellow out. I mean well. Despite our . . . um . . . susceptibility to accident, I do enjoy your company. We were companions once, if you remember."

Caroline drew a breath, let it out. "You don't deserve it, you know. My help."

Henry toed at the carpet. "I know, Caroline. I'm sor—"

"I don't believe you," she snapped. "Some cheek you've got, coming to *me* of all people—asking *me* for a favor, after what you did. I should shove you out the window and be done with you. You cannot possibly understand what I went through

after you left. What you did to me, by leaving. Actually—"
She made to rise.

"Wait!" Henry held up his hands. "Wait, please. The sooner I find the diamond, the sooner I might leave you in peace. The French Blue—it's not just any jewel, my lady. I cannot share details—"

"Of course you can't."

"But suffice it to say you'll be doing old St. George a solid favor by helping me. Or, at the very least, not impeding my search."

Caroline turned her head away from him at that. Like he had that night in his brother's chamber, Henry watched the working of her throat as she swallowed, hard. When she spoke, her voice was tight.

"My brother," she said at last. "If I help you, does that mean you won't pull out his fingernails, either?"

Henry hesitated. "If he cooperates—"

"I don't care if he cooperates. I want your word that you won't hurt him, no matter his role in the theft of the diamond. No matter how your hunt for the thief plays out."

It was a bad idea to promise such a thing; if she knew all that was at stake, she would know he *couldn't* promise to keep William safe.

But there was a lightness, a spark in her eyes that hadn't been there a heartbeat before. He didn't dare hope she was just as eager as he to know, once more, the love they bore each other as companions, but he *would* dare to believe she was willing to give his proposal a try.

"You have my word," he said. Something fizzled at the base of his skull as Henry spoke the words—a warning.

He ignored it.

"You may not poke, but you may look." Caroline lifted the tray from her lap and set it aside. "You might begin by climbing out that window. Go round the house, and knock on the front door—yes, Mr. Lake, you must—so that you might call on me like a sane gentleman. I shall receive you in the drawing room."

Ten

As Lake's rotten luck would have it, Caroline's brother, William, the Earl of Harclay, was reading the paper in the drawing room when Henry was announced. He was glad he had not risked searching the earl's dressing room; clearly he'd risen not long after Henry escaped.

"Mr. Lake," the earl drawled, looking up from his paper. He didn't bother to stand. "How early you are! And that costume. Tell me, do you wear black because it is the color of your soul?"

Lake bowed, wincing at the sharp pain in his leg. "Apologies for the hour, my lord. I have come to call upon your sister the dowager countess."

The earl pursed his lips. He lowered the paper. "Have you, now? I'm afraid she's not yet awake. I would tell you to come back at a more . . . appropriate hour, but Lady Caroline is recently returned to London, you see, and keeps a very busy schedule of appointments."

The earl's lazy, self-satisfied confidence set Henry's teeth on edge; he wanted, very badly, to reach out and throttle the man. Alas, such things were not permitted in drawing rooms, but if they were, Henry would've done it, and soundly, too.

"Any new leads on our thief?" Harclay asked, crossing one leg over the other with luxurious ease. Henry couldn't help but feel the gesture was meant to mock him. "My offer of aid stands."

Henry managed a tight smile. "Of course it does. And how helpful you've been thus far."

"Bah, you flatter me," the earl smiled. He still did not ask Henry to sit. "Doubtless with Lady Violet on the case, you and Hope will have the diamond back in no time."

"Let's hope so," Henry ground out. "We've all got a quite bit at stake, haven't we?"

"Yes, we do indeed," the earl replied.

Henry rocked back on his heels, and glanced out the window. He felt warm about his collar.

He wondered, for the hundredth time, where a man like Harclay might hide a fifty-carat gem. Henry searched this room top to bottom an hour ago; he found nothing. But it had to be here, the jewel, hidden away somewhere in this house. If only he knew where! How tempting it was to think this knotty problem might be solved today. Hope could go back to his bank, and Henry to his work in Paris; the earl to Lady Violet, and Caroline to her hard-won widowhood. She'd never have to see Henry again.

Something heavy moved over Henry's chest at the thought of leaving her once more, as if his heart were caught under someone's thumb.

The earl cleared his throat, glaring at Henry over the paper. "She's not coming."

"I—"

"And even if she were, Caroline is just out of mourning; she is a creature of delicate sensibilities besides. I am her guardian now, and I shall protect her from those who would do her harm."

Anger, mingled with shame, pulsed through Henry. "I would never wish to hurt the lady." Not if I could help it.

The earl looked at him for a long moment. "I'm not sure that I believe you. You see, Mr. Lake, while you may believe yourself to be quite mysterious, and dashing, and rather overly tall—irresistible to the opposite sex, in short," the earl leaned forward, and murmured, "I know better. You aren't what you say you are. And I'll be damned if I let you near my sister."

"Talking about me behind my back, are you?"

The earl and Henry turned at the sound of Caroline's voice. She was standing in the doorway, lazily tapping a pair of muddy canvas gloves against her palm. She wore a plain muslin gown rubbed an uneven shade of green about the knees and elbows. Her dark hair was piled haphazardly on top of her head, the stray wisps at her ears and neck lending her a windswept appearance.

The morning sun set fire to her profile, burnishing those wisps bronze and gold. The shoulders and arms of her gown seemed to glow in the harsh light, and for a moment Henry thought she might stretch her wings and fly away; she was an angel, a goddess.

He looked at her, his pulse drumming inside his skin. He would never get past looking at her; it would never get old.

The diamond, he told himself. Remember you are here for the diamond.

But what did a diamond matter, when an angel was in the room?

"Ah, Caroline! Good morning, sweet Sister. Mr. Lake here was just leaving."

Caroline glanced from Henry to the earl and back again. Her eyes were dark with confusion; she looked at Henry pleadingly, as if to say *you promised, you gave me your word*.

"Yes, of course," Henry said, and bowed. "My lord, my lady. Good day."

But Caroline grabbed him before he could get past the door. "No. Mr. Lake—er—has kindly offered to help me in the garden this morning. Lovely day for it."

The earl opened his mouth to protest, or perhaps to ask when, exactly, Lake had the chance to promise such a thing, but Caroline slipped her arm into the crook of Henry's and quickly led him from the room.

Henry cleared his throat as they made their way to the back of the house. "Sorry about that. I wasn't expecting to see your brother. Isn't he something of a—?"

"Rakehell? Yes, absolutely. You'd *think* men like him wouldn't wake until four after a night out carousing. But alas, William was always an early riser, no matter his prowling the night before. I should've warned you."

He followed her down the narrow servants' staircase and through the kitchens, busy with preparations for the day's meals. Caroline nodded and smiled at the staff as she passed, pausing with the housekeeper to tell her yes, yes, the pudding was lovely last night, might she have another made for this evening?

The morning sun was bright and clean, staring them down from a wide-open sky as they stepped outside. To their right were the mews, fragrant as ever; Caroline led him to the left to a low brick wall that bisected the property. Passing through an iron gate of elaborate scrollwork, she and Henry stepped into the garden.

By London standards it was enormous, and like Caroline's hair, wild and fashionably unkempt. A brick pathway wound about the shrubs and blooming trees, great heaps of hydrangea and purple snapdragons edging out onto the path's well-swept expanse.

"You don't think your brother's stashed the diamond away here, do you?" Henry asked, voice low.

"I don't know where the diamond is," she replied, gaze trained on her feet. "But he's suspicious of you, Mr. Lake. He'll be watching us today. If he sees you gardening with me, he'll think you're harmless and, even better, boring. I'm hoping he'll leave us alone, eventually, so that you might do your work unimpeded. Besides, I do have some flowers to plant, and it can't hurt digging about—maybe we'll find more than roots and worms.

Just ahead, an elderly gentleman was reaching into a tree dotted with white blooms. He smiled when he saw Caroline; she introduced him as Mr. McCartney, the man who'd served the family as gardener for—well, for as long as she could remember.

"Come out to work again, m'lady, 'ave ya?" he asked, wiping his brow with the back of his wrist.

"With this weather I couldn't resist. I dug up the ivy bed yesterday—oh, I know you said you'd get to it, but I figured since I had the time—but now we can put in those peonies you've been growing in the kitchen. How pretty the pink will look against all that purple."

Mr. McCartney glanced dubiously at Henry. "Is 'e gonna help ya?"

Henry glanced dubiously at Caroline. "*Am* I going to help you?"

Caroline turned to him. "If you'd like."

"I would like to, very much, though I confess I know little about . . . er, the earthly arts?"

Caroline smiled, one eye squinted against the sun as she looked up at him. "To quote a man of our mutual acquaintance: 'Then I shall teach you.'"

"I hope I'm better at gardening than you are at the waltz."

"That makes two of us." She turned to the gardener. "I do hate to inconvenience you, Mr. McCartney, but if Mr. Lake might borrow your gloves, I'd be forever grateful."

The gardener handed his well-worn gloves to Henry; excusing himself to gather Caroline's peonies, McCartney hiked up his wheelbarrow and shuffled out of the garden.

"Well, then." Caroline wiggled her fingers into her gloves. "Shall we begin?"

Caroline had always considered a garden a place of refuge and reflection, a tiny square of Eden where, at least for a little while, she might wring her body and her mind of whatever it was that plagued them. She treasured the solitude, the sense of freedom the out-of-doors afforded; her mind would clear and her knees would ache, and there was comfort in knowing she would sleep well that night.

Today, though, was an entirely different story; while her knees ached, her mind was anything but clear. Indeed, her thoughts were a riot as she watched Henry clumsily dump a handful of peonies into a misshapen hole in the ground.

Why she had agreed to let Henry sniff about for the jewel on her watch, she hadn't a clue. Normal people invited gentleman callers to tea; normal people told ex-lovers who'd stolen their virtue and their sanity to sod off. Really, what was wrong with tea and sodding off? Why couldn't Caroline have picked one or the other, instead of the garden?

And what did the diamond matter to her, anyway?

She could tell herself she did it for William, so that he might be spared whatever sorts of medieval torture Henry liked to administer to his enemies; saving her brother was certainly reason enough to agree to Henry's request.

But it wasn't *the* reason she'd done it. Caroline didn't know what *the* reason was, exactly, except that it had little to do with William, and even less with honorably saving someone from torture.

Besides. She hadn't been entirely honest with Henry. It was true she hadn't been aware of William's plans to thieve the French Blue from Mr. Hope's ball.

But that bit about not knowing where William might be hiding the diamond—well. That was something of a gray area.

"I take it you still enjoy your gardens," he said.

"I do," she replied. "When I was young, it was just an excuse to get outside and away from my mother's tedious friends. I started to feel at home in our garden. And there's nothing like the satisfaction of seeing your work come to life."

"Literally." He smiled.

She smiled, too. "Literally."

"There." Henry leaned back on his haunch. "How's that?"

They were kneeling beside one another in a bare patch of earth—well, Caroline kneeled, and Henry crouched in an awkward half kneel, one leg bent, the other stretched out before him, stiff—toward the back of the garden; the sun streamed through the leaves of a young tree above, dappling Henry and Caroline in light and shadow. She'd been very careful not to touch him all morning.

She watched him curl a stray lock of hair behind his ear; he stained the pale strands with mud from his glove as he pulled away his hand.

Realizing, suddenly, that he was looking at her looking at him, Caroline turned to the peonies. They sagged against the black earth like a boxer after a fist to the face.

"It's—"

Henry laughed. "Terrible, isn't it?"

Caroline laughed, too, and reached for the stranded stems. "Here, let me show you again. Dig a little deeper."

Henry slipped his enormous hands into the earth, cupping a small mountain of dirt that he tossed silently aside. She ventured another glance at his face; sweat dripped down his forehead and temples, catching on the leather thong of his eye patch.

She looked away. His sweat—his aliveness—unsettled her.

"Deep enough?"

Caroline peered over his arms. "That should do. Add a bit more manure—"

"The smell makes me gag. I think we've got enough manure in there."

Rolling her eyes, Caroline bit back a grin as she grasped the trowel stuck in the small pile of manure and lifted a healthy scoop into the hole.

"I didn't know your sensibilities were so delicate," she said.

Henry grinned. "Not so delicate that I wouldn't take a handful of that lovely stuff and drop it down the back of your dress."

"I'd like to see you try."

He looked at her for a moment, eyes gleaming with mischief, and then, quick as a snake, his arm darted out and his fingers pawed at the nape of her gown, holding it open as he reached for the manure with his other hand.

"Don't you—stop it!—you wouldn't—dare!" Caroline tried to fight off his grip, breathless as her belly tightened with laughter. She ducked, swatting at his hand, but he held the back of her dress just out of reach.

"You," he panted, "issued the challenge! What sort of gentleman would I be if I didn't accept it?"

Caroline grabbed a handful of manure and, turning, splattered it against Henry's chest. He looked down, his eyes and mouth wide as he surveyed the damage.

"This is my best coat. My *only* coat!" he said. "Oh, you're going to regret that, my lady."

And then he was trickling manure down the back of her gown—"It's cold! It's cold! Stop it, this instant!"—and she was arching away from his touch, screeching and laughing, and Henry was laughing, too. His laughter was rich, deep, entirely male; entirely satisfied.

She flung manure at him, speckling his face and hair until at last he clamped both her wrists between the fingers of his left hand. By now they were both laughing so hard neither of them could speak; Caroline's laughter came in great, silent sobs, her ribs aching against the force of it.

She couldn't remember the last time she laughed this hard. It was the kind of laughter that was childish and gleeful, the kind that made her feel grateful for being alive; a reminder that life's littlest joys could also be its greatest.

Henry's sigh still tripped with laughter some moments later. He wiped his face with the back of his hand, and for a minute appeared as if he might be ill.

"Try not to use your nose," Caroline said. Her eyes were blurred with tears.

"It's *in* my nose."

"You deserved it. I've got it in places I cannot mention in your presence."

"You started it."

She grinned. "I did."

Looking down they realized, at the same time, that Henry still held her wrists. He released them, wiping the manure from his breeches; a moment later he was rolling back his shoulders and shrugging out of his coat.

They looked up, meeting eyes. His face was flush with laughter; the dimple in his left cheek was egregiously adorable. Her belly dropped to her knees.

The air between them seemed to twist and tense, pulling them closer, coaxing them to fall into one another. Caroline's lips felt warm, alive with the need to be kissed.

Oh, kissing Henry—*that* had been life's greatest pleasure.

In the silence that stretched from his body to hers, something moved. Neither of them dared give it voice, but that sensation, that *feeling*, was there nonetheless.

He was leaning close now. She leaned, too, the manure in her stays shifting as she drew closer to Henry. And closer. And closer. Their noses almost touched—

"'ve got the rest ov th' peonies, m'lady, 'pologies for th' delay, but that witch ov a cook chased me off w' a spoon—"

Mr. McCartney drew up his wheelbarrow beside Caroline, his face wide with surprise as he took in the scene before him. Quickly she and Henry fell back from one another, looking down at the dirt as if they'd like to hide in it.

Cheeks burning, Caroline smoothed the soiled expanse of her skirts. "I'm afraid we're going to need more manure, Mr. McCartney."

"Right then. I'll . . . see t' it." And then, after a pause: "E'rything all right, m'lady?"

"Yes, thank you."

The gardener shuffled back to the house. For a moment neither Caroline nor Henry made to move.

What the devil just happened? Had they *really* almost kissed? And here, in her brother's garden of all places, a spot visible not only to the house but to their neighbors' houses as well?

How foolish! How positively wanton of her.

Turning away from Henry, Caroline patted her hair, cheeks flaming.

"Well." Henry coughed. "Back to the peonies, then."

In her quest to smear Henry with manure, Caroline realized she'd tossed the blooms aside; they now lay scattered about the ground at her knees.

He reached over her legs and gently gathered the stems in his hand, shaking stray manure from their roots. His movement tugged the cuff of his shirtsleeve up his arm, revealing the shapely angles of his bare wrist. The bronzed skin was covered in a pale sheen of gold hair.

She looked away.

"Hold them upright in the hole there," she said, gathering a scoop of dirt in her cupped hands. "No, not like that—to the left—to the *left*, Mr. Lake—here, let me show you."

Caroline dropped the dirt and reached for the flowers. Henry slid his hands to the roots while she held the stems. Her arm brushed the bare skin of his wrist; they both moved to reposition themselves at once. Caroline tried to ignore the pulse of heat that shot through her at the sudden contact.

"I'll hold them," she said. "You fill in the dirt."

Henry scooped earth into the hole, carefully, slowly, patting it into place about the plants with gentle fingers as if he was afraid he might harm them. Caroline watched, mesmerized by softness of his touch. There was something distinctly primal, and private, about the juxtaposition of his strength and the gentleness of his hands. He could easily crush the blooms, could have easily crushed Caroline's wrists with a flick of his fingers if he'd wanted.

But he'd handled her gently, reverently almost. Strange this care he took not to hurt her, when a decade ago he'd hurt her in the worst ways without apology.

There was something different about this thirtysomething Henry. When he was young he was rough, and unaware of his nascent strength; she remembered the way he'd knocked into her on their wedding night, bruising her nose. He didn't yet possess the enormous body he'd received in his seventeenth year (he told her he'd grown a foot—*a foot!*—in the span of a few months); he was very much the proverbial bull in a china shop.

But this Henry—this Henry was self-possessed, certain in his strength and able to control it. He proceeded with knowledgeable care, and great patience.

"Here," he said, "you might leave the plant, let's see if it stands on its own."

To her surprise, and her pleasure, Henry had done a decent job of planting the flowers.

"Not bad," Caroline replied. "I wouldn't say it's perfect—"

"It's not." Henry frowned. "Needs to go a bit more to the left."

And so he patted and prodded the earth until he was satisfied, crossing his arms about his chest with a small smile.

"There. *That* is perfect."

His smile was infectious, and even though she knew she couldn't, and most certainly shouldn't, invite him to stay, she patted him on his knee and said, "Yes, perfect. We've only got fifteen more to go."

Eleven

H enry wished they had another fifty peonies to plant. He didn't want to leave.

It was well past noon when he and Caroline planted the last of the flowers. His back ached—though, curiously, his leg did not—and sweat was dripping into his eye.

He had to resist the temptation to try kissing Caroline again. This temptation was infinitely more difficult to resist than the first.

She'd always been a beautiful woman to him. But digging about in the garden, squinting against the sun and sweat, and caked in manure, Caroline was positively radiant.

All morning he'd watched her from the corner of his eye. He couldn't help it; there was something magnetic about her energy, her enthusiasm for her peonies.

And her laugh—Good Lord, he hadn't realized how much he missed that sound until he heard it again. It made his heart unfurl in his chest; it made the armor of his grief loosen.

The hours passed as minutes. He dug, she set down manure and watered the earth with the tin watering can he refilled at the troughs outside the mews. While they chatted and poked fun at one another, they spent a goodly portion of the morning in contented silence, lost in the task that was now, sadly, complete.

He helped Caroline to her feet, and with their hands on their hips they surveyed their work. In the midday heat, the garden seemed more alive than ever, green leaves and bold-faced flowers arching like cats toward the sun.

"It looks beautiful," Henry said. "You were right about the pink against the purple. It's a lovely contrast."

"Thank you," she replied, rolling up her shoulder to wipe her cheek. "And thank you for playing along with my ruse."

"Thank you for saving me from your brother," he said, grinning. "I get the feeling he doesn't like me very much."

Caroline looked up at him. "He doesn't. I wouldn't take it personally; William doesn't like most people."

Henry bent down to retrieve his coat, shaking off the excess manure. He loved this coat. It was probably ruined, and yet he didn't care. It was well worth a morning spent here, laughing with Caroline. He wished he could spend every morning like this.

But you can't, he reminded himself. You are here for the French Blue.

And Caroline would never have him besides.

"Mrs. Simmons would faint if we trailed all this"—Caroline held her soiled gown between her thumb and forefinger—"this mess of unmentionable substances through the house. Let's go toward the mews; you might go out that way."

Henry looped his first two fingers into the collar of his coat and flung it over his shoulder. "Splendid. You know how I feel about front doors."

He followed her through the garden and mews, toeing aside bits of manure as it fell through the jungle of Caroline's garments to the ground. He bit back a smile at the memory of her face as he'd held open her collar, the way she'd scrunched her eyes shut against the force of her laughter. It made him feel light inside, to know he'd made her laugh.

The nape of her neck shimmered with perspiration. He thought of that night in his brother's room. He had to look away.

"What's that?" he asked, pointing to a small, irregularly shaped structure tucked into the far corner of the garden. Its walls were done up in paneled wood, painted a dark shade of brown; a turret of windows sat proudly atop the sloping roof. Through the doors, flung open to receive the warm weather, Henry could make out the sparkle of crystal, the dim outlines of furniture and tables.

"William's garden folly," Caroline replied, stopping to admire the view. "I helped him and his architect design it. It's meant as a place for peace, for solitude and reflection, but I think my brother uses it for rather less . . . noble pursuits. He's done it up in the Turkish style, pillows and sofas everywhere."

Henry grinned. "Solitude and reflection, indeed."

"It's more a harem than a folly," Caroline agreed with a shrug. "Must be something about all this fresh air that puts his—ah—*friends* in the mood."

They made their way through the garden, past the mews and kitchens. Caroline stopped beside the gate, thrown open to a shadowy, narrow lane beyond, and curled her fingers into the gate's wrought iron scrollwork. She looked down at her boots as she scuffed aside a stray pebble.

Henry did not want to leave.

"Lady Caroline," he said, bowing. "You have provided most able instruction. Then again, I am a most able student."

She grinned, turning her head to glare at him from beneath her lashes. "Humble as ever, Mr. Lake."

"Bah, humility is so boring."

"And you," she scoffed. "You're anything but boring."

"Yes," he said.

Yes, and do you like it? he wanted to say.

The quick flash in her eyes told him she might.

Henry hesitated, scrambling to think of something to say. Parting really *was* such sweet sorrow; when on God's green earth would he stop having to learn that lesson?

"Thank you, my lady. For agreeing to help me."

She looked at him for a moment. "You're welcome, Mr. Lake."

Untangling her fingers from the gate, she turned, rolling back her shoulders as she walked; dried clumps of manure fell from the back of her gown.

"Though you must promise never to challenge me to a manure fight again!" she called over her shoulder.

"I promise!"

That was the only promise he could afford to make.

Henry spent the rest of the afternoon in the kind of daze he'd only felt while reading a good book: one foot in this world, the other planted firmly in another, a place composed of thoughts and feelings that were largely the product of his imagination. But they were real somehow, these things. They were true.

And that scared him, in a way he hadn't been scared in a long time.

An impermeable wall separated this world and that of Henry's imagination; a wall in the form of Caroline's brother, the Earl of Harclay, and the fifty-carat gem he'd stolen from Thomas Hope—and from England.

If it were business as usual, Henry would hunt down the French Blue by any means possible. Subterfuge, slitting throats, sex—it was all fair game. Hell, if it were business as usual, Henry would've likely already had the jewel in hand.

But he'd sworn to Caroline he'd refrain from such business, no matter how usual or useful. And this presented an obvious problem: without the diamond, Henry couldn't negotiate with the French, couldn't save the lives of a hundred, a thousand British soldiers, couldn't serve England as he should.

Henry had to tread carefully; quickly, too. As long as he was in London, he was putting them all at risk. And he'd already been the cause for enough hurt as it was.

He took a bath.

And then Henry Lake did what he did best. He pasted a big, furry beard to his face and tucked his queue into a wig and, alongside Mr. Moon, brooded over a tankard of ale in that deliciously sordid Cheapside tavern, the Cat and Mouse.

His right eye—the good one—twitched at the sourness of the ale.

"So, to be clear, we're looking for those short, hairy acrobats again. The ones with bad teeth, rough hands?" Moon murmured, glancing about the low-ceilinged tavern.

"Yes," Lake replied. "This is their favorite watering hole. We need only wait."

"Shouldn't be too difficult, considering every man in here—and woman—fits that description."

"The women aren't *all* that hairy, are they?"

Moon raised his eyebrows at the bar behind Henry.

Henry turned, gaze falling on the barmaids working behind the counter. "Heavens," he said, turning back to his accomplice, "even I can't grow a moustache like that. I don't know if I should be frightened or jealous."

"Jealous. Definitely jealous." Moon sipped his ale. "D'you really think the earl'll fall for this? He doesn't seem the type to intimidate easily, especially if hairy drunkards are doing the intimidating. Why don't we just—ah—*coax* the earl into telling us where he's keeping the Blue, and be done with it?"

Lake looked down at his ale, studiously avoiding Moon's gaze.

"The girl!" Moon nearly cried. "And the honey! You did it!"

"You sound surprised."

"Oh, but I am! Frankly I didn't think you capable of such . . . er, finesse."

Henry sighed. "I don't know why I'm even talking to you about this."

"Because you need my help, that's why," Moon said. "Although it does put us in a bit of a pickle. Can't torture your beloved's brother, no matter how much he deserves it."

"She's not my beloved."

"Keep telling yourself that." Moon scratched at his fiery red goatee. "And she won't help us?"

"She's agreed to let me have a look about the earl's house without interference. But she's not to be involved beyond that," Lake said, more savagely than he intended. "I gave her my word—never mind, I shouldn't be discussing this with you, and at the lovely Cat and Mouse of all places."

"Right," Moon said, taking a long pull from his mug, "back to the hairy acrobats, then."

"Yes, the acrobats."

The plan was simple, really; probably too simple, but it was the best Henry could come up with in his dreamily addled state. The earl was in disguise when he'd hired the acrobats to terrorize Hope's guests; the short-statured fellows hadn't a clue who Harclay was. Which meant, of course, they had no recourse when it came to collecting the twenty-five pounds Harclay still owed them.

But if Lake tipped them off that their employer was none other than William Townshend, an *earl*, and a wildly wealthy one at that, Henry knew the acrobats wouldn't hesitate to show up at Harclay's door for all of fashionable Mayfair to witness.

Harclay's Hanover Square mansion was enormous, and enormously impressive; it wouldn't take long for the acrobats to deduce that the earl had more—much, much more—to give than the twenty-five pounds he promised them.

With any luck, those limber scalawags would harass Harclay for money, for favors, for more money—hell, with more luck they might even blackmail him, threaten to reveal him for the thief and liar he was. Thus beleaguered, his honor at stake, the earl might come to regret stealing the diamond, regret setting his plot in motion. Maybe—and this was a very big *maybe*—the acrobats' harassment might convince the earl it had been a bad idea to thieve the French Blue, and to return it post haste to its rightful owner, Thomas Hope, before he was found out, his honor destroyed.

"We're playing with fire, you know," Moon said. "Once we tip off the acrobats, it will be difficult to control them. They could stake out Harclay's house, follow him, find out who his friends are, and whom he loves. They could use that information as a weapon against him. What if they threaten Lady Violet's life, or your lady friend his sister's?"

"She is *not* my *lady* friend," Henry ground out. "She's not mine, period. How many times do I have to tell you that?"

Moon rolled his eyes. "Of course. My mistake, sir, apologies. But the fact remains—after we tell the acrobats who their employer is, it'll only be a matter of time before they discover his secrets. They could demand virtually anything from him if they threaten to kidnap, or harm, or even kill his sister. You said yourself that Harclay is very protective of her."

A surge of anger rose through his chest to pool at the base of Henry's skull. Just imagining those blackguards handling Caroline brought his baser instincts to life; his fingers tightened around his mug. The earl may be protective of his sister, but Henry would kill anyone who so much as harmed a hair on her head.

"She's not to be involved," Henry repeated, low, steady. "Besides. If those bastards weren't smart enough to recognize the earl, they won't be smart enough to use Lady Caroline against him."

Moon nodded, though the bent of his brow suggested he wasn't entirely convinced. "Yes, sir."

Henry took a long, vicious pull of ale, wiping his mouth with the back of his hand. "But I want you to keep an eye on her, just in case."

"Of course. I assume nights, too?"

"Especially nights. If you so much as see a cat lurking about that wasn't there before, you're to come to me."

By now Moon's eyes were wide as saucers. He nodded again.

They waited and drank, and drank some more, twilight fading to darkness as the hours passed. The Cat and Mouse filled to bursting with London's most devotedly seedy population; in the corner behind Lake's left elbow, a gap-toothed lightskirt plied a lucrative trade.

Still no acrobats.

It was well past midnight when Mr. Moon at last succumbed to ale and exhaustion, his head resting in the crook of his arm on the table. He snored, and not at all softly.

Henry grimly conceded to his own exhaustion. He lifted Moon up by his armpits, "There, that's a good lad, one foot in front of the other," and carried him toward the exit.

Weaving their way through the crush of bodies, Henry was just about to thrust Mr. Moon out the tavern door when he felt a strange rush of air at his back.

It was vaguely familiar, that rush, as was the scent that trailed in its wake: labdanum, a pungent smell, wood and smoke, a vainglorious one, so big and so potent it was said to be worn by Caesar himself. Henry knew that scent. He just couldn't place it.

Henry wheeled about, Mr. Moon's limp body falling from Henry's arms to the ground with a muted thud.

He saw nothing, save the same faces he'd looked at for the past five hours: powdered faces, greasy faces, bruised ones.

The scent overwhelmed Henry once more, and then there was a voice at his ear, so quiet and whispery he wondered if he'd imagined it.

Soon, it said.

And then it was gone.

Henry searched the room frantically, but even with the advantage of his height he could see little beyond the threshold; the lighting inside the Cat and Mouse was dim at best, nonexistent at worst.

There were shouts by the door; someone was yelling about moving the body that blocked the tavern's entrance. Henry took one last look. No sign of sinister scalawags, spies; nothing out of the ordinary.

Henry collected Mr. Moon and stalked into the night.

Twelve

Brook Street, Hanover Square
The Next Day

"A dinner party?" Caroline put a hand to her hip. "Really?"
William looked up from the invitation he was penning. "Yes, really. Tomorrow evening. Don't look so surprised, I'm not *all* rotten."

"When was the last time you hosted a *dinner party*? Do you even know how?"

William glared at her. "Of course I know how. Besides, I've got Avery to help, and you."

Caroline stepped into her brother's cigar-scented study and slid the pocket doors closed behind her. It was late afternoon; the sun burned through the shutters' half-lidded slats with mean intensity, casting the room in burnished bronze. She held up a hand against the light and took a seat across from William.

"I know why you're doing this," she said.

He didn't bother to look up from his paper. "And why is that?"

"You're baiting Lady Violet. Admit it. You like her. Why not just give back the diamond and seduce her the regular way? Wine, flowers, a bauble—try buying it this time—more wine."

"Because," William replied, "like me, Lady Violet revels in the chase, and like me, she would lose all interest if said chase ended on so unimaginative a note as that. Besides, I'm not ready to return the French Blue. It's rather thrilling, to know a priceless diamond once worn by the kings of France is sitting at the bottom of one's—"

"Don't tell me." Caroline held that hand up to her brother. "I may have my suspicions, but I'm enough of an accomplice as it is."

"Very well."

"But you should give it back. The diamond. Soon."

His eyes flicked to meet hers. "All right, all right. Now are you going to help me with these blasted invitations? I haven't a clue what to say."

Caroline straightened her shoulders. "Under one condition."

"Yes?" he said wearily.

"Since you seem to be keeping your enemies—or at least your victims—quite close, invite Hope, and Mr. Lake, too, to this little dinner of yours."

"Hope, yes," William said. He arched a brow. "But Lake? There's something about him. I can't explain it, not really, except I have a bad feeling about that man. He's not who he says he is."

"Of course he's not. No one in London is these days." She put a hand on the desk. "Please, William."

He groaned. "If you insist."

"I do."

"Very well. Now come here, and tell me what to write."

Caroline sidled over to the other end of the desk. Looking over her brother's shoulder, she saw a piece of paper peeking out from under the one upon which he now labored. It was covered in his crooked, angry scrawl.

She could only make out the last line—*Yours, H.*

Curiosity prickled at the base of her skull. William only ever used that signature—informal, intimate—in his letters to Caroline.

Only this letter wasn't meant for Caroline.

While William shuffled through a drawer for more ink, she discreetly lifted the top page to peek at the one beneath it.

Dearest Lady Violet—

*I find myself in an insufferable position: not only have I
not quite finished seducing you, but I also owe you a
great deal of money. Please join me for dinner tomorrow
evening at half past eight. Bring your aunt Georgiana
and Lady Sophia; others of our mutual acquaintance
shall join us.*

*I shall be serving both the brandy and the champagne
that you so liberally enjoyed. Perhaps after we again
indulge, we may settle our accounts?*

Yours, H

"What are you looking at?" William returned to the desk.

Caroline dropped the paper. "What? Me? Nothing, it was
nothing. Here, what you've got so far for the invitation is, um,
less than ideal."

She struggled to contain her excitement as she helped her
brother pen the invitations. William liked Lady Violet. *Liked*
her. Never mind the obvious problem—that the earl had stolen
the French Blue from about Violet's neck, and in so doing had
jeopardized her friend, Thomas Hope, and her future—but William, infamous rakehell that he was, might actually be in love.

The Next Evening

For the second time in almost as many days, Henry Lake was
reduced to using the front door.

He tried to focus on his plan to sneak off from the party
and snoop about the earl's private quarters, his dressing room
especially. Over and over, he ran through the series of events
in his head, when he'd make his move, what he'd say. Work
had always been his distraction, and tonight he desperately
needed to be distracted.

But when he'd stepped into the welcoming front hall of
Harclay's house, Caroline was there, waiting to receive Henry.
He saw her color rise with pleasure, and his heart rose along

with it. Her gloved fingers slid into his palm with well-practiced ease, a current of feeling moving through him from this place where they touched. Her eyes were honey brown in the low light, warm, like velvet, a perfect foil to the pale pink of her gown. She looked happy to see him.

And all that focus, the work, the drive to distraction, dissolved in the space of a single heartbeat as Henry felt himself falling into her gaze. He didn't want to fall, he couldn't fall; there wasn't time, and it was dangerous besides.

But he fell, and kept falling, until she surrounded him. Her scent—lilies, and skin—her awkward greeting, and even more awkward stumble as he escorted her to the drawing room; she filled him, body and mind, and he felt soft in all the wrong places.

Henry passed the half hour of champagne and conversation in a daze. Wherever she was, he would look up and meet eyes with her across the drawing room. She would look away, blushing, adorable and impossibly lovely, and he would have to bite the inside of his lip, and dig his fingernails into his palm, to keep from looking again.

The French Blue, he tried reminding himself. It could be here, in this very house, right under his nose; hidden in the walls, perhaps, or tucked into some corner he hadn't had time to search.

Caroline laughed, the sound sending a rush of pleasant warmth through him. Henry tensed, and felt inexplicably, strongly jealous of Hope, who stood beside Caroline, smiling.

She wasn't Henry's; she owed him nothing. And yet he felt possessive of her, protective, too. If he had his way he wouldn't share her with anyone.

Lady Violet and the earl were ensconced in a far corner, whispering naughty nothings while they all but groped one another. Violet's cousin, Lady Sophia, a rosy-cheeked debutante with a wicked gleam in her eyes, kept trying—and failing—not to look at Hope. Hope was blushing, tugging at his mess of curls.

Henry blinked. Good God, had Cupid poisoned the well? It seemed Henry's wasn't the only desire that thickened the air in the room. He was at once relieved—there was a certain camaraderie in being laid low by longing—and annoyed with himself. He should be taking advantage of the earl's weakness, his state of distraction; instead, Henry was busy indulging his own weakness.

A weakness that went by the name of Lady Caroline Osbourne.

The dinner gong was struck, and Henry escorted Lady Violet to Harclay's cavernous dining room. Silently he prayed he might not sit next to Caroline.

And then he prayed that he might.

Flipping back his tails, he took his seat beside Caroline (he was on her right; to his left sat Lady Sophia). In the light of the silver candelabra, Caroline's diamond earbobs winked and flirted; Henry stared at the tender skin of her earlobe, wondering if she would like it if he took that skin between his teeth.

He winced at the familiar tightening in his breeches.

"Are you unwell? The champagne not to your liking?" she asked.

"Fine, quite fine, thank you," he said gruffly, and finished what was left in his coupe in a single gulp.

They spoke quietly—gossip, the weather, all polite things. Henry watched the earl watching him. Caught between them, Caroline played the perfect hostess, filling awkward silences, diffusing antagonism whenever it arose.

Halfway through the third course, the earl turned to Violet; Caroline turned her gaze on Henry, pleading.

"You promised," she said, low.

"I know," he replied. "You look lovely, by the way. I haven't had a chance to tell you."

"Don't change the subject."

He grinned. She blushed. "So what if I am? But you do look beautiful. That color suits you."

Her eyes raked (hungrily, appreciatively, he'd like to think) over his evening kit. He'd paid a tailor several months' salary to have it made up in three days' time, in the hopes that Caroline might look at him just as she looked now. The bright, crisp white of his cravat and waistcoat; his Pomona green velvet coat; the black satin breeches; she took it all in, biting her bottom lip as she did so.

He hoped she liked it. Really, really hoped she liked what

she saw. Mr. Moon had approved, but it was Caroline's opinion that mattered. That Henry craved.

"And you," she said, mirroring his grin as her eyes flicked over his costume one last time. "Passable, I suppose."

Just like that, in a room full of family and friends and footmen, they were alone, her voice low, his lower, as they grinned at one another. Was he imagining her burn, the same burn that coursed in the space between his blood and his bones? She couldn't like him, or feel for him the things he did for her. He'd left her, he was maimed, a cripple, scarred on both sides of his skin. Why did he even try?

Because of the way she was looking at him, now. He wanted to reach out and touch her face, hold her chin in his palm.

Her brother the earl cleared his throat, and Caroline's blush deepened as she looked away and the spell was broken. Henry looked up and saw Thomas Hope glaring at him from across the table. He straightened in his chair, tugging at his cravat; yes, the diamond, of course.

Dinner passed in a whirl of dishes and desserts; Caroline rose, and the ladies rose with her, bowing out of the room; then, cigars and brandy, the three of them—Hope, the earl, and Henry—sizing one another up through the haze of smoke.

"My offer of aid stands, Hope," the earl said, rolling his cigar between his thumb and forefinger. "The news of the stolen diamond bodes ill for my fortunes as it does for yours. I've men and money at my disposal. You need only ask."

Henry met Hope's eyes across the table. The earl had a set of stones on him, Henry had to give the man that; to offer aid in the search for the jewel, when he knew, and they knew, that he'd stolen it himself, was nothing if not ballsy.

Two can play this game, Henry thought, the table jumping as he stubbed out his cigar in an engraved silver ashtray. "We've men and money of our own," he said. "Besides. I rather enjoy the hunt. Not as much as I enjoy the kill, of course. The kill is my true skill."

It was a ridiculous and melodramatic speech, but there was something about the earl that set his teeth on edge, and made him feel particularly vengeful.

If Henry hadn't given Caroline his word, he would've strangled her brother right then and there.

The earl wore a small smile of triumph; Hope appeared frustrated, utterly defeated; and Henry felt too many things to possibly list.

The earl stood, draining the last of his brandy. "Let's join the ladies, shall we? My new billiards table has just arrived. It's proven quite amusing; even Caroline likes to play."

Caroline liked to play indeed, though she proved she was just as accident prone at sport as she was at life in general. Five minutes after the gentlemen entered the room, Caroline managed to launch a cue ball at Sophia's mother's head; Lady Blaise went down with a muffled cry, her overturned lace-edged petticoats like the layers of a flaky confection from Gunter's.

The party broke up after that. The earl, in all his thieving deviousness, swept Lady Blaise into his arms and gallantly carried her to her waiting coach; the ladies Sophia and Violet hurried out the door after him. Mr. Hope took his hat and gloves from the butler and without a word stalked into the night, which left Henry and Caroline, alone, in the front hall.

She was weeping openly now, bottom lip wobbling as tears rolled down her cheeks.

"Lady Blaise is going to be just fine," Henry said, drawing up before her.

"I know." Caroline wiped at her face with the edge of her wrist. "I just. I feel terrible. I'm such an ungainly mess, I shouldn't be allowed in public, or around other people—"

"Stop." Henry stepped forward. "It was an accident. Besides, you taught us all a valuable lesson: find cover whenever it's your turn to play."

Caroline scoffed. "Thank you," she said. "That doesn't make me feel any better, but thank you for trying."

A breeze wafted in through the front door, carrying with it the barest trace of a strange, heavy scent.

That scent.

A scent that made Henry stiffen. He knew it. It caught inside his head, a vague memory he couldn't quite place.

"Do you smell that?" he asked.

Caroline sniffed. "Smell what?"

The scent dissipated, if it was never there. "Nothing," Henry said, looking down at her. "I must've imagined it."

Heavens, but she was lovely, eyes wide and wet.

Without thinking, Henry reached forward and swiped away a tear with the crook of his first finger. Her skin was damp, and warm; alive.

Caroline froze; realizing what he'd done, Henry froze, too.

Caroline looked up at him, her long, dark lashes wet with tears. He felt wild with the desire to touch her again, but he couldn't move, and neither did she. The air between them tightened, urging them closer, pulling, challenging, teasing. If he took one step forward, just one more step, he could crush his lips to hers, hold her face in his hands . . .

She was afraid; he could tell by the uncertainty that darkened the wet pools of her eyes. Tears rolled silently down the sides of her face, seeping down her throat as she bent her neck to look up at him.

"My lady," he whispered. Of its own volition, his traitorous first finger unfurled, guiding the other four to cup her face in his hand. Desire shot through him, tightening the muscles in his legs, his back, and inside his chest.

Her lips parted, slightly. "Please," she breathed.

"Please what?" His voice was gruff.

Behind them the sounds of the earl's conversation with Sophia and her mother floated through the door; Caroline and Henry were safe, for a moment at least.

Caroline scoffed, her lips curling into a tiny smile. "Please don't address me like that. *My lady.* I hate it."

"It's what you asked."

"I hate it."

"How should I address you, then?"

Her eyes flicked to his lips. "I don't know."

Henry's fingers moved to her ear, her hair. Caroline didn't move into the caress, exactly, but she didn't pull away, either. Her face was tense, pained as she looked up at him.

His eyes moved to her throat. No woman on earth had a more elegant neck; a more enticingly erotic vulnerability there, in the soft sinews that moved against her skin in time to her scattershot pulse.

Henry dipped his head, testing her. Still she did not pull away. Her breath was sweet against his skin.

It was stupid.

It was dangerous.

It was rascally, and unforgiveable.

But he was going to do it anyway.

Before he could think better of it—they were in her *brother's* front *hall*, for God's sake!—he tucked his hand around her head and coaxed her to him, pressing his lips softly to her throat.

Thirteen

Caroline's eyes fluttered shut.

And in the space of a single heartbeat, she was lost in the tenderness, and the heat, of Henry's kiss as his mouth moved to cover her own.

She'd sensed his rising desire all evening: across the drawing room, and at the table during dinner. He vibrated with it, his eye darkening in a strangely familiar way that made Caroline's belly turn inside out.

She recognized his longing in her own. Ever since they'd planted the peonies together in the garden, she hadn't stopped thinking about him, and how hard they had laughed. She hadn't had that much fun in an age; really, since she'd climbed through the window of his bedchamber back in Oxfordshire after she'd married him in secret.

There were no more diverting things in England than climbing through windows and secret weddings, after all. Oh, and manure fights.

Those, too.

Caroline had fought the rising tide of her desire for Henry. She'd tried reading, and walking, and replanting half her brother's garden; but even days spent in the sun, her hands thrust up to her wrists in dirt, couldn't keep her from thinking about his half smile, the pale skin of his wrist.

She hated him for making her feel like this.

She hated herself for allowing him to. She'd been so careful to avoid moments like these, men like him.

And yet the shiver that darted up her spine when he brushed his knuckle across her cheek was impossible to ignore. The *memory* of his touch was its own kind of sweetness; but the *reality* of it was overwhelming, a different sort of sweetness, poignant, unbelievably lovely because it was happening here, now; and neither of them could take it back.

His mouth was warm and soft against her own, possessive. His fingers were moving in her hair, trailing ribbons of fire along her scalp. He kissed her slowly, carefully, as if they weren't standing in her brother's front hall, stealing a caress; as if they had all the time in the world.

He backed her against the wall, his legs spread wide to trap hers between them. He surrounded her; even through closed eyes she could sense the enormity of his body, the enormity of his longing.

Caroline tasted the salt of her tears on his lips. His scent, the lemons and the spice, filled her head.

Heat bolted through her, pooling between her legs. Henry's lips pressed and asked and answered, moving from one corner of her mouth to the other. Both his hands were on her face now, angling her head so that he might kiss her more deeply. His palms felt rough, calloused against her skin.

Where have you been? she wondered. Why did you leave?

And why do I feel this way about you after what you did to me, how stupid you made me feel?

But Caroline knew he wouldn't answer her questions. She would probably never have the truth.

She did, however, have this kiss. And she couldn't have given that up if she wanted to.

Henry stilled at the sound of approaching footsteps. Caroline's entire being cried out at the loss of his caress, even as panic unfurled in her chest. Her eyes flew open.

Oh God, she thought. *William.* If he caught her kissing Henry, he'd kill them both right there in the hall.

She pulled away. "My broth—"

Henry pressed a thumb to her lips, glancing over his shoulder. A beat passed. Caroline's heart pounded in her ears. Henry still pinned her to the wall.

With feline stealth he grasped her by the elbow and whirled her around the corner. Soundlessly he opened the door to her brother's study, using his body to urge Caroline inside as he closed the door silently behind them.

Henry held her against the wall beside the door, his body pressed to hers as he waited. They were both breathing hard.

The darkness inside the study was complete and close; through the door Caroline could hear William conversing with the butler, Mr. Avery, in low tones. More footsteps, a few more words, and then all was quiet.

Caroline was about to let out a sigh of relief when Henry took her mouth with his, resuming the kiss he'd begun in the hall. Hungrily he edged his body against her own, one hand on the wall beside her head, the other on her neck, his thumb grazing her jaw as she rose to meet his caress. Fire streaked through her, the kiss deepened, and he was opening her mouth with his lips, his tongue gliding to meet her own.

She couldn't tell if her eyes were open or closed. Everything was dark, and unbearably warm, but her body was alive, exquisitely, painfully so, as if her sight had lent its wide-eyed strength to her sense of touch.

Her hands went to his chest. She should push him away.

Instead her fingers reveled in the crisp thickness of his shirt, the velvet lapels of his dinner jacket. The muscles of his chest tensed beneath her careful touch. Oh, how she loved the feel of him, the firm softness of his flesh.

The kiss was wild now, and she could feel the gentle press of his cock against her belly. The heat between her legs flashed with pain. Twelve years later, and she still wanted him the way she had in the wanton throes of adolescence.

Twelve years later, and he still wanted *her* the same way. Or so she guessed from the hardness jutting out from his thighs.

The wallpaper scraped the back of her neck. It would leave a mark. He was always marking her. She should stop, and put an end to this madness. They could be caught.

But the thought of getting caught didn't frighten her as it should. Instead it titillated her, and stoked the desire that pounded through her body.

Even as her heart beat a staccato note—*no*, it seemed to say, *no*—she couldn't stop the kiss. It seemed a sacrilege, after all the years of her loneliness, to give up on a kiss like this one. A kiss that she felt in her bones. A kiss that swallowed her whole, and made her glad to be alive.

Funny, but the last two times she felt so glad were with Henry.

Although she refused—*refused*—to believe that meant anything.

His lips trailed from her mouth down the slope of her jaw, lingering on the tender place where ear met neck, before moving to her throat. Caroline sighed; he made an urgent, guttural sound, halfway between a growl and a groan. She felt his chest vibrate with it.

Behind closed lids, her eyes rolled back with pleasure as his teeth found purchase in the skin there. Her head, too, fell back, and hit the wall with a solid thud.

She froze.

He froze.

The house seemed to go still around them.

"Are you all right?" he whispered.

Caroline cracked open an eye, covering the offended spot on her skull with her fingers. "Yes." She winced. "And no. That hurt like the devil."

Her lips felt swollen, and so did her heart. Her eyes must have adjusted to the darkness of closed lids, because she could see Henry, suddenly, like a ghost materialized from the dark. Startled, she drew back; he was enormous, and very close; his one eye glowed, a pale moon that threw no light into the blackness.

For a moment they listened, waiting for the telltale footsteps, waiting to be found out.

And in that moment, Caroline was back in Henry's bedchamber, and it was their wedding night. How nervous they had been, terrified that his father's valet would find them entwined on the floor, or that his mother would return home from the ball and come to tuck her youngest son into bed (he was, after all, her favorite). She felt the same elation, the excitement, the thrilling intimacy of a shared secret.

But she was naïve then. She wasn't this time around.

Henry's hand moved to cover her fingers on her head. The other was still splayed on the wall beside her face. In the darkness she met his gaze. His touch, this time around, was a bit more gentle. Different, but the same.

"Caroline? Caroline, is that you?"

William's voice echoed through the gallery on the other side of the door. Heart in her throat, Caroline ducked beneath Henry's outstretched arm.

"Caroline. I heard something that sounded suspiciously like you banging your head against a wall. Are you there? And are you bleeding this time?"

Henry's eye went wide. "How did he know?" he hissed.

Caroline looked up from smoothing her skirts. "It happens more often than I care to admit," she whispered. "There, the window—tonight you don't have a choice, you'll go out that way."

He ran a hand over his hair, the other on his hip as he hobbled toward the window. His limp, it seemed, had come back to haunt him.

He hooked the fingers of both hands into the bottom casement and, with a small grunt, opened the window. Caroline gulped at the sudden rush of cool night air; it prickled against her skin.

Arms above his head, Henry leaned against the casement; Caroline drew up beside him, the breeze playing at her mussed hair. For a moment they stood at the open window, trying—and failing—to catch their breath. Drops of rain pattered softly on the ground below.

She didn't know what to say after an episode like *that*; heavens, she didn't know what to *feel*.

Henry couldn't keep his hands off her. That was good.

He knew what to do with those hands.

That was better.

But he was still Henry Lake, and his expert hands did nothing to change the fact that he'd broken her heart ruthlessly, rottenly, a decade ago.

She should push him out the window, as she'd threatened to do that morning she caught him snooping about William's house. He deserved it.

Henry leaned into the open window, hands still above his head. From the corner of her eye she watched the muscles of his arms flex against his coat. Her throat was tight, suddenly, her pulse hard.

"I don't know what you want me to call you," he said, looking down at his shoes. "I want to wish you good night."

She swallowed. "Please, Henry." Please kiss me again. And again, and again. "Please leave me be."

"I can't."

"You must." For both our sakes. He must know as well as she that nothing good could come of intimacies like this.

That he'd hurt her too badly for her to ever trust him again.

He dropped his arms. Just before he made to jump, he turned back to her. Taking her neck in the palm of his enormous hand, he pulled her to him and planted a kiss on the crown of her head, just where she'd hit it.

She closed her eyes against the hot press of tears.

When she opened them, Henry was gone.

Caroline stepped out into the hall, giving the door one last tug before it reluctantly *thwump*ed into place behind her.

"Caroline, there you are!" William strode toward her, brow furrowed. "What were you doing in my study?"

"I, um, got lost?"

William crossed his arms over his chest and leaned a shoulder against the wall. "Try again. A better lie this time."

Caroline cleared her throat. "I was rifling through your papers, stealing your money, and, um, using your secrets to blackmail you. There. Better?"

William smiled. "Much."

"You played your role as host with appalling good grace, dear Brother."

"Thank you." He bowed. "And you were a marvel of a hostess."

"Well"—Caroline made to move past him—"to bed, then. It's exhausting, being a marvel."

"Caroline." He grabbed her by the elbow. "Where is Mr. Lake?"

She blinked. "Mr. Lake left with Mr. Hope, not a quarter of an hour ago. Didn't you see him? Or were you too busy fondling Lady Violet?"

"I wasn't fondling her." He appeared regretful as he said this.

Caroline attempted to pull away. William only pulled her closer. "Careful with him," he said, softly. "He's after me, Caroline. And men like Lake are cruel when it comes to getting what they're after. I don't mean to question whatever it is he feels for you—"

"It's nothing."

"But if he can, he'll use you to get to me. I know he's tall, and eye patches are all the crack this season, but that dashing exterior hides a hound. And he's caught my scent."

Caroline waved away his words. "That's a horrid metaphor, first, and second, you've nothing to fear, for I wouldn't let that man touch me with a ten-foot pole."

William's brow shot up. "Is that why your hair looks like that? Because he touched you with a ten-foot pole?"

Caroline turned to the beveled mirror on the far wall. She started at the woman staring back at her. Pink cheeks, pinker lips, a lopsided lock of hair falling across her forehead. Soft eyes.

An obviously well-pleasured woman. One who'd been kissed, and kissed quite thoroughly.

Caroline's throat tightened all over again. She was embarrassed, yes, that her brother should see her in such a state.

But more than that she was afraid. Fear gripped her heart, like ice-cold fingers giving that overworked organ a savage twist. The woman staring back at her wasn't the placid, self-possessed dowager Caroline imagined herself to be. She wasn't the twenty-nine-year-old woman who had learned her lesson about love, and knew better than to allow it to destroy her again.

This woman, the one with the traitorous high color, the one who'd agreed to help Henry Lake find the French Blue, was a fool.

Caroline wrangled her elbow from William's grasp and, excusing herself, darted up the stairs.

She sent Nicks away and, closing the bedroom door softly behind her, brought her hands to her face. Her skin burned.

She did not see the figure separate from shadow until it was too late.

Fourteen

---✦---

Henry paced across the room, each footfall like a clap of thunder. The floorboards shook and moaned beneath his stride.

Mr. Moon jumped back at a particularly vengeful step.

"I swear, you're worse than that black-toothed Genoese opium eater," Moon said, straightening the vials he'd overturned. "It's been, what, an hour since you saw her last?"

"I don't know who you're talking about," Henry growled, clasping his hands behind his back to keep them from shaking. His lips smarted and stung, alive with the memory of Caroline's kiss.

What a fool he was, careless, to succumb to the desire he'd worked so hard to suppress. All those years of sacrifice, of keeping her safe, far from the violence of the life he'd chosen— all that work, dashed in a single instant, by a single touch.

He shattered everything he touched.

He had no right to touch her.

But he couldn't help it. The desire to see her, touch her, possess her was overwhelming. That kiss, that embrace that was supposed to slake his desire for her, merely stoked it to unbearable heights.

She'd felt it, too. He'd known she had. He also sensed her frustration, her anger. He understood why she asked him to stay away.

And yet.

"For the love of God," Moon said, "go back to her already! There's nothing wrong with missing the woman you love—"

"She's not my woman. And I am most certainly not in love."

How is she feeling, he wondered. How is her head?

Moon rolled his eyes. "Right. But would you just go back to her, and leave me in peace? You might continue your search for the jewel, too."

"I've searched the house." Lake turned on Mr. Moon. "And she doesn't want me to go back to her. She doesn't want me, period. She said so herself."

"And you believe her?" Moon cocked a brow.

"Of course I believe her!" Lake said. "What else am I supposed to do?"

Moon smiled. "Call her bluff, and kiss her soundly."

Henry placed his palms on the windowsill. He'd kissed her, all right. Soundly, passionately, stupidly.

"I'm too busy," Henry said gruffly. "If you've forgotten, that bloody diamond is still missing, and Napoleon's still winning the war. I've a rather busy schedule."

Moon sighed noisily. "Go see her."

"I can't."

"If I may take a moment to applaud my powers of persuasion, sir—have I ever been wrong about members of the female sex?"

"Yes," Henry said.

"You know I'm right." Moon sighed. "Have it your way, but don't blame me when you wake up in hell tomorrow morning. If you don't get some sleep, and soon, you're going to end up dead. And the only way you're going to be able to sleep is if you go to her already!"

Henry growled once more and rolled his eyes and shouted his denials. But as he paced away the minutes, he felt a growing terror at the prospect of spending another sleepless night in this room.

And so, like any insomniac experiencing a bout of unrequited affection, he got desperate.

He got stupid.

He got on his horse, and rode for Hanover Square. He told himself he went to make sure she was all right.

To make sure she was sleeping soundly, and safe.

But the burn in his lips, the stretch inside his chest, told a different story.

Caroline's window was open, glowing with the light of candles and lamps within. His stomach clenched; she was still awake.

It was quiet in the narrow lane that ran alongside the house to the mews. Later Henry would recognize it was too quiet, and strange he didn't hear voices floating down from Caroline's window.

But he was too distracted by the prospect of speaking with her again, too excited, to notice the silence that surrounded Harclay's house.

Without a backward glance, Henry mounted the gate and tore through the mews, scaling the wall in record time. Despite the morbid exhaustion that weighted down his limbs, he landed with hardly a thump inside the warm dimness of Caroline's chamber.

A chamber that was empty.

"Caroline?" he called, softly. "It's me, Henry—Henry Lake."

As if there were other Henrys who climbed through her window, uninvited, at all hours of the night.

He cringed.

The bed was made, the counterpane tucked in immaculate angles around the corners of the mattress. There, on the escritoire by the opposite window, a neat stack of letters was ready for the post; a ream of clean-edged paper sat beside it.

All was where it should be.

Only, it wasn't.

The gilded cut glass inkwell hung precariously over the edge of the escritoire, leaking droplets of blood-black indigo onto the Persian carpet. Beside the growing puddle rested a swan feather quill, mangled about the middle as if someone had stepped on it.

His nostrils recoiled at that vaguely familiar scent. It was stronger now. Labdanum—pungent, unmistakable.

Henry's blood went cold; the back of his skull prickled

with terror. In a searing rush the memory came back to him. He'd smelled it that morning in the woods, twelve years ago.

The morning he'd defied orders, and made a mistake.

A mistake that cost the life of a young woman.

A mistake that changed the course of his life, and had him running from England, from everything he loved and held dear.

From Caroline.

Caroline.

He tucked his hand inside his jacket, fingers curling around his pistol.

The door to Caroline's dressing room was slightly ajar, maybe an inch or two; a beam of light cut a widening yellow lane across the floor.

Slowly Henry approached, heart drumming. He fitted the trigger into the crease of his first knuckle. Pain shot up his leg. He ignored it.

He edged his boot against the door, and was about to kick it back when it opened suddenly, sending him stumbling back into the room. Henry tore his loose hair away from his face, righting himself as his eye fell on a man, tall, black-haired, dressed in an exquisitely tailored evening kit.

He was smiling, wickedly.

His teeth, white, even, gleamed with the pearlescent fervor of a full moon. They were a striking foil to his lips, thickened and a smidge raw at the edges of his mouth.

For a moment his rage flared so violently Henry could taste it in his mouth.

Henry knew this man. Knew him well, from his childhood days spent in the Lake family's quiet Oxfordshire neighborhood.

The Marquess of Woodstock stood across the room, his bony, enormous hand wrapped around Caroline's neck. Her skin, mottled blue and red, bulged between his fingers, as if he were giving her throat a good squeeze.

The man's face was long, a misshapen oval that righted itself as Woodstock grinned.

He looked at Henry with piercing eyes, light blue, that, together with the wild black locks curled about his brow, lent him a bizarrely rakish air.

"Hello, Mr. Lake." He turned to look at Caroline. Henry noticed her face pulse a shade hotter; Woodstock was choking her. "Say hello to Mr. Lake, Caroline. He's missed you terribly, you know."

Henry released the safety on his pistol, aiming it at Woodstock's broad forehead.

Woodstock's fingers clawed at Caroline's throat. She cried out, a high sound that Henry felt in the center of his chest.

"She's got a lovely neck, doesn't she?" Woodstock asked. He turned back to look at Henry. "I'll break it."

Henry held up his hands. His gaze never leaving Woodstock's, he crouched down and dropped the pistol; rising, he tapped the pistol with his foot, sliding it across the floor.

Woodstock caught it beneath the sole of his polished boot.

"That's better," he said. "Don't you think, Caroline?"

Caroline let out a strangled sigh as Woodstock loosened his fingers. He did not remove them from her neck. The skin there was bright pink, dappled white where he'd squeezed her especially hard.

"Caroline," Henry said, voice low, "are you all right?"

Her eyes glittered in the dim light. She gave a little nod. "All right."

Henry turned his glare to Woodstock. "Tell me what you want. Let the lady go and I will give you whatever you ask."

"Twelve years ago," he replied, "you murdered a young woman in the woods on my estate. She was helping me with a bit of . . . well, we shall call it precious cargo. That woman was my wife. I am here to return the favor."

Fifteen

T he realization hit Henry viscerally, a blow to the ribs.
Precious cargo. The guns. The stockpile of arms hidden in the woods.

Woodstock was the traitor. The French agent he'd been tasked to root out that fateful, bloody morning twelve years ago.

The morning Henry lost everything.

That strange scent, the labdanum—that was Woodstock's cologne. It had to be.

Henry's mind raced. Woodstock was a *peer*. A marquess, and an enormously wealthy one at that. He owned the better half of Oxfordshire; Henry remembered, vaguely, his parents entertaining the marquess—Woodstock's father—for dinner once. The ruckus surrounding the months-long preparation had driven his father to drink, and nearly undone his mother.

"My God," Henry murmured.

The Marquess of Woodstock, a turncoat. The flower of English aristocracy, of landed wealth and gentle manners, was a bloody traitor. How had Henry not known? All this time, how had he not seen what was lurking just beneath his nose?

But more than that, Henry longed to know why.

Why? he wanted to scream. Why turn his back on a country

that blessed him with every imaginable privilege, with a title and a fortune, with honor, with family, a legacy won by battle half a millennium before?

Never mind the damage Woodstock could have wrought while in Old Boney's employ. The man sat in Parliament; he had access to all kinds of sensitive information, to national secrets, to scandals. Whatever Napoleon had paid Mr. Woodstock, he'd gotten his money's worth.

But why?

Henry met Woodstock's gaze. The man grinned, dipped his head. Henry gritted his teeth to keep from pummeling that grin from his face.

"Because I could," Woodstock said, shrugging. "The same reason I now work for myself. Why not? Oxfordshire can be so very dull. It made things interesting, to switch sides. Besides"—he smiled at Caroline—"being a turncoat makes for some rather lovely bedfellows."

A pause.

"Twelve years it took me to find you," Woodstock said at last. "And all of a few days to find her."

Henry gritted his teeth, took a deep breath through his nose. What an idiot he'd been. "Hyde Park. You saw us together there."

"It was the fashionable hour," Woodstock replied. "Everyone saw you there. I saw the way you looked at her. All this time she's been right under my nose. And then you gave me all the evidence I needed tonight, kissing her in the front hall. How clever, to choose a woman who belongs to someone else."

"She doesn't belong to anyone," Henry ground out. He prayed fervently, he prayed harder than he'd ever done before, that Woodstock would not do further harm to Caroline. This was his cross to bear.

Woodstock scoffed. "You're smarter than that, old man. Though I cannot say that I blame you. She is lovely. And good. Too good for you."

Henry's fingers gathered into fists. He felt sick with rage. He'd never torn apart a man with his bare hands.

There was a first time for everything.

He took a deep breath through his nose. He had to stay calm. Had to play along nicely, for now at least.

"Your masters in Paris have been very busy slaughtering

their neighbors," Henry said. "Surely you've had better things to do than chase me about the Continent."

"Surely, yes. But I didn't want to do those things. I wanted you. You'll be happy to learn I stopped working for the French after your little—what shall we call it?—oh yes. *Accident*. Something about having your wife shot dead before your eyes by a careless boy changes a man. My superiors, as you call them, were rather unsympathetic to my situation. I work for myself now."

A beat of dread pulsed through Henry. "She was an agent of our country's enemy, Woodstock, same as you—"

"She was not," Woodstock spat. "She merely provided aid when I needed it. She was innocent."

Henry swallowed. "If she aided you, that makes her your accomplice. Traitors, the both of you."

"Traitor or not, you did not mean to shoot her."

"No." Henry took a sharp breath through his nose. "I didn't. I'm sorry I missed my mark. I'm sorry I missed *you*. But I am not sorry she is dead."

Again Woodstock smiled. "That is where we differ, isn't it, Mr. Lake? For I am very sorry she is dead. As I'm sure you'd be sorry if your lady love the dowager countess was shot through the head."

Caroline's eyes bulged with terror. "Henry?" she rasped.

"Ah!" Woodstock crowed. "She doesn't know about you, does she, Mr. Lake? But then I suppose killing an innocent woman in cold blood is something you would keep to yourself."

Henry balled his fists at his sides. Even as he'd sworn to keep her far from the sordid details of his past—even as he'd sworn never to admit to her the things he felt—she deserved to know.

"Go on," Woodstock said. His pale eyes glittered. "Tell your tale of woe."

Henry met eyes with Caroline. *I'm sorry,* he pleaded. *I'm so sorry.*

"Down at Oxford I was recruited to serve His Majesty in the war against France," he began. His words were thick, low, each one torn unwillingly from memories he'd locked away. "The morning you and I—after we—I walked you home. When I got back to my parents' house, a boy waited for me with summons from my commanding officer.

"A French spy was working in the area at the time. We made it our business to uncover his identity, root him out. That evening a coded letter from the spy had been intercepted. The messenger carrying the letter had been interrogated, but he revealed nothing. My officer decoded the letter. It revealed the location of an arms stockpile—bayonets, pistols, gunpowder—used by French spies working in London. My orders were to wait for nightfall, when I'd meet up with other recruits to search for the stockpile, and destroy it. If we were lucky, the stockpile would lead us to the spy and we could destroy him, too."

Henry swallowed, hard. "I was impatient. Eager to prove myself. I had you, Caroline, I wanted to start a fam—" He swallowed again. "I had no inheritance, no money or land of my own. I needed to make my own way in the world. I thought I could take care of the guns and the spy myself, even as I knew the guns would be heavily protected. Guarded. I thought I could make a splash with the officers, a coup no one would ever forget."

"I did not forget," Woodstock said.

Henry looked down at this feet. "I did not wait. I went into the woods just as the sun rose, armed with two pistols. I found the stockpile. And I found her."

The memory overwhelmed him then: the clear sky above, the forest lush with summer growth. That strange, strong scent in his nostrils as he took the girl in. She crouched in a small hollow carved out of the roots of an oak, filled to the brim with guns; she was young, and pretty, her dark hair loose about her shoulders.

Young, pretty, dark haired. Just like Caroline.

The girl was alone, or so he thought. And she held in her arms an enormous rifle, fitted with a bayonet that glinted with sinister intent in the pale morning light.

"She—the girl—looked up at me. I didn't know what to do, who she was, why she was there. A shot rang out—"

"That was me," Woodstock said. "I saw it. Everything. I saw you kill her."

"The girl took off running. More shots. I knew there were others in the woods with her. I saw them ducking in and out of the trees—the traitors. I had a clear shot at one of them—he was reloading his gun behind a tree, spilling powder everywhere. I had a clear shot, and I took it. Only it wasn't his scream that filled the woods. The girl, that one with the bayonet, she'd jumped in front of the man just before I'd pulled the trigger."

Henry looked up at Caroline to see a tear fall, silently, down the slope of her cheek.

Despite the tightening in his throat, he pushed on. "The man left her, took off running. The sight of her, facedown—"

A sight that had haunted him for more than a decade. This girl—she'd been someone's daughter. She'd worn a ring on her left hand; she was someone's wife, perhaps someone's mother.

Yes, she was a traitor. But she was also someone's everything.

He remembered, vividly, imagining it was Caroline lying facedown on the forest floor, a bullet in her chest, blood seeping through the delicate fabric of her bodice. Her dark hair sticky with blood, a gruesome halo.

It could've just as easily been Henry's wife, a bystander caught in the crossfire. A victim of his violent, dangerous doings. His mistakes.

Caroline, *his* everything. His collateral damage.

He could not bear the thought of Caroline being harmed, or worse, on his account. He'd sworn, at that moment, to keep her safe. Keep her far from the bloody business in which he was engaged. He was a fool, he was impatient and unwieldy, and his foolishness would only end up hurting her. It was too late to leave the service besides, and now he had a debt to pay, a wrong to make right.

He had decided, quickly, what he would do. The choice he would make.

He took a deep, trembling breath. "I came under heavy fire. So I ran. I could not destroy the arms. I did not discover the identity of the spy or his accomplices. I only managed to kill a girl, and frighten the neighbors. I bungled my mission, embarrassed my officers. And because I failed, because I saw what my mistakes, and my profession, could do to the people I loved, I had to break my vow to you, Caroline. I had to leave."

Caroline let out another cry; Henry's blood leapt, and his body leapt with it.

With violent stealth, Woodstock kicked the pistol from the floor into his hand and pressed it to Caroline's temple. He clucked his tongue. "Not another step, Mr. Lake."

"You're hurting her."

Woodstock's smile curled evilly into his cheeks. "That's the point."

"Kill me," Henry said. "Take me. I'm the one who killed your wife. Kill me and call it even."

"Such a tidy ending that would be for you! But alas, the pain would be too brief. You must suffer, yes, but living can be so much more painful than death if it's done right. And I intend to do it right, Mr. Lake. For your sake. And for Lady Caroline's."

Woodstock released the safety on the pistol. Caroline stiffened, eyes squeezed shut against the blow sure to come.

"Wait!" Henry cried. "Wait. I have something that might interest you. A trade."

Woodstuck narrowed his eyes. "A trade?"

"A fifty-carat diamond, in exchange for Caroline's life."

"It's that diamond all the papers are talking about, isn't it?" Woodstock cocked a brow. "Thieved from some idiot's ball?"

Henry's heart hammered against his ribs. "Yes. The French Blue."

Sixteen

Caroline's breath caught in her throat. Inside her chest her
lungs burned.

It was impossible to tell what shocked Caroline more: the content of their conversation, Henry stripped of his secrets by this
silver-tongued stranger, or the fact that Henry had left her not
because he didn't love her, but because he loved her too much.

The mistake he'd made, why he'd left her. Twelve years ago
he left her because he *had* to. Because he'd accidentally killed
this man's wife, and he feared the same might happen to her.

Henry's leaving had nothing—and everything—to do with
Caroline. He did not leave because he got what he came for (a
toss—well, several tosses—in the sheets); he did not leave
because he found her dull or ugly or unworthy of his handsome enormity.

He left because he loved her. Because he would give up
everything, his family and his name and future, to keep her safe.

He loved her then, as ardently as she'd loved him. All the
time they'd lost, the misunderstandings, the secrets, the pain—it
was almost too much to bear.

And now here he was, offering up a priceless jewel in
exchange for her life.

It made her feel like weeping.

And she would have wept, had a stranger not been threatening her at gunpoint inside her bedchamber.

"The French Blue," Henry repeated. "It's yours, if you leave her in peace."

"You have it?"

"I—"

A hesitation. Slight, hardly noticeable.

Except Woodstock noticed.

Again he clucked his tongue. "You were going to lie to me, Mr. Lake. Good thing you did not."

"I can get it. I *will* get it. I swear to you, Woodstock—"

"When?"

Henry hesitated. Caroline thought her heart might burst. "Soon. Give me a chance to get it. The diamond. And then I'll give it to you."

More silence.

Please, she prayed. Please, Henry, don't get shot.

As if he had control over Woodstock's gun.

She did not dare reach out herself, try to wrest the gun from Woodstock; she'd read enough novels to know startling a man with a pistol usually ended in blood. A very dramatic amount of blood.

Caroline nearly jumped when Woodstock let out a little laugh. He stepped back, removed the gun from her head, loosened his grip on her throat. She gasped for air. "What have I to lose? Surely you are not foolish enough to attempt to kill me before all of London, and during the season at that! I know where you live. I know where *she* lives. And you aren't going anywhere until you find that gem. Soon, then. I'll be watching you."

Henry's words were a rush of relief. "Good. Thank you."

"Remember you swore," Woodstock said, teasingly.

"I did. And in return you must swear not to harm her. Lady Caroline. You are not to go near her, or this house. She is—"

"Not yours."

"No." Henry ran a hand through his hair. "She's not yours, either. So stay away from her, or I'll kill you."

Caroline looked away. The savageness of Henry's threat sent a shiver down her spine.

Woodstock sighed. She could practically hear him rolling

his eyes. "Fine, fine, I'll stay away from her. But know this, Mr. Lake. You don't find the French Blue, and *soon*—well, I'm afraid the terms of our little arrangement shall no longer stand."

"I'll find it," Henry ground out.

A pause. "What will you do?" Woodstock asked.

"About what?" Henry said.

"The blood on your hands? The thousands of men—good men, innocent men—who will die because you choose her over them? I know you mean to use the French Blue as leverage against the French. You won't be able to negotiate for the lives of your men if you don't have the stone."

Caroline's heart skipped a beat. So that's what Henry had been talking about—doing a favor for old St. George. He meant to trade the diamond for the lives of his soldiers on the Continent.

He would not be able to make such a trade if he gave the jewel to Woodstock.

He would choose her life over the lives of his men.

"Let me worry about that," Henry replied.

"The diamond," Woodstock said calmly. "Or Caroline. Your choice. I get one or the other. Don't keep me waiting."

Only when the last of Woodstock's footfalls faded into the blackness beyond her window did Caroline resume breathing. She gulped at the air, thirstily, like she'd been held under water these last minutes; the sudden onslaught of sensation made her dizzy, bright dots blurring her vision.

And then Henry was folding her into his enormous arms, holding her against him as he smoothed her hair, pressed his lips to her forehead, asking if she was all right, was her throat all right, could she breathe all right? His heart beat furiously, violently, against her ear. She closed her eyes, listened as her heart began to beat in time to his.

She buried her face in his chest, stifling the sound of her grief; she couldn't hold back, couldn't stop if she wanted.

Years of unshed tears, of unspoken heartache and unrequited affection burst from the dark places where she'd hidden them and inundated her being. She was powerless against the onslaught. She let herself drown in it.

All this time she assumed the worst of Henry. That he never loved her, that he'd been in love with someone else. That he used her, abused her trust, thought she was strange, repulsive even.

Her affection hadn't been unrequited, after all. He'd been in love with her, ardently, those years and years ago. The kind of ardent love she felt for him, once.

And felt again now, witnessing him forsake everything so that her life might be spared. *Henry chose her.* Turned his back on his men and chose her life over theirs. One life in exchange for thousands.

The fact that he'd chosen her—without hesitation, without a second thought—made her heart swell in the most wonderful, most hopelessly painful, way.

There were a thousand questions she wanted to ask him, a thousand things she wanted to say. I wish you'd told me. I wish you'd taken me with you. I understand why you left, but it hurts—knowing your reasons.

She didn't know where to begin.

But she knew, in that moment, what had to be done.

"You can't do it, you know," she whispered.

"What's that?" he said.

"Give that man the French Blue. I won't let you."

Henry's shoulders fell. He turned his head and looked out the window, revealing the chiseled architecture of his throat and jaw.

His gaze returned to her. "Your patriotism is inspiring, Caroline, really, but I'm afraid you don't have much choice in the matter."

"Choice?" She lifted her chin. "But there's no choice to be made."

The look in his eye changed, loosened. "My point exactly."

"That's not what I meant."

"I know what you meant."

"One life in exchange for the possible slaughter of thousands?" she said. "That guilt will weigh on us both."

He cocked a brow. "Do you always go to bed in so Shake-spearean a mood?"

"Only on Thursdays."

"Well then, Lady Macbeth, you might take your perfumes

of Arabia and go to sleep. I hope you wake in a less suicidal disposition."

She bit her lip, let out a scoff. "I'm not going to let you do it."

"I know you won't," he said softly. "But I'm going to do it anyway. Who knows, we might win the war in the meantime, and then it won't mean anything to lose the jewel to Woodstock."

"It means something to Thomas Hope, and Lady Violet. They'll lose everything. Perhaps we might outwit Woodstock together. Defeat him so you don't have to give up the diamond. We can do it together—"

"I'm sorry, Caroline," he whispered. "I won't put you in danger. Not if I can help it. I'm sorry."

"I know," she replied. "What you did for me—it's extraordinary. Let me return the favor. Let me help you. I'll tell William everything; if he knows we're in danger, he'll give back the diamond, you can take it to the French—"

"And let Woodstock have you?" Henry untangled her from his arms. He looked down and met her gaze. "Considering the things I just confessed to you, Caroline, do you really think I'd let that happen? I'll handle Woodstock on my own. It's too dangerous, you being involved. I won't see you hurt. Besides, I don't trust your brother. If he knows Woodstock threatened you, he might confront him, try to kill him on his own. Woodstock is a well-trained agent, and deadly; your brother, despite his bravado, doesn't stand a chance. Which is why I can't pay the marquess a call tomorrow and take care of him myself. He'll be watching our every move. No, it's better if we keep the earl out of this for the time being."

A beat of silence passed between them.

At last Henry looked away, tugged a hand through his hair. "I have a plan in place to loosen the jewel from your brother's grasp. Once I have the French Blue—"

"You'll do what you think is right." Caroline offered him a small, tight smile. "Just like you did twelve years ago."

He met her eyes. "Do you not think I made the right choice then?"

It was her turn to look away. "There was no right choice, Henry."

There was no right choice now.

Seventeen

———— ✦ ————

O nce Henry had gone and the house was quiet, Caroline flung the counterpane aside and scurried to the door. She listened; not a sound.

She snuck out into the hall, wincing as she stubbed her toe on a sinisterly placed chair. Hopping to her brother's door, she ducked to peek inside the keyhole.

The room was dim, lit by a pair of candelabra.

And it was empty. No doubt William was out somewhere peeling off Violet's clothes. In his carriage, perhaps, or maybe the stables. The way they were looking at one another tonight at dinner—heavens, it was a miracle the box hadn't burst into flames.

She let out a sigh of relief. At least William had not heard the exchange between Woodstock and Henry.

At least their secret was safe. For now.

Caroline crept into the bedchamber and closed the door softly behind her. Even with the windows open, the room smelled just like his chamber from childhood: like *boy*. A close, slightly musky, slightly sour smell that made her smile— he'd been so cute as a boy, and so naughty!—as she moved across its carpeted expanse.

With shaking hands, she plucked a taper from the candelabra. Its light sputtered and flashed in her unsteady grasp. She opened a narrow door at the far end of the room and stepped into William's dressing room. Rows upon rows of drawers neatly lined the walls; their mahogany surface shimmered in the candle's wavering light.

Caroline turned to a wide drawer, a little above waist height. Its copper pull was the only hardware in the room marked with fingerprints.

Perfect. It was *the* drawer.

For as long as she could remember, William had hidden his most treasured possessions in a top drawer amid his stockings and socks. When they were little, it had been a drawer in his ancient bureau that had to be tugged, quite viciously, to get open. Back then he'd hidden money, biscuits, and bugs in his not-so-secret drawer. Caroline would dig through it every Monday after luncheon, when William was at his shooting lessons. Sometimes she'd steal the biscuits; most times, the bugs.

She'd take them back with her to the garden, where they belonged.

As he got older, he'd hide slightly less innocent objects in the drawer of his bedside table here at their father's London house. A copy of *Fanny Hill*, read so many times its pages were limp with fatigue; a flask; a girl's garter, festooned with tiny pink ribbons.

Caroline had been so tempted to ask about that garter. But then William would've known she'd been snooping about his drawer, and moved his secrets elsewhere. And she liked knowing his secrets.

Holding the taper aloft, Caroline clasped the cold metal pull and slid open the drawer. Neat stacks of silk stockings sat shoulder to shoulder, each pile an alternating color: first white, then black, cream, and navy, white again.

Careful not to drip wax onto the stockings, Caroling began nudging her hand between the soft stacks. Her fingers probed and poked, feeling between each sock carefully, patiently—for she knew she could never rearrange these garments as neatly as had William's valet.

She found a few trinkets, old love letters that had very little to do with love. Nothing exciting. Not at all what she was looking for.

Taking the taper in the opposite hand, she began her search anew. She dug deeper, the stockings gliding between her fingers softly. It made her think of Henry, and the glide of his silken hair in her hands.

Her knuckles brushed something hard, irregularly shaped. Her pulse jumped. She chased it to the corner of the drawer, where she was able to grasp it with her fingers and coax it to the stockings' silken surface.

Caroline rolled it to the center of her palm. It felt cold, and heavier than she imagined it would. Dead weight.

The French Blue winked and flashed seductively in the taper's yellow light. Caroline stared at it, transfixed, her heart in her throat as her eyes raked hungrily over the diamond. It was *enormous*.

The jewel appeared black from this angle, like the mummified heart of a child (how morbid, she thought); she turned her hand, and the diamond winked white, purple, translucently cerulean, a shade lighter than the sea.

A strange kind of desire prickled inside her chest; her eyes watered because she hadn't blinked, not once; she was caught in the diamond's seductive pull, in the tide of her longing to possess it.

It was unimaginably thrilling, to think the kings of France once kept this jewel in their own secret drawers; that they once wore it in the halls of Versailles as a complement to their dazzling costumes. It had seduced kings, this diamond, and had doubtless aided those kings in seducing women, wives, mistresses, favors. The French Blue had been witness to a world, and a way of living, that no longer existed. There was something terribly romantic about that. A world long gone, the regret and anger at its passing—Caroline knew these things well.

She held the stone for several minutes, its underside warming to her palm. Her eyes, still swollen from her encounter with Woodstock, began to sting once more.

It was all too much. The things she felt, the events that occurred. The threat the Marquess of Woodstock made against their lives.

He was too much. Henry Beaton Lake.

In her palm, Caroline held the power to put an end to his troubles, hers, too. The diamond could change everything. It could buy the lives of a thousand of Henry's men. Or it could buy her life, a return to her peaceful, if dull, widowhood.

But it could not buy all those things. She knew, no matter how much she pleaded with him, no matter what she said, Henry would trade the diamond to Woodstock.

There was no right choice, but Caroline knew that out of all the options available to her, this was the wrong one.

She couldn't let him do it.

Which meant she couldn't give him the French Blue. Not yet. Not until she could either convince him to take the jewel to the French, or hatch a plan of her own to outwit Woodstock.

She could take the stone to Thomas Hope. As far as she could tell, he was its rightful owner—for the time being, at least. But Thomas and Henry were old friends; if she gave the diamond to Hope, chances were it would end up with Henry.

And then he'd make the trade with Woodstock, and they would all have blood on their hands.

He broke her heart once. She would not let him do it again by choosing her life over the lives of his men.

Caroline's fingers curled around the diamond. She had time; a few days, at least, to convince Henry to trade the diamond to the French, or to beat Woodstock on her own.

She hadn't a clue how she would do either of those things. She couldn't offer herself to Woodstock, confront him; Henry would know of it before she took two steps out the door. She could not go to the French with the diamond; she was not acquainted with any traitorous spies, as far as she knew, anyway.

But she would try.

She would be strategic in her choices. When to reveal the diamond's location, who to tell.

Caroline brought her fist back up to the drawer. She uncurled her fingers. The diamond stared at her, innocuously, from the center of her palm.

She buried it between the third and fourth stacks of William's stockings.

Her head snapped up at the sound of footsteps on the stairs in the hall. Quickly she smoothed the mess she'd made and darted from William's rooms. She ducked behind that sinister chair in the hall just in time to see William pass by, a soaked—and shivering—Lady Violet in his arms.

He used his foot to shut his bedroom door behind them.

Well, then. At least someone's lust would be slaked tonight.

Caroline collapsed against the chair and let out a long, low breath. The skin on her throat burned with the memory of Woodstock's hardened grip.

Her lips sang with the memory of Henry's kiss.

Her head spun. Days ago she'd been a simple widow, dedicated to the simple pleasures of her simple life. Now there was a price on her head, a sinister Marquess on the hunt, and an ex-lover whom she kept kissing, despite the risk to her sanity, her safety.

Now there was no untangling herself from the things she felt for Henry. His confession, the sacrifices he'd made on her behalf—they should have brought her peace.

They brought her pain instead.

Eighteen

Henry hadn't even landed on his feet after launching through the window when Mr. Moon's voice sounded from across the chamber.

"That was a rather long interlude. If you don't mind my saying, sir, good for you."

Henry met his eyes.

And told him everything. About Woodstock's sudden appearance, his traitorous past, his threat to Caroline.

The moral of this tale of woe, as the marquess so eloquently put it, was that they—he and Moon—needed to redouble their efforts to coax the jewel from Harclay's grasp.

When Henry was finished, Moon blinked and let out a long, low whistle. "That's bad news, sir. Very bad."

"I was an idiot," Henry panted. "I knew from the moment I stepped foot in London that I was being followed. I was so careless—so careless to be seen with her—after all this time, the care I took to keep her safe, away from who I am—"

"What's done is done," Moon said. "Besides, we might outwit that bastard Woodstock before he has the chance to make his move. Why don't we do it the old fashioned way? Grab him at night, a little laudanum, a blow or two to the head. And once we have him in our possession, I've a . . . a friend, you see, he's a gaoler down at Newgate. An imaginative one, too—he owes me a favor."

"A favor?" Henry arched a brow.

"A favor. I don't think he'd mind doing a bit of—er, work on the marquess, if you catch my meaning."

Henry shook his head. "If only it were that easy. Woodstock is watching us; he's a trained agent, dangerous. Smart, too. There's no way we could take him on our own; he'd see us coming from a mile away. Besides, if we made an attempt on his life, and we failed, he'd go after Caroline."

"Right." Moon's face was grim. "Our plot with the acrobats, then—it's more important than ever that we coax the jewel from Harclay's grasp. Lucky for you, I've made contact with them."

Winded—wait, why was he still winded, launching through windows was his *craft*, damn it!—Henry bent over, hands on his knees.

"With the acrobats?" he said hopefully, looking up.

Moon nodded. "They'll be performing at Vauxhall tomorrow evening."

A rush of poignant relief flooded through Henry. It was still a long shot, but having the acrobats persuade the earl to hand over the diamond meant Henry didn't have to; it meant he did not have to involve Harclay in Woodstock's scheme; he would soon, with a little luck, be in possession of the jewel.

Which meant he could trade it to Woodstock in exchange for Caroline's life.

It also meant Henry might at last end, however unsatisfactorily, this business with the French Blue in a matter of days, and be back in Paris by the end of the week.

He wasn't entirely sure how he felt about that. Especially after the difficult truths he'd revealed to her.

He prayed Woodstock had not bruised her neck.

"Excellent. We'll corner them before the show starts, let them know Harclay's their man." Henry stood and ran a hand along his jaw. "Better yet, I do believe Harclay keeps a box at Vauxhall. We can point him out to his minions, so that they can put a face to a name. It's better if the acrobats know who they're looking for. I'll make sure the earl is in his box."

Moon arched a brow. "And his sister?"

Henry turned to the mirror and began untangling the disheveled knot of his cravat. "Good night, Mr. Moon."

He could feel the heat of Moon's glare on the back of his head.

He was glad for the low light in the room; for Henry's face burned. Moon wasn't a fool; he knew that Lake knew that Moon knew about his growing attachment to Caroline. Or something like that.

But Moon was nothing if not professional, and so he dropped the wool stockings he'd been folding into a drawer and exited the chamber, quietly, leaving Henry alone with the violent tangle of his thoughts, with the achingly sweet memory of Caroline's kiss on his lips.

The Next Day

While Mr. Moon saw to the acrobats backstage at Vauxhall Gardens, Henry waited outside the wrought iron gates of Harclay's Hanover Square mansion.

Luckily Caroline's maid had forgotten to close the windows in her bedchamber, and Henry was able to catch the last stages of her toilet. He let out a sigh of relief.

She was safe. She was whole. Woodstock had kept his word, for now at least.

It was more than a little strange, watching her like this, and perhaps even a bit disturbing. But Henry couldn't help himself; looking away would be akin to seeking shadow on a chilly day rather than turning one's face up to the sun.

Caroline sat at her vanity as a round-bosomed maid saw to her hair. Henry watched as Caroline held her fingers to her ear, hooking a pearl earbob into the lobe. He imagined what the skin there would feel like between his thumb and forefinger: soft, silken, like a lamb's ear.

He watched her smile at something the maid said. He felt himself smiling, too. He watched her turn down the lamp on her bureau; moments later, he watched her alight the house's front steps on the arm of her brother.

The breath left Henry's lungs. He felt as if he'd been socked square in the gut.

Heavens, but she was beautiful. The kind of beautiful that made his heart swell.

Caroline wore a gown of pale pink satin that shimmered in the waning twilight. It matched the color of her cheeks, a shade lighter than the peonies they'd planted together in the garden. His excitement dimmed, for a moment, when he noticed the gown's high neck; Woodstock had left his mark on her.

Henry would have his revenge. He just had to be patient.

Henry was so distracted that he forgot, for a moment, that he was supposed to be hiding in the shadows. As Harclay helped Caroline into the waiting carriage, he glanced over his shoulder; Henry ducked just in time, heart jolting to sudden life.

He was never sloppy in his work. And his breeches had never felt quite so tight.

What the devil was wrong with him?

Shaking the haze of desire from his head, Henry stole through the streets after the carriage, following its progress toward the Thames. He breathed another sigh of relief as Harclay's lacquered vehicle crossed to the south bank, toward Vauxhall.

Good, Harclay had received Hope's invitation. He would be in his box.

Caroline would be there, too.

Despite its swollen size, Henry's heart leapt inside his chest. He would have to tread lightly. He'd put her through hell these past days, but at least he would see her, could ask after her nerves, her throat, her head.

Besides. Tonight might be the last time he saw her. If all went to plan, the diamond would be his. And what happened after that had nothing—and everything—to do with Lady Caroline Osbourne.

After a quick meet with Moon—"it's done, sir, our hairy friends are in play"—Henry went up to Thomas Hope's box, where he found his host ensconced in what appeared to be awkward conversation with Lady Violet's very pretty, very *young* cousin, Sophia.

They were both blushing like debutantes—Sophia had an excuse, as she *was* a debutante, but Henry had never seen Hope quite so pink—but before Henry could ask any questions, the earl and Caroline arrived.

They stood between the open curtains of heavy red velvet

that marked the entrance to the box, Caroline's eyes wide with uncertainty as they moved over the crowd. At last they landed on Henry; she blinked, lips parting. And then she looked away.

Henry drew his brows together. There was something in her eyes—fear, it looked very much like fear—that unsettled him.

"My lady." He bowed over her hand. Her fingers felt cold, even through the fine kidskin of her glove.

"Mr. Lake," she said. "Lovely to see you again."

"Yes," her brother drawled, his face screwed up in an unfriendly smile, "how lovely. Tell me, are you to star in tonight's show?"

"William!" Caroline hissed.

"What? I daresay he'd make a rather dashing addition to the acting troupe." Harclay turned back to Lake. "There's something . . . thespianlike about the eye patch, don't you think?"

Thespianlike. *Ha* bloody *ha*. Henry gritted his teeth against the impulse to sock his lordship in the face, so that he might be forced to sport an eye patch of his own.

"I think you've had too much of that dreadful punch," Caroline replied, giving him a gentle tug. "Let's go sit. Mr. Lake, my sincerest apologies."

She didn't look at him as she said it; nor did she offer him so much as a parting glance as she led her brother to the front of the box.

For a moment Henry stood by the curtains, the chill of embarrassment prickling his nape. It was the only thing that tempered his rising anger at the earl's insult. Really, the man was insufferable; Henry felt sorry for Caroline, having a scalawag brother like that.

Henry passed the first show in brooding silence. It was a lewd comedy, something he would've typically enjoyed (along with Vauxhall's infamously stout arrack punch) had a persistent feeling of unease not tightened inside his chest.

How was Caroline feeling? He understood her terror, he did. But did she not know he would protect her from Woodstock? He would die before he ever let the man touch her again. He'd never let him near her. His distress over these things was acute; she was suffering, and it was his fault.

And then there was the kiss they'd shared in the dark warmth of her brother's study. He wanted her to have enjoyed the kiss as much as he had, for reasons he didn't entirely understand.

While everyone else took their seats at the front of the box, Henry lingered at the back, arms crossed about his chest. He tried to watch the show, really, he did. But his gaze kept landing on the slope of Caroline's covered neck, and his thoughts returned again and again to the feel of her in his arms the night before.

Henry did not deserve her. He didn't deserve much of anything after what he'd done to her, to his family. And the regret—the pain in his leg pulsed brightly as the familiar weight of his regret settled over his heart.

He should leave her be. He *would* leave her be, once he had the diamond in hand.

The diamond. He had to focus on the French Blue. If all went to plan, it would be his in a day or two, maybe less.

And then he could pay off Woodstock, and get the hell out of London. Leave her to her well-deserved peace.

The first act drew to a blessed end. Henry moved into the shadows put off by paper lanterns hung from the ceiling. The earl moved to speak with Lady Violet; Caroline, taking advantage of her momentary freedom, darted through the curtains and into the gallery outside the box.

He didn't have to think. It was instinct; it was impulse. Henry darted after her.

Where was she going? He could only guess that his presence upset her; heavens, the woman had been nearly choked to death the night before on his account. He did not blame her for running.

Still, he had to make sure she was all right. He wanted to be the one to comfort her if she was not.

She moved quickly, urgently, as if the building were on fire. The crowd was thick and boisterous, but she made fast work of weaving through bodies, and only managed to trip, once, when she pummeled down the stairs.

Henry's stomach lurched along with her, and he was about to leap through the crush when an elderly gentleman, red-faced, potbellied, caught her. His eyes raked hungrily over her as he righted Caroline on the landing.

So Henry wasn't the only one aware of her quiet, exquisite loveliness.

His hands curled into fists at his sides.

She thanked the man, and continued her progress down the stairs. Henry followed her, aiming a black look at the potbellied gentleman as he passed. If he wasn't so eager to get to Caroline, he would've done quite a bit more than that.

Lake drew up at the bottom of the stairs. Vauxhall Gardens stretched out before him, a wide expanse of green beneath a darkening bluebell sky. Lanterns dotted the landscape like stars blinking awake; down here the air was warm but fresh, the very best a London spring could offer.

People milled about the pathways that converged at the theater. Caroline moved through them with a bit more difficulty now, legs snapping unevenly as if her impatience had risen to panic.

Henry followed her more closely, his brow furrowed, pace less polite than before. He wanted to be close in case she fell.

He could smell the clean freshness of her perfume.

At last she stopped, placing a hand against the trunk of a nearby tree as she bent at the waist, the other hand on her stomach.

She exhaled sharply and her back collapsed with the release of whatever it was she'd been holding in.

Henry spoke at the same moment he reached for her.

"Caroline."

Startled, her eyes flew to meet his. She was trying, hard, not to cry.

"Caroline," he said again, his hands sliding around her wrist.

She pulled away from him, stumbling back from the tree. "I'm sorry," she replied. "I can't."

Henry stepped around her, blocking her exit. He looked down at her and she backed away from him and his heart clenched at the idea that he was scaring her.

"Caroline, wait." His voice was edged with panic. "What happened last night—I am sorry—if there is anything I can do, know I will keep you safe—"

She looked over his shoulder at a passing couple. Henry took her wrist once more in his hand and tugged her through the row of trees onto a narrow pathway, this one quieter, more secluded. Henry drew Caroline up before him, his hands on her elbows.

"Are you all right? Tell me what's wrong. Now."

She swallowed. Hesitated.

"Don't force me to pull out your fingernails. I'll do it, I swear," he said.

A shadow of a smile crossed her lips, and then disappeared.

"We should get back," she said. "William will notice we're gone, and think the worst."

"I don't care what William thinks. Something is wrong, I see it in your eyes, and I know it's about last night. Me. Us."

Her gaze flashed as her eyes flicked up to meet his. "It doesn't matter."

She was wiping at her eye with the bottom knuckle of her thumb. He tried to reach out to help but she batted him away.

"Doesn't matter?" He drew back. "Of course it matters."

"Your secrets," she said. "I can't stop thinking about them."

He raked a hand through his hair. "I never meant—you know I never meant to hurt you, Caroline. Not when I left. Not when I told you everything last night."

"I know. But these secrets—the time we've lost—" She looked away.

When he'd torn himself from her life, Henry had been comforted by the idea that a girl so lovely and lively and *good* would surely be scooped up by the season's most eligible bachelor.

Of course, he'd never imagined that eligible bachelor would end up being his best friend. But that was beside the point.

Twelve years, they'd lived this way. The pain lived on in them both.

"They are secrets no longer," Henry said. "Now you know. You know everything. You know about Woodstock. You know the mistake I made. You know why I left."

She shook her head. "But for so many years, I thought you'd lied to me. I used to think you were a scalawag, a scoundrel. All that time I leaned on the only friend I had. My husband, Osbourne—it comforted me to know at least someone was honest with me."

Hurt, tinged a shade darker by his anger, by jealousy, tightened inside his chest. Before he could think better of it his fingers were tightening around the soft flesh of her arms and he was holding her against him, his face inches from hers.

"Honest?" he lashed out. "I'm no saint, I'll admit that. What I did was unforgivable. I'll never forgive myself, Caroline. And you shouldn't, either. I wasn't honest then, yes—I couldn't be, not with men like Woodstock on the loose—but neither were you. We betrayed each other."

She drew back. "How did I ever betray you?"

The words came before he could stop them. "Were you in love with him? The whole time we were together—did you love him?"

"Who?" Her eyes widened. "Osbourne? My hu—"

"Yes, Caroline," Henry spat. "Your *husband*. You married him less than two *months* after I left. How could you marry someone so quickly, if you weren't in love with him before?"

Her face contracted, a wince of pain, as if she were anticipating a blow to the face. *Why are you doing this?* he screamed at himself. *Stop, you idiot, stop! She's been through enough; she's lost enough on your account.*

But he couldn't stop. He needed to know.

"Is that what you think?" she said softly.

"I don't know what to think," he replied. His breath was coming in short, hot spurts. "You married my best friend, Caroline. In practically a fortnight—"

"It was longer than that."

"Not much. If I didn't know better, I would say you were relieved to have me out of the way."

She was weeping now, silent tears seeping from the corners of her eyes. He felt each one as a nail struck through his breastbone. He hadn't meant to ask these questions, not here, not now.

But he couldn't trust himself when it came to Caroline. And so the questions came.

"I can't stop thinking about your secrets," she said, "because I keep one of my own. I had to marry him, Henry." There was a desperate edge to her voice. "I knew him, our families approved. He lived close by."

"You didn't have to marry him so quickly."

"Yes," she looked up at him. "I did."

"Your father? Did he find out about—about what we'd done?"

"No."

"Then why?" he said forcefully. "Why did you have to marry Osbourne so quickly? When you were already married to me."

"Because, Henry," she replied, her voice rising. "I was with child. *Your* child."

Nineteen

Henry's eye unfurled with understanding. His grip loosened on her arms. The high color of his anger faded, replaced by a pallor that shone in the yellow light of a lantern above.

His brows unhooked; the grooves in his forehead loosened. His lips parted and came back together, as if he had a hundred questions, and didn't know which to ask first.

Caroline looked away. She'd never meant to tell him. What did it matter now? And this wound—opening it again was too much to bear.

But he'd shared his secrets, and so she felt compelled to reveal her own.

She closed her eyes against the sting of her tears.

"It was a girl," Caroline said. "She died before she was born, a month too early."

"Oh, God," he said. He pulled her against him, as if he might embrace her.

She stepped back. "Please don't."

"Oh, God," he repeated. "Caroline, I'm—I'm so sorry. I don't know what to say—Christ. I'm sorry you had to do that. Do it alone."

A beat.

"Did you"—his voice was threadbare—"get to see her?"

She scoffed, splattering her tears as she shook her head. "Red hair, just like yours. She was beautiful. Tiny, these little bones, like a kitten's."

Another beat. And then he said: "I wish I could have seen her."

Caroline looked up at him. "I wish that, too."

His grip tightened on her arms now.

"Caroline," he said. "I had—I didn't know. I had no idea. If—"

"Osbourne knew," she nodded. "He knew all along. Knew when I married him. He did it for you, you know. He loved you, and didn't want your child born . . . to parents who weren't married."

Henry's grip tightened again. Her skin pinched in protest.

He looked down at her. His eye was wet, but no tears fell.

"I didn't want this for us," he whispered. "We were—I was so young, I didn't know what I was doing. I should've been more careful when we—when it—"

"You wouldn't be so regretful if you saw her face." Caroline bit her lip. "I would've wished for better circumstances, yes. But she was perfect. I'll never regret her."

She looked away. She couldn't bear the hurt she saw in his eye.

"Did she have a name?" he asked.

Caroline closed her eyes again. Her throat tightened.

"Yes," she said, and shook her head.

Yes, she had a name. But Caroline hadn't the strength to speak it. Not tonight.

They both looked up at the sound of approaching footsteps. A woman with a strangely broad chin and the shadow of a moustache came into view. She took one look at Caroline and stopped dead in her tracks; her eyes moved to Henry, whose face hardened with recognition.

He looked down at Caroline. "I'm sorry—I—"

"Go." Caroline stepped back, eyes trained on her hands.

He hesitated.

"Go."

Henry dipped his head. "This conversation is not over," he murmured in her ear.

And then he turned and disappeared into a nearby box-wood.

He was good at that, the disappearing.

Twenty

The next day dawned warm and bright, a poignant contrast to the shadows and secrets of the night before. Standing at the window of her bedchamber, Caroline inhaled a lungful of air, let it out, slowly, through her nose. She would do right by Henry, by her brother, by England.

She would gladly sacrifice all she held dear—her life included—for everything and everyone she loved. Henry had done it for her; she would return the favor.

Not that she loved Henry. Heavens, just *thinking* it made her heart palpitate. She'd left all that in the past, and for good reason.

Yes, Henry had left twelve years before because he loved her. And that revelation should have brought comfort, satisfaction, closure.

Instead, it loosened feelings she'd locked away more than a decade ago. Potent feelings. Dangerous feelings. Feelings that had no place in the life she'd worked so hard to rebuild.

No matter what happened in the days ahead, she and Henry—they would never be together. It was impossible. And these things she felt for him would only hurt her, as they'd hurt her that summer long ago.

William met her in the drawing room later that morning, and begged her to play the terrible chaperone for he and Violet. He was to take her riding.

In the enormous family coach, Caroline dutifully followed William as he led his sinister-looking phaeton—lacquered a daring shade of pearlescent black—through Mayfair's crowded streets. Violet sat on the bench beside him, her color high, lips curled into an irrepressible smile.

All the while, Caroline's mind raced. How to convince Henry to trade the diamond to the French? How to outwit Woodstock without putting Henry or William at risk?

How to do these things, knowing the choice she made would separate her from Henry forever?

Henry, the handsome man, the honorable man, the man who would rather die than see her hurt or unhappy. The man who had sacrificed everything so that she might live a happy life, a peaceful life.

Just a few short days ago, Henry had been the enemy, the bully who left her without explanation twelve years before. She'd begged him to leave her be. She'd sworn to stay away from him.

But now—everything was different. It had all changed in the space of a single night. A confession, a threat, and suddenly her world was turned upside down.

Warm things, strong things, moved inside her heart. She did not dare give them name.

But they were there. And they scared her for their forcefulness, their familiarity.

Thus distracted by her dark thoughts and mutinous heart, Caroline did not see the object of her distress until he swung open the carriage door and soundlessly leapt inside. The vehicle continued to jolt and weave through the street; the coachman hadn't seen him.

She started, heart in her throat as she watched Henry land on the seat across from hers.

"Windows," she breathed, "are one thing. Moving carriages, Henry, are quite another."

Henry's eye narrowed; Caroline looked away, face burning.

"This afternoon," he said. "Have you any plans?"

Caroline drew back. "Well, I— Aside from the usual, no—"

"Good." He leaned forward, suddenly, and took her hand in his. A shiver, not entirely unpleasant, shot up her spine as his thumb stroked the ridge of her knuckles. "I want to see you. We need to talk."

"I don't want to talk."

"I do," Henry said. "Let's get out of London for the day."

He didn't have to say what they were both thinking. Out of London, out of danger. Away from Woodstock.

"But he'll be watching us."

"Let him watch. We may be getting out of London, but we're going in the middle of the day in a marked carriage. We aren't going very far."

She looked at him a long moment. "Your plan to win back the French Blue. It hasn't worked."

Henry cocked a brow. "How do you know that?"

Caroline blinked. Henry couldn't know she'd found the diamond. Not yet.

"You wouldn't want to get out of London if Woodstock was no longer a threat."

Henry looked at her for a long moment. "My plan hasn't worked *yet*. It's only a matter of time. I want to talk to you before things get . . . busy."

Before she could protest, he was pressing his lips against her cheek. It was a quick kiss, a chaste one, but her body leapt nonetheless.

And then, just as quickly as he'd appeared, Henry was gone. Her hand flew to her cheek, the skin burning.

The coach drew up before her brother's house on Brook Street. William leapt from his phaeton and stalked toward the coach, yanking open the door.

"Where is he?" William growled. "I know he was in the carriage with you, Caroline, so where did he go?"

If only she knew.

She met William's gaze; he looked nothing short of murderous. She squared her shoulders. Henry was her secret, and hers alone.

"I don't know what you're talking about," she replied steadily, holding out her hand. William took it, gave it a good squeeze. A warning.

Twenty-one

---✦---

That Afternoon

It was just as she feared. Henry's plan wasn't working.

Which meant she had to come up with one of her own.

Caroline paced the drawing room for hours, racking her brain for a solution, a way to keep the French Blue out of Woodstock's hands without sacrificing her life, or Henry's, or the lives of all his men.

She came up with nothing. The harder and longer she thought, the more frustrated she became. She cried, she cursed, she choked on her helplessness.

And nothing came of it. Yes, she was a widow, a gardener, and as such lacked experience in things like espionage and blackmail.

Still. She'd seen enough operas to warrant the invention of at least one murderous plot, hadn't she? She had the diamond if she needed it. Surely there was no more powerful a bargaining chip than a fifty-carat stone?

And still nothing. Her lack of creative prowess was depressing.

Caroline paced until her legs and head hurt, and, collapsing on the sofa, decided a break was in order. Hoping to clear her mind, she picked up the dreaded novel she'd been trying to read for an eternity.

A half hour later, Caroline glanced up from her book—she was only on the fifth page, and beginning to think she'd lost the ability to read—and nearly jumped out of her skin.

Henry was leaning through the drawing room's open window, arms crossed on the wide sill. The afternoon sun outlined the hunch of his enormous shoulders in blinding white; his hair glinted bronze. Strands of it hung loose at his temples.

He was looking at her. His eye was soft. So were her insides, suddenly, looking back at him.

"Good afternoon, Caroline."

She closed the book around her finger. She sat a little straighter. "Good afternoon."

"Don't worry," he said. "I'm going round to the front door. You just looked very pretty reading there on the couch. I had to stop and admire the view. How is it?"

"It? What?"

He nodded at the book in her lap. "The book."

"Oh." Her ears burned. "Um. It's decent. Terrible, actually. Quite bad. Can't seem to get past the first few pages."

Henry grinned. His dimple puckered.

That goddamn dimple. Really, it wasn't fair.

"And your neck. It's feeling better?"

"Much, thank you."

"Splendid."

"So," she said. "No new developments since I saw you last?"

He looked at her. Then he pushed away from the sill and stood—the drawing room was on the ground level, and the windows opened directly to the street—and gave his sleeves a little tug.

"I'll be at the door in a moment," he said.

Caroline rose, heart in her throat as she squared her shoulders.

She glanced in the mirror on the near wall, and smoothed her hair. There, better.

A beleaguered Mr. Avery showed Henry into the drawing room.

Avery nodded his head. "My lady." It was more question

than greeting, as in, my lady, shall I let him in, or shall I deliver a blow to his belly?

"It's all right, Avery. Mr. Lake comes in peace."

The butler reluctantly ducked out of the room. And then Caroline was alone with Henry. He stood by the door, hands clasped behind his back.

"Thank you for seeing me." He had the grace to blush as he said it.

"I—well. I . . ."

Frankly she didn't know how she felt. Or maybe she just didn't want to *admit* to the excitement that skittered in her pulse. The relief she felt, knowing she wouldn't have to slog through another page of that book.

"Well, then." He cleared his throat. "I'd, um, I'd like to ask you—to. Er. Bah, this is embarrassing."

A beat of uncomfortable silence stretched between them as Henry ran his palm across the back of his neck. His throat flushed with color.

Oh.

The realization struck her like a cue ball to the head.

Henry is nervous.

It made her smile, his show of nerves. Her smile wasn't a leer; she wasn't poking fun.

She was flattered. And charmed. *Utterly* charmed.

His eye flashed up to meet hers. "While we wait, there is no better way to pass the time than to . . . um . . . spend it with each other? I thought you and I might take a turn at the Botanic Gardens. The, um, ones at Kew? With the pagoda? Only if you'd like to, of course; I know how you enjoy your gardens, and I would like to take you, because, um, you like them."

Her smile deepened.

"I do, too!" Henry burst. "I like the gardens. I like—them. You. Kew. Very much?"

His hand was thrust in his hair now. He closed his eyes and took a breath. "For the love of God, Caroline, put me out of my misery, one way or the other. Please say yes."

Ah, that *look* on his face! The hopeful softness in his eye was shameless, and he knew it.

"I'd feel better if we left London for a bit, if you were with me . . . please, Caroline, I want to spend today with you."

She would never tire of hearing him speak her name. The rumbling rush of his voice, its masculine force softened around the hard *C* of the first syllable.

And the Botanic Gardens! It had been years since she'd last visited.

Henry took yet another step closer. The spice of his cologne filled her head. "Please, Caroline." His voice was low. "I don't want you to be alone today. Not after what happened— What we— The things we discussed last night."

She met his eye. It was sharply green in the bright afternoon light. Pleading.

She set the book down, quietly, on the table beside the sofa.

The Botanic Gardens were a maze of pathways and grottoes and hidden alcoves; Caroline navigated them with ease, the pounding of her heart slowing as the familiar, loamy scents of dark earth, and green leaves, loosened the stranglehold of her nerves. She was acutely, painfully aware of Henry's presence beside her.

People stared as he and Caroline passed. She bit back a smile; she'd forgotten what it was like to walk about in public on Henry's arm. He was enormous, for one thing, twice as tall as most men and just as wide, and enormously handsome, more mysterious now with the patch and the limp.

A limp that, curiously, seemed to come and go. Then again, Caroline didn't exactly trust her senses when in his presence; they were at once heightened and severely—tragically—muddled.

The afternoon sun had disappeared behind a thick layer of cloud. A rumble of thunder broke out over their heads. They kept walking.

They'd met in her parents' garden, Caroline and Henry, more than a decade ago. Being surrounded by this riot of green, the familiar smells, made Caroline think of the first time she'd seen him.

She remembered it as if it were a moment ago: a cold rush of heat had pulsed through her as her heart had labored to break free of its moorings in her chest. The world had gone still; she couldn't think, couldn't breathe; she had been dizzy, lost in the depthless, darkening pools of his eyes. He'd been breathing hard, nostrils flaring; his forehead was slick with sweat. For a beat she'd been overcome by curiosity. What did he feel like, there? She had wanted to run the pad of her thumb across his brow, wipe the moisture on her skirts.

"Caroline," Henry was saying, "look."

She blinked, the image of him at eighteen dissolving into the face she saw now. Henry at thirty, marred, different. But the eyes—the eye—it was the same; a few more wrinkles at its edge, but the darkening interest, the heat was still there.

"Look!" he said.

"What? Where— Oh. *Oh*," she breathed, her gaze following his outstretched arm. There, spread out before them in a misty copse, was a field of bluebells in egregious bloom. Again thunder rumbled; the sky was darkening, and in the copse the light was low and gray. The air was potently still. She could smell the approaching rain.

Blue-violet blooms dusted the copse like snow, silent. Caroline was aware, suddenly, that she and Henry were very much alone.

"It's lovely," she said.

"Yes," he said. "How lucky we are, to catch them while they are in bloom."

They were whispering, as if their voices might cause the blooms to shrivel, the breathless quiet to shatter.

She untangled her arm from his and walked into the copse; the bluebells brushed her skirts as she trailed her palms over their bent heads. Their freshly sweet scent filled the air.

Henry followed her out into the copse, his footfalls soft on the wet ground. She felt his eyes on her back; the skin on the nape of her neck grew warm.

"Robert Dudley lived at Kew," she said. "Queen Elizabeth's Robert. She gave him a palace here."

"Perhaps Good Queen Bess and her paramour visited this very wood together. I wonder what they talked about."

Caroline grinned down at the bluebells. "Or if they talked at all."

"Feisty one, wasn't she, Gloriana?"

"I'd like to think so." She drew to a stop in the middle of the field, hands on her hips as she surveyed the trees about them. "The palace she gave him is gone now, but I imagine it was a lovely place, full of intrigue and art and all these beautiful people. The two of them, Robert and Elizabeth, at the center of it all."

"But she would never have him for a husband," Henry said.

"She *couldn't* have him," Caroline replied. Her throat felt inexplicably tight. She watched as Henry tickled the bell of a nearby bloom. His fingers were enormous, and strong, but he handled the flower carefully, his touch soft as he coaxed the bell between his thumb and forefinger. He could rip it to shreds, the flower. But he didn't.

"There's an old rumor," she said, "that Dudley and Elizabeth's secret name for one another was 'Eyes.' His must've been irresistible."

Henry smiled. "Dark."

Caroline smiled back. "Dangerous."

"Deadly. Didn't he plot against her? Betray her by marrying someone else?"

"Yes," Caroline said. "But heavens, she was Queen of England! She knew better."

"Maybe she knew better," Henry said, his gaze intent, "but it couldn't be helped."

"She should've known a man with eyes like that was trouble."

Henry's voice was quiet. "And him. He should've handled her heart with more care."

Caroline looked away. To hear him talking like that made *her* heart clench. She knew—God, she knew—how Elizabeth felt for Dudley.

And no, it couldn't be helped.

A beat of silence stretched between Henry and Caroline.

"You come here often? To Kew?" he said at last.

"Not as often as I'd like," she replied. "I've missed it. Quite a lot, actually. Osbourne preferred to keep to his house in Oxfordshire. London was a bit much for him, I think."

Henry looked down at his boots. "I'm sorry," he said softly. "I didn't know about . . . everything. What had happened. He was always a good friend, Osbourne. Better even than I knew, I suppose."

"He was good to both of us."

"He was." A pause. They drew to a slow halt. Henry was looking at her now, his one eye clouded as it searched her face.

The pause lengthened, and became something else altogether. An entreaty. A well of feeling.

"I'm sorry about what I said last night," he began. "I know you probably didn't want to talk about the past, and I forced you. I've been so jealous of Osbourne all these years. Angry. I shouldn't have brought it up. I was the one who left. And the child . . ."

Slowly, carefully, she touched her fingers to the kerseymere sleeve of his coat. She fought against the tightness in her throat.

"I would've written if I could," she said.

"I would've left something if I could." He covered her fingers with one of his own. "I thought I understood your grief. I thought I understood *you*." He scoffed, looked down. "I was wrong."

"You left because you had to, Henry," she said. "And I did what I had to do."

A pause. He looked up and met her eyes. "Do you ever think about what she would be like? Our daughter?"

Her vision blurred with tears, and she felt them hot on her face; then Henry was gathering her in his arms, and she let him absorb the sounds of her grief in his chest. He was shaking. Still he held her, tightly, her arms to his breast, his arms wrapped about her body, holding her yet closer.

Our daughter. The daughter they had created together.

"All the time," she said.

The release wasn't violent; for both of them it was quiet, and thorough, and whole. She remembered how safe she'd felt in his arms at seventeen, how his strength had thrilled her.

And now that she was witness to his grief, to the tenderness that lurked just beneath his hardened surface, she felt safer still. Because he was the only person in the world who felt this grief as she felt it. She wasn't afraid to bare it here, in the circle of his arms.

A different kind of safe. Less thrilling. But perhaps better.

Henry wiped her eyes with his neatly folded handkerchief, and then he wiped his own.

He took a long breath through his nose; he looked up. "Let's walk. The rain isn't far off now."

Without waiting for her reply, he looped her arm through his and led her out of the copse. Neither of them spoke until they were back inside the gardens, and strolling across a wide lawn, on the far side of which rose the famed Great Pagoda.

"Ah, the pagoda," Henry said. "It's . . ."

"Rather phallic, I know," Caroline said with a small smile. "But it's an attractive phallus, don't you think?"

"Please." A flush rose, swiftly, from Henry's neck to his cheeks. "Please don't ever—just. Those words, together. I can't."

She blushed, too, even as she grinned. "Since when do you have a prudish bone in your body?"

"Since I turned thirty."

He smiled. She smiled. They smiled at each other.

C aroline blinked at the fat raindrop that hit her forehead and rolled to rest on her eyelash. She brushed it away with the knuckle of her first finger.

Henry tilted his head. "Looks like—"

Rain, great sheets of it, released from the swollen sky like a long, low breath. It plodded on the leaves of the trees above; it pummeled the ground with muted thuds.

Henry rolled back his shoulders and shrugged out of his coat; holding it above his head, he wrapped an arm about Caroline's shoulders and pulled her against him.

"Quickly!" he said over the rising tumult of the rain.

"The Orangery," she replied. "This way!"

Beneath the shelter of his coat, they scurried across the lawn.

"Your leg," she panted as they ran, "is it all right?"

"My leg?" Henry looked down, as if he'd forgotten it was there. "Oh, yes. Er. It's quite well, thank you."

They were an ungainly pair, to say the least; they tripped and skipped and mauled one another as they attempted to remain side by side under his coat. The tightness in Caroline's throat loosened, and was replaced by laughter.

Henry, too, was laughing, poking her with the jutting edge of his hip. She poked back. He laughed harder.

By the time they reached the Orangery, Henry's coat was soaked through, and so were Caroline's skirts. They lurched through the glass doors in a muddy, untidy mess; several patrons stared as Henry shook out his coat. Caroline tried very hard not to keep laughing.

He turned to her, mouth stretching into a half grin. His hair, usually combed back into a ribboned queue, stuck to his forehead; his cravat was hopelessly mussed.

She decided she liked seeing him like this, soaked, disheveled, his clothes plastered to his body. It suited him. Him, the Viking-pirate in the horned hat.

Mostly it suited the daringly cut muscles that arched on either side of his torso.

"You look a fright," she said, eyes sweeping appreciatively over said muscles. "I do, too, don't I?"

"Yes," he said. "Here, let me help."

Placing his one good coat over his arm, he tugged Caroline behind a sickly looking potted lemon tree.

"I can—"

"No," he said, "I will—"

"Let me—"

"Let *me*—"

She fought off his hands, giggling as he made one last swipe for the strings of her bonnet. The giggling seemed to ease the soreness in her eyes and throat after all that crying, although now that soreness reappeared in her ribs as she laughed yet harder.

"Really?" she said.

"Yes," he replied, his grin deepening into laughter, "really."

Henry was looming over her, his face alive with amusement as he reached for her, teasing. "Now hold still."

"What's this?" Henry asked. He lifted a squab from the bench, revealing a velvet-lined compartment beneath.

Caroline leaned forward in her seat, swaying in time to the carriage. They were on their way back to London; rain pattered pleasantly on the roof. "I'm not sure. Perhaps William hides his lady friends in there."

Henry lifted a bottle from the compartment. "Brandy," he said, peering at the label. He took the cork in his teeth. "Want some?"

He held out the bottle.

She grasped it. "It would be rude, and most unkind, to let you drink alone."

Caroline sipped tidily, then winced, coughing as she wiped her mouth with the back of her hand. "The bottle," she sputtered. "It's half empty. Wonder where William was going when he drank all that brandy?"

Henry grinned as he took the bottle and drank. "I'd venture he didn't drink it all by himself."

She arched a brow. "Lady Violet?"

"Girl does like her liquor."

"Those two." Caroline sighed with a shake of her head. Already the brandy was at work, warming her body against the chill damp of her clothes. She felt giddy, and exhausted, after spending the day in Henry's company.

The subject of Woodstock's threat, of the missing diamond, hung heavy, unspoken, between them.

But Caroline didn't wish to discuss it now. This afternoon. There would be time enough for the heavy things later.

The afternoon was theirs. Her sides hurt from laughing so hard, and so often. Her spirit felt lighter, having shared the burden of her secret with Henry at last.

Henry held out the bottle. "More?"

She waved him away. "Go ahead."

He twisted the cork back into place and set the bottle down into its hiding place; he covered the compartment with the squab. And then he turned back to Caroline.

"Thank you," he said. "For today. I'm glad you came. After everything that's happened these past days, I didn't want to leave you alone. To your thoughts and fears, I mean. I've been doing this for a while now, but the violence—it stays with you, no matter how hard you try to forget it."

She swallowed. "I'll be all right."

"I shall make sure of that," he said firmly. And even though everything was decidedly *not* all right, and probably never would be again, the conviction in his words made Caroline feel the tiniest bit better.

Just a few short days ago, she wouldn't have thought it possible—not after he'd left her to fend for herself a decade before—that Henry would make her feel safe.

But wasn't that what he'd always tried to do, no matter the cost to himself?

The thought caused a flutter to rise in her chest, a pleasant, ticklish feeling.

She looked at the knot of her folded hands in her lap. "I'm glad you asked me to come. Though it was hardly difficult to say yes—the Botanic Gardens are to me what that sordid tavern is to you. Heaven."

Henry smiled. "A sordid tavern is hardly heaven. Though if the ale is decent . . ."

Caroline bit her lip.

"Don't you remember," he asked, "when we were in the garden at your parents' house, how you'd talk about Kew? You wanted to visit, badly, but no one would go with you."

"I remember." She blinked. "And so do you."

"I remember everything," he said softly. "It's all I had, when I left—what I remembered. I've been remembering for twelve years."

Caroline felt her cheeks flush with heat. She'd like to blame the brandy.

She knew better. There was no mistaking that feeling, the flutter that became a full-on rush of blood to her heart.

"What have you been remembering?"

"You, mostly."

She met his eye. "Henry—"

It was a warning. A plea.

"I regret many things, Caroline," he said. "But I will never regret you."

Her gaze moved over his shirt, still stuck to his skin in a most revealing fashion. Did she regret *him*? Having to let him go, perhaps.

But there were some things about which she felt less certain. Namely, the passion they shared. And his criminally handsome person.

Henry's broad chest rose and fell, straining against the transparent fabric of his shirt. She took her bottom lip in her teeth.

"What?" he asked innocently. And then, looking down upon that *shirt*: "Oh, dear, look how *wet* my shirt is. I shall just *have* to remove it . . ."

With deft fingers he coaxed one button free, then the next, and the next, the revealed skin a vibrant foil to the white of his shirt. A smattering of pale, wiry hair covered his chest. She was tempted—*so tempted!*—to reach out and touch it.

The side of his mouth quirked up in that saucy half smile of his as he watched her watching him. He held out his arms, baring his chest to her.

"Would you care to complete the task, my lady?"

With a disbelieving scoff, Caroline crossed her arms about her breast and fell back against the squabs, glaring pointedly out the window. "You're shameless, Henry. Absolutely shameless."

"You're sure you don't want to give it a go? My shirt, that is."

Caroline rolled her eyes. "No, thank you." And fought an enormous smile.

Twenty-two

———◆———

H enry was in love with her.

It happened as he helped Caroline down from the carriage. The conviction hit him squarely in the center of his chest, like a bullet shot straight through the heart; a sudden, shocking thing, though later he would recognize it had been there along, this feeling, and only then, in that moment, had she knocked it perfectly into place. Like an obstinate dead bolt, coaxed at last into its lock by the proper key.

It was the warmth of her hand in his, the dark wisps of hair that caressed the back and sides of her nape, the bloom of embarrassment (and arousal, he'd like to think) staining her cheeks. The intelligent, and censorious, gleam in her eyes as they met his.

He liked teasing her. Mostly because he adored making her smile in the midst of all the doom he'd brought to her doorstep. It was hardly decent of him, playing at getting naked in her brother's carriage, but then when had either of them—Henry or Caroline—ever wanted to be decent?

Decent was boring. And Caroline Townshend (she would always be Townshend to him) was anything but boring, even if she refused to indulge in a bit of midafternoon nudity with him.

She turned to him and smiled. For a moment he couldn't breathe.

"Careful," she said, and reached for his shirt. She slid the top button into its tiny hole. The tip of her first finger brushed his throat. "I daresay I am the only woman in London immune to your chest hair."

Oh, heavens. He was *very much* in love with her.

He smiled, an enormous thing that hurt his face. They were standing close. Too close, considering all of Hanover Square could see them.

"I'll have you know I'm rather proud of my chest hair. Took me thirty years to grow it."

She laughed, a high, delighted sound. "Quite the accomplishment."

Henry glanced over her head at the stern façade of her brother's house. On cue, the front door swung open, the earl's palm wrapped tightly about the brass knob as he moved out onto the front step. His eyes were black and hard as they took in Henry.

Henry's smile faded a bit. As if he didn't have enough enemies with which to contend; he'd almost forgotten how much Caroline's brother loathed him.

He stepped back. Reading his face, Caroline glanced over her shoulder.

She turned back to Henry. "I should go."

The light was fading; during their ride back to London, the sky had cleared, and now it was bare, a darkening blue too late for sun, too early for stars; the surrounding buildings blocked a view of the sunset.

Caroline's skin shone in the soft light, and a small breeze tickled the wisps of hair at her neck. It was spring.

And Henry was in love.

He looked at her a moment too long. He was tempted to reach out and take her hands, but Henry had no doubt the earl would challenge him to a duel if he so much as *looked* at Caroline the wrong way.

Henry stepped back, clearing his throat. "Right. I don't want to keep you. Good evening, my lady."

He strode out into the street in a daze, his pulse racing, thoughts whirling. The floral note of her perfume lingered in his nose; he imagined he could taste it.

It was the one thing he swore he wouldn't do, falling in love with Caroline. He swore he'd stay away from her, from London; he swore these things to keep her safe.

He'd left her twelve years ago, to keep her safe.

And now her life—his, too—was in danger.

He closed his eyes against the panic that sliced through his chest.

He was in love.

And he was in trouble.

He made a sharp turn into a narrow lane; the evening traffic on Regent Street was distracting, and Henry needed to think.

Soon, very soon, Woodstock would lose patience. He'd hunted Caroline for more than a decade; his revenge would not wait. Henry would not let him kill her. Not while he still had breath in his body.

More than once Henry contemplated holding a gun to her scalawag brother's head, demanding he hand over the diamond. But that would mean bringing more violence to Caroline's doorstep; and doubtless the earl, being the cocky man he was, would assume Henry would not dare shoot him.

And he'd be right. Which meant Henry would be forced to tell Harclay about Woodstock. All hell would break loose, and someone—all of them, probably—would end up dead.

No, he would not confront the earl. Not yet. Henry's plot with the acrobats was still in play; if he could get the French Blue without having to threaten Harclay himself, it would be best for everyone.

He would have to wait. And keep watch over Caroline.

He couldn't bear the thought of her coming to harm—again—on his account. Her, the woman he loved.

The woman who, knowing his luck, he'd end up hurting all over again.

Still.

He *loved* her. He'd been an idiot to think falling for her again was anything but inevitable. It had taken him all of an afternoon to fall in love with her a decade ago; an afternoon of bright yellow sun, laughter, and a promise to meet her in the garden the next day. He kept that promise, and met her by the secluded folly on her father's estate; he met her there the next day, and the next, and the next, always in the morning, always early, so eager to see her, and laugh with her, and tease her.

She was an earl's daughter; she came with a ten-thousand-pound dowry. He was a third son, with no position, no money, and nothing to offer.

Now, ten years later, Henry could boast of a position, and a good one, an honorable one, but serving king and country was hardly a profitable affair. He had very little money, and less to offer a lady like Caroline, who, as a dowager countess, was accustomed to a lifestyle that Good Queen Bess, his fellow feisty ginger, wouldn't scoff at.

Even if Henry could somehow defeat Woodstock, and save Caroline's life; if the earl stopped being a jackass, and handed over the diamond; if Henry negotiated successfully with the French, and in so doing helped end the war; even if all these things came to pass, what did he hope would come of his affection for Caroline? That she would forgive him, and forget about the widowhood she so fiercely defended, and love him as he loved her?

They had nowhere to live. He couldn't retire. Agents like him had no choice in the matter; most died young. He wouldn't subject Caroline to the horrors of his life as an agent; he'd already put her life at risk, and he'd been in London only a week. He wanted better for her. She deserved better than he could give her.

He was in love with her.

But he would be damned if she fell in love with him. It wasn't fair. It was dangerous.

He would protect her, even if it killed him. He would focus on the diamond, and his duty, and head back to Paris, where he belonged.

Henry blinked, realizing he'd walked farther—and faster—than he'd intended. He stood at the end of a barrel-ceilinged walkway that led out onto a small, nondescript square. It was prematurely dark here, the buildings lining each side of the square blocking what little light was left.

The hair at the back of his neck prickled to life. Henry turned his head, slowly; he peered over his shoulder; the passage behind him was quiet, eerily so.

That's when he smelled it.

A musky scent, masculine, like burnt wood.

Labdanum.

Woodstock. He was here.

Henry's pulse rushed cold. He turned this way, then that, hoping to catch something, the edge of a coat, someone disappearing into the hedge, but the square met his wild search with silence.

"Show yourself," Henry growled.

Still nothing.

He held up his hands. "Show yourself," he repeated.

Henry turned toward the quiet rustle behind him. A man emerged from the shadows of the passage, sweeping the beaver-skin hat from his head and tucking it into the crook of his arm. He was of medium height, medium build; fair skin; with a mop of close-cropped hair that was neither blond nor brown, but both. His eyes were brownish-hazel-green-yellow; he wore breeches and a coat of nondescript quality and color. He looked like a middling barrister, minus the wig.

Conspicuously inconspicuous.

Which meant, of course, this man was anything *but* a barrister. He was an agent.

And while that was hardly comforting, at the very least he wasn't the Marquess of Woodstock. Henry let out a silent sigh of relief, his arms falling to his sides.

"You've been following me," Henry said, and turned to face the man.

"Yes." His accent was scrubbed clean of any inflection, any quirk that might mark him, tie him to a place. "I understand you have—or *used* to have—something that might be of interest to me."

Henry arched a brow. "To you?"

The man smiled. "To me. And my superiors."

The man reached inside his jacket and produced a neatly folded newspaper, which he handed to Henry. Henry held it open between his thumb and last finger and glanced at the latest headline detailing Hope's missing diamond.

Lake looked up at the agent and passed back the paper.

"Are you the thief who stole it from Mr. Hope's party? The French Blue?" the man asked.

"Depends." Henry crossed his arms.

"Depends?"

"What will you give me?"

The man stuffed the paper into his coat. "The French Blue rightfully belongs to the Republic. It was stolen from us twenty years ago. We shouldn't have to give you anything."

Henry grinned. "But you will."

"We are willing to negotiate, yes."

"Willing to negotiate." Henry scoffed. "Don't play coy, good sir, for I know your *superior* would trade his bollocks for the missing crown jewels."

The man blinked. "We shall discuss terms when you produce the French Blue. It is our wish to conclude this business quickly. If you do not have the jewel, we will find out who does, and negotiate with him."

He flicked his wrist and a small, thick-edged calling card appeared between his fingers. He held it out to Henry. "My solicitor. He knows how to contact me."

Ducking into his hat, the man bowed and said, "Please make it known His Majesty the prince regent has France's wish for continued good health."

"How lovely. Except we both know Prinny drank away whatever health he had back in the nineties. Nevertheless, I shall pass your wishes along."

The man turned and disappeared into the passage's gaping darkness. Henry watched him go, trying not to wince at the sudden, fierce ache in his leg.

As if Woodstock's threat did not place Henry under enormous pressure already; now this, a reminder of what he would lose should he find the diamond, and trade it to the marquess. All those men—his men—fighting for England on the Continent; Henry would not be able to negotiate with the French for their lives.

They would lose—even England could lose—if the French Blue went to Woodstock in exchange for Caroline's safety.

Nothing—nothing—mattered more than that. Her. Caroline.

Tugging a hand through the hair at the back of his neck, Henry limped into the deepening twilight. How to keep both his promises to England and to Caroline, to himself—that was the question. A question that, at the moment, didn't seem to have an answer.

Henry let out a sigh of frustration. Even Hamlet, in all his ghost-seeing grimness, wouldn't envy Lake's current debacle. He'd faced *madame guillotine*, master swordsmen, but facing the fact that he had to betray his country to keep her alive—that he would leave her again, after falling for her once more—

That was too much to bear.

Twenty-three

—◆—

The Next Day

Her usual afternoon stroll in Hyde Park interrupted by a bout of foggy drizzle, Caroline was ducking into her carriage when she heard a voice, sickeningly familiar, ring out behind her.

"My lady!"

She turned to see the Marquess of Woodstock approach, a gruesome little smile splitting his face as he offered a sweeping bow.

A charge of terror moved beneath her skin, leaving a metallic taste in her mouth. Had he come at last to claim his prize, exact his revenge? But it had been only a few days—she thought they had more time—

"My lord," she replied, her voice high, unsteady. The drizzle was turning into rain, pattering dully against the ground, the top of the coach.

Her eyes flicked over Woodstock's head. Where were—?

"They're not here," Woodstock said.

She drew a breath through her nose. "They will be, soon."

"That gives me ample time to make good on my . . . promise, if I should so choose."

Nicks, who had been standing quietly beside the vehicle, stepped forward, sensing something was wrong. The marquess narrowed his eyes, slipping a hand inside his coat.

Caroline stepped back. "Into the carriage, Nicks. You're getting wet."

"But I—but—you are too, m'lad—"

"*Now.*"

Nicks shot Caroline a pleading look; Caroline ignored it; at last Nicks climbed into the vehicle.

"Why don't you do it, then?" Caroline hissed, closing the door behind her. "Why don't you take me now and end this ridiculous game you play?"

Her heart was in her throat; she felt wild, and a little dizzy. The rain soaked her bonnet; it hung limply against her cheek.

Was this it? The moment she ceded her freedom, and her life?

She would do it.

She would do it if it meant saving Henry's career, all those men fighting for him on the Continent.

She realized how afraid she was to die.

Woodstock's smile returned. "I confess I am rather enjoying myself, watching the lot of you chase your tails. And the anticipation of the things I shall do to you . . ."

He reached out, brushed a thumb over the slope of Caroline's chin. His touch was cold, his skin clammy; she recoiled from it, and he laughed.

"Soon, my lady," he said. "Tell your *paramour* I shall come for you very soon."

And then he turned and stalked into the gloom.

B eing confronted with the very real prospect of dismemberment and death, Caroline realized she had to do something. Anything. Now.

For days now she'd racked her brain in an attempt to outwit Woodstock. She'd come up with nothing on her own.

But this—this changed everything.

She did not want to die; she did not want Henry or his men to die, either.

Which meant they had to defeat the marquess.

They—she and Henry and Moon—had to try, at least. Together.

Assuring Nicks the strange man in the park was an old friend, Caroline changed into dry clothes and laced up a pair of sturdy boots.

Gathering her reticule and umbrella in the front hall, she turned and was nearly mauled, for a change, by her brother, William, as he skipped down the stairs.

"Good God, William, what's gotten into you?" Caroline wheezed, hand on her chest. "I didn't know you were one for skipping."

"I wasn't skipping," he said. He turned to the mirror and with his fingers slicked back a rogue lock of dark hair. Dressed in an evening kit of black velvet coat and breeches, he appeared every inch the rakehell.

Caroline knew he was up to no good.

"Yes, you were," she said.

"I was not."

"Were, too."

"Was *not*."

Caroline met his eyes in the mirror. "What's the occasion?"

"Almack's."

Even as her pulse leapt—excellent, William was out tonight, which meant he would not notice that she would be, too—Caroline narrowed her eyes.

"Almack's? You've reached a new low, William, trolling for your prey at the assembly rooms. Every debutante in there wears a padlocked chastity belt."

William turned to her. "For your edification, sweet Sister, I have no interest in unlocking said chastity belts."

"I don't believe you."

"I'm escorting Lady Violet Rutledge and her mother. Oh, and her cousin—Lady Sophia. *She's* the one with the chastity belt, though I daresay Thomas Hope's made quick work of it."

"Mr. Hope and Sophia Blaise?" Caroline cocked a brow. "Didn't see that one coming—a banker and a debutante."

William shrugged. "Violet thinks it's innocent enough, but I know better. I see the way that millionaire rogue looks at her. He's enamored."

"You look at a lot of women," Caroline said. "It's never innocent, the way you look. But what do you know of being enamored?"

She was baiting him, and he knew it. He was smiling.

But not his usual wicked smile, the devil flashing in his dark eyes. It was a quiet smile. Secret. And he was blushing. William never blushed.

"Well, then," Caroline said. "I do so hope you enjoy yourselves. Keep out of trouble."

"Please, Caroline, it's Almack's. We couldn't find trouble if we wanted."

Caroline put a hand on his shoulder. "You're William Townshend. Trouble finds you."

"Not tonight." Henry looked at the umbrella she held in the crook of her arm. "Any plans for you this evening?"

"No, no, I've got a bit of a headache, and the rain, and . . . um. I was just—I was just coming back from the park, you see . . . early to bed, I suppose."

William eyed her for a long moment; it took Caroline every ounce of resolve to not wince, or burst out laughing at the ridiculous jumble that was her excuse.

But it appeared William was rather more enamored of Lady Violet than he was suspicious of his sister, for he bent forward, planted a kiss on Caroline's forehead, and dashed out the door.

Watching him descend the front step, Caroline noticed the puddles in the street below were stewing and still; the rain had stopped, but not for long. She ducked her head outside. The sky was gray and low.

The perfect evening to slip through the empty Mayfair streets unnoticed.

Twenty-four

—◆—

Henry bolted upright in bed at the sound of footsteps by the door. His entire being ached with exhaustion.

Sending Moon to patrol Caroline's window, Henry had spent the previous evening huddled in a corner at the Cat and Mouse, convincing those hairy acrobats to make their move already. It had been a delicate operation; he didn't want to give himself away, but he managed to coax from them a promise they would confront the Earl of Harclay soon. Which meant the diamond might be loosened from his grasp as early as the next evening, and this sordid business at last concluded.

Having returned home well after the sun rose, Henry had attempted to get some sleep that day.

Considering thoughts of Caroline haunted his waking and sleeping dreams, he did not get very much at all.

His hands were on his face; his fingers fumbled as he attempted to tie the leather thong of his eye patch at the back of his head.

He opened his eye and his breath caught in his throat.

Caroline. She was here.

* * *

"Good God, Caroline," he said, running a hand through his adorably mussed hair, "I know everyone else wants to kill me, but you, too? If I weren't so bloody knackered I'd cry. How'd you get in?"

Already she felt the familiar tug at the ends of her mouth. She leaned against the doorframe, crossing her arms.

"I found your associate, Moon he called himself, lurking beneath my window. He escorted me here and kindly allowed me entrance. I don't mean to offend, but was he the woman at Vauxhall, the one—?"

"Yes," Henry said, grinning. "He makes a far less compelling female than he'd like to believe, I'm afraid. Something about the jaw, and his moustache . . ."

He sat up against the pillows, the counterpane falling into his lap. He wasn't wearing a shirt (why would he be? she wondered vaguely); Caroline watched his nipples pucker at the chill evening air that came in through the cracked window. In the thin gray light his chest and shoulders appeared smooth, the skin pulled taut over muscle and bone, the slopes pleasing, masculine, inviting. The barest trace of spice tickled her nostrils.

She swallowed, hard. A moment ago she felt as if she were standing at death's door, but now, seeing Henry and his muscles and his naked chest, her body felt glaringly alive, as if she'd not only inhaled smelling salts but also ingested them.

Henry followed her gaze to his chest. His grin faded as he tugged the counterpane back into place. "I'm, um, terribly sorry, Caroline, you startled me, and I forgot that I was naked—without clothes, that is; here, let me get a shirt . . ."

Eyes trained on her feet, Caroline shook her head. "I won't be long. I've come to offer my aid in untangling this mess with Woodstock, and the diamond. I've too much at stake; I can't just wait for you to end up dead, trying to rescue me."

"I won't end up dead."

"Your men will, if you trade the French Blue to Woodstock. Let me help you, Henry. Please."

He released a long, low breath. "You know I'd never allow you to put yourself in harm's way on my account," he said slowly.

"I want to help. If not for your sake, then for Violet's, and my brother's. I can't sit still, knowing how much trouble we're all in."

Caroline heard the scrape of skin; she snuck a glance at Henry to see him cross his arms across his naked chest. Though those arms and that chest bulged with muscle, the freckles that dotted his skin made him look boyish, somehow. God, those freckles, they did something to her . . .

She looked away.

"For your brother's sake, Caroline, and for yours, I beg you stay out of this, and keep yourself safe. Besides, what makes you think Moon and I haven't had any luck concocting a plan to destroy Woodstock on our own?"

Caroline scoffed, toeing the fine layer of dust that covered the floor. "It can't hurt to have more help, can it?"

"Yes, it can, if it puts you in danger. I won't have you ending up hurt, bleeding out in the middle of the woods like—like that poor girl. I cannot accept your offer."

"You left everyone and everything you loved," she said. She turned her head to look at him. "You left to protect me. Let me return the favor."

He returned her gaze steadily. "Doesn't matter now, does it?"

"Oh, for God's sake, Henry. You're no martyr. Of course it matters. Let's work together. Defeat Woodstock, so you might trade the diamond to the French, and save the lives of your men."

"One problem," Henry replied. "We don't have the French Blue."

"We will."

He cocked a brow. "You sound awfully confident about that."

She hoped—prayed—her burning cheeks did not give her away.

"I am confident in us," she said. "Don't you even want to try to defeat Woodstock? He's a traitor—"

"Of course I want to defeat him. But your life is at stake, Caroline. If I move against him, and I fail—I'm sorry, Caroline, but it's too dangerous. No."

"No?"

"Yes. *No.* Not this time."

With a petulant huff, Caroline crossed her arms and snuck a glance about the room. Her eyes caught on the chairs drawn up before the fireplace; she saw one of Mr. Moon's wigs—long, blond curls—hanging from an armrest.

She didn't know what she'd do with a wig, or how it would help her outwit Woodstock. But it was a wig, a disguise, and surely a disguise was a step in the right direction? She darted across the room and snatched the wig, making a break back toward the door.

"I'm going to defeat Woodstock," she panted, "and you can't stop me."

Henry tossed aside the counterpane and leapt from the bed. "Watch me," he growled.

She glanced over her shoulder to see him lunging for her.

That wasn't the only thing she saw.

Her pulse gave a little shriek of pleasure.

He was completely, utterly, fabulously naked; not so much as a sock marred the pale perfection of his person. Heat flooded her face as she reached for the doorframe—wait, why am I running from that? she wondered vaguely—but Henry was too quick, too strong.

He curled an arm beneath her ribs and caught her, heaving her against him with a breathless grunt.

Caroline made one last grab for the door, but Henry held her fast, wrapping his other arm around her torso as she attempted—and failed—to slither free of his grasp.

She wanted to tell him to go to hell, to set her down. His touch felt dangerously delicious; she knew she had to escape, quickly, before the ability to resist him abandoned her.

Caroline elbowed him, or tried to, at least. He scoffed—"nice try"—and pressed her against the wall, stilling her movements as he twisted her free arm behind her back.

His breath tickled the hair at her temples. A shiver worked its way down her body as she struggled to catch her breath.

"Give me the wig," he said.

"Not this time," she mocked, holding it closer to her chest.

He pressed his body against hers. "Caroline. What the devil d'you think you're going to do with a wig? Give it to me."

"No. Not until you let me help you—"

"Hand it over. Now."

"No-o!"

And then he was reaching in front of her, his fingers on her belly as he grabbed at the stringy curls, and she was wrenching away from him, her insides seizing with laughter.

"Give," he panted, "*it!*"

"You can't," she said, "have it!"

Caroline doubled over, unable to breathe between great sobs of laughter, and Henry took advantage of her momentary weakness and grabbed the wig from her hand.

He was laughing, too, tugging the wig onto his head and dangling the curls against her face, making her laugh harder.

"I'd like to see you steal it now," he said, drawing to his full height.

Caroline let out a sigh of relief as her laughter subsided, closing her eyes against the tears. She fell against the wall.

She wondered what it was about Henry, exactly, that made her laugh so hard she cried. This was the second time in as many weeks; it felt as lovely as it had that first time in her garden with the peonies. Her sides ached, her eyes burned.

When she opened her eyes they fell, naturally, on Henry.

He was naked. In the throes of her laughter she'd forgotten that fact.

And naturally her eyes wandered from his face to his shoulders and chest, down the sinewy ridges of his torso and hips. They followed the narrow trail of darkening hair from his navel to his groin, coming at last to his sex.

It hung, soft and careless, from between his legs, nestled against a thatch of wiry, red-gold hair. Even as she looked at it—marveled at it, really, it was the first time she'd seen a man's cock since she came face-to-face with this same one more than a decade ago—it began to stiffen in apparent appreciation, and grow, its smooth surface becoming engorged with veins, color.

Henry, it seemed, had also forgotten he was naked, and just as his sex sprung to vibrant, sudden life, he tugged the wig from his head and held it over the offending organ, turning abruptly away from her.

"I'm sorry," he said. "I didn't want . . . I didn't mean for you to see that."

With some effort, Caroline tore her gaze from Henry's buttocks. They were very pale, round; where thigh met backside, the skin puckered into two tiny, deep dimples, adorable and childlike, just like the dimple on his cheek.

She swallowed for the thousandth time, and drew to her feet. She cleared her throat. She had to tell him, if only to do something, keep herself from shoving Henry back onto the bed, and having her way with him.

"Woodstock," she said. "I saw him. Today. We're running out of time."

Twenty-five

—◆—

A pulse of rage, hot and blinding, shot through Henry. He stepped forward, towering over her. "Are you all right? Did he harm you?"

"I'm fine. But we've got to defeat him, Henry, before he comes after us. He grows impatient—"

"But how did he get to you? I sent Moon—"

"You said it yourself—Woodstock is a trained spy. I don't know how he got to me. But he knew I'd be unguarded, for a moment at least. We don't have much time."

Mr. Moon, something of an expert in the field of eavesdropping, suddenly appeared in the doorway, a pair of trousers in hand.

"I'm sorry, sir," he said. "I was following her, I was, but then I, ah, had to answer nature's call—"

"It doesn't matter," Caroline said. "Woodstock didn't hurt me. But he will if we don't move quickly."

"*We* are not doing anything," Henry said, casting Moon an evil look as he exchanged the wig for the pants. He turned around, shuffling into shadow. Stepping into the trousers one leg at a time, Henry's heart clenched; he blew out his cheeks. He hated the idea of involving Caroline, now more than ever.

Moon, ever the diplomat, cleared his throat. "Perhaps three minds are better than two."

"Absolutely not."

Caroline squared her shoulders. "We might come up with some ideas—"

"About the wig?" Henry turned back to Caroline.

Caroline picked at her skirts. "Well. No, not really. I'm not sure what I was thinking about the wig."

"Woodstock demands either you or the diamond—the choice is clear." He looked to Moon. "We should make it."

Ignoring him, Caroline stood. She turned and began to pace before the window, hands clasped behind her back. There wasn't much room to move in either direction; the chamber was small, the house hardly the Hanover Square mansion to which she was accustomed. It made her movements appear frantic: three steps in one direction, turn, three steps in the other.

"What about a hired assassin?" Caroline said. "Surely you know one or two of those?"

The corner of Henry's mouth curled upward. "Even if they did exist—which, strictly speaking, they do not—assassins are more trouble than they're worth. Rough lot, they are, most of them drink gin to break their fast. Half the time they're the ones being stabbed in the eye, rather than the other way around. Trust me, even if I kept assassins in my employ—which I do not, remember, because they do not exist—I wouldn't call on them for this."

"He's right," Moon said, toeing at the edge of the faded rug. "By the time these nonexistent assassins sobered up, it'd be too late. We've got to make our move, soon, before that bastard—pardon my language, my lady—changes his terms again."

"There's that *we* again," Henry ground out.

Caroline fell into her chair with a sigh of despair so ardent her lips sputtered. "Really, the two of you are the best England has to offer, and you haven't thought of anything?"

"I have," Henry replied. "I'm going to give the French Blue to Woodstock. That's always been the plan, Caroline. It still is."

She tugged at a loose curl, winding it about her finger. "There's a better plan. We just haven't thought of it yet."

She looked away from him, brow furrowed as her gaze

flitted to the ceiling, as if she might find the answer there. Henry glanced out the window. Rain lashed against the pane. The diamond weighed heavily on his thoughts. He would be glad to be rid of it, whether it went to Woodstock or to Bonaparte.

Henry turned back to her when she suddenly stirred. Caroline looked down at the lock of hair in her fingers, then she looked up at Mr. Moon.

He was busy brushing out one of his wigs. This one was blond and wavy; Moon draped it over his fist, running the silver-handled brush through it with great care.

Caroline's eyes lit; Henry watched the spark of an idea unfurl into something else. Something she was obviously excited about.

She rose. "Tell me, Mr. Moon," she said, sidling up beside him, "exactly how extensive is your wig collection?"

Moon shrugged; he didn't look up from his brushing. "Sizeable. Why?"

Caroline met Henry's gaze. "Then you'll have a wig that matches my hair."

Mr. Moon turned to survey Caroline's tumbling locks. "Your hair is an unusual color—darker than most brunettes, a bit redder. But I suppose I have something close." He grinned at Henry. "Are you going to dress my superior as your twin?"

And then, suddenly, his face fell as the realization dawned upon him. He looked at Caroline. They were the same height; not exactly the same build, but Moon was nowhere near the hulking monster Henry was.

"Oh," Moon breathed. "*Oh. I'm* going to be your twin."

Caroline tapped a finger to her lips. "My body double, as a matter of fact."

"That's bloody genius," he replied, lips curling into a wicked smile.

She looked pointedly at Henry. "Isn't it, though?"

It was all he could do not to roll his eyes. Pushing his hand into the hair at the back of his head, Henry sighed. "And how does this bloody genius plan of yours work?"

"You agree to Woodstock's bargain," Caroline said, eyes dancing with mischief. "Tell him you'll hand over the diamond. You won't, of course, but you still bring it to him—"

"Wait, wait," Henry said, waving away her words. "Not two steps in, and already your plot has a serious hole. We don't have the diamond."

She crossed her arms over her chest. "Yes, we do. I do, I mean. My brother does. I know where he's hiding it."

Henry blinked, his heart tripping inside his chest. "What—wait—wait, Caroline. The diamond—you mean to tell me you know where it is?"

"I do." She held her chin high, the soft plane of her jaw pearlescent in the low light of the fire. "And I will give it to you under two conditions. First, that you agree to my bloody genius plot. We shall require the French Blue for its success. Second, you must swear to keep it from Woodstock's grasp."

For a long moment she stared him down, willing him to defy her. That *look* in her eyes—the determination, the challenge, the spark—it was formidable.

And arousing as hell.

Henry needed that diamond. They all did. But he could not tell which choice would make him the bigger fool: accepting Caroline's offer, or refusing it.

"All this time, you've known where the diamond was?" Henry asked.

"I had my suspicions," Caroline replied. "Suspicions I confirmed not long ago."

Hands on his hips, Henry poked the inside of his cheek with his tongue. "Whether you know where the stone is or not, it's always been my plan to give the jewel to Woodstock—"

"I won't let you do that." Caroline turned, stepped toward him. "There's too much at stake, Henry. All the lives you could save—what do I matter, when weighed against all the good you could do with this diamond?"

He stepped closer, too close, the words escaping his lips before he could think to control them. "You are the *only* thing that matters. Not that you're a thing. But you matter to me, very much." He spoke savagely. "I won't do it, Caroline. Tell me—is there anything I can do to change the terms of your offer?"

Caroline shook her head. "No. Either you let me help you, or the French Blue stays where it is."

Henry glanced at Moon. Moon shrugged. "I don't have any

ideas to outsmart Woodstock. You're going to lose the diamond, sir, if we don't think of something, and soon."

"Please, Henry," Caroline pleaded. "I want to help."

Involving Caroline in his dealings with Woodstock was Henry's worst fear realized. For twelve years he'd protected her from him; he'd sacrificed everything to keep her safe, keep her far from the danger that followed him day and night.

And now she would step into the lion's den beside him. He would try, heavens, he would try, but Henry couldn't protect her from Woodstock at such close quarters. The thought of losing her, and to Woodstock—

Henry swallowed, hard. He looked at Caroline, lovely, her eyes lively as she plotted with Moon. She didn't understand the danger in which she placed herself. But he wouldn't stop her; he couldn't.

All he could do was play his part, and play it well, and pray that if he did not escape Woodstock's grasp unscathed, she might.

"I have your word, Henry, that you won't trade the jewel to Woodstock?"

Henry tugged a hand through his hair, let out a long, low breath. "You do."

"Splendid. To my brother's house, then."

The thunderous clap of hoof beats sounded behind Caroline; whoever it was, he rode like the devil. The ground began to tremble beneath her feet. It was dark here in the alley, too dark even for shadow; she could hardly make out the line of Henry's shoulders as he limped ahead of her.

The hoof beats grew louder, imminent. In a flash of sudden, violent movement, Henry turned and with his body wedged her against a nearby wall, his knee thrust between her thighs. She let out a cry; he covered her mouth with his hand, and pressed his body more firmly against hers.

The horse hurtled past them, so close Caroline felt the great *whoosh* of wind it trailed in its wake. She watched in wonder as the horse and its rider disappeared down the alley. It could've been the darkness, or the wavering of her senses with Henry so near, but she could have sworn the rider rode the horse without a saddle, his fists tangled in his mount's inky mane.

A horse thief, perhaps? She hoped the rogue hadn't pillaged her brother's stables.

Henry released her. "Sorry about that," he panted, smoothing back his hair. "But he would've run us over. I didn't mean to scare you."

"It's all right," she replied, even as the unease in her belly pulsed brighter. The last echoes of the horse's hoof beats faded. Peering one last time down the alley, Caroline turned in the opposite direction and made for Hanover Square.

Henry held the taper aloft as Caroline opened the door to William's dressing room. Her heart skipped a beat when her eyes fell upon the drawer.

It gaped open; stockings hung haphazardly over its sides and covered the floor, as if it had cast up its accounts. Caroline toed aside the silk and the cotton and the wool as she darted for the drawer. Glancing inside, she felt sick.

She didn't have to dig to know the diamond was gone.

A cold rush of panic moved through her limbs. She covered her face with her hands. Their plan, the wigs, the defeat of Woodstock . . . their hopes, dashed in the space of a single heartbeat.

What were they going to do without the diamond?

Henry appeared at her side. "What? What is it?"

"The French Blue," she replied. "Someone took it. It was here, not a few days ago . . ."

"Wait," Henry said. "William kept the French Blue here, in his sock drawer? A priceless, fifty-carat diamond? In his *sock drawer*?"

"It's a long story."

His eye reflected the taper's flame in a single pinprick of light, a tiny star floating in the darkness of his pupil.

"May I?" he asked.

Caroline nodded. He passed her the taper and stepped toward the drawer. His face was a study of hard planes as Henry tore at the drawer's remaining contents, a flush of anger creeping up his neck to his chin, his cheeks.

"It's not here," he said at last, resting his elbows on the

open drawer. He pressed his thumbs to the place where his eyebrows met, and closed his eye.

"You think that man, the one on the horse—"

"Maybe. Could your brother have moved it elsewhere? To a safe, perhaps"—he scanned the mahogany cabinets lining the drawing room walls—"or another drawer?"

"No." Caroline slumped against the cabinets. "William would keep the French Blue here, in that drawer, or nowhere at all. It's gone."

"I apologize for the language I am about to use. But shit. This puts us back to where we began." He took a deep breath. "Just *shit*."

Caroline swallowed, silently cursing herself for not taking the diamond when she had the chance. "Henry, I'm so sorry."

He turned his head and opened his eye. "It's not your fault. Stop apologizing. We'll hunt it down, the diamond, though I may be forced to cut off your brother's fingers this time around."

"Fine by me." Caroline sighed. "That scalawag deserves it."

And then, after a beat: "You won't really, though, will you? Cut off his fingers?"

One side of his mouth quirked up. "No, I won't really."

"Good," she said with a sigh of relief. "We can still do it, you know—put our plot in play without the diamond. Tell Woodstock you've agreed to hand me over—"

"No," Henry said, savagely. "I won't go near that man without the French Blue in pocket. If something goes wrong—and knowing our luck, it will—we'll need the diamond as protection against any threat Woodstock might make to your life."

Henry rose and dug a hand into his hair, gathering the golden strands between his fingers. She watched, transfixed. Even in his shimmering anger he was handsome.

"I've got to go," he said. "In the meantime, I won't have you feeling guilty about this. Promise me you won't?"

She met his eye. "Let me come with you."

"*No.*"

The vehemence of his reply startled her.

"But why—?"

"Stay here, Caroline. Let me sort this out. If I find anything, I shall come to you, straightaway." He paused. "Thank you. For trusting me."

*   *   *

Caroline was reaching for the knob when the kitchen door swung open, sending her flying—where else?—into Henry's arms.

Avery stumbled into the hall, hair and costume askew. "Oh, oh, my lady, I am terribly sorry! Are you all right?"

Caroline remained plastered to Henry's chest. The bones in her shoulders vibrated in time to his heartbeat. She inhaled, deeply, the spicy scent of his skin filling her head.

He set her on her feet. He touched her as if she were a stranger; efficiently, tepidly. It made her stomach hurt.

"Yes," she said. Her gaze swept over his person. "What about you?"

Avery opened the door the rest of the way. At once half a dozen men swarmed around him, each one dressed in Harclay livery. A tendril of panic unfurled in her chest.

The butler's eyes flicked over Caroline's head, to Henry.

"Tell me," she said. "Is it William?"

Avery met her gaze. "It's Lady Violet. She's been kidnapped. The acrobats, the ones at Mr. Hope's ball—they kidnapped her."

She heard Henry draw a breath behind her.

"The acrobats?" Henry asked. His tone was carefully neutral.

"Yes," Avery snapped. "Took her right in the middle of a dance at Almack's. Gone, just like that."

Twenty-six

———— ✦ ————

Henry's heart fell to the floor between his legs with a *squish*.

Oh God, he thought, this is all my fault, this isn't how things are supposed to happen. He hadn't seen it coming.

Moon had; Moon had warned Henry that this could happen, that tipping off the acrobats—telling them the bearded man who owed them money was the wildly wealthy Earl of Harclay—could endanger Caroline, or Violet, or both. That the acrobats could use the women as blackmail against Harclay, threaten their lives, kidnap them.

Henry offered a prayer of thanks that it hadn't been Caroline. And then he cursed himself, silently, fluidly, for being so stupid as to put her in harm's way with Woodstock. Just the *thought* of her being harmed, taken—it would be his fault, all of it—made his vision blur with rage.

He was thirty-two years old, for God's sake, and had been playing at this espionage business a solid decade or more. He should know better. He should better protect the woman he loved. Had he learned nothing, being forced to leave her as he did? Had he not learned to take more care?

His hands curled into fists at his sides. "Do we know where they took her?"

"No," Avery replied. "The earl is in pursuit. Didn't even have time to saddle his horse."

"What do they want, the acrobats?"

Again the butler looked to Caroline. She gave him a small nod. *Go on.*

"Not entirely sure, sir. No doubt a sizable sum of money."

Henry blinked. It all came together in a sudden, startling flash of clarity. *Of course.* The rider in the alley. The missing diamond, and the kidnapping.

Yesterday, Hope told Henry he'd frozen the earl's accounts at the bank until his lordship produced the French Blue. It meant the earl had little, if any, access to the money their friends the acrobats were demanding.

The earl did, however, have the diamond. If he were as enamored of Lady Violet as Caroline seemed to think he was, he would trade his bollocks to get her back; he would trade a gem worth upwards of twenty thousand pounds.

What was that line the earl had used with Violet? Oh yes. *It's only money.*

The rider who had nearly mauled Henry and Caroline in the alley was none other than the earl himself. After the kidnapping, he'd no doubt made a mad dash from Almack's back to his house in Hanover Square, where he dug the diamond out of his drawer; when Henry and Caroline had seen him tearing down the lane, William was heading away from the house, after Violet, the diamond tucked into his coat pocket.

Henry guessed the acrobats were hiding out in Cheapside. The Cat and Mouse, most likely.

He had to get there before Harclay traded away the diamond. If the acrobats got hold of the French Blue, it would be lost forever; pawned, sold. Caroline would die, and so would his men.

He turned to the butler. "You'll stay here, and guard the lady. Lock the doors. No one comes in or out. Keep her away from the windows—an interior room would be best."

He turned to Caroline. She appeared as if she might burst into tears at the slightest provocation. His stomach clenched. If he made it out of this alive, he would never, ever forgive himself.

He took her elbows in his hands. She was shaking.

"Please," he said, giving her arms a gentle squeeze. "Stay here. I'm going to help your brother find Violet. If there is any news, I shall see that you receive it straightaway. But you must stay here; the streets are not safe."

"All—right, all right," she stammered.

Henry made for the door. At the last moment Caroline lunged for him, giving his sleeve a gentle tug. "Take care, Henry," she said.

"I will," he said.

And he meant it.

Two Hours Later

Horse nickering with exhaustion beneath him, Henry watched from the shadows as Lord Harclay helped Violet up the front steps of her family's crumbling Grosvenor Square manse.

She looked worse for the wear, gown spattered in blood, hair askew, but she was home, and in one (disheveled) piece. Harclay had successfully negotiated with the acrobats for her release. What drunk idiot wouldn't forfeit a girl, even a pretty one, for a blue diamond that was practically the size of a plum?

By the time Henry arrived at the Cat and Mouse in Cheapside, it was too late. The air was acrid with singed gunpowder, an acrobat lay bleeding on the tavern floor, the deal was struck. Violet was in William's arms, and the French Blue clenched in an acrobat's greedy fingers.

It was too dangerous to go in after the diamond. Even with a man down, there were still three acrobats with which to contend, and while they were short of stature, they were strong, and quite drunk, and far more limber than Henry ever hoped to be.

He'd begged. He'd pleaded and threatened. This wasn't how the plot was to go. He hadn't had time to call in more men, to bring something—anything—with which to negotiate.

It was a losing fight.

It disappeared, the French Blue, two decades ago, in the beginning tumult of the Revolution. Now, if Henry didn't act quickly, it would disappear again.

He'd have Moon canvass London's shadiest pawnbrokers in the morning, its more discreet jewelers; beyond that, there wasn't much Henry could do. He didn't want to notify his superiors, or the agents working for him; the more people who knew, the sooner the French would discover the jewel had slipped from his grasp, and look elsewhere for their negotiations.

Henry had come to London to find the diamond; he'd planned to exchange it for the lives of British soldiers on the Continent.

But now his plan had changed. There was too much at stake to give up now; in one fell swoop he could spare Caroline's life, and leave her to her hard-won widowhood.

He could not give up now.

Even though he hadn't a clue what to do next.

He closed his eyes and drew a long, slow breath. Hope would be furious, his stock would continue to slide, and Lady Violet's fortunes would fall. So many lives and livelihoods depended on this bloody diamond.

All weighty concerns, surely. He should be thinking upon them, devising schemes and deceptions to win back the stone, and right these wrongs.

He was thinking of Caroline instead.

He hoped she'd heeded his request and stayed at home.

From Violet's front door came delirious cries of relief, muffled sobs; Henry stood watch, lest there be any undue fainting or palpitating of elderly hearts.

When the cries died down and the sobs became giggles, Henry urged his horse into motion.

Mayfair was all but deserted at this hour; the gas lamps were his only company, casting his flickering shadow out before him in sinister enormity. His leg was killing him.

He was exhausted, and hungry, and in pain.

Still. There would be no sleep for him tonight.

He led his horse down the familiar alley. In the dark Hanover Square was eerie, and strange. Windowpanes, blank with drawn drapes, stared down at him with unreadable intent.

All but one windowpane, that is. A single window was open to the cool night air, lit from within by a lamp whose light was reflected in a mirrored vanity.

Wincing, Henry dismounted and tied his horse to the iron

rails of the back gate. Despite the stiffness of his leg, he climbed the gate without disturbing so much as a pebble; he did, however, bite back an enthusiastic expletive when he landed on his bad leg.

He stood beneath the window, craning his neck as he waited for Caroline to pass by, or draw the drapes, or settle on the sill and quote a bit of Shakespeare.

(If only she'd whisper those lovelorn lines: "Henry, O Henry, wherefore art thou Henry?"; he'd be scaling the wall and in her bed in half a heartbeat.)

He heard Caroline move inside the room, heard Nicks's muffled admonitions to go to bed, and get some sleep.

Even as his heart began to pound at the memory of Caroline's mouth pressed to his, Henry felt limp with relief. She was here. She was safe.

He leaned his back against the cold brick, crossed his ankles and his arms, and closed his eyes. He listened. Caroline was in bed now; the maid was leaving the room.

He could smell her perfume. Inside his chest, his heart hiccupped.

She was safe.

For now.

And heavens, she smelled good.

"Caroline," he whispered.

Twenty-seven

———— ✦ ————

Caroline could not sleep.

She rose from bed and made her way to the window. Brushing aside the curtains, she rested her elbows on the sill and leaned out into the night—black, still, enormous.

That's when she heard it. Her name, whispered by a familiar voice.

Henry waited beneath her window, face upturned, his one eye translucent in the darkness. Her heart clenched. He was so handsome.

He was here.

"Can't sleep?" he whispered.

She shook her head.

He hesitated, but only for a moment.

"I've got a few bottles of decent wine back at my brother's," he offered. "Let me keep you company tonight, Caroline. I know you're afraid."

A warm rush of tears thickened at the back of her throat. She *was* afraid, she was exhausted, and she wanted nothing more than to spend the night with Henry.

It was a stupid choice. A bad choice.

But she made it anyway. She didn't want to be alone tonight.

* * *

Not two moments into their ride back to Henry's, a solid sheet of rain descended upon them, pummeling their heads and shoulders, splashing the ground.

Henry rode like the devil, urging his horse through the streets.

When at last they arrived, Henry lifted her from his horse and together they made a dash for the house, slipping in muddy puddles before they fell into the kitchen, the door closing softly behind them.

A fire crackled merrily in the hearth, lanterns lit the space, thunder rumbled outside.

Henry gave his shirtsleeves a good shake.

Caroline pushed back her cloak. Praise heaven her dress was spared most of the onslaught; so were Henry's shirt and breeches, which unfortunately did not cling to his person as they had that day at the Botanic Gardens.

Her gaze trailed up from his waist and chest to his face. He was looking at her.

"Henry," she said. "What are we going to do? If the diamond's gone—"

"I don't know." He ran a hand through his wet hair. "But in the meantime I should like to keep you safe. With me. After what happened with Violet . . ."

A pause.

"Stay," he said. "For a drink. For anything you want. Stay."

"I came the first time you asked, didn't I?"

Was it just her imagination, or was he leaning closer? The space between their bodies was alive, suddenly, twisting with potent possibility. Despite the chill of the rain, Caroline felt warm. Watching a stray drop wind its way down the slope of Henry's neck, she felt warmer.

He overwhelmed her, surrounded her. She couldn't have tucked tail and run if she'd wanted. He was keeping her here.

Like she would ever want to leave.

"Your cloak," he said. She moved to untie the knot at her throat. Henry brushed her hands aside. She looked away when his fingers brushed the skin of her throat. The place between her legs pulsed dully.

She tried not to think about that first night, the night of

Hope's ball. The wild kiss she and Henry had shared in the dim coolness of that chamber. Even now her lips burned.

Upstairs, the door to his room was open. Henry moved through it easily, tossing aside a pair of breeches hung about the back of a chair as he passed.

"Sorry about the mess," he said. "Moon's housekeeping skills have yet to improve."

"But the candles are lit—he's not all bad. No luck finding a valet?"

"No time," he said, and toed a stack of rumpled papers underneath the bed. "Figuring out a way to coax the French Blue from your brother's grasp—without pulling out his fingernails, of course—has proven a time-consuming task. A task at which I have sadly failed."

The window was open, and the soft patter of rain floated into the room. Henry pushed the window closed; the air was cooling.

"Here," he said, and gathered a fistful of newspapers off one of the chairs drawn up before the fireplace. "Sit."

She sat. Henry went to work on the near-extinguished fire, tossing the papers on top of a fresh wedge of firewood. The flames flickered to life, slowly at first, until a blistering fire burned brightly at Caroline's feet, lighting the room.

Outside the window, thunder rumbled; rain continued its assault on the pane. It made for the perfect cozy night in.

Except Caroline felt anything but cozy. Just being in this room—the smells, the bed that loomed over her shoulder—made her feel unsettled, and intensely aware, awake. She felt drawn tight, like the string of a bow just before the arrow is released. Perhaps she should have just gone to bed, as Nicks in no uncertain terms had told her.

She tried taking a deep breath, but only managed to inhale the scent of Henry's soap. Citrus, a hint of masculine smoke. Again that tug between her legs.

"Wine?" Henry asked. "I think we both need a nip after this evening's events. Besides, I've taken the liberty of replenishing my brother's stores with a more palatable selection."

She looked over her shoulder at Henry, who stood at the bureau with a corkscrew in one hand and a gleaming dark bottle in the other. The corkscrew appeared laughably tiny in Henry's square-edged fingers.

"Time to replenish the stores," she said with a smile, "but none for a valet?"

"A man must keep his priorities in order."

"Wine first," she said, "work second, clothes third?"

"Something like that."

He pulled the cork out of the bottle with a deft snap of his wrist. He poured the inky wine into a pair of elegant, etched-glass cups—they weren't proper wine coupes, but they were better than the teacups he'd proffered last time—and held one out to Caroline.

"Cheers to Violet's rescue," he said, offering his own cup as he settled into the chair across from hers.

She touched her glass to his. "Cheers."

They drank in silence. Caroline gulped at her wine; it was delicious, tart on her lips, jammy on her tongue. At once she felt the familiar stirring in her blood, the simultaneous release.

She kept drinking.

"That's good," she said, rolling her lips between her teeth. "Very good, Henry, thank you."

The grin he gave her made the backs of her knees tingle. "Better, now that you're finally calling me Henry." He looked down at his glass, glinting pleasantly in the light of the fire.

She kept drinking. It helped ease her worry, her fear that they'd lost everything by losing the diamond.

There was nothing more to be done tonight. Nothing to do except wait.

"Shall we play a game, then?" she asked. "Cards, perhaps?"

"Caroline," he said. His voice was low, a warning. "You're changing the subject. Quite clumsily, might I add."

She met his gaze. It was getting dark in the room; the molten light of the fire was reflected in his pale iris, turning it a shade darker than amber.

"Please," she replied. "I don't want to talk—not about that, anyway. Let's play."

"Fine." Henry threw back the rest of his wine and set the glass on the floor beside his boots. Rolling up the sleeves of his shirt, he leaned forward, his eye flashing. "A game of truth."

"Truth?" Caroline chased the droplets of wine that were left in her cup. "But you never tell the truth."

"You may choose to tell the truth," he said, "or you may choose to drink."

Caroline straightened. She liked the sound of that. "Then you're going to get very drunk."

"That is the hope," he replied, rising.

He brought the bottle over from the bureau and refilled their glasses.

Twenty-eight

———— ✦ ————

They were on their third bottle of wine. The rain had stopped; the view outside the window was so dark Caroline could see naught but her reflection in the pane.

What had begun as a test of truth had, in true Henry Lake fashion, devolved into a drinking game.

Who is your favorite brother, Robert or Peter?

Peter, he'd said, and gulped at his wine.

Do you sometimes fantasize about killing your brother? he'd asked.

I know *you* do, she'd said, and gulped at hers.

It went on like this for an hour, and then another, the two of them giggling over their empty cups as they refilled them again, and again, and again.

Henry was leaning forward in his chair, allowing the last of the wine to drip from the bottle into Caroline's cup. He set the bottle down at his feet, and looked up to meet Caroline's gaze. His lips were stained red from the wine; his cheeks were rosy pink from the fire; and his hair, dry now, coursed over his shoulders, the pieces at the front tucked behind his ears. His eye patch shone dully in the low light of the fire.

She resisted the impulse to reach out and touch it. It made

her heart clench, to take in all his scarred handsomeness. She longed to touch him. To feel his lips on her skin, and return the favor. Her body ached for it.

The wine had whipped her blood into a frenzy. Her entire being was alive with desire.

Still she made no move. She wasn't *so* foxed as to think it a wise idea.

"Are you all right?" Henry asked, eying her.

"Yes," she said, too quickly. "Why?"

"You look flushed. Shall I open the window?"

Caroline shook her head. "No, thank you. It's just—"

He leaned closer.

She did not pull back.

"Just what?" he murmured.

Caroline looked at him. The words came before she could stop them. "Are you happy?"

She cringed, inwardly, at the awkwardness of her question. Whence had come *that* particular, and particularly intimate, query? And why did it matter to her whether Henry was happy or not?

"Happy?" He grinned. "I'm English. And a ginger. Of course I'm not happy."

"I'm serious," she said. "Are you content, doing . . . whatever it is that you do? Has it made you happy?"

The gleam in Henry's eye hardened. He scoffed, looking down at his empty cup. "Tell me, Caroline, what do you think?"

"I don't know what to think."

He met her gaze through the pale fringe of his lashes. "You know me better than that."

She looked down at her hands.

He drew a breath. The hand cupped about the ball of his knee clenched, fingers curling into the fabric of his breeches.

"No," he said quietly. Even as he said the word, she was sorry for asking the question. Henry was right. She'd known the answer. Perhaps she just wanted to hear him say it. "I'm not."

After a beat he asked, "And Osbourne. Did he make you happy?"

Her eyes flashed to meet his. "George was a good man. An honorable husband."

"Did he make you happy?"

"We were content. I wanted for nothing. I still want for nothing. He was good to me."

Heated silence settled between Caroline and Henry. She felt her body arching into the pull of his sharp-edged curiosity. Her stays were tight against her labored breathing; she longed to be free of them.

"Did he make you come?" Henry said suddenly, the softness of his confession replaced by a savage calm.

Caroline blinked. Her skin prickled with a flush of uncomfortable desire.

She sipped nervously at her wine.

"He didn't?" Henry's eye went wide. "For ten whole years, he didn't?"

"Henry, please—"

"You've never—?"

"I have." Her eyes burned.

Henry scoffed. "Alone? Really, Caroline, that hardly counts." He set down his cup. "I've never made you come. And I intend to remedy that sad fact right now. Finish your wine."

"Henry! I can't just—"

"Finish your wine." His voice, his face—everything about him was dark, shimmering with intent.

Caroline looked at him for a long moment. She swallowed what was left in her cup. Henry took it from her and set it beside his on the floor.

He met her eyes. "I'm sorry it's taken so long," he said, sliding off the chair onto his knees before her, "but I mean to make up for lost time."

Even though Henry was kneeling, he still managed to loom over her. She inhaled, sharply, as he pressed his belly to her knees and took her face in his hands and pulled her to him.

He pressed his lips to her jaw, to her chin, to her ear. Her head fell back, eyes fluttering shut at the white-hot desire that streaked through her. Days, weeks, decades of thwarted longing were unleashed, at last, and she felt she might collapse beneath the delicious weight of her relief.

His mouth moved to take hers. She saw stars as his lips pulled and teased at her own, his thumb brushing her eyelashes as he worked to open her to him. The kiss was slow and measured and lovely; he took his time seducing her. He kissed her carefully, as he always did, though tonight she sensed a humming tension in his touch, as if he was struggling to hold back, struggling not to press for more.

He bit her bottom lip. Shocked, delighted, she drew a breath; Henry dove into her mouth, his tongue stroking, demanding, and she rose to meet him, her hands sliding up his chest, cupping his neck.

He took; she gave. She wanted him to take more.

The wine—or maybe it was his hands, the velvet glide of his mouth—ignited her every sense, and behind her closed lids she lost herself in her desire. The feel of his breath on her skin; his scent, now musky with lust; the calloused pads of his fingers, and the delicious weight of his body pressed against hers; the sound of her heart in her ears—she lost herself in all these things. She'd waited so long to get lost like this.

His lips slid back to her jaw, trailing one long, breathless kiss down the slope of her neck.

"Henry," she breathed.

"Say it again," he panted against her skin. "My name. Say it."

"Henry." He nipped at her throat with his teeth. She thought she might faint.

He ducked his head, and his mouth and his hands moved down, down. His first finger hooked into the sleeve of her gown, pushed it off her shoulder; he did the same with the other sleeve. And then his finger was moving just inside the neckline of her bodice, digging past her stays and chemise to brush the hardened points of her nipples.

Caroline sucked a breath through her teeth as heat sliced between her legs. Henry was coaxing one breast over the edge of her bodice; it spilled into his hand, eager, firm with desire. Nipple met with hardened palm; his skin at once chafed and aroused.

He was pulling down her bodice now, tugging at one breast with his teeth as he freed the other from her stays. She arched against him; her sex throbbed with the need for more, more, always more.

While his mouth teased and stroked, his hands moved down her belly, to her legs, her ankles. Gently he removed one slipper, then the other; they fell with a soft clatter to the floor.

Henry grasped the hem of her gown and pulled it over her

•

knees, his hands gliding up her thighs, thumbs trailing along the inside of her pantalets; *oh, oh, God, he wasn't—he wouldn't—*

He took them off, slowly, patiently, the fabric sighing against her skin as he slid them down her legs; he took off her stockings, too, fingers trailing down her calves, her feet.

He gave her nipple one last bite.

And then he was coaxing one leg, and the other, over the arms of the chair, her knees bent. He pushed her skirts up to her waist. She was bare to him.

He fell back on his haunches, his eyes raking hungrily down the length of her body. Henry put his hands on the inside of her thighs. He pushed, and spread her legs wider. He scraped his thumbs along the sensitive skin just outside her sex.

Caroline's head fell against the back of the chair. She could feel his eyes on her, *there*, on that place where her legs met.

"Caroline," he said. "Look at me."

With some effort she opened her eyes. He looked at her with intensity, his eye sharp, glistening with desire.

"Tell me what you like," he said. "And what you don't."

"All right," she whispered.

His left hand traveled up her torso to cup her breast. He flicked his thumb across the painfully aroused knot of her nipple. Sensation shot through her sex; she cried out. Henry's lips curled into a satisfied half grin.

With his right hand he parted her, fingers tickling her damp curls. And then slowly, languorously, he drew his first two fingers up the length of her slit, tracing the slick curvature of her lips. The tip of his middle finger brushed against the bead at the top of her sex—the very center of all this extraordinary pleasure.

Her eyes clamped shut and her body tensed.

He circled that finger over the bead once, twice, three times. In the space of a single heartbeat she was on the verge of completion.

"Not yet," Henry breathed. "Wait for me, Caroline."

And then those two fingers slipped inside her. Her sex stretched and pulsed around them; she felt full, and incredibly aroused. The heel of his palm pressed up against her flesh, wet and swollen with need.

He pulled his fingers out; slid them back in, more easily this time. She felt another kind of rise inside her belly, this one different from that which swelled at the top of her sex, and yet very much the same. A pulsing, a pressing hunger.

"Do you like that?" he asked.

"Yes," she moaned, opening her eyes. "Heavens, yes."

She watched as he bent his head and, with his fingers still inside her, pressed a kiss to the bead where her lips met. She arched against him, her pleasure now an agony. Watching him kiss her, his lips pressing into her flesh, aroused her yet more.

He turned his wrist, fingers rotating inside her so that his palm faced down. He bent his head lower, his tongue tracing lazy circles of fire at the top of her sex, his fingers moving in and out, in and out, faster now.

Her legs stiffened; she braced herself for the fall.

"Henry, it's happening—soon—I can't wait much longer—"

"Wait."

He pulled away, removing his fingers, his mouth, looking up to meet her eyes. This retreat, it was swift, and beyond devastating. Her entire being pulsed with unrelenting need. She was so close. So very close—

"Why?" she panted. "Please, Henry, I cannot bear it!"

Henry grasped her by the thighs, his enormous hands spanning the width of each of her hips; with a savage tug he pulled her toward him, her back and head falling onto the seat of the chair as her buttocks, now bare, fell into his waiting palms.

Before she could protest, he bent his neck and buried his face in her sex, his tongue moving in and around and back inside her, nicking, caressing.

"Do you like this?" he murmured.

She moaned her reply.

He pressed his lips to the tip of her sex, tongue circling, slow, patient circles, *dear God, oh God*—

Caroline surrendered to the blinding beat of her orgasm, the muscles in her legs clenching as wave after wave of immaculate pleasure coursed through her. Her breathing was ragged; her heart pounded an unsteady beat inside her chest as she gritted her teeth and bore a completion so intense, so powerful, it left her feeling hollowed out, eviscerated.

Henry continued to kiss her, gently, as the throbbing of her sex subsided.

The beat slowed; she came back to her body, heavy, slick with sweat. For a moment she wondered if she would ever be able to move again.

And then she wondered why she'd never felt such release by herself. She could never replicate the magic of Henry's fingers, his mouth. It was the work of a master.

He looked up from between her legs. His lips glistened with her arousal. He made no move to wipe it away.

Again that half grin. The dimple puckered inside his cheek. "Did you like that?"

"Hated it," Caroline said, grinning back.

And then she was sitting up and taking him by the collar and pressing her lips against his. She could taste the salty musk of her body on his mouth. He kneeled between her legs, his hands on her thighs as Caroline kissed him, hard. He laughed against her mouth. Her body pulsed back to life even has the dim remnants of her completion still weighed down her limbs.

She felt wild. She felt a little dizzy. (Was it the wine? The soaring orgasm? The dimple?) She felt like *more*.

Henry took her face in her hands and pulled away, resting his forehead against hers. He was breathing hard; she loved—*loved*—the smell of his skin.

She tried to think about her pride. About Woodstock and his threat. About her brother, that scalawag thief, and about the missing diamond. Her freedom, her carefully mended heart, the loneliness she'd endured. She tried to think about the bitter past.

But it was the swell of the present that inundated her every thought, her every sense. These hours she spent with Henry went too quickly, and she didn't want to miss a thing. She had a feeling they did not have many hours left. Hours like these, anyway.

"You know," he murmured, "I've been waiting to do that to you for years."

She wanted to say yes, yes, I've been waiting, too. But what she said was, "More wine?" and he was grinning, and shaking his head, and pressing his lips to hers.

Twenty-nine

—— ✦ ——

Henry knew he should stop.
Only he couldn't.

Call it the satisfaction of a job well done (she still looked dazed, minutes after the fact), call it a bottle and a half of juicy Bordeaux, call it what you wanted, but Henry couldn't stop kissing her if Old Boney himself were pointing a pistol at his head, threatening to invade England if he didn't let her go.

Henry unleashed years of pent-up longing upon her body. He held nothing back. What he couldn't say aloud, he said with his hands and his mouth. Foolishly he imagined she touched him with the same intent, the same ferocity of feeling.

Foolish, because he forfeited any claim to her affection when he left her twelve years ago. Caroline was passionate, yes; but how could she love him after what he'd done?

Pain sliced through his leg. His grin flattened into a grimace. He'd missed her, God had he missed her, and he'd missed so much. A baby, the birth of his daughter. Caroline had borne the weight of that grief alone. He couldn't imagine the pain.

He'd hurt her.

But she was offering herself to him, freely. He kissed her, and she kissed him back, hungrily, and he knew that if he lifted her in his arms and took her to the bed, she would not protest. Tomorrow she would regret it. A glorious orgasm was one thing; making love quite another, considering all the grief it had caused her when they'd done it last. She'd be hurting all over again, and it would be his fault.

He didn't want to hurt her anymore.

"Henry," she was saying against his lips, "are you all right?"

He pulled away, grasping her thighs in his hands as he struggled to catch his breath. His body screamed at the loss of her embrace.

But it didn't matter. By virtue of her attachment to him, Caroline's life was at risk. She'd became part of his underworld, a world of devils, daggers, and death.

He hated himself for dragging her down. For sullying her loveliness with his sordid past.

And now that the diamond was gone—what in hell was he to do when Woodstock inevitably returned?

Henry tugged a hand through his hair.

"Is it—is it something I did?" Caroline asked. "Did I, um, bite you, or . . . or something?"

Henry let out a short breath through his nose and shook his head. "You were—are—Caroline, you're perfect. I'm so hard, I'll knock over this chair if I try to get up."

The seductive curve of her brow shot up. "Now you're just bragging."

He looked up. Met her eyes. They were soft with satiation, a little tired. In the low light of the fire, their color was depthless. His heart clenched.

I am so in love with you, he wanted to say.

"Is it your leg? I didn't know you could bend it like that."

Henry looked down at his right leg, bent at the knee, just like his left. Except it *couldn't* bend at the knee, the right leg. Or at least it hadn't since it'd been pinned to the poop deck by a fallen mainmast some ten years ago.

He glanced back up at Caroline. Wisps of her dark hair had struggled free of their pins and surrounded her face in a soft halo, burnished gold by the fire.

Reaching up with his right hand, he cupped her face and trailed his thumb across her chin, idly.

Her eyes lit with surprise; her mouth fell open. He pressed

his thumb to her lips, closing them. His cock leapt; it was enormously erotic, the smooth softness of her lips against the pad of this thumb. He wanted her.

He would have to wait.

"I'm sorry, Caroline. Sorry for hurting you like I did. For involving you in this mess."

Her face tensed, like she was peering over the edge of a precipice. "You left behind everything you loved for me."

"I left you," he said savagely. "And our daughter. There is nothing romantic about that. If you hadn't met me—if we hadn't married—none of this would have happened to you."

Caroline drew back. "But it happened. And it happened because—"

"Because I am in love with you."

There it was. The truth. What he should've told her the moment he mauled her in Hope's ballroom those few weeks ago.

A peculiar, high-pitched ringing filled his ears; his clothes felt clammy against his skin; his heart beat loudly in his throat. All this while he waited for her reaction. He guessed she would slap him; he deserved it. But he wanted her to smile, to say it back, to kiss him.

Caroline did none of these things. He watched with rising panic as her gaze moved away from his face, and her body moved away from his. She leaned back, slowly tugging her bodice over her breasts, hooking the sleeves of her gown back onto her shoulders. Her eyes were wet and still, as if she were in a daze.

"Please," he said. "Please, Caroline, say something."

"Henry," she said.

"I'm sorry. I didn't mean to tell you. Like this. At all."

"I wasn't expecting. . . ."

"Of course you weren't." Henry looked at the floor. He scoffed. "Who in their right mind would?"

Her hands stilled. "Henry," she said softly. "I did not know you mourned your past as I have mourned mine. I thought—I don't know what I thought. But at some point I had to let you go. It hurt too much. I never heard from you. No one heard from you. And now I know how you've been hurting, too, and remembering, and feeling the way you do."

Caroline met his eye. "I'm tempted. So tempted, Henry, I am, to let you back in. To care the way I cared once. But never mind my brother, or how we're going to get back the French Blue. You have a duty to England. You're leaving again, you said yourself you're going back to Paris. I can't—I've worked so hard to rebuild myself, my life—"

"I know."

"Why didn't you tell me this before? Didn't you trust me?"

He dug a hand into his hair. "Of course I trust you, Caroline. I just—like you said, I'm leaving, I have to leave, and I didn't know if the truth would help you, or if it'd just be best to leave you be . . ."

He inhaled a deep breath through his nose, willing his heart to slow its frantic thudding. It was only fair, her rejection. She owed him nothing. She was a dowager countess, for God's sake; she was in possession of a title, a fortune, a freedom only afforded to women of her wealth and status. What the devil would she want with a man like Henry? A man who brought danger to her doorstep?

And she was right. He may have been the third son, but he was the son of a baron nonetheless. He had a duty to Caroline, once, a duty he had forsaken. He would not forsake his duty again.

His leg screamed with pain as he settled himself back into his chair. He swiped the bottle of wine from the floor and took a long, desperate pull, wincing as the wine burned its way down his throat. He could still taste her on his lips.

At least he had been able to give her that, he mused darkly.

A heaviness rolled over his chest. He hadn't admitted it to himself; indeed, he'd denied it time and time again, but up until this moment Henry had been hoping to have her alone, like this, their passion transcending the slights and the questions and the impossibilities. Perhaps he hoped she'd run away with him, to Italy, to India; perhaps he hoped she had known all along, and had kept faith he would return.

But she hadn't.

It crushed him, that truth.

If Henry hadn't felt like flinging himself out the window (and not for his usual soft landing, either), he would've laughed. The irony of it, that he'd started this game of truth, only to be defeated by it, did not escape him.

He felt the heat of Caroline's gaze. He looked up.

"Take me home, Henry. Please."

Thirty

Caroline watched the shadows move across Henry's face. His thoughts, his emotions—she could read them clearly.

Watching him suffer like this was tantamount to torture. But what else could she do? She had nothing left to give him. She'd made a promise to herself, and even though it hurt—it *still* hurt, and probably would for a long while yet—to refuse him, it was the right choice.

Never mind the swirling unease in her belly. She'd made her decision.

But that didn't mean his confession hadn't stirred her blood, that she hadn't been waiting for it on the edge of her seat. The words had been so simple, and in their simplicity lovely. Were they true, those words? Oh, how she'd hoped, and how she'd feared, they were.

He was in love with her.

He'd hurt her once, badly. She could not bear to be hurt again. Caroline had fought, viciously, to mend what he had broken. And he had broken her, whether his intentions were good or not. It had taken years, years she would never get back.

Still. Whether or not his words were true, Henry had said them in good faith. He'd looked her in the eye, he hadn't asked for anything in return, he hadn't taken advantage of her obvious arousal. It hadn't been easy to tell her the truth; she could see it pained him.

They walked back to her brother's house in silence. She was too afraid to talk; she knew she'd burst into tears the moment she tried.

So she was quiet. Henry was, too, until they reached the house.

"Not the back door," he said. "It's late enough that the servants might be stirring. Here, I'll see you up."

With no small effort—Caroline was, after all, painfully clumsy—she managed to climb onto Henry's shoulder. Her window was open to the cool, early morning air; she somersaulted through it, banging her elbow on her escritoire as she landed in a heap on the floor.

A moment later Henry landed noiselessly on his feet beside her.

"You didn't," she panted, accepting the hand he offered her, "have to come up."

He pulled her to his feet. "Last time I was here, a certain sinister marquess had snuck into your rooms." Henry glanced over her shoulder. "I must ensure he has not done so again. A moment, if I may."

Henry ducked into the shadows, reappearing moments later with a sigh of relief.

"No sign of sinister marquesses?" she asked.

"You are safe."

The unspoken words hung in the air between them: *for now.*

Henry took a step closer. For a moment they stood, breathless, half an inch apart. He reached up, as if he might cup her face with his enormous palm. Her body cried out for his touch, cried out when he pulled back, his hand falling to his side.

"I should be going," he said, stepping back. "Notify me if you see anything out of the ordinary?"

"Yes."

"Do you promise? Caroline."

She managed a small smile. "I do."

She watched from the sill as Henry lowered himself to the ground. He turned to the window, head tilted back as he moved to look at her. He managed to trip into a nearby bush, arms flailing in an attempt to regain his balance. He did, and then he met her gaze.

"Good night, Caroline."

The burn in her chest threatened to consume her. "Good night."

Caroline's pulse thumped at the crunch of footsteps on the gravel behind Henry. Before she could warn him off, her brother, William, appeared. His dark hair was a sea of wild points and waves; he wore a rumpled shirt and jacket but no cravat, as if someone had torn off his clothes and he'd had to put them back on without the aid of a valet.

His face was a mask of fury.

Caroline's belly turned inside out. This was not good.

William strode purposefully toward Henry. Without slowing his gait, he pulled back his arm and drove his fist into Henry's jaw.

Thirty-one

---◆---

Caroline's scream filled his head as he recoiled from the blow. Cupping his jaw in his hand, Henry straightened. The salty tang of blood filled his mouth.

Well, then. He hadn't been expecting that. What the devil was the Earl of Harclay doing in the drive at half past four in the morning?

The answer appeared at William's shoulder. Lady Violet, eyes and lips swollen, wrapped her fingers around his elbow as if she might hold him back. He pulled free of her grasp.

Breathing hard, Henry met William's eyes. His face was flushed with rage; his lips, too, were tellingly raw.

Henry would've laughed if his mouth weren't full of blood. The gentleman jewel thief and his mark, falling in love, getting naked. It was like something out of a novel; it was absurd.

So was falling in love with the woman you'd left twelve years ago, Henry knew, but he didn't have time to stew properly over which was the more ridiculous scenario.

Not only had Caroline's brother the earl caught Henry sneaking out of her rooms at dawn, but the diamond was missing, and her life was in danger. He had to act quickly, before the French Blue disappeared for good.

The last thing Henry needed was to be sidelined by a dramatic interlude with his lordship.

"You trespass on my property," the earl ground out. "You harass my sister, despoil her under cover of darkness, while she is under my protection. Tell us, what other secrets have you been keeping?"

Caroline was begging them to stop, stop it, or she'd jump from the window.

Henry replied without looking away from the earl. "I'd catch you if you did. Though I daresay your brother might shoot me in the back before I could reach you."

Blood spilled out onto Henry's fingers. One of his back molars felt loose. God, but that would hurt later.

Harclay scoffed. "I would do it gladly, if it meant getting rid of you."

They traded barbs then, Henry and the earl. Henry called William a rotten, cowardly thief (an admittedly feeble rejoinder, but he was bleeding from the mouth, God damn it); he told some lies about the jewel; and then, without warning, Harclay's eyes widened and his mouth fell open, as if he'd been struck squarely between the brows.

"It was you," he said, jabbing his finger into Henry's chest. "You were the one who informed those damned acrobats that I was the man who hired them. It's all your doing—Hope turning me away at the bank, Violet's kidnapping. It was all *you*."

His voice shook at those last words. The earl was seething with rage.

And so was Henry, suddenly. It wasn't his intention for things to play out the way they did. He needed Caroline to understand that.

Shoving his face into William's, he growled, "It was the only move I had to make, and so I made it. I never meant for Violet to be involved; on my honor, I would never place her in harm's way."

The earl did not appear convinced. Despite the cool morning air, perspiration beaded along his hairline and at his temples. The whites of his eyes were bloodshot. He was enraged.

Henry clenched his teeth at the unwelcome swell of sympathy inside his chest. This wasn't supposed to happen; he wasn't supposed to feel this way about the enemy. Henry should be pulling his fingernails out, or at the very least threatening to.

But in the earl's dogged defense of Violet, Henry recognized his own unrelenting fear for Caroline; fear that his actions, and his mistakes, might haunt them both more than they already had. William, rakehell and despoiler of virgins though he was, was terribly, awfully, irrevocably in love.

And so was Henry. He'd like to think he'd tear any man apart who'd caused Caroline harm, same as William wanted to tear Henry apart now. Only Henry was that man, the one who hurt Caroline. He hurt Violet, too, and for what? He was no closer to finding the diamond, to saving Caroline's life, to negotiating with the French on behalf of England's interests on the Continent.

As usual, Henry had made a muck of things. He understood Harclay's rage, his desire to protect the woman he loved. He knew it, and he lived it.

He did not begrudge the earl his anger.

Still, Henry would do as honor demanded. He may not have Caroline after all this was done, or the concessions he'd worked so hard to squeeze from the French, but by God, he'd protect the honor of the woman he loved.

"Today, at dawn," William said. "Farrow Field, just outside the city. I'm sure you know it well. Choose your second. I shall bring the surgeon."

Henry glanced up at Caroline's window. She had disappeared, the drapes sighing as if she'd just brushed past them. His heart clenched.

Henry turned back to the earl. He bowed. "I accept your challenge."

The plunk of gravel broke out behind them. Henry looked to see Caroline skidding toward him, her slippered feet caught in the hem of her dressing robe; it hung haphazardly off one shoulder, baring the other.

That shoulder. It did something to him, made his limbs sing with longing.

Together she and Violet stepped between the gentlemen.

Caroline spun on her brother. "If you hurt him, Harclay, you'll be as good as dead to me. Do you understand? I'll disown you, shame you, throw you to the wolves."

Henry had never heard Caroline speak like this. Savagely,

the words born at the back of her throat. It made his mouth hurt a little less.

He did not dare imagine her defense of him meant anything. For God's sake, he'd just told her he loved her and she sent him packing. But there was the kiss, the one they'd just shared mere hours ago . . .

The earl said something about Henry not being worthy of her affection. That he was a dog. Henry agreed, though he did not say so. No one was worthy of Caroline.

Brother and sister exchanged heated words. Blessedly, Henry's pulse beat so loud in his ears he could block out most of what they said. He couldn't bear to hear Caroline's defense. He didn't deserve it; while the blame lay squarely with William as to why they all found themselves in this mess, Henry had made one mistake after another, and only made the mess worse.

Never mind that he'd confessed his undying love for Caroline (in a terribly romantic fashion, he hoped) and she'd refused him. Crushed his heart and his soul and whatever was left of his hopes.

No, never mind that.

He half wished Harclay lived up to his reputation as an excellent marksman, and at twenty paces shot Henry dead.

The earl disappeared into the fading night, Lady Violet in tow; she'd called out to Caroline, promising that together they would make things right, but Henry knew better.

He just agreed to a bloody *duel*, for God's sake. If it was to be believed, Henry had never fought a duel before. He'd been too busy extorting Frenchmen and fighting for Harry, England, and St. George. There'd been no time for *duels*.

Until now, that is. He may have never fought a duel, but he knew they usually ended badly.

Caroline could not bear to lose her brother; Henry knew this. As much as he loathed the earl, and wished upon him all the plagues of Egypt, Caroline loved him deeply. He was the only family she had left. Not that Henry ever had a chance with her, but killing her brother in a duel would sever what little affection, friendly or otherwise, Caroline still bore him.

Henry let out a long, low breath, tugging a hand through his hair.

Caroline was looking at her hands. The light around them burned from blue to gray; they had an hour, maybe less, before dawn. Her hair hung loose about her shoulders. It was darker than it was when he'd married her; before it had been honey-hued, still brown but shot through with gold. Now it was chestnut, a shade lighter than coffee.

He wished he'd been there to witness the change. Perhaps it had been gradual; he would've noticed it one day in disbelief, the way a parent might look upon a small child and wonder where his baby had gone.

"You did not have to speak on my behalf," Henry said. "But thank you nonetheless."

She looked up. "A *duel*." She said the word as if the very syllables that composed it were as ridiculous as the thing itself. "My brother did always have a flair for the dramatic."

Henry stepped forward. "You need to stay here, Caroline. I'll do what I can, but I don't want you to be there if something . . . happens."

She looked at him for a long moment. He ached with the desire to reach out and take her face in his hands. "You're not going to do anything stupid, Henry, are you?"

"Of course I am. Now go back to bed, and don't you dare follow your brother to Farrow Field. With any luck he'll lock you in your rooms so I don't have to worry."

Caroline crossed her arms, toed at the gravel on the edge of the drive. "But then I'll worry about you."

Oh, God, she was killing him.

"I'll think of something. I can take care of myself," he said. And I can take care of you, too.

He would take care of her. It was all he could do.

When he met his gaze, her eyes brimmed with tears. "You'll think of something," she said. She hesitated, and then she turned and made for the back of the house.

Farrow Field was little more than a stretch of green surrounded on all sides by adolescent oaks. The nascent sun was sharp with late spring, streaming ardently through crisscrossed leaves to blind the men gathered there. The air smelled clean, of dew and grass.

"So," Mr. Moon panted as they made their way back across the field, "have you thought of anything?"

"Not since you asked me two minutes ago, no," Henry said grimly.

"You always work best under pressure. No doubt you'll think of *something* before . . . er, shots are fired. I thought the terms were fair, though twenty paces sounds a bit excessive, doesn't it?"

Henry grunted in reply. Across the field Harclay and his man, Avery, were scrubbing imaginary dust off the earl's gleaming Manton dueling pistol. Henry held its mate in his left hand; it felt beautifully heavy, a heaviness that spoke of expert craftsmanship, of history, of loving use. No doubt the pair cost a fortune; no doubt the earl had gotten his money's worth out of them.

Glancing about the field, Henry breathed a silent sigh of relief. Caroline hadn't come. Thank God she would not be there to see whatever it was that was about to happen. Henry's stomach had roiled itself into a knot; he had a bad feeling about this. About what would come next.

The surgeon seemed to feel the same; on the opposite edge of the field he held his hands clasped at his back and shifted uneasily from one foot to the other. On the ground beside him rested his leather valise of tools and potions.

Mr. Moon cleared his throat. "Are you . . . er . . . going to walk straight, sir? Without the limp, I mean."

Henry started. "I don't know what you're talking about," he said carefully.

Mr. Moon took the pistol from Henry's hand, pretended to inspect it. "I, um, know. I know about your limp, how it comes and goes, depending on your mood. And your aim, it might help to have two steady legs instead of one?"

Henry blinked. And then, after a moment, he clapped Mr. Moon on the shoulder. "You're a much better agent than I give you credit for, Moon."

"Yes, sir," Moon said steadily. "I've been waiting for you to acknowledge that fact for quite some time now. Just because I've a flair for disguise doesn't mean I don't excel at the fundamentals. Sir."

"How long have you known?"

Moon drew a breath and looked up from the pistol. "Oh, forever, I suppose."

Henry bit back a smile. "Do you know why I walk with a limp?"

"Officially? Because you saved Mr. Hope from a falling mainmast." Moon lowered his voice. "Unofficially? Her lady-ship the dowager countess."

"She prefers Caroline."

Now it was Moon's turn to smile. "I know."

"Of course you do."

From across the field came a shout. Henry and Mr. Moon looked up; the earl was ready.

"Moon," Henry murmured, "I've left instructions on the bureau. You're to look after her—find the jewel and trade it to Woodstock—"

"Stop it, sir. Just stop it. I'll have you know I would sell my soul to the devil so that you might win."

Henry laughed, heart rising. "Let's hope the devil does not disappoint us."

"He rarely does." Moon held out the pistol. "I'd wish you luck, sir, but with the devil on our side, I think we both know we won't need it."

Henry took the pistol. "Thank you," he said.

He continued his walk across the field alone. Harclay strode purposefully toward him from the other end of the field. His eyes were like black beads, flat, serious, immune to the potent light slicing through the trees.

Henry's heart began to pound.

Of course he had a plan of last resort. But like all plans of last resort, it was tricky and terrible and not at all what he wanted to do.

Think, he told himself with every step he took. *Think*.

He realized his steps were even. The limp was gone. For now, at least.

Henry met the earl in the middle of the field. Was it stupid to hope the earl's face would break into a smile, that he would embrace Henry and tell him to go forth and make Caroline happy?

Yes, Henry mused, taking in the earl's rageful expression. Definitely stupid.

"I am sorry to have offended you," Henry said. "But I love your sister. I care only for her happiness, her honor."

The earl looked as if he were about to spit. "Caroline deserves better, and you know it."

Avery was calling out to them then, the duel's first commands. Henry turned, his back to the earl's. He bent his arm, bringing the heel of the gun to his shoulder. The knot in his belly tightened.

"Count paces!" Avery cried, and Henry took the first of his twenty steps.

Think. Think. Think.

Oh God, he thought at step thirteen. I'm going to have to resort to my plan of last . . . er, resort.

For a moment he felt as if he were going to be sick.

But this was not the first time Henry thought he was going to die. And so he did what he always did when faced with certain death: he squared his shoulders and drew a deep breath and willed the fear that cluttered his mind to sod off.

Eighteen, nineteen, and then twenty paces.

Think.

Henry turned and raised his pistol. He narrowed his eye, aimed wide.

He pulled the trigger at the same moment Lady Violet stumbled into the line of fire, her admonitions to stop, for the love of God, *stop*, lost in the rising rush of Henry's panic.

Thirty-two

Caroline watched in horror from the far side of the field as the bullet met with Violet's belly. Her forward momentum drew to a sudden, sickening halt, and for a moment she stumbled on her feet, arms flung over her head.

And then she was falling backward, all color draining from her face, features squeezed into a grimace of pain.

Half a heartbeat later a dull *thwack* sounded behind Caroline; she turned to see a raw hole burrowed into the trunk of a nearby tree. She looked across the field.

Henry was looking at her.

His bullet. It had hit a tree.

He'd aimed wide. *Very* wide.

Caroline didn't have time to think about what that meant. She joined the rush on Violet, sprinting beside the surgeon as he lugged his valise across the field.

By the time they reached her, William was already on his knees, holding her against him. Even as he shouted orders and obscenities, he wept, tears plummeting one after the other to the ground like fat raindrops.

A seeping flower of red grew on the bodice of Lady Violet's

gown. She was pale, her lips an unnatural shade of purple; her body was limp in William's arms.

Fear, a violent rush of it, moved through Caroline. If Henry's bullet hit a tree, that meant the shell lodged in Violet's ribs came from William's pistol.

Oh God, she thought. *Oh my God.*

William's shot Violet.

Someone's hands were on Caroline's shoulders, turning her toward him. She looked up into Henry's face, heard his voice as he said her name.

"Caroline," he said. "Caroline, stay here, please, I'll be back directly."

He moved her aside, gently, and then bent to pull William away from Violet. William stood, wiping his face with the heel of his hand as he watched the surgeon kneel beside her.

"Is she going to be all right?" he asked. "Is she going to live?"

Caroline wanted to reach for him, to take him in her arms and hold him until the shaking stopped. But he would only push her away. There would be no consoling him; there would be no consoling anyone who'd shot the woman he loved, perhaps fatally.

The surgeon was calling for William; he returned to Violet's side, and helped administer some sort of potion the surgeon proffered in a glass vial.

"Might I help?" Caroline asked. "I can hold back her hair, or . . . or go and get more help, another surgeon?"

The surgeon waved her away. "Stand back, please, she needs the air."

William was apologizing now, telling Violet that it was going to be all right, that he would make everything all right.

She did not respond; not until her eyes fluttered open, suddenly, and met with William's.

Caroline couldn't be sure, but she thought she heard Violet whisper something.

I hate you, she said. *William, I love you.*

Caroline's eyes blurred with tears.

Violet was still alive a few hours later, barely. William had decamped to her family's Grosvenor Square house; he'd come home to change his shirt and cast up his accounts before returning to her bedside, where Caroline imagined his moods alternated between bitter weeping and drunken stupor.

He'd taken two quarts of their father's best vintage brandy, and not an hour ago sent a note to Caroline, asking for two more.

None of them slept. Caroline longed to send for Henry; he'd escorted her home after the duel, holding both her hands in one of his as she stared out the window, hardly daring to breathe.

When they'd reached Hanover Square, Henry had turned to her. "I'm sorry," he'd said.

"I'm sorry, too," Caroline replied, though she didn't know what, exactly, she was apologizing for.

He ran his thumb across the back of her hand, and then he let her go.

Even now, so many hours later, the skin there still burned with the memory of his touch. She was terrified for Violet, for William. For herself. Surely Woodstock grew impatient, and the diamond was lost, gone forever it seemed. Without the diamond, they had nothing with which to bargain for her life, or the lives of Henry's men.

The terror made her feel lonelier than usual. She would bear it, as she must. But that did not mean she didn't ache for Henry. He would know what to say, how to touch her; he would make her laugh; and he would bring her relief, at least for a little while.

She wanted him, but she knew she could not have him. Not a day ago, he told her he loved her, and she refused him. She was too frightened to risk her heart again, of reliving the devastation and hurt she'd felt after losing him the first time.

No, Henry was not hers to pine over, or to call upon when she felt lonely. He deserved better than that.

But like all stations in life, widowhood brought with it certain benefits, particular challenges. Loneliness was one such challenge. *The* challenge. She'd been lonely for as long as she could remember, but this kind of loneliness was new, and enormous, and eviscerating.

Thirty-three

— ❖ —

Brook Street, Hanover Square
That Night

The light in Caroline's window dimmed, and then went out
altogether.

Sidled up at his perch beside the wrought iron gate, Henry
tossed aside the smooth-edged pebble he'd been rolling
between his thumb and forefinger. He let out a sigh.

Caroline was safe, for one more night, at least.

And now she was asleep.

It was late, somewhere between one and two in the morning. He wondered what had kept her up. News about Violet,
the French Blue? That dreadful book she'd been reading?

Henry knew it was foolish to wish he was the one to keep her
awake. Why would Caroline waste her time thinking about him?

Still he wished it. With his whole being, he wished it.
Knowing she was thinking about Henry made his own sleep-
lessness, the incessant winding of his thoughts over and
around and about her, less pitiful. Less painful.

He took one last sweep of Harclay's property. No sign of

Woodstock, thank God. Lake knew he would come to collect what he'd asked for, soon. He prayed he would have the French Blue to give him. Henry and Moon had torn apart London in the twelve or so hours since the duel, searching for it. With increasing panic, Henry realized seeking out the diamond would prove a far more formidable task than he anticipated.

Digging a hand into the hair at the nape of his neck, Henry gritted his teeth against the heaviness in his chest.

He missed her. He craved her.

He had to see her, if only to make sure she was all right.

He turned back to the window.

H er eyes, sticky with grief and sleep, fluttered open at the soft thud that sounded by the window, then fluttered back shut.

Caroline drew a breath, inhaling a bit of drool along with the air. The carpet felt prickly and hard against her cheek. Her neck hurt, her mouth was unpleasantly dry and thick. He entire body ached; she felt like she'd been beaten from the inside out.

She didn't remember falling asleep on the floor.

There was a quiet rush somewhere above her head, and then she was being lifted into her bed, the ropes groaning in protest as she landed softly on the mattress. She moaned; the bedclothes felt deliciously cool against her skin.

Again her eyes opened. She could not see much; only an enormous shadow, the otherworldly luminescence of a single pale eye that pierced the darkness like a moon in miniature.

"Henry," she whispered.

He pressed a kiss into her cheek. "Go back to sleep, love," he said.

"Stay with me," she whispered.

She struggled to keep her eyes open; she was weary with exhaustion. She turned onto her side, eyes closing once more. Above her came the breathy sigh of a sheet, and a moment later it drifted down upon her, its touch light, lingering.

The mattress dipped; she heard Henry's boots fall to the floor, quietly. A rustle of bedclothes beside her, the sound of him letting a long breath out through his nose.

And then he was gathering her to him, curling her body

into the warm curve of his own. His arm wrapped about her
waist and his nose grazed the back of her neck, breath warm
on her skin. She relaxed against him, falling further from consciousness with each beat of his heart against her back.

She smelled lemon, and laundry, spice.

She fell asleep.

When she woke, the light streaming through her window
was pale gray, soft with the first hint of sun. The air
inside the room was already warm; she felt sticky at her temples and about the nape of her neck.

Caroline opened her eyes, looked across the room.

Henry was there by the window, leaning against the wall.
His shirt was undone, revealing a deep V of skin and freckles
and muscle. She'd never seen his chest in the light. So many
freckles. She liked them, and wanted to trace their pattern
with the tips of her fingers.

She was awake, suddenly.

His arms were crossed about his chest and his good leg was
bent at the knee, the sole of his stockinged foot pressed to the
wall. She recognized this posture from their fateful afternoon
stroll through Hyde Park, just before they'd gone for that swim
in the Serpentine. With a little thrill, she realized it was one of
the many things that made Henry *Henry*, much like the way
he dug his fingers into the hair at the back of his neck, or
hooked stray strands behind his ears; like that half smile, the
one he used liberally, knowing it laid waste to every female in
a fifty-foot vicinity.

She was beginning to know him all over again.

In that moment she felt, strangely, as if they'd never been
apart. She understood the romance of it, of knowing someone
so well, of that someone knowing you.

She wanted, badly, to get lost in the romance, to allow herself to feel the heady loveliness of all this *knowing*. She met
Henry's eye. He was looking at her the way he was always
looking at her. Softly, with feeling.

Caroline looked away.

"How is Lady Violet?" Henry asked. "And your brother?"

"Not well," Caroline bit her lip. "And not well."

From the corner of her eye, she watched Henry lean forward. "They need your help more than I do, Caroline. Go to William. He needs you, especially if—"

A beat of uncomfortable silence settled between them. Caroline didn't want to think about what would happen if Violet died. William would never forgive himself; there was no telling what he'd do.

Henry was looking at her, face hard, eyes soft, color creeping over his unshaven jaw. The stubble was dark in this light; it matched the purple thumbprint beneath his eye. He was exhausted.

She ran her tongue over her teeth. She wished she had some water.

"You aimed wide," she said. "You were going to let William win. You were going to let him kill you."

He returned her gaze steadily. "Doesn't matter now, does it?"

"Oh, for God's sake, Henry. You're no martyr. Of course it matters. What about the lives of all those men you're meant to save? What about the jewel? What about our plot to defeat Woodstock? We couldn't do any of it without you."

"I wasn't going to kill your brother, no matter how much I wanted to. You love him. Losing him would destroy you, I know it would. And I've already destroyed you once. I'm not going to do it again."

Swallowing for what felt like the hundredth time, Caroline resisted the impulse to dash across the room and leap into his lap and kiss him until tomorrow.

He's not yours, she reminded herself. You refused him; you have your widowhood, and your scalawag brother, and your gardens. You made your choice. You cannot go back now.

Caroline plucked at a furred thread in the sheet spread out across her lap, watching as she made a big hole out of a tiny one. Henry sat on the edge of the bed; the mattress ducked and jolted as he tugged a boot up his leg. She snuck a glance; the fabric of his shirt stretched across his shoulders. Enormous shoulders.

"You stayed," she said after a beat.

He stilled. "You asked."

"I didn't ask you to come up," she said.

His foot fell with a muted clap to the floor. He placed his

hands on his thighs, thumbs pointing toward his hips with arms akimbo.

Hanging his head, Henry said, "Can't exactly trust a man like Woodstock to keep his word. He'd touch you just to spite me. So I had to see that you were all right up here. Alone."

"Besides the usual visit from my lover, he usually comes once a week—"

Henry's head shot up.

"Joking! Just a joke."

"Not funny." Henry turned to look at her. "What do you want me to say, Caroline? That yes, I meant to ensure your safety, but mostly I just wanted to see you? That after the duel I knew I wouldn't sleep, and I was looking for comfort, and I didn't know where else to go?" He scoffed. "That man—the man who would say these things—I don't want you to pity him."

I don't pity him, she wanted to say. I love him.

I love him.

But she didn't say those words. She couldn't get them past the tightness in her throat, the fear that shot through her.

Oh, God, she thought. It's happened, the thing I swore never would. I'm in love with Henry Beaton Lake. Again.

His gaze was earnest, and lovely. She couldn't bear it; she looked away. She looked down at his legs.

"Here," she said, sliding across the bed. "Let me help you with the other boot. It's your bad leg, isn't it?"

Henry stiffened as Caroline sat beside him. She was aware, suddenly, just how transparent her chemise was. She pulled the neckline up, toward her chin.

"Does it hurt today?"

"Yes," he said. "It was getting better, and then . . . well."

"You'll let me know if I need to stop?"

Henry dipped his head, a nod. She leaned over him and reached for the boot, its leather stiff, as if it had learned to stand at attention from the solider who wore it.

Henry set his hands on the mattress behind him. As he lifted his leg he drew a small, short breath through his teeth. Caroline guided the boot over his foot and up his calf. The muscles there were taut, flexing against his plain cotton stockings. She resisted the urge to run her thumb along the ridge between his shin bone and muscle.

Caroline grasped the top of the boot with both hands and gave it one last tug.

"There," she said. "All right?"

Her hands lingered on the lip of his boot, right below his knee. She shouldn't be touching him like this; in fact, she should be running for the proverbial hills, to the safety and comfort of her uneventful widowhood.

Instead her fingers slipped into the bottom hem of his breeches. She had to know, suddenly. She wanted to know all of him. The good, the bad, the scarred parts, and the whole ones.

"Caroline," he said.

"Tell me if I need to stop," she repeated.

She hooked her thumb into the brass buttons that fastened the outer seam of his breeches, working each one free.

"Caroline," he said again, a warning. But he did not stop her. She braced herself for what she was about to see.

She slid the fabric up, revealing the ball of his knee. The skin was intimately pale there, there were no freckles, and a smattering of wiry red hair sprung out from beneath the edge of his breeches.

There was no scar. No misshapen bones, or gruesome contortions. Just a knee—an enormous knee, she wouldn't be able to cover it with both hands—the flesh stretched smoothly over the pear of his kneecap.

Caroline inched the breeches farther up his thigh. They wouldn't go far; the muscles there were monstrous. Still no scars, no signs of the injury he'd suffered a decade ago.

Maybe time had been kind to him, for once, and erased the physical evidence. Maybe the damage was internal, a fracture or sprain that never healed properly.

Maybe it was none of those things. She couldn't begin to guess how Henry bore his grief, his relentless regret, all these years. If she'd learned anything, Caroline understood everyone had his own way of coping. She had her garden; perhaps Henry had his knee.

She looked up to his eye patch; the leather thong dug into the skin of his temple. She met his eye. It appeared small with hurt, an edge of fear. A little wet.

"Caroline." He was pleading now.

Leaning over him, she held back his breeches and pressed her lips to his knee, gently.

After a moment, she straightened and rolled the fabric back down to the top of his shin, coaxing each button through its embroidered hole. She tucked the breeches into his boots.

"I hope it feels better," she said.

He inhaled, mouth opening as if he were about to speak.

She leaned in and kissed him on the lips. The ache in her chest heightened. Henry kissed her back, watching her watching him. It was chaste, this kiss, compared to the others they'd shared. His eyelashes fluttered against hers. They did not close their eyes.

He was the one to pull away. He stood and walked softly toward the window. Caroline followed him.

"Thank you," he said, holding his mouth in his hand.

They both turned to the window.

There, far below, a familiar face looked up to them, mouth curled evilly into a smile.

"Good morning, lovers," the Marquess of Woodstock drawled. "Such luck, Mr. Lake, that you are here to see me claim my prize!"

A figure, cloaked in black, struggled in the circle of Woodstock's arm. Caroline narrowed her eyes to get a better look, but in that moment, Woodstock pulled back the figure's hood, revealing a tumble of vibrantly red hair.

Fake hair.

A wig.

"Come down now, the both of you," Woodstock said, holding a pistol to the figure's head. "I would so hate to harm your friend Mr. Moon."

Thirty-four

———— ✦ ————

I n the alley that ran along the length of the house, Caroline swayed on her feet beside Henry. She closed her eyes; her bottom lip trembled.

"Keep breathing, Caroline," Henry murmured in her ear, tucking her behind him. "It's going to be all right. There, that's it, that's better."

Henry's fingers curled into fists at his sides. He cursed, silently, though no less fluidly than he would have aloud.

His own pistol lay at his feet. He should have shot Woodstock the moment he saw him. He should have saved Caroline while he had the chance. For God's sake, he was better than this; a better agent, a better husband.

Could he call himself that, her husband? Or had he forfeited that honor to his old friend Osbourne?

His gaze moved to Woodstock's tall, lanky figure. That smile of his—Henry wanted to tear it off his face.

Mr. Moon squirmed against his grasp; Woodstock had his arm wrapped around his neck, the pistol pressing into the soft flesh of Moon's cheek, dimpling the skin there.

"Are you all right, Moon?" Henry said. He kept his voice low; the house would be stirring soon. He did not have much time.

"A bit brassed off with this one," Moon stuttered. "Otherwise right as rain, sir."

Woodstock's grin deepened. "My patience has worn thin. You can have him back, Mr. Lake, once you give me the lady. Or I suppose I could kill them both, if you do not cooperate." He raised his eyes, peeked over Henry's shoulder. "Hello, darling. What fun we shall have together!"

Behind him, Caroline stiffened. He reached behind and pulled her against him. She was shaking.

Henry glared at Woodstock. "I need more time. The French Blue—we're close—"

"Are you?"

Again Caroline shook. Again Henry felt as if he'd been stabbed through the heart. He'd let her go once. He'd rather be dead than let her go again, and to this man.

Woodstock tightened his grip on Moon; Moon was trying, valiantly, to breathe.

"Stop it," Henry growled, stepping forward.

Again Woodstock clucked his tongue. "I'll stop when I have the diamond. Where is it? I have given you several days to look."

"Give me another," Henry said steadily. "When I find it, it's yours. I swear to you. I've my best men on the case."

"Men like this one?"

Moon made a small wheezing sound, like air rushing out of a punctured bellows.

"*Stop it*," Henry repeated. "I need more time. You've chased after me for twelve bloody years. What's another few days?"

"I've waited long enough." Woodstock's tone turned savage. "Give her to me."

Henry's heart punched against his breastbone. *Never, never, never.* "Don't be a fool, Woodstock. You know as well as I do the power the French Blue buys you. Old Boney's lusted after it for years. You could use it to change the course of the war. Surely that's worth more to you than she is."

Woodstock inhaled a long breath through his nose as he surveyed Henry from across the predawn gloom.

My God, thought Henry. He's going to do it. He's going to give me more time.

"No," Woodstock said at last. "I don't think so, Mr. Lake."

The marquess released the safety on his pistol. He dug it so far into Moon's cheek the poor man gurgled—a choked scream. Henry could see the whites of his eyes. Behind him, Caroline was shaking so hard it was a miracle she remained upright.

"Wait!" Henry cried. His mind raced. "Wait, please. The French have already contacted me. What if I . . . what if I put them in touch with you? They offered a handsome sum—and more—for the jewel. Once it's in your hands it will be easy to trade. You're bored here, Woodstock, and you know it. You're not meant for civilian life. The diamond is your way back in."

Woodstock grinned. "We know each other well. Don't we, Mr. Lake?"

"Unfortunately," Henry replied. "Remember our bargain. It works out in your favor."

The marquess gave Henry another long, searching look. "Very well," he said, pulling back his pistol. Moon slumped against him in relief. "Although this changes the terms of our 'bargain,' as you so adorably call it. Bring me the French Blue, and I will consider your debt paid. In the meantime, I shall keep your colleague here—Mr. Star, was it?—as a token of your good faith."

Henry clenched his fists. "That's not what we agreed to—"

"I don't care what we agreed to. I keep him until you bring me the diamond. Understood?"

Lake eyed Mr. Moon. Moon returned his gaze steadily. *Go,* he mouthed. *Go.*

Henry hated to leave him. But he had no choice.

"Fine," Henry said. "You can expect to hear from me presently."

"Wonderful. I look forward to seeing you both. Good evening, Mr. Lake, Lady Osbourne." He bowed.

Rising, he stepped forward and reached past Henry for Caroline's hand, bringing it to his lips. "Thank you, darling, for a marvelous interlude. I cannot wait to do it again."

Caroline did not cower from his touch, though Henry could feel the tremors that racked her body.

With a small flourish, Woodstock turned and, tugging Moon beside him, disappeared down the lane.

All at once, Henry was turning Caroline to him and taking her face in his hands and whispering his apologies.

Caroline scoffed as she looked down at her bare feet. "Poor Mr. Moon. D'you think Woodstock—do you think he'll hurt him?"

Henry bit his lip. "I'll find the diamond, Caroline. I'll make this right. You needn't worry."

"Of course I need to worry. Between you and William, I haven't got time to do anything else." She looked up. Her eyelashes were wet, clumped together, making them appear darker than usual. "What are we going to do?"

"*We* aren't going to do anything," he replied. "I've a few tricks up my sleeve. These kinds of things always work themselves out at the eleventh hour."

The lies came easily. He had no idea what he would do. He'd searched everywhere for the diamond. He would redouble his efforts, but with Moon gone it was practically futile.

Things were looking very bad indeed.

The neck of Caroline's gown slipped; he saw the remnants of bruises, left by Woodstock not long ago.

For a moment a wash of fury blurred his vision.

"Your neck," he said.

"It's all right," Caroline whispered.

"No," Henry said savagely. "No, Caroline, it's not all right. I'll never forgive myself—"

"Please, Henry." Caroline leaned her head against her chest and sighed. "Enough. Enough of everything, for now, at least. Just hold me for a moment, would you?"

Henry blinked. This—this was more than he ever hoped for, a chance to hold in his arms the only thing he'd ever wanted.

Her. Caroline.

He dug one hand into the hair at the back of her head, careful not to touch her neck; the other he placed on the small of her back. With both hands he pressed her against him, resting his chin on the top of her head.

Henry was so tempted to kiss her.

He didn't.

Caroline melted against him, her arms drawn up against his chest. She was breathing deeply, her nose against his shirt as if she were as desperate for his scent as he was for hers.

Which she wasn't, of course, but he could pretend, for a moment at least, that she might be.

The terrible ache in his leg lessened. Not for the first time since he'd been back in England did he wish he had both eyes. There was too much loveliness here, too much goodness to take in with one eye alone.

When at last Caroline pulled away, Henry pasted a smile on his face. He told her he would find the diamond, and save Moon, and fix everything. He asked several times if she was all right, if she needed anything.

Mostly if she needed him to stay.

She didn't.

He walked her to her window. He watched her clasped hands fidget and fight with one another. She rolled her lips between her teeth.

Henry reached for her, sliding his hand into the hair at her temple. He bent his neck and pressed his lips to the place where her forehead met scalp.

"Leave this to me, Caroline," he said. "Heavens, I am one of His Majesty's most decorated agents. Surely in the face of such genius Woodstock doesn't stand a chance."

"Genius," Caroline scoffed. "I wouldn't go *that* far."

Thirty-five

Caroline handed her hat and gloves to Avery and covered her face with her hands, fingers finding purchase in her eye sockets, sore from lack of sleep.

She hadn't slept in what felt like forever. Not since Woodstock had appeared beneath her window that fateful morning some days ago, pistol in Mr. Moon's cheek.

"Everything all right, m'lady?"

She let out a little moan.

"Right, then," Avery said crisply. "I'll have tea brought up to the drawing room."

"Thank you, that sounds lovely," she murmured, sighing. "Any word from my brother?"

Avery dipped his head, lowered his voice. "He returned home this morning, and has been locked away in his study ever since. He won't see anyone."

"Has he eaten?"

"I'm afraid not, m'lady."

Caroline sighed again. Lady Violet regained consciousness a few days ago; the first thing she had done was send William away, apparently with strict instructions to leave her be.

While Caroline couldn't blame the poor girl—William *had* shot her in the midst of an immensely foolish duel—her heart ached for her brother. Yes, he could be a careless cad, and yes, he could only blame himself for the terrible position in which he now found himself.

But he was in love, with a woman he'd irreparably wronged, with a woman who would not have him.

Caroline could relate to both sides of that equation. She wouldn't wish either on anyone, even her rakehell of a brother.

"I'll see what I can do," Caroline said. "Perhaps I might convince him to take tea with me."

Avery bowed, and disappeared down the hall.

Caroline followed him, stopping before the study's carved oak door. She leaned her ear to the wood; nothing, not so much as the scratch of a quill against paper.

She knocked, softly. "William? William, are you there? I'm taking tea, I thought you might like to join me."

"Later!" came the clipped reply.

"William," she tried again. "You need to eat. Please—"

"Later!"

Caroline jumped at his shout.

Well, then. She'd be taking tea alone.

The silence inside the drawing room was visceral thing, enormous and alive, combing its fingers through the shiny motes of dust floating before the windows. Caroline stirred sugar into her tea, waited for it to cool.

And then she burst into tears.

She'd had no word from Henry. Which meant the diamond was still missing, and Mr. Moon still a hostage. She hoped and prayed Woodstock did not hurt him. That he was alive and well.

Caroline prayed she would still be alive when all was said and done.

It hurt, Henry's absence, his silence. She thought about him day and night. She craved him, so often and so ardently she swore she could smell him, his scent invading her chambers at night.

Like a lovesick Juliet she waited at her window, offering up a series of increasingly desperate prayers that he might gallantly call out to her from below, and climb into her room and tell her he'd found the diamond and defeated Woodstock and turned the tide of the war in England's favor.

Alas, her warrior Romeo did not appear. She wondered where he was, who he was with. If he was getting any closer to the diamond, any closer than she was.

Despite Henry's admonishments to keep away, she searched high and low for the stone. She spent her days visiting pawnbrokers (discreetly, of course), jewelers' shops, even a gambling hell or two.

Caroline would come home exhausted and discouraged, as she had today. As far as she could tell, the trail had gone cold. The diamond was lost.

She did not like to think about what that meant for Henry, or Moon. For her brother, for Violet, for Thomas Hope.

Which she did now, and which made her cry harder.

She was about to sink into rising tide of her self-pity when the drawing room door swung open, slamming against the far wall.

Caroline jumped, spilling scalding-hot tea down the front of her gown. She looked up to see William, his hair and cravat tragically askew, stalking toward her.

His face was lit with—wait, was that *joy*?

Quickly she wiped her eyes, ignoring the sting of the hot tea seeping against her skin.

"I've found it!" William lifted her from the settee and squeezed her so hard she thought her eyeballs might pop out of her head. "The diamond! Caroline, I've found the diamond! And I've got a plan to get it back."

Caroline blinked. For a moment her heart stopped beating altogether; her lungs burned.

"Is that," she wheezed, "what you were doing, in your study?"

William set her down, shoving a sheaf of papers into her hand. "It's taken me all morning and afternoon to devise it. You see, Avery uncovered a bit of gossip about old Louis, the one who's calling himself king now, that he likes to watch women—"

"Wait," Caroline said, blinking. "King Louis? As in—?"

"Yes, *that* King Louis. He's the seventeenth's younger brother, the one who lost his head." William waved away Caroline's questions. "Anyway, you know he's in exile here in England, and I saw him last night, at White's, and I overheard him talking about the diamond. He knows where it is!"

Caroline peered dubiously at her wild-haired brother. Dark stubble covered his chin and cheeks. "Are you sure that's what you heard? You'll have to forgive my assumption, dear brother, but you haven't been exactly of sound mind these past days. An exiled would-be king, one you found at White's, willing to spew his secrets in public? Sounds rather . . . interesting."

"Interesting?"

Caroline coughed. "Farfetched."

William clapped a hand to his forehead and rolled his eyes, a gesture Caroline was quite familiar with from their days in the schoolroom. William still labored, sadly, under the delusion that he was the cleverer of the Townshend children.

Caroline let it go, just this once.

"An earl in need of neither fortune nor fame, stealing a fifty-carat diamond in front of five hundred members of the beau monde—that, dear sister, is farfetched."

"Yes," Caroline said. "But that's you."

Even as William grinned, his dark eyes were serious. He took both her hands in his, crumpling the pages in her hand. "I understand I do not deserve your trust, Caroline—"

"You don't. You still haven't apologized, you know, for almost killing my—er—Mr. Lake."

"I know." The grin devolved into a smirk. "But that apology is going to take hours, days even, and we haven't the time. Hope's fortunes fall by the minute, as do Lady Violet's. I won't see her fall into penury on my behalf. Not after . . . well, everything that I've done. If all goes to plan, I'll have the gem back in Hope's pocket by week's end."

Caroline's heart leapt into her throat. *By week's end.* That meant Henry still had a fighting chance, that their plot to defeat Woodstock might actually work.

For the first time in what seemed an eternity, the warmth of hope peeked around the great mass of her frustration and hurt. All this time she'd ssumed the worst, and had held little faith that either she or Henry would meet with a happy ending.

And now there was a chance that Henry might, if all went well, and Woodstock was bested. He could trade the diamond to the French, and turn the tide of the war.

She ignored the stab of sorrow that pierced this sudden onslaught of relief. Henry's happy ending meant he would successfully complete his assignment, and go back to Paris to continue his work there. Henry would leave London, and Caroline.

It was becoming more difficult to deny the deep and lovely and frightening things she felt for him. Like how she would miss him all over again, when he was gone.

But she would deny them as long as she could, for in admitting these feelings, Caroline would expose herself to the eviscerating heartache of losing him once more. She would become a traitor to herself, to everything she had worked for, to every promise she had made.

There was no future to be had with Henry Beaton Lake. They each had chosen their paths. It was too late to change course now. Not after all that had happened.

But that didn't mean she couldn't help him find the diamond, and in so doing outwit Woodstock, and use the jewel instead to save the lives of Henry's fellow soldiers, Mr. Moon included. It was what she owed him, for keeping faith in her all these years, for aiming wide when William did anything but.

And so Caroline untangled herself from William's grasp and looked down at the pages, scattered with diagrams, timetables, maps. "Tell me more about this plan," she said. "Where is it, the French Blue?"

"Some jeweler or another has it—Eliason, that's what Louis called him. Must've bought the diamond off the acrobats. Anyway. The king and his brother, the Comte d'Artois, are to meet him later this week to purchase it."

"Right," she said. "So we follow the king and Artois, and buy it from Eliason ourselves?"

"Buy the French Blue, or steal it."

Caroline arched a brow. "Stealing it once was enough, don't you think? Better we come up with a new trick."

William shrugged. "Perhaps. Either way, old King Louis is going to lead us to the French Blue. After we lure him into a trap and capture him, of course."

"Of course," she replied. "Shall we drug him as well? Tie him up, slap him for good measure?"

She meant it as a joke; this plan as it now stood was nothing if not absurd, but William tapped a finger to his lips, thoughtfully. "Excellent idea, Caroline. We shall indeed."

William pointed to the papers in her hand. "We'll add it to what I have here. Genius, if I don't say so myself. Look, we'll decorate the house in the guise of a—um—house of ill repute, and lure the king there under the pretense of watching some lovely ladies perform, and then we'll drug him . . ."

Thirty-six

———— ✦ ————

Hanover Square, Brook Street
Five Days Later

The Earl of Harclay's plan was as exceedingly absurd in execution as it was on paper.

It was all Henry could do not to roll his eyes as one disaster after another befell their motley crew of players: Violet, looking worse for the wear, and discreetly casting up her accounts in the water closet every quarter hour; Lady Sophia, her cousin, who managed to drug the earl instead of the king, now sobbing quietly in a corner; Thomas Hope, mooning over Sophia as she sobbed; and then there was the earl himself, dressed as Achilles (for God knows what reason) in a breastplate with egregiously erect nipples.

The idea that the French Blue was found, and within his grasp, was the only thing that kept Henry from going mad. That, and Caroline's presence.

Though she was vaguely costumed as some Greek goddess or another, she wore her shimmering pink toga well; her cheeks flushed a matching shade when she met Henry's eye across the room.

Heavens, but she was lovely. He longed to speak with her, if only to ask how she had been, and if she finished that terrible book already.

But what would it do, to ask her these questions, but deepen the agony of their inevitable parting? These past days, as tonight's moment of judgment approached, an increasing sense of dread had beleaguered Henry, and kept him awake at night. There were too many moving parts, too many risks. This would not end well; not for Henry, not for Caroline. Probably not for Mr. Moon, either, poor bastard. And he did not want to frighten her with his feelings of helplessness. It was better if he stayed away, as she had asked him to from that first encounter at Thomas Hope's ball.

Besides, the both of them were kept occupied by the evening's seemingly endless string of ridiculous tragedies. Even as she flitted capably about the room, he could tell by the set of her mouth that she shared in Henry's complete and utter lack of enthusiasm for this nonsensical scheme.

Henry watched her, wishing all the while he could grab her, and together they could steal away into the summer night's velvety warmth.

But he was needed; it was time to move the Bourbon King, Louis XVIII, toward the front door. To say Louis was fat would be like saying the earl's plan was "somewhat flawed": so gross an understatement as to be an outright lie.

This man was *enormous*. His arms and legs stuck out from the bulbous mass of his belly like sticks from a pudding. Holding him at gunpoint—"What?" Henry had asked, releasing the safety on his pistol. "He isn't exactly cooperating, is he?"—made him sweat profusely, his powdered wig sticking to his forehead.

His brother, the Comte d'Artois, was no better. After shoving King Louis into the first of two hired hackneys brought round to the earl's residence—Henry had recruited the drivers from among the most discreet of Mr. Moon's men—the lot of them made for the city. There, using information begrudgingly provided by Louis, they met with Artois at a darkened corner;

the comte held in his pocket the twenty-thousand-pound note he planned to exchange for the French Blue.

Henry coaxed him into the hack beside King Louis, again at gunpoint; despite lacking a kingdom and a country, the royals proved overly familiar with giving orders, rather than taking them. The two of them, Louis and Artois, were like bewigged, blubbering hippopotamuses.

Hippopotamuses in whose meaty hands the fate of all those gathered here rested.

Henry tugged a hand through the hair at the nape of his neck and let out a short, hot breath. Why they didn't entrust the diamond's retrieval to him and Mr. Moon in the first place, he hadn't a clue. It would have been easier, and far more discreet. They would have a chance—a small chance, but a chance nonetheless—of success.

As things stood now, Henry had a better chance of being eaten by Artois than anyone, including the earl, had of retrieving the diamond.

The knot in Henry's belly tightened. He reached up and pounded the roof, signaling the driver.

King Louis swore this jeweler of his—the mysterious Mr. Eliason, the one who apparently had the diamond—was holed up on a ship in the Docklands.

Henry hated the idea of traveling to London Docks, and at darkest night. Never mind the pickpockets and cutthroats that populated the nearby wharves; he feared the Marquess of Woodstock might materialize from the darkness and snatch Caroline so quickly, so silently, that Henry could do naught to stop him.

But Caroline's brother the earl would not be thwarted, even as he was ill with the aftereffects of his accidental poisoning, and so to the docks they went.

The stench rose up like a fog from the Thames as the hackneys approached. By now Henry's heart was clambering up and down his rib cage. If Louis was telling the truth, they were close, very close, to the French Blue. Henry's every worry, every fear, could be erased in a single stroke, but he was not so foolish, nor so hopeful, as to believe that luck was on their side.

Still, even if the jewel was beyond his grasp, that didn't mean he couldn't protect Caroline. She rode in the hackney behind his; the moment they reached their destination, Henry leapt through the door and waited for Caroline to alight, following her closely as they made their way onto the wharf.

"Is everything all right?" she whispered.

"Hardly," he replied. "Stay close."

The blackness was complete here, blurred by the lantern Thomas Hope held at his shoulder. The only sounds were the limp rush of the Thames, the snap and grate of ships in their docks; no one dared make a noise, their footfalls muted. It was humid, the air, and Henry's palm felt clammy against the warm metal of his pistol as he held it in the waistband of his breeches.

King Louis led them to the end of the wharf, before he turned to the small crowd gathered behind him.

"We cannot take all of you," he said in heavily accented English. "Eliason is a greedy man but he is not stupid. If he sees so many coming, he will turn up his tail and run."

Artois nodded, chins quivering in agreement. "Yes, he will run. We will only take two."

Henry's throat seized with rage. He was so close, so *very close*, to the French Blue, and now he was being turned away, told to entrust its retrieval to these idiots.

He had half a mind to leap past the royals and find Eliason's ship himself. He knew the jeweler would use a sloop, something fast and low in the water, probably something old, inconspicuous. It would not be difficult to find. Doubtless Henry could outwit and outsize Eliason, and any goons he employed as security. Lake could bully the jeweler into handing over the diamond; he could have the French Blue in his pocket in a quarter of an hour, maybe less. Free Moon and be done with the whole thing.

But that would mean leaving Caroline.

And Henry wasn't about to do that, not here, not in this godforsaken swampland. Who would defend her, should Woodstock appear out of the ether? Certainly not her brother, as lovesick and half-dead as he was; and Thomas Hope was, well, hopeless—thoroughly occupied with Lady Sophia's ample bosom.

Henry ran a hand through his hair for the thirtieth time that night. No, he would stay behind, and protect Caroline from whatever—whomever—lurked in the darkness. He was not willing to risk her life, not for the diamond, not for what the diamond meant to him.

Because Caroline Townshend meant more. And so Henry stood down.

Lady Violet did not. Stealing a glance at the earl, she stepped forward, a bit more steady on her feet than she'd been at the house.

"Lord Harclay and I will go with the king," she said firmly.

Hope, of course, cried out in protest, and fought to accompany King Louis and Artois to Eliason's ship. The diamond had technically belonged to Hope when it was stolen, and Hope stood to lose just as much as Henry—that was to say, everything—should the jewel be lost.

Nevertheless, Violet won the argument, swearing to Hope that she would return the French Blue to him. While she spoke with convincing sincerity, Henry didn't exactly share her conviction.

Looping her arm through the earl's, Violet followed the King and Artois. Henry watched the night swallow them. He should follow them, see Harclay's inane plan through, reclaim the diamond for England. There was so much at stake: his future, Caroline's, his men and his country, and all he had worked for these past twelve years.

The weight of this knowledge suffocated him. And yet he did not follow Violet and the earl, and stood instead by Caroline's side.

Caroline.

He could smell her perfume, and sense her rising panic; she was shaking and trying to hide it. Henry swallowed his own; he had to calm her down. He turned to Sophia and Thomas Hope, who stood in a tangled huddle behind him.

Hope was drawing a shawl about Sophia's shoulders; the debutante looked up at the banker with eyes that glittered in the darkness. The way she was looking at him—it was an invitation, a provocation, even.

And Thomas Hope appeared all too happy to be provoked.

Henry cleared his throat. "Well," he said, rocking back on his heels. "Jolly good of Lady Violet and Harclay to do the heavy lifting for us, eh? Come, let's have a nip in the hack while we wait."

Without turning from Sophia, Hope untangled a silver flask from his waistcoat pocket and handed it to Lake.

Henry looked down at the flask, fighting a smile. It was as subtle an admonishment to leave Thomas and Sophia alone as a spoken "shoo, off with you!" would have been.

Henry tucked the flask into his coat and placed his hand on the small of Caroline's back. Her trembling lessened, slightly. "We'll just, er, meet you . . . there, back at the hackney. Do take your time"—here he would've wiggled his eyebrows, if Hope had been watching—"we have all night."

Lake pressed Caroline into motion beside him.

After a beat, she released a stifled giggle. "Good Lord!" she wheezed. "No mystery as to what they'll get up to. I wonder where they'll do it."

Henry snorted. "Right there, if I had to hazard a guess. Luckily we escaped before the show began."

They made for the hackney in silence, the only sound Henry's footfalls on the uneven cobbles. Caroline's slippers made barely a whisper as she moved beside him. Through the gauze of her gown, her skin warmed his palm.

"We should have gone," she murmured at last. "I know this whole mess was William's plan, but you and I—we should be meeting that jeweler, and buying back the diamond."

Henry guided her closer, so that she walked in the cradle of his arm. "You're worried about him. Your brother."

"Of course I'm worried," she replied. "That's all I do anymore, is worry. About him. About you."

Inside his chest, Henry's heart skipped a beat. "You don't have to worry about me."

He could practically hear Caroline roll her eyes. "I know, I know, you can take care of yourself, all that rubbish. But it can't be helped. I think about y—"

She stopped herself. Henry swallowed, hard, and tried not to dwell on what it meant that she *thought about him*.

Caroline refused him, hadn't she? And even if her feelings had changed, and she felt a fraction of what he felt for her, it didn't matter. Whether they won back the French Blue tonight, Henry was leaving, bound by duty and honor to return to Paris. They could never be together, Henry and Caroline. There was no place for such a match in the worlds they had chosen, no time or tolerance for a repeat of the heartbreak they each had suffered twelve years ago.

And yet.

The insistent beat of Henry's desire for her would not be ignored. It was immediate, and overwhelming, the heat from his palm pulsing up his arm to land in his chest, between his legs, in his temples. A million sensations sprang forth from this place where he touched her, where mere layers of muslin and whalebone and gauze separated flesh from flesh.

God, but he could not get past how much he wanted her. How much he loved her.

It could have been his imagination—overeager, as usual, in her presence—but Caroline seemed to curl farther into his touch, pressing her body against his.

She's just frightened, he told himself. Tired.

Still, Henry liked the sense of peace it brought him, surrounding her with his body. Knowing he could protect her, in this moment at least, even if protection wasn't what she was looking for.

When they reached the hackney, waiting just beyond the wharf's edge, Henry nodded at the driver; the man tipped his hat and studiously averted his gaze.

"Find someplace safe," Henry told him. "Out of the way. We're sitting ducks here."

Henry opened the door, and his fingers slid from Caroline's back to her hand. Her fingers felt naked and cold in his palm. Without thinking, he gave them a squeeze as he helped her climb into the vehicle.

He followed her inside, closing the door quietly behind him. It was cool, and dark in here; the hackney's lamps, distorted through the grimy window, offered little in the way of illumination. He took a seat on the thinly cushioned bench across from Caroline. The hackney began to move, slowly, the wheels clapping an uneven beat over the cobblestones.

Henry removed the flask from his coat, unscrewed its top. She turned her head to look out the window, the skin on her swanlike neck burnished gold in the low light. She held her hands in a tight knot on her lap.

"Care for a nip?" Henry held out the flask.

With trembling fingers she took it, and gave it a sniff. She wrinkled her nose. "What is it?"

"Single malt Scotch whiskey. You're not going to like it."

Caroline tilted back her head, taking a goodly pull. At once her face screwed up in a grimace, tongue emerging from between her lips as if she could banish the taste from her mouth. "You're right. That's awful. I don't know why I keep doing this to myself—drinking whatever it is you're offering me inside a coach. Why can't anyone keep a nice sherry beneath the cushions?"

Henry grinned. "Have another sip. It'll help."

Even as she held the back of her hand to her lips, a look of distaste darkening her features, she did as he bid her.

"You're getting better at it," he said, taking the flask she held out to him. "You didn't spit half of it out this time."

Caroline let out a sputtering sigh. "You forget William Townshend is my brother. Debauchery runs in my family. It's only a matter of time before I can drink you under the table."

Henry took a sip, sucked a breath through his teeth. Heavens, but that was a potent brew; no doubt Hope was in need of so vibrant a libation, considering he was nearly bankrupt, his bank teetering on the edge of ruin.

Henry could certainly relate.

He took another pull, a long ribbon of fire trailing down his throat, before screwing the cap back on the flask. He replaced it in his breast pocket, and met Caroline's eyes across the coach. She held her arms tightly about her chest.

The air between them tightened; it was always charged, magnetic, Henry realized, but at this moment the pull was acute, as unavoidable as the past they shared.

"So," she said.

"So," he said.

"Alone again."

"If I didn't know better, Lady Caroline, I'd accuse you of planning this—absconding with me to a darkened corner. Be honest. Do you mean to seduce me?"

Caroline scoffed, glancing once more out the window. He'd asked her that same question twelve years ago, on their wedding night.

He hoped her answer tonight was the same as it had been then.

The hackney had come to a halt; as far as Henry could tell, the driver had led them to a dim, damp alleyway. "That would prove a compelling distraction, wouldn't it?"

He grinned. "I would not be opposed."

"No," she said, turning to look at him once more. His heart rose when he saw she, too, was grinning. "I didn't think you would be."

She looked down at her hands, tangled in her lap. "You don't think they're going to find it, do you? The diamond."

Henry didn't answer. His fingers itched for the flask.

"What are we going to do," she asked, softly, "if they don't?"

"I'll take care of it." *Of you*, he wanted to say. But he didn't.

"This old argument," she said. "Let's not have it again."

Henry watched the working of her throat as she swallowed. "William is going to be fine, Caroline. If he can make it out of Hope's ballroom with a priceless gem shoved in his smalls, he'll make it out of this. And Mr. Moon—he's been through worse. He'll be fine."

Her eyes flashed to meet his. She was shaking again; he could see the trail of goose bumps along her bare arms and chest.

Of course; why didn't he notice it sooner? In their rush to leave Mayfair, Caroline hadn't had a chance to gather a pelisse, a shawl, anything to keep her warm.

Cursing himself, Henry shrugged out of his coat.

"You don't have—"

"I want to," he said, crouching as he leaned across the hackney. She leaned forward, allowing him to hook his jacket across the yoke of her shoulders. He tugged the lapels closer about her breast, wrapping her tightly in a sea of fabric.

"Henry," she said. He could feel her looking up at him.

"Just a minute, are the sleeves all right? Are you better?"

"Henry." The way she said it this time made him pause. His pulse drummed as he looked down.

Caroline's eyes were wet. The space between them crackled with longing, with unspoken things. Henry was glad to have shed his coat; he felt warm under his collar.

Her arm emerged from between the lapels of his coat;

carefully, she dug her fingers into the buttons of his shirtfront, just beneath his cravat. Of its own volition his head ducked into her pull, his mouth hovering an inch above hers. He could see the pearlescent glow of her teeth peeking through her parted lips.

The way she was looking at him—it made his entire being ring with *everything*. Hurt and desire and regret and lust and love.

"Distract me," she said. "Please, Henry, distract me."

And then she pulled him down on her mouth, her lips moving over his hungrily, desperately, as if the world were ending, and this was their last night together.

Thirty-seven

———✦———

Henry reached across the hackney and tugged the curtains closed, his mouth never leaving Caroline's. She moaned against his lips as his arm brushed against her breasts; desire, liquid and hot, arrowed through her.

"Shh," he whispered. "I won't share your sounds—I won't share you with the driver."

His admonition only heightened her excitement. She couldn't ignore it, this desire. She didn't want to.

It was enormously foolish, of course, to give in; how many times now had she sworn not to do exactly that? A hundred, a thousand?

And still she could not ignore it. Her body felt wild with heavy things: worry, fear, a growing dread that this was all going to end badly, that Mr. Moon would end up dead. Nothing could make her forget, she knew, except Henry's hands. His touch drowned all that she didn't want to feel. She liked how she felt in his arms, beneath the assault of his passion.

How much longer would she have him, besides? He was leaving, whether or not William and Violet managed to pry the French Blue from this jeweler's grasp. God, Henry was *leaving*, and Caroline would be a devoted widow again, and she would never be able to touch him like this. He would never touch *her* like this.

The loneliness of that knowledge—it was too much to bear.

In the space of a single heartbeat she pushed him back onto the squabs and climbed onto his lap, straddling his legs. He dug a hand into the hair at the back of her neck, his fingers gliding past pins and braids to work free her curls, which fell heavily about her shoulders.

Caroline held his face as he met her stroke for stroke. It was the kind of kiss she felt everywhere. She burrowed against him, his heart working against her breasts as she plied his lips with her own. He held her close against him, one hand in her hair, the other on the small of her back.

Henry sat up, settling Caroline farther onto his lap. She felt his arousal prodding against the throb between her legs. As she kissed him she inhaled his scent, long, heady draughts of spice and sandalwood, of his skin. She wanted to bite him; she couldn't get close enough.

Her body warmed beneath the gentle caress of Henry's touch. She drew back her shoulders and tugged at the sleeves of his coat. He helped her shrug it off, tossing it aside.

"That didn't last long," he murmured, his breath warm on her skin. He slid his hands up the length of her bare arms and throat, resting just beneath her jaw. He tried to take control of the kiss, moving her head in time to his lips, but she shrugged out of his grasp. This time—this embrace—was hers. Caroline would take what she wanted, and learn what she wanted to know, before Henry was gone.

Before he was gone forever. Again.

He was inching her skirts up her legs, urging the fabric out from under her knees and sliding his palms along the smooth expanse of her silk stockings. Something about the sound of it—the scrape of his skin against her legs, quiet, a happy whisper—made her grin against his lips. It was involuntary, this grin, irrepressible.

"Caroline," he said against her mouth. "Are you laughing at me?"

"I"—*kiss*—"would"—*kiss*—"never."

"Yes, you most certainly would."

And then she really did laugh, and so did he, and in that

second between them, Caroline's heart felt so full she wanted to cry.

She kissed Henry instead.

Her fingers worked at his cravat, unwinding it from about his neck. He held her, softly, on her sides, thumbs hooked into the spaces between the ribs of her stays.

Caroline pressed him back against the seat, unbuttoning his shirt.

"You're certain?" he panted.

"Certain."

She felt him relax. "All right." He held out his arms, grinning. "Do what you must, my lady, I am your willing servant."

"Splendid," she said, pulling away so that Henry could take off his shirt. She watched as he reached his arms over his head; he grasped the back of his collar and slid the shirt over his head. It was dark, but even so Caroline could appreciate the enormity of his physique, the flex of the muscles underneath his arms and along the sides of his torso.

She bit her lip, slid her hands over his chest. "Now stay still."

She remembered their first night together—their wedding night—and she remembered how he taught her to touch him. He hadn't allowed her to finish then. He would tonight.

Sliding her hands down the length of his chest, Caroline leaned forward and covered his mouth with hers. He tensed as her hands found their way to his belly, to the waistband of his breeches.

Henry's hand shot down to catch her by the wrists. She pulled away. *"Stay. Still."*

"I can't. Not when you're touching me like that. You don't have to—"

But his refusal was lost in her kiss. She wouldn't be thwarted. Not when she'd come this far, and there was so little time left to them, together.

He tensed, his body coiled, as she fingered the buttons of his fall. His cock pressed eagerly against her touch. He was enormous here, too; for a moment Caroline was overcome with doubt. What if she did it poorly? What if she hurt him?

Henry would tell her, that's what. She would ask. And he would tell her.

Caroline hadn't a clue from whence this sudden bravery

had come. Wasn't she just swearing, hours ago, that she was too scared to allow herself to feel the things that lurked on the dark side of her heart—the things she once felt for Henry?

And yet.

She felt herself sinking into these lurking things, these delicious, overwhelming, warm-feeling things. She let the weight of her body pull her down into the flood, and she liked it. For these minutes, she would allow herself to admit to liking it.

The front of his breeches fell away beneath her fingers. Henry sucked a breath through his teeth as Caroline wrapped her fingers around his cock. The place between her legs throbbed. With longing, with curiosity.

"Show me," she whispered. "Like you did before."

Henry reached down between them. As he had more than a decade ago, he wrapped his hand around hers, urging it tighter around his manhood. He moved his hand and she moved with him, thrilled by the intimacy of the act, by the eroticism of the power she felt, knowing that she controlled his pleasure.

Caroline kissed him, hard, and he kissed her back wildly. His body arched against hers, his teeth nicked her bottom lip. He was groaning against her mouth, his worry about the driver all forgotten; he was saying her name, whispering it as he kissed her. Her pleasure rose in time to his.

"Caroline." He gritted his teeth. "I'm going to come. Let me go, God, let me go, please, before—"

The words caught in his throat. Quickly she unhooked her fingers and pulled away. Henry covered his cock with his hand and squeezed shut his eyes. He pressed his forehead against hers, sucking a breath through his gritted teeth as he was overcome by his completion.

For several moments neither of them said a thing. The only sound was Henry's rough breathing; Caroline's heart beat loudly in her ears, almost as loudly as the desire that beat between her legs. Had she, in all her twenty-nine years, ever been so aroused?

She closed her eyes, too, and willed herself to memorize the feel of Henry's forehead, damp with sweat, against hers. Willed herself to be aware, immaculately, of this feeling of freedom. The lightness of living in this moment, one heartbeat to the next. No past, no interminable future. Just now, when Henry was all hers, and she wasn't afraid of what that meant.

Caroline felt Henry's eyelashes flutter against her nose. She opened her eyes and saw him looking at her, his pale eye translucent in the darkness. The way he looked at her—it made her heart turn over in her chest.

Her gaze moved to his other eye, the one that was missing. She reached up, feathered her fingers across the patch. The look in Henry's good eye changed, intensified. His nostrils flared with each breath he pulled in.

Caroline didn't know why she did it; only that she was curious, and sad, and that she wanted to know what it was like, to have half the world hidden from view.

She traced her finger over the leather's crackled ridges, like the scales of a tiny fish, and wondered what she would find beneath it. A scar, perhaps, or a red-rimmed hole. What had happened to his eyelashes? Would they have survived, she wondered, if his eye had not?

Her fingers moved to the leather thong pressed into the skin of his temple. Henry pulled back, suddenly, as if she'd caught him with the edge of her fingernail. Caroline looked away, embarrassed.

He reached for the rumpled length of cambric that was once his cravat. Looking down, he went to work tidying himself up, wiping his hands before tossing the cravat aside.

And then he looked at her again. She heard him swallow. His hands were on her thighs again, thumbs inching toward the place where she ached for him, fiercely.

Caroline glanced to the window. She pulled back the curtain: nothing. No sign of William. No sign of anything, really, as the alley was darker than the night from which they'd escaped.

She turned back to Henry. He lifted a hand and pressed his thumb to the place where her eyebrows met.

"You're worrying again," he said. "I thought I was supposed to be distracting you."

Caroline released the furrow she hadn't known was there, brows stinging with relief.

She half laughed. "Distract me, then."

"I'm not going to take you in a carriage, Caroline," he said.

His thumbs inched up her thighs. "But perhaps I might touch you as you touched me?"

Henry didn't wait for a reply. He sat up in the seat, pressing his lips to hers as his hands moved up her legs, pulling her against him. This kiss was slow, luxurious in comparison to the fevered bites and pulls they'd shared just minutes ago. He was being careful now, diligent that he should kiss her thoroughly, and well.

Behind closed lids, Caroline saw stars as his mouth moved to her jaw, her neck. The stubble of his chin tickled her throat; she giggled; Henry growled playfully.

In the throes of her rising passion, Caroline didn't hear the voices approaching the hackney; or maybe she just ignored them.

Either way, she was not prepared for the ominous *clap* of the carriage door as it swung open.

"Mr. Lake." It was Lady Sophia, Violet's cousin. "I— *Mr. Lake!*"

In a flurry of movement, Henry tore Caroline from his lap and settled her behind him, his fingers shaking as he attempted—and failed, of course—to button up his breeches.

Caroline glanced over his shoulder to see Sophia standing openmouthed outside the carriage, eyes wide as saucers as she took in the scene before her. Behind her, Mr. Hope hovered, the limp figure of Lady Violet draped across his arms.

Caroline's blood rushed to ice. After the heat of her desire, the rush left her reeling; for a moment blinding pain flashed inside her head. The agony of being interrupted; the shame of being caught *in flagrante delicto*.

But there was no time for shame. At first glance, it appeared things had not gone as William planned: Violet's head lolled over Thomas Hope's forearm.

Oh God, Caroline thought. Oh, God, William would never let Violet out of his sight. Where in hell is he?

"Is she all right?" Caroline asked, helping Henry shrug into his coat. There was no hope for his shirt, much less his cravat.

"Yes," Sophia panted. "I'll explain everything, but we *need* to *go*. Now."

"What about William? My brother—where—?"

"We need to go."

Henry placed a hand on Caroline's thigh, gave it a good squeeze. He turned to Sophia. "I say, what's that dreadful smell?"

Caroline blinked, her nose twitching as the acrid scent of singed tar, overlaid with the more savory smell of burning wood, filled her head.

Bile rose in her throat. That couldn't be good.

With Henry's help, Thomas—giving his old friend a black look—handed Violet's body into the hack. Thomas and Sophia climbed in after them, squeezing Caroline against Henry, hip to shoulder. His hand was still on her thigh.

"No word of the diamond?" he asked.

Hope shook his head, let out a sigh of defeat. Like Henry, he stood to lose everything—his bank, his fortune—if the diamond was lost. "That fool Harclay set the jeweler's ship on fire. Why, I haven't a clue. The ship will sink, if it hasn't already."

Caroline began to shake. Was William still on that ship?

"Violet told us virtually nothing," Hope continued, running a hand through his mop of dark curls. "We found her running from the ship, choking on smoke. For all we know, Artois could've run off with the diamond before the fire started, or that Eliason chap could've jumped ship with it in his pocket. The French Blue could be anywhere by now."

Caroline jumped when Henry slammed his fist into the roof, jolting the driver—and the hack—into motion. "Bloody perfect," he growled. "We came so close. So *bloody close*."

She rolled her lips between her teeth, struggling to breathe against the panic rising in her chest.

William. Where the devil was he, damn him, she'd box his ea—

An enormous sound—so enormous it was more of a sensation, a force that knocked the wind from her lungs—rent a hole in the darkness. It was like the thunder that followed lightning struck very close: crackling, huge. The horses cried out; Caroline cried out. Henry's arm shot across her breast, bracing her against the seat as the hackney drew to a sudden halt.

Henry leapt from the vehicle, shouting at the driver; the driver shouted something back about an explosion, out there on the river. Hope joined them, holding the door open behind him.

Wordlessly, Sophia reached across the bench and took Caroline's hand in her own.

"William," Caroline whispered. "Oh, God."

Henry turned to her, resting an arm on the door's top bracket. The lapels of his coat stretched open, revealing his bare chest. "Do not move, Caroline, or so help me I will tie you to the seat. There's nothing you can do, not without getting harmed yourself. I'll see to William. You'll have word as soon as I do."

Without waiting for a reply, he turned and dissolved into the darkness.

Caroline sat very still, the backs of her eyes burning with tears. Hope lingered in the open door, telling Sophia to look after her cousin Violet, that he'd given the driver instructions to take them home, under pain of death.

He closed the door, pounded it with the flat of his hand. The hackney jolted forward, eliciting a moan from Violet. Caroline watched the slope of Hope's shoulders disappear toward the river, after Henry.

And then they were alone—she, Sophia, and Violet. The diamond was gone. William was—well, who knew where he was. Henry was going after him, yes, but who knows what would happen—what wouldn't happen? It was possible she would lose them both. She couldn't think about it, not without being strangled by a creeping sense of disaster.

Caroline squeezed Sophia's hand, and looked away from the window to the lifeless body dangling across her knees. "Let's see to your cousin," she said.

Thirty-eight

---◈---

Violet and Sophia's Residence
Grosvenor Square

It was no easy task, dragging Violet up two creaking flights of stairs. Caroline held one arm while Sophia held the other; together they grunted and panted their way through the house.

Climbing up the stairs, Caroline cursed her countrymen and their predilection for large houses; this one seemed to go on *forever*.

By the time they reached the second landing, sweat dripped into her eyes. They paused to catch their breath, wiping perspiration from their brows. Sophia's face was tensed, her eyes hooded, as if she wanted to weep but didn't have the energy.

"Just. A bit longer," Caroline panted, as they carried Violet the last few feet into her chamber.

Sophia drew up just before they reached the bed. "I don't think I'm . . . I'm able to do it."

"Yes, you are. One. Last push." Caroline blew the hair from her eyes, and took Violet by the wrists. "I'm afraid we'll have to swing her onto the bed. There, you take her feet. That's it, Sophia, just like that."

"God," Sophia said. "She's *heavy*."

A count of one, two, three, and Violet landed heavily on the bed, the mattress ducking beneath her weight.

Bent over with her hands on her knees, Caroline said, "Smelling salts."

Sophia nodded, too winded to speak. She held up a finger as she turned and disappeared from the room. A moment later she was back, bearing a fistful of salts.

"Good heavens!" Caroline said, peering at the salts. "How often do people faint in this house?"

"My mother," Sophia said, as if that explained everything.

"Oh, yes, I'd quite forgotten about Auntie George. Swoons often, then?"

"Several times a day since I've made my debut."

Caroline tried not to appear horrified. "I'm terribly sorry."

Sophia shrugged. "Don't be. I do not mean to sound ungrateful, but when she's unconscious I can escape."

Caroline didn't have to ask where Sophia escaped to.

She was escaping to Mr. Hope. His bed, probably. They were an unlikely pair, yes, the banker and the debutante. But in Caroline's experience, the unlikeliest pairs were also the most passionate.

It only took a sniff or two of the salts, and Violet stirred, letting out a little moan. They undressed her quickly, and wrapped her in the counterpane. Violet moaned again when Caroline tucked the bedclothes about her bosom.

Across the bed, Caroline met Sophia's eyes.

"What is it?" Sophia whispered.

"How long has your cousin been ill? The weak stomach."

Sophia furrowed her brow. "A few weeks now. She says it's nothing, but . . ."

Was it possible, Caroline wondered, after all Violet had been through? The wound, the painful recovery?

But Caroline knew better than anyone that anything—really, *anything*—was possible. Her heart clenched; she remembered the symptoms well. The tender breasts, the incessant swell of nausea. She wanted to smile. She wanted to cry.

If something had happened on that ship, William wouldn't only be leaving behind his sister, and the woman he loved.

Caroline wished, violently, that he was all right, that he was alive. If only so he might know. His face, when he heard the news—how priceless it would be!

"You look exhausted," Sophia said, drawing round the bed to loop her arm through Caroline's. "I'll send for the carriage, get you back home. Perhaps there's word waiting for you there about Lord Harclay."

Sophia saw her to the back of the house, where a yawning coachman waited.

"Thank you," Sophia said. "For your help. He's going to be all right, your brother. He made it out of Hope's ballroom with the French Blue. I daresay he'll make it out of this, too."

She pulled Caroline into a hug then, squeezing her tightly. Caroline nearly started, and then, after a moment, she allowed herself to fall into Sophia's embrace. It was an intimate gesture, a familiar one. Caroline wondered if this was what it felt like to have a sister. They would be cousins, she and Sophia, if William and Violet married. Caroline wouldn't mind having a cousin like Sophia. More family. It would certainly make the prospect of her perpetual widowhood less depressing.

With a kiss on the cheek Sophia let her go.

Caroline had to pound on the roof when the carriage passed her brother's Hanover Square house. Tumbling out onto the street, she saw the driver give himself a good smack on the cheek; he'd fallen asleep.

The house was quiet as a tomb, and just as vacant. The butler, Avery, was nowhere to be found; Nicks, as bleary-eyed as the driver, said Avery had not returned since the whole party left hours ago.

Caroline was in bed, staring at the ceiling, when she heard a sudden jolt of noise. Somewhere in the bowels of the house, a door swung open, slammed shut.

She knew right away it was the kitchen door, at the back of the house.

She didn't remember flying out of her room, down the stairs, down again, and yet again; she found herself in the dim cacophony of the storerooms, voices rising and falling as maids and cooks held naked tapers aloft.

"Make way, please," Caroline choked, moving toward the door. She felt sick with anticipation.

There, on a makeshift stretcher, was Lord William Townshend, Earl of Harclay and Caroline's brother.

What was left of him, anyway. His clothes were soaked; he reeked of gunpowder and smoke, scents that waved off him like putrid clouds. His face was bloody, swollen, unrecognizable; sunken in places, like a rotten plum.

She met eyes with Avery, who stood, chest heaving, to William's right. He, too, appeared the worse for wear. Caroline didn't ask; she didn't want to know.

"A little," Avery wiped his face with the sleeve of his coat, sniffed. "He's a little alive."

William and Violet, the both of them a little alive.

A black hole of dread, sucking and deep, opened inside her. It pulled at her organs and turned her blood to ice.

She turned away from it, to keep it from swallowing her whole. In rapid-fire shouts she issued orders to the staff. You, call the doctor, and you, the surgeon, and the chemist. You, boil water, bring him upstairs, stoke the fire in his rooms. No women, we have to strip him. The soap, the laudanum, and yes, two fingers of brandy for me, thank you very much.

Caroline went to work on her second lifeless body of the night. She was apparently good at it, the resuscitation bit. Once they got him in bed, William moaned, just like Violet had; only William's moan devolved into a colorful expletive that made Caroline laugh.

"He's a little more alive," she said. Thank God.

Shirt, breeches, shoes, stockings: together she and Avery peeled back each grimy layer, dropping the articles into a canvas sack one of the footman held, with a look of sincere distaste, at arm's length.

As far as Caroline could tell, William bore no serious flesh wounds; the surgeon would know if any bones were broken, if there was bleeding where the eye could not see.

They made him as comfortable as they could; the surgeon came, and after repeated admonishments that his lordship was in good hands, Caroline and Avery were at last persuaded to take their leave.

"The study," Caroline said. She felt weary, suddenly, a kind of exhaustion that transcended the ache in her body. "I need another drink, and I'll not have it alone."

"Hardly proper, the butler and the countess taking brandy together," Avery said, following her down the stairs.

The butler and the countess, the banker and the debutante, the countess and the spy. What did it matter anymore? Held captive by the romance of being seventeen, and in love, Caroline remembered thinking that these distinctions of class and comportment were silly. The world had quickly taught her otherwise, but now, tonight, she understood once again her youthful conviction.

She and Avery sipped their brandy quietly. Avery refused to sit in Caroline's presence—some rules, he said, upheld civilization itself, and this was one of them—and so he stood across from her, staring into the empty fireplace.

She thought of Henry.

"At the docks—did you see Henry Lake?" she asked. "Or Thomas Hope? They came looking for you."

Avery nodded. "They helped me see his lordship to safety. We escaped just in time, before the ship sank. They are well."

Caroline set her empty glass on the table beside her chair. She breathed a silent sigh of relief. At least Henry was alive. *A lot* alive.

"And our French friends. Them, too?"

Avery ducked his head, a nod.

"How fortunate for France," she said. "I'm sure they'll thank us for saving their most esteemed sovereign's life."

He grinned. A beat passed between them as he finished his brandy.

"My lady." He cleared his throat and turned to look at her. "There's something I'd like to give you. For safekeeping, while his lordship is . . . indisposed."

Caroline met Avery's gaze. He was nervous. Which, of course, made her nervous. He dug into his waistcoat pocket.

Her pulse, drowsy from the brandy, leapt.

It couldn't be—no, it was lost. The chances were laughable, at best, that he held the diamond in his pocket.

He dug about some more.

And then Avery placed the French Blue in Caroline's palm. For a moment her heart stopped beating altogether.

"I got lucky," he said. "That's how."

That's it? she wanted to say. You got lucky? What the devil did that mean?

She knew that was all he would give her. She did not press for more.

Even in the flickering light of a nearby candle, the diamond was starkly compelling. Caroline recognized its flirtatious shimmer, its flashes of vermilion, white, violet. Despite being stashed away in Avery's pocket, the diamond was cold to the touch, and heavy in her hand.

She looked up once more at the butler. "Why didn't you just keep it for yourself? You could've run away with it, easily."

Avery held his hands behind his back. His lips twitched.

Caroline scoffed when the realization hit. "You're just as bad as William is, aren't you, chasing after a thrill?" She rolled her eyes. *"Men."*

Avery gave in to his smile. "Yes, unfortunately I am one."

Caroline sighed, closing her fingers about the diamond. "Well, then. I'll just put this back where it belongs, where it's safest. In my brother's sock drawer."

Only, she didn't.

While the house was still abed, Caroline slipped out the back gate. She pulled her hat low against the ardent rain and made for Henry's house, hand held against the small reticule buried in her skirts. She did not look back.

She trusted her gut.

She trusted Henry.

Thirty-nine

---✦---

S opping wet and smelling of smoke, Henry pushed through the kitchen door of his brother's town house.

He shuffled inside.

And nearly jumped out of his skin at the sound of a familiar voice.

"Pardon me, sir, but what the devil happened to you?" Mr. Moon was at his side in an instant, helping Henry out of his clothes. "And why aren't you wearing a shirt?"

Throat tight with relief, Henry drew Moon into his arms, squeezing him until the poor man choked out a request to be released.

Henry held him at arm's length. He appeared to be in middling condition; his eyes were bruised, and one was swollen shut. His lip was split, and a gash ran the length of his cheekbone. His skin was the color of dirty dishwater.

"My God." Rage thundered inside Henry's chest. "What did that bastard do to you?"

Moon waved away his concern. "You needn't worry—old Brunhilde could serve up a better beating. It was a shameful display, sir, just shameful; I felt quite sorry for his lordship the marquess."

"How the devil did you do it?" Henry marveled. "How in the world did you outsmart Woodstock?"

Moon shrugged, as if it escaping the clutches of a madman were no small thing. "Took advantage of his weakness, his sense of control. He had no idea you and I have been jumping out of windows for years now. I jumped. Granted, it was a few stories up, and more painful than I would ever admit sober—"

"A few stories? But how? Why?"

"It's done." Moon frowned at Henry's costume. "You haven't told me about your missing shirt. Or why you're sopping wet."

It was Henry's turn to shrug. "Some royals, a poisoning, an explosion—it's done, as you say."

"Excellent news, sir. Let's get ourselves cleaned up then; it won't be long before Woodstock knows I've escaped. He'll come looking for us here."

They both turned at the knock on the door.

He was at the door before she mounted the first step. She, Caroline.

"Come in!" he said, reaching out to her. "Let's get you out of the rain."

She brought the scent of it with her into the shadowed entrance hall. Water, earth, a trace of flowery perfume. His pulse thumped.

She drew back her hood, and for a moment Henry was struck dumb. Her dark hair tumbled loose about her shoulders, egregiously lovely, somehow erotic, and he imagined this is what it would look like, after a night in bed with him. A bit mussed, glossy.

God, but she was beautiful. He would never get used to that fact.

He was standing too close to her; he should move.

"Mr. Moon!" she cried.

Moon managed a smile as Caroline tucked him into her arms. They exchanged pleasantries, Moon told her about the jump, and then Caroline turned to Henry.

"Are you all right?" she asked, unbuttoning the front of her pelisse. "You're soaking wet."

"Yes, yes, I'll take care of that in a moment." Henry sprang forward, taking her hat and gloves and placing them on a nearby table.

He turned to look at her. "Caroline," he said quietly.

She looked at her feet and shook her head.

"How is your brother?" Henry asked. "He was worse for the wear when we set him in the hackney last night."

"He's better," she said. "He's sprained both ankles, and his face is bruised. He won't be out of bed for a few weeks, maybe longer. I was going to send word, but he doesn't want anyone to know, not yet. Especially Lady Violet. Says he has his reasons for not telling her—I told him he was a scoundrel—but he made me swear." She forced a smile to her lips. "So you must swear, too."

Henry wanted to keep that smile there, so he smiled himself, and held a hand over his heart. He leaned forward, teasingly. "I swear not to tell Lady Violet, who is probably half-dead with worry, that your brother is alive, and mostly well."

"Thank you," she clipped. "He's a devil, isn't he, William?"

She was biting her lip now, trying not to smile so hard.

That lip. It killed him.

"Well, then," Mr. Moon stepped in. "To what do we owe the honor, my lady?"

Only then did Henry notice that Caroline's outstretched hand was gathered into a fist. Slowly she uncurled her fingers, revealing a blot of darkness in the middle of her palm.

Henry blinked.

And then he looked up at Moon. Moon stared back.

"Our plot against Woodstock," she said. "We might put it into play at last."

Henry nodded at the diamond. "May I?"

"Of course."

Henry held the French Blue up to the thin light that streamed through the kitchen window. The diamond sparkled a thousand shades of watery gray. Propped between his thumb and forefinger it appeared rather small, though no less remarkable; he understood why half the world lusted after it.

Drawing a deep breath through his nose, Henry gathered his fingers around the jewel and held it in his palm. He turned to look at Caroline.

"Thank you for bringing it to us."

Caroline blinked. "I owe you—well, quite a bit. You threw a duel for me, for God's sake. You were going to let my blackhearted brother shoot you, just so I would not have to suffer his loss. You saved him from an exploding ship. This"—she nodded at the jewel—"is the least I can do. So let me do it."

He should have known she would try something like this, do something that would, in her mind, settle her debt to him.

But there was no debt to be settled. He did not throw the duel out of duty, or even decency. Throwing it had felt as ordinary, as obviously simple, as smiling back at a laughing baby. Henry had done it, and he would do it again. For Caroline. Because it meant keeping her safe, and happy.

Forty

— ✦ —

The Marquess of Woodstock's Residence
Berkeley Square, Mayfair

Henry lifted the heavy brass knocker, allowing it to fall with a ringing *thud* on the door. Straightening, he moved his hand to cover the telltale bulge in his waistcoat pocket.

The French Blue. It jumped against his palm in time to his hammering pulse; though it was hardly bigger than his thumb, the diamond felt heavy in his pocket, an unwelcome, ominous weight.

At last. It was time to put an end to this bloody business.

Henry prayed all went to plan; that this plot of Caroline's worked, that they would leave with their lives intact, and the diamond in hand. Even if his audience with Woodstock went badly, it comforted Henry to know he could use the jewel as a bargaining chip of last resort. If the marquess threatened Caroline's life, or made a move Henry did not anticipate, he could always offer up the diamond; even Woodstock, in all his strange-smelling evilness, would be entranced by a fifty-carat gem. Henry would never have agreed to Caroline's plot if he did not have the gem as insurance against disaster.

The front door, lacquered a sufficiently sinister shade of black, swung open, and an officious butler saw him up the stairs to a drawing room of sorts at the back of the house. The chamber was more bordello than parlor, with walls and floors and furniture done in gleaming shades of black, brass, and gray. It was dark; the fire was a smoldering pile of embers, and no lamps or candles were lit.

After ensuring Henry was not armed—the butler was an annoyingly thorough fellow—he turned and made for the door.

"Wait here." He sniffed over his shoulder. "His lordship shall be down presently."

Standing very still, Henry glanced at the window on the far end of the room. Heavy velvet drapes hung on either side of the window; perfect hiding spots for Moon, Henry thought, when he made his move.

He drew a breath through his nose, and willed his heart to be still. His palms were clammy. He was unaccountably nervous. Unaccountably, because he never got nervous; the feeling was as foreign to him as good beer was to the French.

It was because of Caroline—the nervousness. In the past, the fate of nations had been at stake. History. Victory. His life, and those of his best men. But Caroline's life never hung in the balance.

Now it did. And Henry was scared.

"Ah!" came a deep voice, followed by a clap as hands were brought together, the scrape of skin as they were rubbed against one another with glee. "I am so glad you have finally made your choice, Mr. Lake!"

Henry turned to see Woodstock stride into the room, his boots beating an authoritative tattoo against the bare marble floors.

He was smiling. "Your man, Mr. Moon—what a wily one he is! I was just about to take a stroll to your brother's house. Lock you and Moon inside and burn it down. What impeccable timing, Mr. Lake, that word should arrive about your decision just as I was walking out the door."

"I wish to be done with this business," Henry said. "Done with you."

Woodstock made his way to an ebony sideboard. "A drink, to mark the occasion?"

Henry cocked a brow. "Occasion?"

"Your defeat, of course. I've only been waiting twelve years."

"No, *thank* you, I'd rather make the trade so I can leave, get back to work. Your old friend Bonaparte doesn't wait."

"Oh, he'll wait for me." Woodstock pulled the stopper from a decanter. "I admit I hoped your search for the jewel would prove a failure. I so looked forward to becoming acquainted with your lovely companion, Lady Osbourne. Alas, knowing how England will suffer once I have the French Blue—that is no small consolation."

Woodstock held out a heavy-bottomed crystal tumbler to Henry. "Cognac, a '73. A gift from my old friend, as you called him, from his personal cellar." He tilted this head, confidingly. "I think you're going to like it."

In a single, swift motion, Henry reached out and slapped the glass from Woodstock's hand. It crashed to the floor, shards of glass exploding from the point of contact across the room.

Woodstock's smile didn't deepen, exactly; it just curled in on itself with a sinister kind of joy. "Your anger, Mr. Lake, is so satisfying."

He sipped placidly at his cognac, boots crunching on the broken glass as he stepped toward Henry. "I wish to see my prize now," he said, voice low. "Show me what I have won."

Henry glanced at the clock on the mantel. A few minutes before Caroline was to appear; he hoped, fervently, she would arrive without event, safely.

Digging into his pocket, Henry grasped the stone with his fingers and pulled it out into the light. The marquess's breath caught in his throat as Henry held it up to the warm glow of the chandelier.

The French Blue glittered a thousand shades of blue and red and white, a blot of flashing brilliance that refracted the light in a rainbow of brilliance. Henry's heart was pounding; it was difficult to hold the diamond still in his fingers, lest Woodstock see how nervous he was, how terrified that they would be found out, their plot foiled.

"How ever did you find it?" Woodstock asked, his eyes never leaving the gem. "I heard something about that Bourbon idiot, and an explosion down at London Docks. Sounds like your sort of trouble, Lake."

Henry did not answer.

"I'm sure it is a marvelous story." Woodstock smacked his lips. "Since you will not share it, tell me another. How will you live with yourself, knowing you chose your cock over your country? How did you become so broken, that you would make such a choice?"

Henry bit a hole in his lip to keep from breaking Woodstock's face. "I did what I had to do," he ground out.

"Yes, yes of course you did." The marquess held out his palm. "And I shall do the same. Thank you for coming to see m—"

"Wait!"

They both turned at the cry that sounded at the door; a cry that was followed by the crunch of hurried footsteps across the broken glass. Henry's heart nearly exploded at the sight of Caroline, breathless, disheveled, her hair and her dress in convincing—and, he thought grimly, voluptuous—disarray; her bonnet hung precariously from one ear.

"Wait!" She dashed across the room, arms flailing above her head. "Wait, Henry, I won't let you do it."

The marquess's rough-edged mouth broke into a smile as he turned away from Henry. Taking advantage of the momentary distraction, Henry slipped the jewel back into his pocket.

"Why, Caroline, dear," Woodstock drawled, "what a most welcome surprise!"

"Whan in hell are you doing here?" Henry asked. "How did you find me?"

"I've been following you for days," she panted. "I knew you'd do something stupid sooner or later."

"But how—?" Henry sputtered. "I would've seen you!"

"For one who claims to have lived in the shadows all these years, you're not nearly as savvy as you believe yourself to be."

Henry glared at Caroline. Insulting him was decidedly *not* part of the plan.

Caroline swallowed, turning away to face Woodstock. "Please, my lord, take me instead. I won't—I can't let Henry give you the diamond. There are too many lives at stake—take me, please, take me and let's be done here."

Woodstock drew a hand, slowly, down the length of Caroline's arm. Henry gritted his teeth; he could tell she struggled not to pull away, not to wince at the marquess's touch.

But Caroline was brave. She was insulting, too, but she was also bold. She would, he knew, play her part well.

As Henry would play his.

"No," he growled, tearing her away from the marquess. "This is my decision to make, Caroline. You haven't a clue what you're saying, the sort of trouble you'd get yourself into. What in hell were you thinking, coming here like this?"

Caroline pulled her elbow from his grasp. "I was thinking of England. I was thinking of you, Henry. Give him the diamond, and all is lost. Your men, the war, our innocence."

Somewhere, deep inside his terror, laughter stirred. Caroline's speech was ridiculous, and ridiculously perfect. *Our innocence.* He would have to tease her about that later, if, that is, they made it out of here alive.

"Poor dear," the marquess said. "She does have a point, Mr. Lake. Leave her here with me, and you are able to take the jewel to the French. Negotiate for the lives of your men. St. George would thank you for it. So"—he curled a lock of Caroline's hair around his finger—"would I."

"I would rather die than leave her with you," Henry spat. "Take the diamond, Woodstock, and leave us be."

Caroline tilted her chin in the air. "Henry, I'm staying."

"No, you're not. You're leaving with me, now."

But even as Henry reached for her, Woodstock already gathered her to him. His eyes flashed with malice as he looked down upon her, fingering her chin, tucking a stray lock of hair behind her ear.

Henry balled his hands into fists. He couldn't take Woodstock's touching, his fawning, much longer without doing something stupid. Where the devil was Moon?

"Forget the diamond," Woodstock said, turning to look at Henry. "I want her. She stays."

"Take your hands off her," Henry replied. His voice was hoarse with rage. This time he was not playing his part.

Woodstock turned his gaze to Henry. "But she belongs to me now, doesn't she? We all win this way. Lady Caroline comes to me, and you—well, you've got the French Blue, and whatever victory you think you've won for king and country."

He took Caroline's gloved hand in his and brought it to his mouth, running his lips across her knuckles. "Patriotism can be so dull. Wouldn't you agree, darling?"

Henry's pulse counted the passing seconds. Surely five minutes had passed? Moon was supposed to be here, damn it; Henry didn't know how much longer he could hold back.

"But what of the power the diamond would bring you, the things you could buy with it?" Henry said. "Your rage blinds you."

"Very good, Mr. Lake, very good!" Woodstock dropped his hand from Caroline's face, sipped at his cognac. "Of course I wanted whatever—*whomever*—it was that would kill you to give me."

He took a step toward Henry. "I wanted to break your spine and your spirit." Suddenly his voice was low, savage, spittle flying. "I wanted to destroy you by destroying everything you loved. And I have. I have, Mr. Lake. I've destroyed you. You think you know hate now. But I'll destroy her, too, and then you will know what hate really is. It fills you up, and rots you from the inside out. England's most dedicated agent, rotten. Just like me. Her most dedicated enemy."

Henry made a great show of rolling his eyes. "Are you done yet? I've heard my fill of these sorts of speeches—the villain at last explaining his motives, puffing out his chest at another hero vanquished. I'm vanquished, Woodstock. I'm rotten. You've turned me into what you are—a traitor, worth less than a dog. Come, Caroline, let's be off."

Again he reached for her; again she pulled away. "Go, Henry," she said. "Go."

Woodstock sipped at his cognac, eyes glittering like the cut glass tumbler he held to his lips. He was enjoying this; he did not want his moment of triumph to end.

"Tell me," he said. "Is the lady as feisty as I think she is? I suppose I shall have to restrain her, for the first few weeks at least."

Henry's fingers curled so tightly into his fists he felt the bite of his nails against his palm. He couldn't stand this much longer; he did not trust himself to hold back. If Moon did not appear, and soon, Henry would kill Woodstock, and in so doing probably end up dead himself.

Lake glanced one last time across the room. He nearly cried out with relief at the appearance of a lithe figure there in the corner; a figure with long, dark hair. The figure turned, silently closing the window behind him before turning back toward the chamber.

Finally. He—she—was here.

He prayed, harder, that neither Caroline nor Moon would not be harmed, playing their parts.

Moon's feet made no sound as he made his way into the chamber. With his right hand he swiped an engraved silver candlestick from a nearby table; ah, so he would not use his usual dagger. Interesting choice. Henry bit back a cry when Moon caught the edge of the table with his hip; Henry could not see his face—the room grew darker with an approaching afternoon storm—but he could just imagine his grimace. Caroline's clumsiness was rubbing off on Moon.

Woodstock caught Henry looking; to stop the marquess from looking over his shoulder himself, Henry stepped forward and jabbed his finger into Woodstock's chest.

"I'll come for her," Henry said, doing his best to play the panicked lover. He did not have to try very hard. "And when I do, I'll kill you. If she doesn't do it herself."

Woodstock grinned. "She is feisty, then. Splendid."

Behind Woodstock, Moon approached, candlestick held fast in hand.

Henry refocused his gaze on Woodstock.

"How dare you describe her as 'feisty,'" Henry said, knowing as he said it that it was a poor excuse for a rejoinder. He was too nervous to be witty. "Caroline is a lady, the widow of an earl!"

"Yes," Woodstock purred. "And this lady—she is mine."

Henry blinked back the rage that dimmed the edges of his vision. He should just reach out and strangle Woodstock himself.

"Which lady," Henry said slowly, "do you mean? There seem to be two of them present."

He nodded his head at the figure drawing up behind Woodstock. Moon held the candlestick over his head, poised for attack.

Alarm flickered in Woodstock's pale eyes as his head snapped about. His nostrils flared as the realization hit him. He looked at Caroline, looked back at Moon. In the low light the two of them appeared identical, dark hair curling over proud shoulders, bonnets framing their faces with scalloped lace and delicate ribbons.

It was the perfect ruse.

Caroline had been right. Woodstock was taken entirely off guard.

His eyes, wide, slid to meet Henry's.

Moon did not hesitate. Seizing upon Woodstock's indecision, he brought the candlestick down, hard, on the back of his skull.

Woodstock's eyes went wider, so wide Henry thought they would pop out of his head. He wavered for half a second on his feet; Henry knew Woodstock was far too wily an opponent to allow him a full second—that devil would think of something—and so Henry drew back his arm, and was about to drive his fist into the man's face when Caroline stepped in, and did it first.

Bold indeed. Henry remembered the sting of her slap that first night, after Hope's ball. Caroline landed a solid blow, doubtless from years of practice on that idiot brother of hers.

There was a dull, squishy *crack*; a spatter of blood, eyes rolling back; and then the Marquess of Woodstock collapsed on the ground in a heap of gangly limbs.

The three of them—Caroline dressed as Caroline, Mr. Moon dressed as Caroline, and Henry—peered down at the body.

"Did I do it?" Caroline whispered, flapping her hand. "Is he unconscious?"

Henry fell to his knees, straddling Woodstock's lifeless torso. He cuffed his chin, for good measure.

Wiping his brow, he panted, "Now he is. Let's go. Before we're found out."

They moved quickly; Henry and Moon carried the body to the window. Before he could tell her to wait, he'd catch her in the alley below, Caroline was leaping through the window, a smile of satisfaction lighting her face as she turned to look up at him.

"I learned from the best," she said.

Henry rolled his eyes, and then rolled out after her.

B y the time the hackney pulled away from Newgate Prison, the evening was getting on. A high half-moon floated in a darkening bluebell sky; well past ten o'clock, but still light enough to see the gleam of Caroline's skin across the vehicle.

Her skin, flawless, just like the night sky.

Henry had always loved that about London—the long summer days, when one could emerge from dinner to see the city swathed in soft northern light. It wasn't the same in Paris. Paris seemed endlessly dreary against nights like this one.

Henry drew down the window, inhaled a long draught of air.

Beside him, Caroline let out a small sigh.

"What is it?" Henry asked.

"Disappointed it's over, that's what."

Henry leaned forward, put his elbows on his thighs, and covered the ball of her knee with his palm. "You played your part with aplomb, Caroline," he said softly. "But you are a lady, remember? A dowager countess. You're not going to waste your widowhood clocking fellows in the face, are you? Surely you've got better things to do."

She was smiling now. If Moon weren't swaying in the carriage beside him, Henry would have slid his hand up her leg, watched her smile widen, her head fall back on the squabs.

Inside his chest, his heart clenched. The heat of her skin seeped through her gown into his palm; she looked away, out the window.

Back at Henry's brother's house, they congratulated one another. Caroline joined Henry and Moon in a toast to their victory, and was a dear not to mention how terrible the champagne was, even though her eyes watered at its sourness.

Henry couldn't tear his gaze from her face.

This was their last night together. They'd solved the puzzle; Woodstock was gone, the diamond was in Henry's possession. Negotiations would begin with the French tomorrow, after Henry delivered the good news to his commanding officer; he would promptly be sent back to Paris, probably by the end of the week. In the war against Old Boney, there was no time to waste.

He no longer had a reason to pester Caroline, call upon her, expect her to call upon him. The French Blue had brought them together, and now that the diamond would go to Napoleon, Henry and Caroline would once again be parted. She would be a respectable widow once more. And he—he would go back to his work, his men, his duty. He would be in a world so far removed from hers it might as well be the moon.

Tonight's victory was proving a bittersweet one.

But tonight—Henry and Caroline still had tonight. It was too depressing to think about what happened next, without her. So he would think about tonight.

He hoped the minutes might pass slowly, so that he might savor them.

He hoped Caroline would stay with him. He would do anything she wanted—play cards, drink wine—as long as she stayed.

Only, she didn't.

"Time to go, I'm afraid," she said, setting her half-empty glass on the bureau. "Henry, would you walk me home?"

Forty-one

Henry stalked through the darkness in silence.

"Why so," she panted, "serious? Eager to be rid of me?"

He looked at her from the corner of his eye. "You were the one who wanted to leave," he said gruffly.

"Don't you know? I only did that so that we might have some time alone."

Henry cocked a disbelieving eyebrow. "You did?"

"Of course I did. Couldn't hurt Moon's feelings by asking him to make himself scarce."

"That would've been a tad obvious, yes." Henry grinned.

"Dear God, Henry, could you please slow down?"

He did as she asked. She slipped her arm through his and drew him close. She could smell just the vaguest hint of lemon, but it was enough to fill her head—and then her body—with longing.

Together Caroline and Henry made their way through Mayfair's quiet lanes and squares, careful to muffle their footfalls in the spaces between cobbles.

Only when the stately façade of her brother's house appeared did Caroline's heart resume its beating. Relief, warm like wine, washed through her. The backs of her knees tingled; her footsteps slowed.

They'd won. With her help, Henry had defeated Woodstock, and ensured the success of his plans for the diamond.

Playing her part had been her confession. She loved him; she hoped he understood.

Just outside the mews gate, she bent at the waist, resting elbows on knees as she caught her breath. Beside her, Henry leaned his back against the wall, let his head fall back, too. His enormous chest rose and fell, rose and fell; Caroline watched through the curtain of hair hanging in front of her eyes.

She felt flush with victory, yes. Even now she smiled at the memory of their deception, and its success. Henry's greatest enemy—well, the only enemy she knew about, anyway— would be locked away, buried in a hole so deep he would never be found again. Another traitor to England, as good as dead.

And Caroline had helped capture him. She, a dowager countess, a gardener, a widow.

The French Blue would be used as Henry had always intended: an enticing piece of diplomatic bait, in the hopes Old Boney would exchange British prisoners, perhaps a Spanish city or two, in his quest to collect the crown jewels.

Henry would do his duty by England. That duty, of course, would bring him back to Paris, where he would continue his work. He was too good, too experienced, to be allowed to stay in London; Caroline had no doubt his loss these past weeks had been felt, acutely.

Pain, black and swelling, punctured her relief. She'd always known he would go back. But that didn't make it hurt any less.

These two things warred inside Caroline: her love for Henry, a love she could no longer deny, a love she'd all but admitted by helping him win back the French Blue; and the need to protect herself, to keep her carefully tended wounds— wounds that, after twelve years, had never fully healed—from opening again.

But Henry had opened them, and she knew it was too late to stanch the bleeding. She felt rent in two, equal parts love and fear, longing and sadness. The euphoria of having him near, and being so in love, was tinged with an ache Caroline knew well.

She smoothed her hair behind her ear, and looked at Henry as she drew upright. Tonight. It was all they had left. The wild chase that had brought them back together was done.

But they still had tonight.

Henry held out a hand to her, and she took it. He brought her close, his fingers entwining with hers as she stepped into the wedge of shadow put off by the wall.

"Caroline," he said quietly. Would this be the last time, she wondered, that she'd hear him speak her name? "Thank you. I was an ass to believe I could do this alone. Without you."

She grinned. "I only had to tell you three hundred times that I could help. At last, I get my due! Tell me, is the Alien Office looking to recruit new spies? I daresay I'd be smashing at it."

Henry tugged her closer, set her hand to rest against his chest and covered it with his own. His heart beat strongly against her palm. Desire pulsed, dimly, low in her belly. "What about your gardens? And that book! You still need to finish that book."

"Oh, that book," Caroline sighed, looking up at Henry. "I have that dreadful book, and you'll have Paris."

His grin faded. He squeezed her hand, ran his tongue along his bottom lip. For a moment he looked away. "I hope— sincerely—that I have not caused you overmuch pain, coming to London like this. I never meant to take captive your life, you know. It just . . ." He shrugged, that half-grin of his returning full force, dimple and all. Caroline thought she might faint. "Happened. I don't regret it, Caroline. No matter what happens next, I don't regret it."

Tears pricked at her eyes. It was her turn to look away. "Tomorrow. This is going to hurt tomorrow, Henry."

With his other hand he cupped her face, his thumb brushing her eyelashes. "I know," he said. "You and I—it seems the world conspires against us, doesn't it?"

Caroline scoffed. "An understatement if there ever was one."

She looked up and met his gaze. He was still grinning, and that gaze—it was as full as she felt.

"I've waited for you," he whispered. "And even if we were only together for a little while, it was worth every minute of the twelve years I waited."

The lump in her throat was so enormous she could hardly breathe. "I've waited too, Henry."

Again his grin smoothed into seriousness. "Promise me, Caroline, that you won't wait anymore. That tomorrow you'll start over."

A beat. "But tonight?"

He dug his hand into the hair at the base of her skull. He looked down at her for a long moment, his pale eye swirling with emotion. "Tonight I want to be with you, Caroline. If you'll have me."

Tears burned against her closed eyelids. Tears of relief. "Yes," she breathed.

And then Henry was curling his body around hers, pressing her back to the wall as his mouth came down on hers. His arm propped on the wall beside her head, he kissed her hard and well and sure. He surrounded her, his body, his scent, and she drank deeply, wrapping her hands around the nape of his neck, her fingers tangling in his hair as she pulled him closer, closer; he was never close enough. Desire flooded her every vein and sinew, pulsing between her legs and in her chest. She wanted him, badly.

By now she knew his kiss, and he knew hers, and Caroline thought she could stand here, just like this, for hours, days even, and be kissed by Henry Beaton Lake. He took her bottom lip between his teeth, guiding her mouth against his own by holding her chin between his thumb and forefinger. She untied the ribbon of his queue, releasing his hair to fall over his shoulders and down his back. His unfashionably long, pale red hair. She'd miss it.

But she wouldn't think about that now. If she had learned nothing else, Caroline understood that the bad—that tomorrow—would come anyway, whether or not she thought about it today, protected herself from it.

And so she wouldn't think about it. She wouldn't think at all; she would know, and touch, and lose herself in Henry, and this moment.

"Not here," he whispered, trailing his lips down her throat. "Where can we go?"

"The folly, in the garden," she said. "We've just got to get over the gate."

Henry made quick work of that, hoisting Caroline up on his shoulders so she might climb to the other side. He followed, landing soundlessly on his feet.

She took his hand as she led him into the gardens.

Peonies and wisteria perfumed the air; a bright moon shone down upon the garden folly, still and silent, its curious windows gleaming silver one way, blue another.

Caroline drew open the doors and led Henry inside. It smelled of wax, recently lit tapers; William must have come out earlier that evening to take some air. The light from the moon illuminated the folly just enough, outlining the wrinkled edges of the pillows in downy halos. It streamed through the high windows and caught the chiseled planes of Henry's face.

He was looking at her, intently, intensely, so much so that she looked away. Her eyes burned with tears. Why was she crying? It made no sense. She didn't want to cry, not here, not now, on their last night together.

He wiped away her tears with his thumbs, murmuring, "It's all right, Caroline, it's all right," in her ear.

The murmur turned into a kiss. Henry held her by her face, she held on to him by his wrists, his lips setting fire to her skin.

They kissed for a long time, until Caroline's lips were raw, and her desire soaring.

Her hands dove between the lapels of his coat, urging it over his shoulders. He took off her cloak; he trailed a hand down the back of her gown, unhooking each button slowly, carefully, her heart screaming to be released.

He undressed her like this: slowly, savoring every bit of lace, each embroidered eyelet.

But she—she undressed him quickly. He laughed at her impatience, and nicked her naked shoulder with his teeth.

Henry held her against him when they were at last done with one another's clothes, his fingers trailing down the skin of her back as he kissed her collarbones and neck.

Head thrown back, Caroline allowed him to toss her onto the mountain of pillows, a small laugh of surprise escaping her lips. The pillows felt at once foreign and impossibly soft against her naked body; she sank into them, the heaviness of her limbs a vibrant counterpoint to the liquid desire running just beneath her skin.

Henry fell onto his knees before her. He put his hands on her and parted her legs; his hair gleamed white in the light from the windows as it dipped between her thighs.

The breath caught in her throat as his hands slid up the inside of her thighs and his mouth met with her sex. A slow kiss, perfect, one that had her crying out, the muscles in her legs burning, tightening.

One kiss, and she was already on the edge, already gritting her teeth and closing her eyes and clenching the pillows in her hands.

Another kiss, and she came apart.

It was so immediate, it happened so quickly, Caroline felt as if she were flying. The fiery pulses overtook her, *poundpoundpound*, filling her heart and her ears, her hands tugging at Henry's hair.

He was climbing over her, even as she gasped for air. He placed his forearms on either side of her head, brushing back the hair from her eyes. His belly pressed against hers, he was pushing her legs wider with his hips.

Henry took her moans of pleasure in his mouth, his lips wild now, and impatient.

She was still coming when he entered her. She couldn't tell if the pain was good pain or bad, the intensity of it all. It had been so long—years—since she'd been with a man. Henry went slowly, kissing her as he slid inside her. The pain dissolved as he sank to the root, then vanished altogether. Pleasure, only pleasure now, and so very much of it.

He reached back and wrapped her trembling legs about his buttocks, thrusting deeply. The hardened points of his hips scraped against her belly; he was taking her nipples in his mouth, first one, then the other and back again.

Caroline closed her eyes, and surrendered.

She met him thrust for thrust, her body as eager to know as his. Oh, God, this was as lovely as she remembered. Better, now, because they knew each other, knew their bodies.

Henry moved onto his side, taking her with him. His thrusts became slower, luxurious. She could tell he was holding back. He didn't want this to end.

She would not think about the end.

His hands moved over every inch of her skin, her sides and her back and the backs of her thighs. Caroline could not get enough of his enormous shoulders, the way his muscles moved beneath her touch.

Henry was on his knees now, keeping Caroline on her side as he pressed her legs together and drew them up by her chest, entering her this way. It felt different. It felt wonderful.

He had her breast in one hand; with the other he was touching the tip of her sex, urging her toward completion once more. She yielded to his touch, yielded to the rising wave when it hit her at last. She closed her eyes against the fullness she felt, the sense of wholeness.

Henry's movements grew more urgent, and then he was pulling out of her, covering himself with his hand. Caroline watched his face tense, his eye squeezing shut. His lips were gathered in a white line; he breathed in short, hot spurts through his nose.

How different from last time—the first time—this care he took. How foolish they'd been then, and young, and lost in each other. Not that she wasn't lost now.

She reached up and took his face in her hand. His eye opened. It was narrow with satiation, the green of his iris burning gold in the darkness. It was overwhelming, the intensity of being looked at like this, knowing she was the spark that had lit this man on fire.

Inside her chest her heart felt swollen, and strangely quiet. As if, in this moment, the eye of the storm, it was content.

Henry ducked his head, pressing a kiss into her palm, and then he fell onto his back and reached for his shirt, tidying himself up.

When he was done he propped himself up on his elbow, guiding Caroline onto her back beside him. He ran his fingers in slow, lazy circles across her belly. The tenderness of his gesture made her heart swell.

"Elizabeth," she said. "I named our daughter Elizabeth."

She watched the working of his throat as he swallowed. "After Gloriana?"

"Yes." Caroline took his wandering hand in her own and

held it against her skin. "It was the red hair—I'd like to think she would've been a feisty one, like you, and the queen."

"Elizabeth," he said, trying out the word. "It's lovely."

She squeezed his hand. "I'm glad you like it. When I was pregnant, I would visit Kew often—it was the only time Osbourne and I stayed in London—and I thought often about Queen Elizabeth, and Dudley, and you and me."

He met her eyes. His somehow managed to be soft and hard all at once. Hard, as if he was struggling to hold something in. Soft, as if that something was a great sadness that threatened to overwhelm the levee inside him.

Caroline smiled, brushing her nose against his chest. She inhaled, closing her eyes. This scent—his scent, male, skin, soap—God, how she would miss it.

As if reading her thoughts, Henry pulled her to him, surrounding her with his warmth. She melted against his skin, burrowing into the place between his arm and torso, his hand splayed across the small of her back, protectively.

Together they were still.

She didn't fall asleep, not exactly. Instead she floated in the comfortable darkness behind her closed lids. Time could pass slowly, quickly, not at all; she was in Henry's arms, that was all she knew, and in those minutes, that was all she needed.

Forty-two

———— ✦ ————

"I don't want to go," Henry whispered, sometime later.

"Stay, just a little longer," Caroline replied, her breath a warm rush against his skin.

He pulled her closer. How many hours did they have left? he wondered. These moments—they would be the ones he'd remember, when he was back in Paris, alone.

Henry supposed he should be grateful he had new memories, memories of caresses, things said and done. Leaving her the first time had been excruciating. Leaving her again—God, but he couldn't breathe.

At last the darkness burned to gray. He hadn't slept; Caroline had been equally restless until she finally fell asleep some time ago, her breathing deep and even.

The good-bye would be too much to bear, and awkward besides. What could he say to her, that he hadn't already said? She never told him she loved him—had never spoken it aloud, anyway—and he did not wish to force a confession, or pester her once more with his own. Would they embrace, meet eyes, murmur wishes of luck and fortune and peace?

It would be a lie. There would be no peace for either of them; they both knew that.

Carefully he untangled her limbs from his own, and settled her comfortably in a nest of embroidered pillows. He tucked her gown about her torso and legs—wouldn't do to have Mr. McCartney discover her naked as the day she was born—and smoothed the hair from her face. His fingers lingered on her cheeks, indulging one last time in the softness of her skin.

She was so beautiful.

His hand fell. He slipped off the edge of the sofa.

With a wince, Henry pulled his breeches over his hips. Despite drinking deeply of Caroline's body, it seemed his own lusted for more; he was hard as a rock, his erection straining painfully against the fall of his breeches as he worked to button them.

He ducked into his shirt, waistcoat, boots—damn it, why were his hands shaking?

He made for the door. The sun was rising now, burning away the gray. At the threshold, he paused, glancing one last time over his shoulder. The light caught on Caroline's dark eyelashes; a stab of longing left him breathless.

He had to leave. They couldn't be together. Had the twelve years he'd spent away from her taught him nothing? Caroline deserved better than the violent, peripatetic life he'd chosen. She craved solitude, and stability, above all else.

Henry had to leave.

One foot in front of the other.

He gritted his teeth and did as his will bade him, heart clenching as he stalked across the grounds. He glanced at the gardens as he passed.

The peonies Henry and Caroline planted together were in full bloom, the dusky pink flowers so heavy, their stems bowed out onto the path.

Henry looked away, the flowers' earthy scent filling his head, and made for the street.

Forty-three

---◆---

Russell Square, Bloomsbury
Several Days Later

As was his usual habit, the lieutenant general was conducting business from the palatial manse in which he'd installed his mistress—and most decorated spy, Lucy Joplin—some years before.

Henry applauded the general's genius; one must, after all, give credit where credit is due. Russell Square was in a well-kept but not-quite-fashionable part of London; no one much cared for the comings and goings of the not-quite-fashionable people who lived there.

Which was a good thing, because today the house was a beehive of activity. Clerks and footmen and agents darted in and out of various rooms, closing doors behind them with careless force. Henry watched from the end of the long hallway as a young man, caked head to toe in sweat-streaked mud, was led, limping, out of one such room to the kitchens.

The hairs at the back of Henry's neck stood to attention. Something had happened. There was news. Big news, from what he could tell by the sudden rush of voices that filled the hall.

He slipped his hand inside his coat, his fingers tapping the telltale bulge inside his waistcoat pocket. Hopefully they had not suffered a defeat, an indignity, that could have been prevented by the French Blue.

Henry had waited for what felt like an eternity: for four days, the general was incommunicado, and only this morning had returned to Russell Square. An assignment, perhaps, or something to do with this big news that had everyone so stirred up. Still, the general's absence—his silence—was surprising, considering he assigned Henry the task of obtaining the jewel years ago; it was a major victory for England, now that the Alien Office was in possession of it.

And Henry was rarely made to wait besides.

He tapped his foot impatiently against the polished marble floor. The ache in his leg had returned suddenly, the pain just short of agony. He leaned the back of his head against the wall and closed his eye.

He saw Caroline, her lips, her swanlike neck, the pile of dark hair swirling atop her head. He saw her eyes flutter shut as he ducked between her legs, her body rising to meet his kiss—

"Lake, old boy, no time for sleep on a day like this!"

Henry started at the familiar, mottled shout. The general—known to the beau monde as Baron Richards—leaned out of a nearby room, waving his arm.

"Come, come!" he said. "And make quick work of it!"

Henry shuffled inside the room, a high-ceilinged parlor that had been repurposed as a rather feminine-looking office: buff-colored walls, carpet, and cut-velvet drapes. Everything was pink, right down to the trinkets that littered a generously sized desk in the middle of the room.

The general clapped Henry on the back, a smile curling at his thin lips.

Henry peered at him, warily. "I don't think I've seen you this jolly since you first met Lucy. Tell me, what's happened?"

"Ah, but a drink first," the general replied, sidling up to a makeshift sideboard at the other end of the office.

Henry arched a brow. "You're beginning to frighten me, sir. Is this a good news drink, or a bad news one? I must know if I am to be celebrating, or fortifying myself against horrors yet to come."

"Sit down, old boy, and I'll tell you."

He lowered himself into the chair; a spike of pain shot through his leg, and he sucked in a breath through clenched teeth. But God, it had never hurt so ardently, his leg. It was nearly unbearable.

The general frowned at Henry as he passed him a snifter of brandy. "You've seen the surgeon I told you about, the one in Calais?"

"I have," Henry nodded, swirling his brandy. "Seems I am beyond repair."

His superior officer took his seat behind the desk, his gaze never leaving Henry. His light brown eyes were soft with sympathy, concerned lines etched into his broad forehead. "I didn't know it had gotten so bad."

"Keeping busy helps—it's all this sitting still that's the worst. When I feel it most," Henry replied. He took a long pull from his snifter, a pull he hoped did not betray his desperation. "So, keep me busy."

The general arched a brow. "I've a feeling you've been doing a fine job of that yourself, Lake."

Henry met his eyes. Setting his snifter on the edge of the desk, he dug inside his coat.

A moment later, he placed the French Blue on the desk with a hollow *thwunk*. In the bright afternoon sun, the diamond glittered and winked flirtatiously, a translucent shard of light.

The general choked on his brandy. Pounding his fist against his chest, he set aside his brandy and plucked the diamond off the desk.

"By the prince regent's bollocks," he coughed. "You've actually found it. How—?"

"You know I'm not going to answer that question."

The general held the jewel up to the light, wincing as the diamond flashed directly in his eye. Henry watched as his initial disbelief faded into something that looked suspiciously like dismay.

His stomach clenched.

"I thought—," the general began. "From your missives, I

thought the jewel was lost. And the papers, what with all the news of it being stolen from Thomas Hope's ball—I thought—"

Henry grinned, a rueful thing. "But I found it. We can begin negotiations with the French straightaway. They've approached me, and they're quite eager—"

"Wait, wait," the general held up a hand. "Does this have anything to do with the capture of the Marquess of Woodstock? We found him in a hole at Newgate. Apparently he's the one we've been looking for—the spy back in Oxfordshire. What was that, ten, twelve years ago?"

Henry set his hands on his thighs and squeezed. This wasn't how he imagined his conversation with the general would go. He wanted to leave London—leave *her*—as quickly as possible, before he changed his mind, or drowned in his grief. Already this was taking too long.

"Yes," Henry ground out. "I had a vendetta of—*ahem*—a personal nature to settle with his lordship. I won. Thought he'd do well at Newgate. Although I fail to see how Woodstock is more important than the French Blue. He hasn't worked for the French for years now."

The general set down the diamond and clasped his hands, leaning his elbows on the desk. "We broke him, easily. Just the *threat* of pulling out his fingernails, and he spilled the names of a dozen of Old Boney's agents, working here in London. It's a victory of enormous proportion."

Henry started for the second time that day. "Woodstock—he *broke*?"

Heavens, if only he'd known it would be that easy!

The general nodded. "So far, we've rounded up six traitors. A seventh is in custody up in Norfolk. A bang-up job you did, Lake."

Grasping his brandy, Henry took one long, last pull. "Well. This is certainly news."

"Excellent news. News worthy of a promotion—several promotions, in fact."

Henry blinked. "I don't like the sound of that."

"No," the general said, rising, "I didn't think you would. Which is why I am offering you a pension, in addition to a rather large token of my personal gratitude. I believe you'll find it satisfactory—it's certainly enough to provide a comfortable retirement."

Henry's heart lurched. "Retirement?"

The general walked around the desk, planting a hand on its surface as he looked at Henry from beneath his furry brows. "This is the biggest intelligence victory we've scored in a decade. Perhaps even longer. You've done well by your country, Lake."

Henry blinked again. Retirement *did* sound lovely. But what about his work? England was still at war, lives were at stake, the future map of Europe was at stake; there was so much to be done . . .

"My work," he said at last, looking up at the general. "I can't just leave it. And retirement—I'll get fat, and lazy . . ."

The general's eyes warmed; he grinned. "You've given England twelve years, and half your body besides." He nodded at Henry's leg, stretched out stiffly before him. "You've groomed Moon; let him go back to Paris. I'll put my best men under his command. No doubt he'll miss you, but I think it's time you sat on your fat ass and enjoyed yourself for once."

That also sounded lovely—enjoying, rather than punishing, himself.

Henry didn't know what to do. So he laughed, a deep thing that made the sides of his torso ache. Inside his chest his heart felt light, the vise grip of his grief released at last. The throbbing in his knee slowed, then disappeared altogether.

He could not wait to see Caroline's face when he told her the news.

The general was laughing, too, and then he was pouring Henry another drink, and then another, and they were having toasts to being potbellied old men.

When Henry had drained his third brandy, he set the snifter down and nodded at the French Blue, still winking from the general's side of the desk. "But what about the diamond?"

The general's grin widened into a smile. "We've just received word that Wellington took Salamanca. Defeated that libertine Marmont—apparently he is wounded, but we can't yet confirm that bit; it's why I've been indisposed these past days. Wellington's marching on Madrid as we speak. The diamond—well, we may not need to use it. The tide's finally turned in our favor, Lake." He let out a long breath, tucked an arm behind his back and looked down into his empty snifter. "Finally, all our work has come to fruition. Your men—with any luck they'll be coming home soon."

Henry sat back in his seat. This was so much good news as to be laughable. What in hell had he done to deserve a day like today? Perhaps the devil had at last agreed to the bargain Henry had been trying to make for twelve years. Anything, he had sworn, I'll give you anything if Caroline is happy.

Henry was going to make her happy.

"You take the French Blue," the general said, making his way back to the desk. He slid the diamond across the desk's gleaming surface. "I task you with being its keeper; you must safeguard it at all costs. It would serve us to keep the jewel in England for a while longer yet. Save it for a rainy day, as the saying goes. Just keep it safe, hide it if you must, should things take a turn for the worse in Spain. Perhaps return it to your friend Thomas Hope for safekeeping? After that horrid episode in his ballroom, no doubt he'll have the most heavily guarded vaults in all Europe."

Henry didn't realize he was shaking until he held the gem in his hand. It took two tries to tuck it back into his pocket.

The general set down his snifter. Henry rose to his feet and met the general's gaze; he shook his head and scoffed.

"Forgive me, sir, but you're sure this isn't a hoax?" Henry asked. "I really am not worthy of retirement. There's so much left to do . . . "

The general waved away his words. "None of us is worthy, Lake. Or maybe we all are. I haven't quite decided which one it is yet. Regardless, after you secure the jewel's safety, use your pension and go buy a manor. A house, a cottage—whatever your pleasure, buy it. Marry your lady, and bring her there. The two of you can get fat together having twelve children."

"Lady?" Henry said, eye trained on his boots. "How did you—?"

"For one so infamous for his disguises, you certainly have trouble disguising what you feel for her. It's written all over your person. Your face, the way you sit. It's frightfully obvious."

Henry sighed. Why was everyone so intent on pointing out the look of love he apparently bore? He'd spent plenty of time looking in the mirror; he hadn't seen it.

Then again, he hadn't seen how quickly he would fall in love all over again with Caroline until it was too late, and he was in *way* over his head.

"Thank you, sir," Henry said, bowing. He made for the door.

"I hope you'll name your firstborn after me!" the general called after him.

Henry scoffed again. "Never! Harold is a terrible name, and you know it!"

"At least the dog!" the general called, roaring with laughter. "Surely you can spare a dog?"

Henry stalked out of the house and onto the street, mind racing. There was still one obstacle to his happiness, and to Caroline's. One that seemed as dauntingly insurmountable as Woodstock, Henry's work, Caroline's grief. If not more so.

He would call on the Earl of Harclay first thing the next morning. William was an early riser. With any luck Caroline would still be abed; Henry knew she took her breakfast in her chambers.

That would give Henry plenty of time to convince Harclay that he was good enough for his sister.

Henry had a feeling he'd need it.

Forty-four

Brook Street, Hanover Square
The Earl of Harclay's Residence

Henry hoisted himself onto the small terrace and tapped the knuckle of his first finger against the window.

Inside the breakfast room, the earl started. Dropping his fork with a muted clatter, he pressed his lips together and met Henry's eye.

Henry shrugged, pointing at the cremone bolts that locked the window casements in place.

William glowered. After a beat, he dropped his napkin on the table and hobbled over to the window. Henry noticed his face was still mangled, the bruises taking on a greenish sheen; a flush of red marred one of his eyes.

Whatever happened on that ship that night in the Docklands, it was clear William had come very, *very* close to losing everything—including his life.

The earl turned the knob, bolts clicking out of place.

"I'll get it," Henry said, and bent to open the window.

"You know," William said, ducking out into the morning,

"the last time you snuck into my house, I challenged you to a duel. And here you are again, asking for more."

Henry ran a hand through his hair. His heart tripped inside his chest; God, but he was nervous. "I was hoping we could talk. I didn't want to wake her ladyship your sister; she cannot know I came to see you."

The earl cocked a brow. Henry waited, breathless. He wouldn't blame William for turning him away, telling him go to go to hell. The earl adored his sister, and only wanted what was best for her.

A one-eyed Viking with a penchant for violence—well, no one wanted his sister to end up with the likes of Henry Beaton Lake.

But Henry had to try. He wouldn't let Caroline go without a fight. And he was determined to do things the proper way this time around—no sneaking about, no secret weddings.

He would do right by Caroline, even if that meant losing her all over again.

"Fine," William ground out. "You have five minutes before Avery returns with my papers."

He turned and hobbled back to his seat, settling his napkin into his lap. As was his usual habit, he did not invite Henry to sit.

Henry ducked into the breakfast room, done up in vibrant shades of plum. The strong morning light flooded the room in pale yellow beams, illuminating motes that danced high above the earl's head.

William sipped at his coffee, and looked up at Henry, expectantly.

Henry cleared his throat and drew his hands into a tight knot at the small of his back. Rocking back on his heels, he said, "I've come to ask for your sister's hand in marriage."

The earl let out a small scoff. "That's easy. My answer is no."

"I thought you might say that."

"Then why, Mr. Lake, have you come at all, if you knew what my answer would be?"

Again Henry cleared his throat. His face felt hot; doubtless his whole person was one shade of red or another. "Because I was hoping to convince you that I'm worthy of her. That I could make Lady Caroline happy."

"Do you believe her to be *un*happy, Mr. Lake?"

"I think we both know she's been unhappy for some time, my lord."

The earl's face fell at that; he knew it was true. He focused his gaze on his coffee; Henry noticed the neat, black stitches that held together his left eyebrow.

"Caroline is a private woman," William said softly. "She does not share much with me. I confess she has worried me these past years. I remember coming home that summer from Eton—I was, what, fifteen then? Anyway. She was different. Sad. She'd changed."

Henry squeezed his hands so tightly, the knuckled snapped and popped.

"She's been that way ever since. Until—" William's gaze flicked to meet Henry's. He let out a long sigh of dismay. "Until you came along, I suppose."

Henry ignored the pulse of hope that leapt inside him. "Don't sound so excited about your sister falling in love."

"I know what you are, Lake. What you do. And men like you don't marry ladies like Caroline. What will you do, take her to live in a filthy garret in Paris?" The earl rose suddenly, the napkin falling from his lap as he made his way to the window. Glancing over his shoulder, he said, "She loves children, you know. Wants to have a few of her own."

The words came before Henry could stop them. "And I want to have children with Caroline. More than anything, that's what I want. To be with her, make her my wife. Make a home together."

"And how, Mr. Lake, do you propose to do that, with a soldier's wages?"

Henry stepped toward the earl. "Through a variety of unlikely and frankly preposterous circumstances, I have secured a decent income. It's small—but it's mine, and I want to share it with Caroline. I've retired, you see—"

The earl whirled about, face screwed up with disbelief. "You? You've retired from whatever sinister games you play?"

"Trust me, no one is more shocked than I am. I took a quick inventory of the terms of my income, visited Mr. Hope at the bank. He helped me draw up a few documents—"

"What do they say, the documents?"

Henry looked down at his boots, scuffed, worn, smudged with dirt. "That I can afford to buy a new pair of boots. Hoby's this time, maybe they'll last a bit longer. New boots, and perhaps a manor. A small one. But it will be ours."

Lord Harclay paused, and then: "That doesn't change the fact that you lied for a living."

"No, it doesn't," Henry replied steadily. "But I don't anymore. I intend to become a perfectly boring gentleman farmer."

"You don't mean that."

Henry set a finger on the table. "Forgive me, my lord, but I bloody do mean it. With all my heart. Question me on everything else, on my past, my family, my occupation. But don't question my intentions, for they are good."

The earl looked at Henry for a long time, sizing up the truth of Henry's claim. All the while Henry's pulse skipped and jostled; the room felt warm suddenly, the sun beating down upon him. The anticipation was killing him; he felt a burn crawling up from his stomach into his throat.

"No," William said at last, gaze trained on a spot in the garden outside the window. "You cannot have her."

Henry felt as if he'd been delivered a blow. Panic threatened; he gritted his teeth, and willed himself to press forward.

"Please," he said. "I love her."

"Is that the spy talking, or the boring gentleman farmer?"

Henry slammed his fist into the table. The china and silverware jumped, falling back to the table with no small clatter. Damnation, he hoped he didn't wake Caroline; his temper was getting the better of him.

"I'll beg, and I'll grovel," Henry growled. "And if that doesn't work, I will leave your house, and I'll leave your sister alone. I won't do this without your blessing, not—" Henry stopped just short of saying *not this time*. "But Christ in Heaven, my lord, put your sister and me out of our shared misery. I want to ask Caroline to be my wife. I want to ask her to marry me."

William turned away from the window.

To Henry's very great relief, his lordship was smiling.

"Ow," William said, gently fingering his stitches. "Smiling hurts my face."

"I'm—sorry, I suppose?"

"Don't be," William stepped toward Henry, and held out his hand. "Yes. My answer is yes."

As if in a daze, Henry allowed the earl to take his hand and pump it thoroughly. "But I—um—don't understand. What—how—?"

"Appealing to the vanity of a man like myself is not a clever move, but it is a smart one," William replied. "I needed to hear you say you meant to do this honorably, besides. The bit about not marrying her without my blessing—well, be still my beating black heart. Get your affairs in order, and then you have my permission to ask Caroline to marry you."

The earl was a man transformed, his dark eyes warm, lips trembling as he fought back that painful smile.

"I've caused my sister an awful lot of pain these past weeks," William continued. "I owe her—and you—an apology. The duel . . . well, that was not my finest hour."

It wasn't much, but Henry knew it was no small thing, for the Earl of Harclay to admit wrongdoing. William eyed Henry, waiting for his absolution. Oh, how Henry would love to toy with him, give the blackguard a taste of his own medicine, but alas, he was not willing to risk his hard-won victory.

And so he gave his lordship's hand one final squeeze, pulling away.

And in his empty palm, Henry placed the French Blue.

William started with such surprise that he nearly dropped the stone.

"Now it's my turn to ask why," he said, his voice suddenly hoarse.

"You're trusting me with her ladyship your sister," Henry replied, and nodded at the diamond. "And in return, I'm trusting you to do the right thing."

"The right thing?" William looked up from the French Blue. "You mean give it back to Hope. But why don't you—?"

"Because Thomas Hope will appreciate the poetry of it—the man who stole from him, returning what he stole. I'm sure you'll come up with some ridiculous plan or another.

"Oh," Henry said, "and one more thing. D'you happen to know where your sister hides things? You know, her version of your sock drawer. I need you to find something for me."

Forty-five

───── ✦ ─────

A Few Days Later
The Earl of Harclay's Residence, Hanover Square

Stepping into the cool dimness of the entry hall, Caroline wiped her brow with her sleeve. She tugged the gloves off her hand and shook them out over a potted palm.

Goodness, but the July heat was terrible. She couldn't remember a day as warm and bright as this one; a poetic counterpoint to the heavy chill that permeated her being.

But Caroline was in no mood for poetry, not even that rascal Lord Byron's feisty verse. The only thing that helped her cope with the loneliness, the sense of uselessness, was working in William's garden.

She worked all morning, well into the afternoon. The peonies she'd planted with Henry had grown riotously, and while she cut back the rest of the garden, she could not bear to trim them. In fact, she could hardly bear to look them, or even be near them, their fresh scent a poignant reminder of the manure Henry had shoved down her back.

Henry. Caroline had expected the pain to hit her in a few

weeks' time, when the reality of his absence set in. She was not prepared for the immediate onslaught of grief; it greeted her the moment her eyes fluttered open that morning in the folly. She was naked and sore and somehow aroused. She'd reached for Henry, but he was gone.

For the second—and last—time, he'd left her.

Even now, three days after the fact, Caroline struggled against the burn of tears. She was a widow; now she had the solitude, the space to do as she pleased. She was alone. It was exactly what she wanted all these years.

She had never been unhappier. Without Henry she felt lost, and more than a little bored. If men were forced to live the lives available to women, Caroline mused darkly, no doubt they'd start a revolution. *Liberté, égalité,* and a little excitement, for God's sake.

A little more freedom, to have a little more fun.

Not that Caroline would have any more fun, if she were possessed of more freedom. There was no fun to be had, not without Henry.

Again tears threatened. She was about to give in to them when she caught sight of the brass salver, placed on the edge of a nearby table.

It was Avery's salver; he used it to deliver correspondence and calling cards to Caroline and William.

Only the square package resting on the salver was most conspicuously *not* a letter, or a calling card.

Curiosity prickled at the back of her neck. The package was small, the size of Caroline's fist; wrapped in brown paper, it bore no stamp, no mark.

She lifted it from the table and turned it over in her hands. The wrapping was sloppy; aside from that, the package offered no clues.

"Avery?" she called. "Avery, are you there? What's this package on the table? Is it for William?"

No answer. The house was quiet. William was still unwell; he'd dismissed half his staff to the family seat in the country, so this quiet was nothing out of the ordinary.

Still, Caroline had the funniest feeling about this package.

She started at a rustle, over there by the drawing room door. Was that a footstep, a sigh, the curtains moving in a breeze?

"Avery," she tried again, peering past the door. "Is that you?"

She waited for an answer, but none came.

She looked down at the package in her hands, hesitated. Her curiosity was tempered by the knowledge that William probably ordered all manner of illicit objects. Perhaps she didn't *want* to know what was inside.

Oh, who was she kidding.

Of course she wanted to know.

Caroline tore at the paper, crumpling it in a ball and dropping it onto the salver. The box was red leather, its edges boasting tiny designs embossed in gold leaf.

A jeweler's box.

Her pulse leapt.

She glanced about, guiltily, as if she were a child again, daring a foray into cook's biscuit tin.

She flipped the tiny latch with her thumbnail. Her heart turned over in her chest.

There, nestled in the blue satin inside the box, was a piece of tattered green ribbon, tied in a circlet.

"Marry me."

Caroline turned at the sound of a familiar, rumbling voice.

Henry emerged from the shadows of the hall.

Henry.

He was here. He was back.

The light caught on his pupil, smattering the green with flecks of gold. The look he gave her was pleading, soft.

Her eyes blurred with tears as he fell to one knee before her. He took her free hand and held it in his own. With his other hand he reached for the ring, holding it between his thumb and forefinger.

"Henry," she breathed. Her hand shook inside the warmth of his palm. "What are you doing?"

He looked up at her, one side of his mouth rising into a smile; his dimple was thrown into egregious, adorable relief.

God, that dimple.

"Caroline," he said, holding up the ring. "I'm asking you to marry me. Again. Marry me, please. Please, Caroline, say yes."

She plucked the ring from his fingers. "How did you find this? I haven't—no one knows—"

"Your brother knows," Henry replied. "Funny, both of you

claim to have outwitted each other with your hiding spots. But you know all about William's sock drawer. And William knows exactly which pair of boots you use to ferret away your secrets."

Caroline blinked. "You—and William—my brother helped you find the ring? Knowing what you meant to do with it?"

Henry dipped his head, a nod.

"But William hates you." Henry reached up, swiped a tear from her cheek with the pad of this thumb. "He tried to kill you in a duel, remember?"

"I remember, Caroline. Of course I remember. But we've since made amends. I had to bribe him, of course. He doesn't want to let you go."

Caroline drew back. "Bribe him? But—"

"I'll explain everything, Caroline. Just know that William gave me his blessing."

She started to cry in earnest then. Henry took her face in his hand, wiping away the tears as they rolled off her bottom lashes.

"I love you, Caroline," he said. His voice was low, earnest. "I promise there will be no more leaving. Marry me again. I want to marry you in front of everyone this time. Your family and mine. Our friends. Even people we don't like, let's invite them. I want everyone to know that I am yours, and you are mine. Trust me. Marry me."

Caroline swallowed. "But your work—and Paris—you said yourself that it was not possible to be together—"

"I hate to boast, darling, but I'm retired now"—Henry held up a finger at her gasp—"with the intent of becoming the fattest, most boring gentleman farmer England has ever had the misfortune of knowing. I intend to buy a pile and a bit of land, and while I haven't a clue what to do with either of those things, I *do* know I would like to share them with you."

Caroline looked down at him, her chest rising and falling as she struggled to breathe through the tightness in her throat. She swore she'd never let him close again; she swore she'd never open herself to another. How badly he'd hurt her the first time, the second; the pain of his absence was fresh in her mind, considering she'd been drowning in it just moments before.

She'd be a fool to trust him.

Except—

Except he'd proven himself to be everything she'd ever

wanted. Everything she dreamed of. He wasn't the selfish liar she believed him to be. No—he was honest and generous and fun and good God his hands and loyal and, above all else, he was in love with her.

They'd both been lonely.

They did not have to be lonely anymore.

Caroline didn't know she was nodding until she saw Henry's eyes spark. "Yes," she whispered.

His smile was delirious now, and she was falling to her knees on the carpet, and Henry was digging his hands into her hair and pulling her to him and telling her he loved her, he loved her, God, he loved her.

The kiss was hard and wild and a bit slobbery, considering all the tears. When at last Henry pulled away, he held up the ring.

"May I?"

Caroline's hand trembled as he slid the ribbon onto the fourth finger of her left hand. As it had been twelve years before, the ring was a bit loose; it felt smooth against her skin, and she toyed at it with her thumb.

"Before the wedding I'll have something real made up for you," Henry said. "Perhaps an emerald, or a sapphire! Yes, a sapphire, I—"

Caroline pressed her fingers to his lips. "I don't want another ring. I want you, Henry," she paused, looked into his eyes. "I love you."

As she said the words, a great weight rolled off her chest, a weight that had smothered her joy. Now that joy flooded her being, bubbling inside her like laughter.

Henry grinned. "Heavens, woman, I've only been waiting a decade to hear you say that! I was beginning to believe you never would."

"Let's not wait anymore," Caroline replied, smiling against his lips as he kissed her, and kept kissing her, until at last she surrendered.

Historical Note

The French Blue vanished from historical record following its theft in Paris from the Royal Warehouse in autumn 1792. It reappeared some two decades later in 1812 London, in association with French émigré and jeweler John Françillon; in his papers, Françillon described an enormous, and enormously unique, blue diamond that was at the time in the possession of another jeweler (you may recognize his name from the pages of this book!): Daniel Eliason.

There are a variety of scenarios that point to the French Blue's whereabouts between 1792 and 1812; according to Richard Kurin's excellent *Hope Diamond: The Legendary History of a Cursed Gem*, it's possible Caroline, Princess of Wales, inherited the stone from her father, the Duke of Brunswick. If this had indeed been the case, Kurin posits the duke—under duress while at war with Napoleon—had the stone recut sometime around 1805, before sending it to his daughter in London for safekeeping.

While it's impossible to know, exactly, how the French Blue crossed the Channel, I'd like to think this the most likely scenario; a scenario I explored in my previous book, *The Millionaire Rogue*.

Henry Beaton Lake, the hero of this book, tracks down the jewel so that he might make a strategic trade with the French—a trade that would save British lives. While the diamond was many things—mysterious, beautiful, even dangerous—it was not, as far as my research tells me, used as diplomatic bait during England's war with Napoleon.

Of course, as a fan of James Bond (Daniel Craig slays me, every time!), I couldn't resist inserting a spy into the murky history that surrounds the French Blue in the early nineteenth century. The opportunity to incorporate the French Blue into the political and military action of 1812—the battle of Salamanca, Wellington's march on Madrid—was far too tempting to resist.

It is true King Louis XVIII and his brother, the Comte d'Artois, lived in exile in London following the Revolution. They would return to France in 1814 during the Bourbon Restoration. That they frequented White's—and had a penchant for nubile women—is, as far as my research tells me, purely fiction.

For more on the Hope Diamond, check out Richard Kurin's *Hope Diamond: The Legendary History of a Cursed Gem* and Marian Fowler's *Hope: Adventures of a Diamond*, both of which proved indispensable to my research for this trilogy.

Turn the page for a preview of the
first book in the Hope Diamond Trilogy

The Gentleman Jewel Thief

Now available from Berkley Sensation!

One

City of London, Fleet Street
Spring 1812

T he evening's winnings in his pocket and a small, if indiscreet, smile on his lips, Lord William Townshend, tenth Earl of Harclay, strode into the bank. At once a gaggle of bespectacled Hope & Co. employees gathered at his elbow. One peeled back his coat while complimenting Harclay's cologne, even though he wasn't wearing any ("a vigorous choice, my lord, most vigorous!"); another took his hat and gloves and bowed, not once but three times, and appeared about to burst into sobs of gratitude.

Biting back a sigh, Harclay continued up the familiar wide staircase, polished with such enthusiasm as to make it impossible to climb without the aid of the sturdy balustrade. He admired the zeal of Mr. Hope's bankers, he really did. But to be greeted as if Harclay were Julius Caesar, triumphantly marching on Rome—it was a bit much, considering he came not to conquer Pompey, but to deposit a thousand or two.

And Mr. Hope—ah, he was an altogether different breed.

It was why Harclay had, upon his accession to the title some eight years before, chosen to transfer his not inconsiderable wealth to the then-unknown Hope & Co. For Mr. Hope possessed qualities Harclay was hard-pressed to find in his English set: Hope was foreign and exotic and infinitely odd, but more than that, he was possessed of a sort of magnetic brilliance that was at once off-putting and entirely hilarious. That Hope had, through wise investment, nearly doubled Harclay's fortune—well, the earl considered that quite secondary.

The doors to Hope's office were flung open to welcome him, and he strode into the cavernous room—more a museum, really, with a Japanese samurai suit of armor squatting in one corner and a passel of Persian rugs rolled up in another. Above Mr. Hope's enormous desk hung a monumental Botticelli, which, despite Harclay's admiration, was a bit indecent for a place of business, considering it depicted a breast-bearing goddess.

And then there was Mr. Hope: tall, broad, imposing in that strange way of his. He stood and, though Harclay waved him off, proffered a short but lyrical bow. Behind them the doors swung shut and Harclay let out a small sigh of relief.

"My dear Lord Harclay," Mr. Hope said. "To have braved such hellish weather to seek my company—why, after a brandy or two I'd blush! Speaking of . . . ?"

Hope raised an eyebrow to a stout pine sideboard crowded with crystal decanters winking seductively in the dull morning light.

"Good man, it's not yet noon."

Mr. Hope blinked. "Nonsense. In the north it's common knowledge a nip in the day keeps the doctor at bay. Please, do sit."

As Hope busied himself at the sideboard, Harclay folded his tall frame into a rather wide but rickety antique chair. It groaned ominously beneath his weight.

"I say, is this chair sound? I would hate to damage the"—he cleared his throat—"*lovely* piece."

Hope waved away his words, setting a heavy blue crystal snifter before him.

"Ah." Hope smiled, landing in his own chair, snifter pressed to his nose. "I daresay it will withstand its current burden, all things considered. It once belonged to Henry VIII—did you know he weighed over twenty stone at his death?"

"I did not," Harclay said, shifting his weight so that it rested not on the chair but on his own legs. "However did you manage to discover such a treasure?"

"That profligate prince regent of yours," Hope said. "Idiot fellow's so deep in debt he'd sell his own bollocks for a fair price. Whatever is left of them, anyway."

"Fair point," Harclay replied.

"No matter." Mr. Hope took a long, satisfied pull of brandy. "Assuming you have not come to discuss the prince's rather epic stupidity—in which case I am *most* happy to oblige you—how might I be of assistance this morning, Lord Harclay? A withdrawal, perhaps?"

Harclay shook his head. "Not this time. A deposit, actually, and a rather large one."

He placed his snifter on the desk. Reaching into his jacket pocket, he produced a stack of banknotes, each signed by its respective debtor and stamped with the credentials of various banks and agents.

Harclay watched in amusement as Hope struggled to smother his surprise. The banker coughed, pounding on his chest, and finally managed to wheeze a reply.

"Good God, my lord, did you ransack the royal treasury? Bankrupt the local gentry?" He lowered his voice to a whisper. "Not a duel, surely? Winner takes all? I hear blood wages are quite the thing."

Harclay laughed. For a brief moment he thought of his Manton dueling pistols, gleaming, gorgeous things that were his constant companions during a rather raucous youth. Alas, they had remained in their velvet-lined box for some time now, but Mr. Hope's toes would positively curl if he knew how often those guns had been Harclay's saving grace.

"No, no," Harclay said. "I'm afraid it's just a bit of luck I've come across at White's, games of chance and all that."

Mr. Hope scooped up the stack of notes and rifled through them. Harclay could tell the banker was biting his tongue to keep from exclaiming at the number of zeros on each note.

Hope clucked his tongue. "Tsk-tsk. Those gentlemen friends of yours should know better than to gamble with *the*

Lord Harclay. Hell, even I've been warned about you. Something of a legend you've become; they say your luck never runs out. That your stakes are impossibly high."

Harclay, legs aching, leaned as far back as Henry Tudor's priceless chair would allow without splintering into a dozen pieces. "My companions at last night's table were"—here that secret smile returned to his lips—"in a rather generous mood."

"Well"—Mr. Hope held up the stack of notes with a smile—"all the better for you, my lord, though your accounts are already robust, yes, *most* robust. Many gentlemen of—ah, your particular age and station have quite the opposite problem, I'm afraid."

"Indeed," Harclay replied. He was hardly surprised. For all their swagger and impeccable breeding, most of his friends were frightfully broke. Harclay pitied the poor fellows and helped when he could; nonetheless, there was no helping his set's near-complete lack of intelligence and savvy, and the temptation to best them time and time again proved far too enticing.

"Very well," Mr. Hope said. He clapped the long edge of the notes against his desk to gather them into a neat pile. "I shall see to this at once."

"Excellent," Harclay said and made to rise. "And it goes without saying—"

Mr. Hope pressed his thumbnail to his lips. "To the grave, Harclay. Can't have word of your companions' most sizable losses getting to the papers or, worse, to their wives."

"Gratitude, good sir, I do appreciate your discretion," Harclay replied. He was about to turn and exit the room when Mr. Hope held up his hand.

"And one more thing," the banker said. "I assume you have not received the invitation I sent, some days ago? Post is dreadful this time of year, what with all this rain washing out the roads, and I know a man of your stature would never be so rude as to send a tardy reply."

Harclay detected the slightest trace of irony in Mr. Hope's words and replied with no small measure of his own. "I abhor rudeness, Mr. Hope, above all things."

For a moment Mr. Hope studied Harclay, his dark eyes twinkling, but the earl merely returned Hope's gaze with a measured amount of disinterest.

Of course Harclay had received the invitation, and, as he had done with all others from Mr. Hope, he had blatantly, rudely ignored it, as had many of his friends. The banker was rich beyond imagining, indeed, with the tastes and fine manners of a gentleman, but alas bore no title; the more rigid of Harclay's set zealously scorned Hope while harboring a secret envy of his fortune and freedom.

That Hope did not have the good luck to be born into a blue-blooded family mattered not a whit to Harclay. No, his reason for ignoring Hope's invitation was rather more mundane. Every year, on the first Friday of May, Hope hosted the most extravagant and hotly anticipated ball of the season. Hope, in usual form, attached to each ball a sufficiently ridiculous theme. Last year, the more adventurous of the *ton* arrived dressed as popes, assassins, and breast-bearing courtesans for "The Murderous Medici"; the year before, it had been "One Thousand and One Nights in the Emperor's *Hareem*," whatever that meant.

Harclay would rather forfeit his tongue, or even his manhood, than attend such a spectacle. The same tedious conversation with the same tedious debutantes; the crush of rooms and the smell of damp, drunken bodies; the spirited dances and inevitable swoons: all this glory, but raised to fever pitch by daringly cut costumes, cunningly crafted masks, and Hope's rather impressive cellar of cognacs and brandies.

No, Harclay mused, no, thank you indeed.

"I know you haven't attended many of my humble soirees in the past," Mr. Hope said, reading Harclay's thoughts. "But this year, I'm doing something a bit different."

"Oh?" Harclay said, with a longing glance toward the exit.

"Oh, yes," Mr. Hope replied, a sly grin on his lips. "Imagine it, if you will: the glory days of Versailles, when the Sun King, Louis XIV, ruled over the most splendid and sumptuous court the world has ever seen. The feasts, the silks, the pomp—*the jewels*."

A pulse of interest shot through Harclay so quickly he struggled to catch it before it showed up on his face. Jewels? Now, this was something interesting—something different, new, unexpected.

"I'll let you in on a little secret," Mr. Hope said, lowering his voice. "After much searching, I do believe I've managed to locate one of the French crown jewels."

"The French crown jewels?" Harclay drawled in his best monotone. "Didn't they disappear ages ago, at the start of the Revolution?"

Mr. Hope smiled. "Don't play dumb with me, my lord, for you are as familiar with the tale as anyone else. We know a band of thieves broke into the royal treasury shortly after poor King Louis XVI and Queen Marie-Antoinette were arrested. The thieves, and the jewels, seemed to have vanished overnight. And now, nearly twenty years later, one of said gems has resurfaced."

"But how—?"

Mr. Hope daringly waved his finger. "A gentleman does not kiss and tell."

Harclay furrowed his brow. "I believe that applies to something else entirely—"

"As I was saying," Hope said, nearly perspiring with excitement, "I've managed to purchase the *very same jewel* worn by the King of France!"

Harclay paused, trying in vain to contain his curiosity. "Which jewel, exactly? Surely not—"

"The French Blue? Yes, that's the one. It is the crown jewel of my collection, so to speak."

Harclay made a show of an enormous yawn, though it did nothing to still the rapid beating of his heart. The French Blue!—a treasure indeed. It was rumored to be the size of an apricot, and the most brilliant diamond ever discovered. Harclay had, of course, heard whisperings of the curse attached to the stone; but these only increased his interest. An enormous diamond, worn by kings and cursed by their royal blood? *Marvelous!*

"I plan to display the jewel at the ball, Friday next. I've hired half the British army to guard them," Hope said with a smug scoff, "but it will make quite the splash, the jewel, don't you think? Oh, do make plans to attend, Lord Harclay. 'The Jewel of the Sun King: An Evening at Versailles'—really, how could you resist?"

Harclay let out a well-practiced sigh of resignation. "Perhaps," he replied. "I've a busy season ahead, you see; I make no promises. And my valet, he's been unwell, and I can't very well attend in the nude . . ."

But Mr. Hope smiled beatifically at Harclay's excuses, knowing he had won over the reluctant earl; as if he knew he had been the first to pique Lord Harclay's interest in a very, very long time.